Myths, Gods & Immortals
Odin
New & Ancient Norse Tales

This is a FLAME TREE Book

FLAME TREE PUBLISHING
6 Melbray Mews, Fulham,
London SW6 3NS, United Kingdom
www.flametreepublishing.com

First published 2024

24 26 28 29 27 25
1 3 5 7 9 10 8 6 4 2

ISBN: 978-1-80417-932-1

Publisher's Note: The stories within this book are works of fiction. Names, characters, places, and incidents are a product of the authors' imaginations. Locales and public names are sometimes used for atmospheric purposes. Any resemblance to actual people, living or dead, or to businesses, companies, events, institutions, or locales is completely coincidental.

A Note on Spelling: You may notice variation in this book in the spellings of Norse names. Sometimes they are spelt according to the Old Norse (e.g. the nominative singular with the -r suffix, or using diacritics) and sometimes in the anglicized simple style, especially the more well known names. We have opted for *local* consistency within an author's work over complete consistency, in order to retain deliberate stylistic identity.

Cover art by Flame Tree Studio based on elements from Shutterstock.com: MaksimVector, Tiny Art, baon, omnimoney, Liliya Butenko, Andrei Metelev, Vlue.

Extracts from classic texts in this book derive from: *The Poetic Edda*, translated by Henry Adams Bellows (New York: Princeton University Press: Princeton, American Scandinavian Foundation, 1936); *The Prose Edda* by Snorri Sturluson, translated by Arthur Gilchrist Brodeur (New York: American-Scandinavian Foundation, 1916); and *The Story of Egil Skallagrimsson*, translated by W.C. Green (London: Elliot Stock, 1893).

A copy of the CIP data for this book is available from the British Library.

Printed and bound in China

Myths, Gods & Immortals
Odin
New & Ancient Norse Tales
FLAME TREE
PUBLISHING

Contents

Foreword

Carolyne Larrington

Odin, or Óðinn in Old Norse, is the leader of the gods, known by a myriad different names. He is the Old One, the General, the Hanged One, and attracts many other epithets. He and his brothers, Vili and Vé, created the universe – either by lifting the land out of the sea or by building the cosmos out of the dismembered corpse of the giant Ymir. Odin and two companions (Loki and Hœnir) shaped men and women out of wood, giving them breath and life.

Odin rules in the great hall Valhöll (Valhalla) where the heroic dead reside. Here they spend their days in fighting, feasting and waiting for Ragnarök, the final great battle against the giants and their allies. Odin is the god of war. Although he does not fight himself, he initiates combat by casting a spear over the assembled armies, consecrating those who are about to die. He understands battle strategy and imparts it to his chosen heroes. He helps them in various ways, giving advice about fighting or horses. Yet, he will always betray them at the end, appearing before their final fights to signal that their time is up and that the Valkyries will shortly bear the dead heroes off to Valhalla.

Odin knows that Ragnarök is coming – but is it inevitable? He journeys among men and ventures into the realms of other beings, seeking someone who knows of an alternative story, one in which he and the other gods will survive. He travels as an old man, a wanderer, with a cloak drawn down over his one remaining eye, questioning and learning. But the story is always the same: the wolf, Fenrir, is waiting to devour him.

God of wisdom, Odin knows many secrets and prizes both arcane knowledge and the simpler maxims of men. You should check your supplies before the winter, he observes in one poem; at feasts you should not eat or drink too much, neither talk too much nor sit in silence. You should be cheerful and generous, be good to your friends and relentless to your enemies. Odin traded his missing eye for hidden knowledge; for a drink from the Well of Mímir at the foot of the World Tree (Yggdrasil). He also hanged himself on that tree, suffering for nine days and nights without food or drink, pierced with a spear as a sacrifice of himself to himself. Through such suffering he gained knowledge of the runes – the technology of writing that enabled gods and men to record what they knew for future generations.

Odin is also the god of poetry. In legend he ventures deep into the mountain fortress of the giant Suttungr and sweet-talks the lovely Gunnlöð into allowing him three sips of the mead of poetry. This brew, made of blood and spittle, endows those who drink it with the skill to compose verse. Odin did not restrict himself to little sips, however; he swallowed down the contents of all three vats of mead before transforming himself into an eagle and flying back to the home of the gods, hotly pursued by Suttungr, also in bird form. The mead was regurgitated into a vat that the waiting gods had ready, but some he shot out behind him as a defensive strategy: the sustenance of the bad poets.

As the end of the world draws near, Odin's son Baldur is killed through the machinations of Loki. As a father he grieves for his lost boy, but he grieves all the more for his understanding that this is an early indicator that Ragnarök is approaching. The day is coming when the warriors training in Valhalla will march out – but to no avail. They will lose and the great wolf, jaws agape, will devour Odin. It will be for Odin's son Vidar to avenge his father, setting his foot on the wolf's lower jaw and tearing him apart. And thus the old world will die.

Such are Odin's roles in Norse myth. In legendary history he owes his rulership to his cunning. As the leader of a band of refugees fleeing Troy, he brings his people to Scandinavia and persuades the inhabitants to worship them as gods. He appears in the genealogies of the kings of Scandinavia and of England, pitched somewhere between Noah and the first historic monarch. Our modern apprehension of Odin owes much to Wagner's characterization of him as Wotan in his mighty operatic cycle, *Der Ring des Nibelungen*. At the start of the opera, Wotan is at the zenith of his powers, having commissioned the building of Valhalla by two hard-working giants. But thanks to his bad faith and double-dealing, by the end of the cycle he is sitting in that same hall with the branches of the World Tree piled up around it, waiting for the great conflagration that will bring the end of the gods' rule, leaving the world to men.

The modern conceptualization of Odin-Wotan has its roots here. He represents the ending of the old order, the last gasps of a patriarchal power that still seeks to hang on to his authority. In Neil Gaiman's *American Gods* (2001), he is a conman, a grifter, playing a long game in order to bring about a mighty battle that will replenish his power through blood-sacrifice. In the Marvel Comic Universe he has had enough and is aiming to hand over his power to his son, the mighty Thor. Yet he continues to signify wisdom, shrewdness, pragmatism and many other qualities that are greatly needed today. He still inspires the poetic imagination, supplying the stuff of stories and breathing life into poetry. And his dignity and courage as he faces the fate that he realizes cannot be circumvented, his confidence that the world will rise again and go on without him, hold a lesson for us all. The stories that follow bring many different facets of Odin to light, retelling old tales and inventing new ones to celebrate the High One in his many guises.

Ancient & Modern: Introducing Odin

by Charlie Shotton

1.
Origins as Old as Time

Of old was the age / when Ymir lived;
Sea nor cool waves / nor sand there were;
Earth had not been, / nor heaven above,
But a yawning gap, / and grass nowhere.
From *Völuspá* (*The Prophecy of the Seeress*), from the *Poetic Edda* (trans. Henry Adams Bellows, 1936)

is name has sailed through the waves of time for thousands of years, with many praising him upon marvellous acts of war, calling to him for answers, seeking his blessings with sacrifice and following a path in life dedicated to his knowledge and teachings.

He was a being, born from the womb and seed of giants, whose eternal essence surrounds knowledge, power and wisdom, none of which came to him, or his followers, without struggle and sacrifice. Of all the beings throughout the cosmos, of all those who ventured throughout the nine worlds of Yggdrasil, none stood more glorious or better known than the Allfather, Odin.

Odin is known by many names, each inspired by various aspects of his persona and demeanour, or by his acts of legendary grandiose. The name Odin has also been written and translated into different languages, from the original Old Norse to modern-day English. His being has been depicted in poems, sagas, folklore and tales from ages past and brought into contemporary pieces of artwork from paintings and literature to films and comic books. The interpretation of Odin, the one-eyed wanderer, has mostly stayed consistent, with images and descriptions portraying him as a titan, a kingly being who wielded such great wisdom and magic, a figure who put himself through immense struggle and torment for the betterment of mankind as well as his clan of higher beings.

In some instances, Odin travelled through Midgard as a frail, kindly old man in disguise to observe his followers, often simply watching, other times intervening, passing on wise words or even jesting and tormenting his pagan children for his own amusement.

But where did Odin's story begin? Much like other fantastical tales of godly beings and religious figureheads, his origin is part mystery and part historical epic that transcends thousands of years.

THE PROSE EDDA AND THE POETIC EDDA

Odin, the Allfather, stands as one of the most enigmatic and influential figures in Norse mythology, with roots growing deep into the cosmic fabric of ancient northern European belief systems. To uncover the mystery surrounding Odin's beginnings, we must explore the deep, rich narratives of the *Prose Edda* and the *Poetic Edda*. These are the primary sources that provide a glimpse into the complex lore and history of Norse pagan beliefs.

Snorri Sturluson (1179–1241), an Icelandic scholar, compiled the *Prose Edda* in the thirteenth century. This huge piece of work is essential for comprehending the tales and legends of the Norse gods, and most notably Odin. The *Poetic Edda*, on the other hand, is a collection of poems that were contributed anonymously from the same period that adds to our understanding of Norse mythology. It is a collection of poems with deep narratives. This collection is one of the most valuable and important sources on Odin, the gods and the very nature of Norse mythology and pagan beliefs. The *Poetic Edda* is part of the Icelandic manuscript, *Codex Regius* (Royal Book). These poems give life to Odin and Norse mythology and without it, perhaps Odin would not exist in today's world.

Its translation to English has been debated, due to the Old Norse language being difficult to interpret. However, there is a general understanding the *Poetic Edda* consists of 21 poems with 11 being part of the *Codex Regius*.

Many of these poems feature almost everything we know of Odin, with the wider narrative of the poems setting him as the main protagonist, as his presence in the poems are typically during events of great importance and significance. The book is divided into sections, and one of the most well-known poems in the *Edda* is the very first, *Völuspá (The Prophecy of the Seeress)*, which provides a prophetic account of the world's birth, the events leading up to Ragnarök, and the aftermath of this calamity.

Other notable poems include *Hávamál (Sayings of the High One)*, *Hymiskviða (The Lay of Hymir)*, *Vafþrúðnismál (The Lay of Vafthrudnir)* and *Grímnismál (The Lay of Grimnir)*. *Hávamál*, especially, is regarded as wisdom literature and is accredited to Odin. The poem offers counsel, ethical lessons and insight into Norse cultural ideals.

THE BEGINNING OF THE COSMOS

In the beginning of the cosmos, there was a land of fire and a land of ice. Between them lay a void – an abyss of darkness and mystery – called Ginnungagap. The world consumed with flame, flowing stretches of volcanic lava and clouds of ash is known as Múspellheim, and the land that screeched with torrents of ice and freezing winds is Niflheim, with this world often overlapping and being recognized with the other Norse world, Hel. These two worlds existed long before the creation of Earth, or as it is more favourably known in the history of Norse cosmology, Midgard.

The abyss between the two elemental worlds began to transform into a new one as Múspellheim and Niflheim grew closer, with the streams of Niflheim flowing into the void and meeting the fires of Múspellheim. And so the void of Ginnungagap was formed into a new place of being.

The creation of Ginnungagap is written about in the *Gylfaginning* – the first main entry in the *Prose Edda* (trans. Arthur Gilchrist Brodeur, 1916):

"...Ginnungagap, the Yawning Void." Then spake Jafnhárr: "Ginnungagap, which faced toward the northern quarter, became filled with heaviness, and masses of ice and rime, and from within, drizzling rain and gusts; but the southern part of the Yawning Void was lighted by those sparks and glowing masses which flew out of Múspellheim."

Flowing through the newly formed Ginnungagap were icy rivers; however, these rivers, known as Élivágar, were of poison. From this poison, the life of the very first giant being, Ymir, was sprung.

Ymir was a frost giant and alongside him, of all creatures, a cow was also created. This new icy landscape trapped other giants, almost frozen in time waiting to be released from their cold prison. The cow was called Auðumbla and is said to have produced rivers of milk from its udders from which Ymir fed. Auðumbla wandered the land and came upon a giant named Buri, who was stuck in the ice. The cow licked the salty ice for three days and freed Buri onto the world. This marked the very beginnings of Odin, as Buri had a son named Bor, who married Bestla, a giantess, and together they had three sons: Odin, Vili and Vé.

As Bor's sons gained power and stature, they saw Ymir as a threat to the growing order of the cosmos. Odin, Vili and Vé planned to confront and eventually kill Ymir. This act of divine parricide was the catalyst for the creation of the nine worlds.

The three brothers attacked Ymir while he was sleeping, and the scope of the cosmic wrath is vividly described. Ymir's blood gushed like a torrent, drowning most of the other frost giants. Only two stood and survived against the flood of blood. Bergelmir and his wife boarded a hollowed-out tree trunk and became the new leaders of the giants but cast out into their own realm.

After killing Ymir, the three brothers used Ymir's body, which was gargantuan in its nature, to shape the human realm. Ymir's flesh represented Earth (Midgard), his blood the seas, his bones the mountains, his fangs and jaws the rocks and cliffs, and his skull the sky. The gods used Ymir's brows to form a protective barrier around humanity. It is written in *Grímnismál* (trans. Bellows):

Out of Ymir's flesh / was fashioned the earth,
And the ocean out of his blood;
Of his bones the hills, / of his hair the trees,
Of his skull the heavens high.

Mithgarth the gods / from his eyebrows made,
And set for the sons of men;
And out of his brain / the baleful clouds
They made to move on high.

This famous Norse tale symbolizes the common and recurring theme of the Norse beliefs. The never-ending cycle of creation and destruction.

THE FIRST OF THE GIANTS AND NORSE GODS

Odin's family tree and the ancestorial connections between the Norse gods is expansive, magical and ancient. The deities that the pagans worshipped each held their own characteristics and stories. And with the very first Norse gods that were not of the race of giants have an epic tale of blood and warfare. Out of that came the creation of the nine worlds of Yggdrasil.

We talk of frost giants – Ymir and Buri – being the two notable and first to live among the cosmos, but what would they have looked like?

Ymir is depicted looking eerily similar to how humans look today. In paintings and illustrations, he is seen suckling at the udders of the cow that followed his inception as fair-skinned and muscular, but not as an otherworldly being or giant (Jötunn). The later depictions of the giants to how they may have been perceived during the times of Norse pagans and Vikings will undoubtably differ. Most deities throughout time have been showcased as titans; beings that are taller, stronger and hold a distinct prowess compared to mankind.

Ymir could reproduce asexually, and from the sweat of his armpits and from between his legs many other giants were created. These offspring would then birth the first of the Aesir.

ODIN AND THE AESIR TRIBE

Odin is the chieftain and leader of the Aesir tribe. The most famous gods we know today are part of the group, with the likes of Thor, Loki, Baldur, Frigg and Freya all being prominent in the Norse myths. Many of these gods are directly related to Odin, while others represent other emotions and symbols of life.

Thor

Thor, the thunder god and Odin's son, is a powerful and beloved figure in Norse mythology. Known for his tremendous power, fearlessness and fierce temper, Thor holds the mighty hammer Mjölnir. He is a protector and guardian of both the gods and humans, fighting giants, trolls and other monsters that roam the realms. His chariot, pulled by the goats Tanngrisnir and

Tanngnjóstr, symbolize his link to fertility and the cycle of life. Thor's deeds are depicted in various stories cementing his status as a beloved and iconic Norse deity.

Loki

Loki, the complex and intriguing trickster god, is a key figure in Norse mythology. Loki is known for his cunning and unpredictable nature, which resulted in both havoc and redemption. His parentage is unusual, as he is both Jötunn and Aesir. Loki's role in crucial events – such as Baldur's death and Fenrir's binding – influence the course of Norse mythology. Despite his chaotic impulses, Loki is vital to the gods and to Odin, as he represents the duality of deception and resourcefulness.

Baldur

Baldur, the radiating god of beauty and light in Norse mythology, is Odin and Frigg's son. Revered for his extraordinary compassion and knowledge, he is widely regarded as the most adored of the Aesir gods, but perhaps not as much as his father. His mother, Frigg, obtained oaths from all beings of Yggdrasil to protect Baldur from harm, but his terrible fate unfolds when Loki interferes, resulting in the favoured god's death. Baldur's death becomes an impactful moment, symbolizing the fragility of life and the certainty of fate.

Frigg

Frigg, the queen of the Aesir and Odin's wife, is a goddess of motherhood, wisdom and foresight. Her maternal role is highlighted by her worry for her son Baldur, and her skills to see what is yet to unfold are alluded at in several myths. Frigg's influence extends to the hearth and home, representing the ideal of a protective and nurturing mother goddess.

Frey

Frey, a fertility god linked with prosperity and abundance, did not belong to the Aesir gods but to the Vanir. Frey is the twin brother of Freya and the son of Njǫ̈rd, and the ruler of sunlight, rain and harvest. He holds many renowned possessions, including the ship Skíðblaðnir and the boar Gullinbursti. Frey's benevolent influence extends to love and peace, making him a highly worshiped Norse deity.

Freya

Freya, the enchanting goddess of love, beauty and fertility, is like her twin brother a member of the Vanir. She is also associated with death and conflict. Her stunning necklace represents her beauty and appeal. Freya's chariot, driven by mighty cats, depicts her connection to love and battle. Her varied nature distinguishes her as one of the most powerful goddesses in existence.

Heimdall

Heimdall, the watchman of the gods, is a sentinel deity who possesses extraordinary senses. He guards the rainbow Bifröst bridge and ensures Asgard's protection. His expansive vision and hearing make him an invaluable guardian against potential threats and a close friend and adviser to Odin. Heimdall is the one who sounds the Gjallarhorn to signal the start of Ragnarök. His origins are shrouded in obscurity, and his purpose as a vigilant protector emphasizes his importance within the divine order of the Aesir.

THE WORLD TREE YGGDRASIL

The cosmos in Norse mythology is filled with nine realms, each a marvellous spectacle with its own landscapes, rules and leaders. These nine realms are just as important as the ones who occupy them.

The world tree Yggdrasil sits at the centre of everything. This monolithic tree, with deep roots and vast branches that hold the nine worlds, is the essential component that connects cosmological beliefs. Yggdrasil's branches rise high into the heavens, supported by roots that extend deep into the Well of Urdarbrunnr. Each branch has a realm where the gods preside, as well as homes for various other beings and creatures from Norse mythology, such as giants, dwarves and those who can wield magic that can change fate. Yggdrasil also contains the realm of humanity known as Midgard.

The wellbeing of Yggdrasil is inextricably linked to the wellbeing of the cosmos. According to the sources, when Yggdrasil is disturbed or damaged, it is an indication that the beginnings of Ragnarök are commencing.

Norse mythology presents the cosmos as being comprised of nine realms, but other worlds and areas appear in its writings and sources. These areas lie in other parts of the existing nine realms, with some only accessible to those who are worthy. They include the halls of Valhalla where dead warriors celebrate with Odin;

Fólkvang, a place where Freya receives some of the warriors who have died in battle; the everlasting void Ginnungagap; the Bifrost – the rainbow bridge that connects the realms of Asgard and Midgard, guarded by Heimdall; and finally Odin's seat, Hlidskjalf, that allows him to observe the goings-on across the nine worlds as well as a place of reflection and solitude for him and him alone.

Asgard

In Odin's kingdom, high in the sky, the enclosure of the Aesir is a heavenly realm of order and civilized nature. Asgard is home to the Aesir gods and goddesses, who include the Allfather Thor and Baldur. It sits at the top of the pantheon of Norse kingdoms for its paradisical nature. Its glittering halls and palaces, vast riches, harmonious weather and awe-inspiring landscapes truly make it a place people wish to live. Far beneath Asgard lies Valhalla, the halls echoing with the laughter, fighting and cheering of the almighty fallen.

Midgard

The word 'Midgard', which translates as 'Middle Enclosure' in Old Norse, refers to humanity's position in the cosmos. Midgard sits in the centre of Yggdrasil, and above it is Asgard, with the two of them connected via the rainbow Bifrost bridge. We are all too familiar with what Midgard looks like today, but Earth's landscape during the Viking age (793–1066 CE) and further back in time was one of icy fjords and dense forests, without the civilizational advancements we know and often take for granted. Midgard for the Norse pagan people, and to the gods, is a stage for mortal beings and endeavours. It serves as the intersection between divine and earthly affairs, with each struggle and triumph humanity faces echoing through the branches of the world tree and influencing the order of the cosmos.

Vanaheim

The home of the Vanir, Vanaheim is the realm of love and fertility. However, little is known about Vanaheim, as sources provide scarce detail on its appearance. Only few sources mention this realm, with both the *Prose Edda* and *Poetic Edda* detailing it as the place where the god Njǒrd was raised. Vanaheim functions similarly to Asgard, providing a safe haven for those who live there. We know it is a place that sees conflict with the Aesir tribe, with an exchange of hostages leading to a tentative peace and the integration of the Vanir into the cosmic affairs of Asgard.

Jötunheim

Jötunheim is where giants roam, rule and slaughter. A desolate, bitter and empty homeland, it is not a place many dare to visit. The giants of this realm are sworn adversaries of the Aesir tribe. The rocky landscape is barren, with deep forests and icy vistas covering the expansive world. Both the *Eddas* state that winter is never-ending in Jötunheim, leaving no fertile or habitable land. The realm's giants feed on what they can from the rivers and forests. The struggle and hostility between the giants and Odin's clan was everlasting. Thor would frequently visit Jötunheim to slay the giants, which was considered to be one of his favourite pleasures. The giant's resting place, their palace, is known as Utgard. It is carved from ice and snow, and presiding on its throne is the beastly leader, and biological father of Loki, Laufey.

Alfheim

Mythology, fantasy and myths often share similar beings and creatures. Elves frequently appear as mystical entities across many religions and beliefs, and Norse mythology is no different. The elves in Norse pagan beliefs live in the land of Alfheim. These demigod-like beings are elegant creatures who are fairer than the sun. Their description suggests that their abode is a realm of beauty and tranquillity. Alfheim is ruled by the Frey of the Vanir tribe, implying the elves too are beings of fertility, love and nature. Alfheim is surrounded by magic, with the elvish race casting both wicked spells to harm humans, causing illnesses and healing abilities to aid in their woes. Like Vanaheim, the elvish world is not widely written about, with its location considered to be very close to Asgard.

Niðavellir

Dwarves, like elves and other supernatural entities, play an important role in Norse mythology. Their homeland is Niðavellir, where they dwell in underground caves and caverns crafting great weapons, armour and trinkets for themselves and the gods. In fact, they have smithed many of the Norse deities' weapons and equipment, including Thor's hammer Mjölnir, Frey's ship Skiðblaðnir, the ring Draupnir and spear Gungnir, both of which belonging to Odin. The dwarves are said to despise daylight and prefer to spend their time in mines and forges. Their skin is stained with grease, dirt and muck from the work they carry out, with no care to keep themselves clean. Niðavellir is a testament to the intricate layers of Norse mythology and paganistic beliefs, where craftsmanship thrives in the depths of the earth, and hard labour and expert makings are celebrated and valued.

Niflheim and Múspellheim

These two worlds we have touched on and the part they played in the forging of the cosmos. Niflheim, a realm of primordial ice and mist, stands in stark contrast to Múspellheim's fiery essence. Both play a key role in the balance of the cosmos, with Nilfheim's icy breath contributing to the formation of the world, and Múspellheim denoting the cyclical narrative of creation and destruction with its present role in the events of Ragnarök.

Helheim

With Odin's realm of Asgard representing a heavenly confine, with the halls of Valhalla emphasizing the idea of an afterlife for those who are worthy, the less fortunate dwell in Helheim. Ruled by the goddess Hel, this land of the dead is a location for those who did not die in combat, and is characterized by the river Gjöll and the bridge Gjallarbrú, guarded by the monster hound known as Garmr. Helheim is not a place of retribution but rather a destination for those whose path did not bring them to Odin's tableside in Valhalla. Helheim, 'The Realm of Hel' in older Norse sources, is referred to as Hel. The names Hel and Hell, the Christian underworld of endless torment and suffering, derive from the same root in the Proto-Germanic language where Christians and Anglo-Saxons used the same word to define and allude to the region of suffering in their faith. The realm of Helheim is a dark, brooding and dreary place beneath the roots of the world tree. However, where the Christian idea of Hell is a nightmarish, endless life of torture and misery, Helheim in the Norse sources describe it as a limbo for the dead, where there is neither peace nor endless pain. According to the few sources, a fence surrounds Helheim with only one route in to reach its centre.

ODIN: HIS NAMES

Odin is known for his many names, each describing who he is and what he represents. The Old Norse translation of his name is split in two. 'Odr' and 'Inn'. The first part, 'Odr', means frenzy and fury. Even dating back before 2,000 BCE of the Proto-Indo-European times, his name simply represented raging and possessed. These all emphasize who and what Odin is. He is a god of war, violence and rage. This is spread across his epic sagas in the *Poetic Edda* and the *Prose Edda*, with accounts of this titan of war killing the first Jötunn with his brothers, and the god taking part in the many battles of the devastating end of all, Ragnarök.

But that is not all Odin is. He is more than a being who wants death and destruction. For Odin carries the heavy burden of preventing Ragnarök at every chance he gets. He lusts for knowledge when wandering the realms of Yggdrasil.

'Odr' also stands for inspiration, mind and spirit. These are brought forth throughout the several sacrifices the Allfather makes, whether hanging from a branch of the world tree, stabbed with his own spear, or when he rips his eye from his socket as an offering to Mimir. Odin's rewards for these deeds were extraordinary and helped shape pagans in new ways.

'Odr' also means poetry, and this is written about in the second part of the *Prose Edda*, *Skáldskaparmál*, where Odin drinks the Mead of Poetry. The latter part of the translation of his name, 'Inn', is indeed a suffix – meaning 'the' or 'the one'. So, when put together, Odin means; 'the frenzy one', 'fury one', 'the one of poetry' or 'inspired one'.

Grímnismál

In *Grímnismál*, the fourth poem in the *Poetic Edda*, Odin speaks and proclaims his many names and what he has been known as. The tale begins with King Hrauðungr and his two sons, Agnarr and Geirrǫðr.

One day, the brothers went out on their boat to fish, but the sea and weather had ulterior motives. A ferocious storm swept them out to sea and they became washed ashore in a new land. After recovering from the ordeal, they came across a man and a woman, and each fostered one of the siblings. The man fostered Geirrǫðr and the woman fostered Agnarr, and as time passed the man built them a ship.

However, when the brothers presented themselves on the beach, the man took Geirrǫðr aside and spoke to him privately. The man whispered in his ear words of deceit, pitting Geirrǫðr against Agnarr. The brothers climbed aboard the ship and set out to sea to meet their father at his harbour. They arrived, both pleased with their journey and excited to see their father after all this time, who had not yet heard of their arrival. What should have been a joyful moment for both brothers did not come to fruition. The words the man spoke sparked Geirrǫðr's next actions. At the front of the boat, Geirrǫðr leapt ashore and without hesitation pushed the ship back out to sea. Agnarr was taken further and further out towards the horizon, never to be seen again.

Geirrǫðr marched towards his father's settlement and was welcomed with open arms. Unfortunately, events took a dark turn when King Hrauðungr died and Geirrǫðr laid claim to the throne, ruling and becoming famous throughout the land. Years passed and Geirrǫðr had a son who he named Agnarr, after his brother. When the prince turned ten, King Geirrǫðr held a feast with his kin, but eyes were watching on. Henry Adams Bellows writes in his work the tale of these events.

"Seest thou Agnarr, thy fosterling, how he begets children with a giantess in the cave? But Geirröth, my fosterling, is a king, and now rules over his land," Odin asked Frigg. For the foster parents who aided them after coming ashore were Odin and his wife the goddess Frigg. The two had played a marvellous game to see which son would become more successful. Frigg turned to Odin and said, "He [Geirrǫðr] is so miserly that he tortures his guests if he thinks that too many of them come to him." Odin saw Frigg's statement as a lie, and declared a challenge to prove she was in the wrong. Frigg sent her waiting-maid, Fulla, to the king and spoke that a sorcerer among them would try to undo him, and that no man or dog would set upon him. Being in a position where he felt threatened, King Geirrǫðr did not share his food and ordered for the capture of the sorcerer who was feared by all, or supposedly so. The sorcerer wore a blue cloak and was questioned. He gave his name as Grímnir and that is all he spoke. The king ordered for him to be tortured until he gave more information on his motives and who he was. The method of torture involved Grímnir being placed between two fires until he spoke. Shocked by this appalling act, Prince Agnarr brought Grímnir a full horn of mead to drink and heard what he had to say. This is where the verse of *Grímnismál* begins:

Hot art thou, fire! / too fierce by far;
Get ye now gone, ye flames!
The mantle is burnt, / though I bear it aloft,
And the fire scorches the fur.

"Twixt the fires now / eight nights have I sat,
And no man brought meat to me,
Save Agnar alone, / and alone shall rule
Geirröth's son o'er the Goths.

Hail to thee, Agnar! / for hailed thou art
By the voice of Veratyr;
For a single drink / shalt thou never receive
A greater gift as reward.

The land is holy / that lies hard by
The gods and the elves together;
And Thor shall ever / in Thruthheim dwell,
Till the gods to destruction go.

Grímnir goes on to tell of the realms of Yggdrasil and the gods, deities and beings who inhabit it, detailing Odin's Hall, where a "wolf hangs before the west door and an eagle bends over it", as well as accounting how the Earth was created from Ymir's flesh. The names of the gods and goddesses go on and on, with this poem acting as a history lesson for the ten-year-old prince.

Grímnir then goes on to tell of his many names and reveals his identity as the Allfather himself.

A single name / have I never had
Since first among men I fared.

The tale ends with King Geirrǫðr, now knowing Odin was in his presence, wanting to release the Allfather. However, King Geirrǫðr's sword was on his knee, half-drawn, while the king was seated, and surprised by his knowledge and fear of the consequences of what he had done to Odin, stood quickly and proclaimed to release him from the fires. The king's sword fell from his lap with the hilt pointing down. Suddenly, the king tripped on his own foot and fell upon his sharp blade and was killed. Odin, now free, had accomplished what he wanted and disappeared leaving no trace. Agnarr was made king and ruled for years with the knowledge of what Odin had told him.

Translations

The many verses and stanzas in *Grímnismál* detail Odin's various names that encompass all of who he is, for which Henry Adams Bellows provided some translations (not all could be deciphered):

Many of the names are not mentioned elsewhere, and often their significance is sheer guesswork. As in nearly every episode [Odin] appeared in disguise, the number of his names was necessarily almost limitless. Grim: 'The Hooded'. Gangleri: 'The Wanderer'. Herjan: 'The Ruler'. Hjalmberi: 'The Helmet-Bearer'. Thekk: 'The Much-Loved'. Thrithi: 'The Third' [...] Helblindi: 'Hel-Blinder' (two manuscripts have Herblindi: 'Host-Blinder'). Hor: 'The High One'.

Sath: 'The Truthful'. Svipal: 'The Changing'. Sanngetal: 'The Truth-Teller'. Herteit: 'Glad of the Host'. Hnikar: 'The Overthrower'. Bileyg: 'The Shifty-Eyed'. Baleyg: 'The Flaming-Eyed'. Bolverk: 'Doer of Ill' [...]. Fjolnir: 'The Many-Shaped'. Grimnir: 'The Hooded'. Glapswith: 'Swift in Deceit'. Fjolsvith: 'Wide of Wisdom'.

Sithhott: 'With Broad Hat'. Sithskegg: 'Long-Bearded'. [...] Sigfather: 'Father of Victory'. Hnikuth: 'Overthrower'. Valfather: 'Father of the Slain'. Atrith: 'The Rider'. Farmatyr: 'Helper of Cargoes' (i.e., god of sailors).

Nothing is known of Asmund, of Odin's appearance as Jalk, or of the occasion when he 'went in a sledge" as Kjalar ('Ruler of Keels'?). [...] Oski: 'God of Wishes'. [...] Jafnhor: 'Equally High' [...]. Omi: 'The Shouter'. Gondlir: 'Wand Bearer'. Harbarth: 'Graybeard'.

ODIN'S PURPOSE

Odin's name has true meaning which symbolizes the wise god's purpose. As the chief of the gods, he inherited an important role in the newly formed cosmos. The *Prose Edda* defines him as a god with several attributes, the most notable of which are wisdom, magic and war. The thirst for knowledge is emphasized in well-known and staple tales, such as the sacrifice at Mimir's Well, which we will explore in depth on pages 41–44. This self-inflicted wound shows Odin's determination to acquire knowledge at any cost, emphasizing the Norse belief in the value of intelligence.

The *Poetic Edda* dives deeper into Odin's identity through many poems that shed light on different facets of his personality. Odin communicates his wisdom to humanity through the *Hávamál*, or the 'Sayings of the High One'. The stanzas in these poems illustrate the god's link to the runic alphabet, which Odin is granted after his sacrifice by hanging from the World Tree, revealing the mystical and practical sides of runes – the ancient Norse system of writing and divination.

Odin's role as a shaman is also reflected in the *Poetic Edda*, where he is described as a practitioner of seiðr, a type of Norse magic linked with divination, shapeshifting and fate. This aspect of Odin's personality adds levels of complexity to his divine nature, as he engages in acts that contradict traditional gender norms and societal expectations.

The narratives in the *Prose Edda* and the *Poetic Edda* intertwine to create a vivid picture of Odin's varied personality. He is more than just a battle deity or a wise Aesir ruler; he is a cosmic force forever linked to the very fabric of creation. His journey from primordial chaos and murderous ruler to the builder and father of an organized cosmos again highlights the pattern of cycles and rebirth in Norse beliefs.

Odin's Legacy

Odin's beginnings continue to have impact on the Norse people's cultural and religious activities. The desire for wisdom, the value of sacrifice and the understanding of all things being connected are common themes throughout Norse society. Odin's role as the Allfather and primary figure in Norse religion reflects cultural ideals, such as courage, knowledge and duty.

Fate is a common reoccurrence in the Norse myths and Viking beliefs, with many Norse pagans believing their fate was to enter Odin's halls to drink and feast with him and other fallen brothers after dying in battle.

However, no one can know their true fate, whether it is to die in battle or not. Not even the gods could know their fate, not even Odin. This ability to see the future only some knew. In Norse mythology, it was those of the Vanir tribe who only possessed the vision to see what was yet to come. This type of magic was brought to Odin and the Aesir, intended as a gift, but what would unfold would mark a defining event surrounding Odin and all Norse gods.

THE AESIR-VANIR WAR

The Aesir-Vanir War, a significant event in Norse mythology, is a captivating story about divine strength, diplomacy and cosmic equilibrium. This mythical war, described in the *Prose Edda* and the *Poetic Edda*, details complex interactions between two sets of deities, the Aesir and the Vanir, as well as Odin's essential role in forming the Norse cosmos.

The Aesir and Vanir tribe of gods each had their own set of rules and traditions. This is said to be the primary reason for their separation into two distinct groups.

The Aesir's abundance of deities represented might, strength and wisdom, all of which Odin also showcases. The Vanir, a group of gods and goddesses, wanted to use magic and cunning to their advantage. The conflict that broke out between them is similar to any other war. One side sought control due to fear of the other. This fear would result in hatred, suffering and death.

Prior to the war, both groups coexisted peacefully, with Odin and the Aesir residing in Asgard, and the Vanir calling Vanaheim their home. This great conflict took place near the very beginning of the gods' history, but it is not as well-known as the events of Ragnarök. However, the events of the war between the gods made an impact on the Viking and Norse Pagan people and their entire perception of their beloved gods.

The Beginning of the War

The Vanir tribe were skilled in magic, and their magic was something the Aesir and Odin could not fully fathom or believe. Their magic is known as 'seiðr' and is related to the ability to predict and influence fate or someone's future. This rather shamanistic magic occurred with the user in a ritual trance where they connected to other entities and worlds that otherwise could not be seen.

The conflict arose with the burning of the Vanir goddess Gullveig. This Vanir goddess was a sorcerous who came to

Asgard to preach her talents and offer her wisdom of magic to the Aesir people. Gullveig offered anyone who desired it to unravel and change their fate. The Aesir gods marvelled at this because they could not control what was yet to pass and Odin especially sought out this power.

Perplexed and intrigued by this opportunity, the Aesir gods began to ask for simple things, such as the chance to know small events of their futures and fates. However, this sparked debate and conflict amongst the Aesir deities. Their squabbles and disputes led them to assume that Gullveig had come to Asgard to intentionally pit them against one another.

The Aesir gods attempted to quell their fury by seizing and attacking Gullveig. They stabbed her body with spears, before placing her on a pier to be burned. This attack on the goddess is depicted in *Völuspá* and showcases the violent nature of the Aesir as well as the power these deities had at defying death:

"The war I remember, the first in the world, When the gods with spears, had smitten Gollveig, And in the hall of Hor had burned her, Three times burned, and three times born, Oft and again, yet ever she lives."

In astonishment, the Aesir gods released Gullveig, who could not be silenced for good. The Aesir's belief of Gullveig being an evil force set to doom their tribe was reinforced. Upon release, Gullveig returned to her people and told them what the Aesir had attempted. The Vanir were outraged with the attempt on Gullveig's life; their deep upset would have to be resolved, as they had sent the goddess to Asgard to simply teach their ways.

For this torment, the Vanir prepared for war, filled with vengeance and hatred. Odin was quick to respond and began preparing himself and his people for the conflict. Odin always sought new wisdom and knowledge, but did not seek the Vanir's magical wisdom. His greed for war and triumph was a far greater alure.

Odin was the first to initiate the start of the war by tossing his spear into the Vanir. The great war between the Aesir and Vanir had begun.

With the Vanir's use of magic, which the Aesir tribe still did not completely comprehend, the Vanir began to gain an advantage in the battle. As Asgard's walls and other landmarks crumbled into rubble and dust, the Aesir unleashed the full force of their gifts and powers, wreaking havoc on the Vanir and their realms.

Both sides were beginning to become equal in their skill, each tribe saw heavy losses and destruction to what they held most dear. Both groups began to realize that neither could claim victory. They grew bored of fighting and started to debate who was to blame for the conflict in the first place.

Odin, as the Allfather and the leader of the Aesir, was instrumental in managing the complications of the Aesir-Vanir War. His knowledge and awareness, earned through countless hardships and sacrifices, established him as an important meditator and strategist. According to the *Prose Edda*, Odin, recognized the destructive nature of the conflict, the two factions declared a truce and exchanged prisoners to end the hostilities.

Exchanging Hostages

In exchange for the Vanir deities Njðrd, Frey and Freya, who were sent to Asgard, the Aesir deities Hœnir and Mimir were banished to Vanaheim. However, this seemingly peaceful end to the war was the start of other troubles between the Norse gods.

Njðrd, along with his son Frey and daughter Freya of Vanir, were welcomed into Asgard and began teaching the magic that was intended to be a gift to Odin and his people. Hœnir and Mimir began to provoke the Vanir at their new home in Vanaheim, and Hœnir was appointed as one of their leaders, while Mimir, one of the wisest gods, stood by his side as an adviser. Mimir would advise and delegate authority over crucial decisions. He advised Hœnir to step back as the appointed decision-maker and let others debate and decide such important matters. Hœnir was viewed as a god of force and ferocity rather than a wise leader, especially compared to the Vanir's previous batch of rulers. The Vanir felt duped – they had received an inferior peace offering in this arrangement to end the war.

To seek vengeance and revenge, the Vanir beheaded Mimir and returned him to Odin. However, Odin did not grow violent or spark hateful speeches and acts of war this time. For the Allfather had been learning of the new ways of magic and could bring the living back from the dead. Odin revived Mimir's head by preserving it with herbs and magical charms and gave the head the ability to speak. He would keep Mimir's head close to him with him giving council, advice and great knowledge.

The Meaning of the Great Conflict

One of the most important consequences of this war was the incorporation of the Vanir into the Aesir pantheon: notably, Njǫrd, the god of the sea, and his two children, Frey and Freya, symbolizing the harmonious union of the two families. This integration represented an ingrained moment in Norse mythology – the interconnection of cosmic forces and the value of balance.

The *Poetic Edda* adds depth to the story by presenting poetic tales of the conflict and its aftermath. *Völuspá*, the *Prophecy of the Seeress*, alludes to the Aesir-Vanir struggle and foretells the gods' ultimate demise during Ragnarök. This apocalyptic vision includes elements of fate and inevitability, mirroring Norse beliefs about the cycle of existence. Odin's participation in the war is more than just that of a mediator. His role represents his greater purpose as a cosmic architect and balancer. After all, he did shape the very fabric of the realms from Ymir's body. The incorporation of the Vanir into the Aesir tribe is consistent with Odin's ultimate objective of establishing order. The war, while chaotic, eventually adds to the larger cosmic harmony envisioned by the Allfather.

Völuspá

Völuspá has been interpreted as a tale being told to Odin, an account of events he took part in. *Völuspá* begins with the seeress, a lady blessed with prophetic powers who summons Odin. Her request to Odin sets the stage for a cosmic revelation, implying that what follows is more than just a historical tale but a heavenly insight into the past, present and future. In Norse mythology, Odin is respected as both the chief of the Aesir and a seeker of knowledge.

These events are mentioned in the very first poem of the *Poetic Edda*, *Völuspá*:

Hearing I ask / from the holy races,
From Heimdall's sons, / both high and low;
Thou wilt, Valfather, / that well I relate
Old tales I remember / of men long ago.

I remember yet / the giants of yore,
Who gave me bread / in the days gone by;
Nine worlds I knew, / the nine in the tree
With mighty roots / beneath the mold.

Of old was the age / when Ymir lived;
Sea nor cool waves / nor sand there were;
Earth had not been, / nor heaven above,
But a yawning gap, / and grass nowhere.

2.
Mores and Morals: A Meeting of Paganism and Christianity

Here were dreadful forewarnings come over the lands of Northumbria, and woefully terrified the people: these were amazing sheets of lightning and whirlwinds, and fiery dragons were seen flying in the sky…the woeful inroads of heathen men destroyed God's church in Lindisfarne island by fierce robbery and slaughter.
– From the *Anglo-Saxon Chronicle,* Eleventh Century

he classic tales in the *Poetic Edda* and *Prose Edda* tell of Norse mythology and Odin's life. The beliefs, their meanings and the societal rules of pagan culture would have opposed greatly different opinions for the diverse groups of people across the continent of Europe. Christianity, at the time, viewed paganism with such abhorrence that wars were fought over their differing beliefs and ways of life.

There are many entries of both *Eddas* that feature Odin, but some are more famous than others, with certain myths truly presenting his ethos and purpose. The ending of the Aesir-Vanir war saw almost a restart of the culture of the Norse deities, which circles back to the constant theme of life starting over, with new ideas, morals and fates coming into play. Seeing what this conflict brought about, Odin was now aware that not all problems needed to be solved with war and violence. Now was the time for him to become more than that. These stories present him in his ultimate form, expressing all aspects of his nature, from his eagerness to learn to his selfish acts of heroism. Odin's most defining moments are depicted in the stories of his quest for knowledge and, hand-in-hand, the sacrifices he makes to reach that goal.

The main myths in question are focused on and retold using passages from sources in the *Codex Regius*. Complete tales include 'Odin's Sacrifice of His Eye', the knowledge of runes in 'Nine Days of Hanging' and finally the doomed end of the world in 'Ragnarök'.

ODIN'S SACRIFICE OF HIS EYE

This first tale is not actually described in the main sources written by Sturluson; rather, it is a narrative that has been retold and interpreted from various other sources within Norse mythology. This sacrifice is only mentioned as a retelling in stanza 28 of *Völuspá*, with the Völva, also known as a seeress, recounting the ancient lore of the cosmos:

Alone I sat / when the Old One sought me,
The terror of gods, / and gazed in mine eyes:
"What hast thou to ask? / why comest thou hither?
Othin, I know / where thine eye is hidden."

I know where Othin's / eye is hidden,
Deep in the wide-famed / well of Mimir;
Mead from the pledge / of Othin each morn
Does Mimir drink: / would you know yet more?

Unlike the famous story of Odin hanging from Yggdrasil, his sacrifice at Mimir's Well is a broader representation of Odin's quest for knowledge and is a culmination of the main thematic elements in other Norse myths. It goes to show that Norse mythology has many gaps and missing pieces, much like many other religious and historical accounts, and emphasizes both the significance of the Allfather's purpose to gain as much knowledge as possible and how Odin's very essence has survived thousands of years with considerable consistency.

Mimir's Well

Yggdrasil, the world tree that connects the realms together, stood bold, and Odin gazed with his two eyes at the almighty wonder of it all. Yet, Odin's sight only stretched so far. The King of the Aesir, while content with the state of his realm Asgard, and the other eight lands that Yggdrasil held, longed for something more. His thirst grew stronger with each passing day as he travelled across the realms. During this time, he learnt of a place that would give him the knowledge he sought.

Mimir's Well was a sacred source of wisdom from which only those who are worthy could drink. The waters possessed unimaginable knowledge of the cosmos and the fate of all kinds, both gods and mortals alike. Odin was transfixed by the powers granted by Mimir's Well and journeyed to the roots to become powerful with the knowledge of mysteries of existence. "But at what cost?" he thought. His quests for knowledge thus far had all come with a price, but that did not matter to him. He cast all apprehension aside and made for the roots where the well and its guardian were situated.

"What brings you to my sanctum, Odin?" Mimir questioned the Allfather with a trace of curiosity.

"Why do you ask what you already know, Mimir? In your well flow the answers I seek. The understanding of the cosmos, the fate of my kind, you and all who dwell across Yggdrasil's branches and roots." Odin stood and saw a faint smirk form on Mimir's face.

Mimir came close to Odin and faced him. "You are most wise at this very moment but there is more to learn. But to do so, a price must be paid."

"I am no stranger to paying great costs," said Odin.

Mimir's next words were spoken with gravity. "This price is no mere currency or material wealth. A sacrifice of oneself must be made, but you know this. But what part of you do I deem worthy for my well's power and foresight?"

Mimir turned and walked towards his well. Odin followed closely and gazed upon its magnificence. The water glistened with an otherworldly luminescence, which lured Odin. He saw the very core of Yggdrasil coming from its depths and stood in awe of its power.

"Is this where you have gathered your wisdom and knowledge, Mimir?" Odin asked. "Why not share this with me and my people?"

"Because only those who are worthy may have what I do. Your fate is to give me what I want and be rewarded, not for me to share this out of my own good will with your kind or with the mortals you helped to create."

"Then tell me," said Odin. "What is it you want from me?"

"From you I require something deeply integral to your being. You have made a long, arduous journey traversing your realms to reach me, and now you must make an even tougher decision," said Mimir.

Odin looked at him, slightly unnerved and with high anticipation of his next words. "Give me your eye," Mimir stated. "Your all-seeing eyes are perhaps your greatest asset. Cut one from its socket and I shall allow you to drink the core of Yggdrasil and become as wise, perhaps wiser, then even myself." Mimir paused and tried to gauge Odin's emotions of the request. Odin hid any hint of fear or distress.

"What say you, Aesir ruler?"

Odin looked at the well and the waters within it and turned back to Mimir. "I am a creator. Without me, mortal kind would not exist and praise me as they should. I have helped sow the seeds of existence throughout the lands and travelled to learn all there is to know. And what I have learnt is the destruction of all creation, Ragnarök." The air fell silent and Mimir's face suddenly had a look of worry. "I know you fear it too," Odin continued. "I have grown very fond of what I have helped to build, and I understand my burden of knowing the end of all beings comes with the task of trying to prevent it."

Mimir was impressed with the Aesir leader's determination in his words. "So, you will cut out your eye and cast it into my well?"

"I will do what I must to save all who wander the realms," Odin said, undeterred. He approached the well and saw his reflection in the water. He saw not only his face but also the waters dancing and shimmering with ancient knowledge, only furthering his determination and conviction of his sacrifice.

Odin's sacrifice

Odin paused, surveying the cosmos with a gaze that transcended mortal limitations. He felt the winds whispering through the branches of Yggdrasil, speaking of fate and destiny. Underneath his cloak, Odin withdrew his mighty spear, Gungnir. He raised his hand and with this motion the atmosphere became electric with arcane energy. He felt his eye, the source of his divine perception, begin to radiate and a bright glow pulsated from it. He pointed his spear to his eye and sliced it from its socket. Blood dripped down his cheeks, but Odin made no cry of pain.

He held his eye in his hand and took one last look. Without hesitation, Odin threw it into the water and it sank into the depths, consumed in the magical essence and never to be seen again.

Mimir stood next to Odin and gifted him a horn. "Drink the waters and become all-seeing."

Odin took the horn and filled it. He gulped down the contents and as soon as the horn left his lips, a surge of transcendent insight swept into him. The cosmos unfolded before him, with its fate and destiny now clear and present in his mind. Mimir did not say a word. His silence was filled with a nod of acknowledgement that Odin was truly worthy of having the burden of cosmic knowledge.

The Aftermath of the Sacrifice

Following the great sacrifice, Odin's perspective on existence changes dramatically. The world around him is no longer limited by mortal perception; rather, it emerges as a multifaceted tapestry of interwoven threads.

The sacrifice of Odin's eye is a watershed point in Norse mythology, representing the innate link between insight and personal sacrifice. It emphasizes the Norse idea that true enlightenment is not an easy path, but one that demands the relinquishment of oneself, an acknowledgement that the quest for great truths comes at a cost that goes beyond materialism. Odin, now marked by his sacrifice, emerges from the hallowed area at Yggdrasil's roots with renewed purpose. His remaining eye, a statement of divine wisdom, conveys the cosmic mysteries he has discovered. The sacrifice became legendary, and the unmistakable mark on the Allfather's face revealed the depths one must go to achieve real wisdom.

As Odin ascended from the roots of Yggdrasil, the nine realms resonated with his enlightenment. The gods of Asgard, the giants of Jötunheim and the mortals of Midgard all perceived a subtle shift in the cosmic equilibrium. Odin's sacrifice echoed throughout the lands, leaving an everlasting mark on the collective consciousness of the Norse inhabitants.

Following the transformative event, Odin once again took on the mantle of wanderer and continued to journey through the realms with a sagely purpose. His interactions with beings from all realms were now instilled with a fresh sense of awareness and knowledge. In Asgard, Odin's hall was brimming with those telling of the legendary act at the well, absorbing the essence of his sacrifice. The tale is a critical component of the rich history of Norse mythology. It represents the interconnectivity of wisdom, sacrifice and destiny, inspiring individuals who consider its significance to undertake their own journeys of self-discovery.

NINE DAYS OF HANGING

There are few stories that are as profound as the saga of Odin hanging himself from the world tree, Yggdrasil, for nine days and nights. The tale is an integral part of Odin's quest for wisdom, a sacrifice as famous for the Norse pagans as the story of Jesus being nailed to the cross for Christians. There are, in fact, several distinct similarities between the two stories regarding the harrowing torture both deities endure. Odin's sacrifice is denoted as fully being self-inflicted, without being forced in any way by his enemies. Jesus's sacrifice, on the other hand, while he knew what he was about to suffer – with such brutality and violence from being lashed by Roman soldiers and paraded through the streets carrying his heavy cross to the nails being slammed into his hands and being hanged on his crucifix – was all carried out by those who feared him.

The word 'Yggdrasil' can be broken down into two meanings: 'Ygg' meaning 'death' and 'Drasil' deriving from the old Norse term meaning both 'gallows' and 'horse'. In turn, Yggdrasil translates to 'Dead Gallows' and it is possible that it gets its name from Odin hanging on its branches. The 'horse' translation in the context of the myths symbolizes Yggdrasil as the mount Odin rode on his travels through the nine realms.

The similarities between the tales of Odin and Jesus Christ are more apparent due to the time period in which the *Eddas* were written. The *Prose Edda* dates back to 1220 CE and is imbedded with Sturluson's Christian influence throughout. Sturluson added his own details that extenuate the Norse mythology at times, and within the prologue of the *Prose Edda* he included the biblical version of creation, including Adam and Eve, and the story of Noah's Ark and the great flood.

The roots of this myth can be uncovered in *Hávamál*, a section of the *Poetic Edda* where Odin tells the story through poetic verses. Once again, Odin is after great knowledge, and the wisdom he seeks involves the secrets of the runes and language itself. Stanzas 138–164 detail Odin hanging and finding the runes, or songs as they are called in the translation. Nine songs, one for each day the Allfather hung there, as well as precious mead poured from Óðrerir, which gave him greater wisdom. The Christian influence shines again with Odin describing eighteen rules, much like the Ten Commandments.

The poem is as follows:

I ween that I hung / on the windy tree,
Hung there for nights full nine;
With the spear I was wounded, / and offered I was
To Othin, myself to myself,
On the tree that none / may ever know
What root beneath it runs.
None made me happy / with loaf or horn,
And there below I looked;

I took up the runes, / shrieking I took them,
And forthwith back I fell.

Nine mighty songs / I got from the son
Of Bolthorn, Bestla's father;
And a drink I got / of the goodly mead
Poured out from Othrörir.

Then began I to thrive, / and wisdom to get,
I grew and well I was;
Each word led me on / to another word,
Each deed to another deed.

Runes shalt thou find, / and fateful signs,
That the king of singers colored,
And the mighty gods have made;
Full strong the signs, / full mighty the signs
That the ruler of gods doth write.

Othin for the gods, / Dain for the elves,
And Dvalin for the dwarfs,
Alsvith for giants / and all mankind,
And some myself I wrote.

Knowest how one shall write, / knowest how one shall rede?
Knowest how one shall tint, / knowest how one makes trial?
Knowest how one shall ask, / knowest how one shall offer?
Knowest how one shall send, / knowest how one shall sacrifice?

Better no prayer / than too big an offering,
By thy getting measure thy gift;
Better is none / than too big a sacrifice,...
So Thund of old wrote / ere man's race began,
Where he rose on high / when home he came

The songs I know / that king's wives know not,
Nor men that are sons of men;
The first is called help, / and help it can bring thee
In sorrow and pain and sickness.

A second I know, / that men shall need
Who leechcraft long to use...

A third I know, / if great is my need
Of fetters to hold my foe;
Blunt do I make / mine enemy's blade,
Nor bites his sword or staff.

A fourth I know, / if men shall fasten
Bonds on my bended legs;
So great is the charm / that forth I may go,
The fetters spring from my feet,
Broken the bonds from my hands.
A fifth I know, / if I see from afar
An arrow fly 'gainst the folk;
It flies not so swift / that I stop it not,
If ever my eyes behold it.

A sixth I know, / if harm one seeks
With a sapling's roots to send me;
The hero himself / who wreaks his hate
Shall taste the ill ere I.

A seventh I know, / if I see in flames
The hall o'er my comrades' heads;
It burns not so wide / that I will not quench it,
I know that song to sing.

An eighth I know, / that is to all
Of greatest good to learn;
When hatred grows / among heroes' sons,
I soon can set it right.

A ninth I know, / if need there comes
To shelter my ship on the flood;
The wind I calm / upon the waves,
And the sea I put to sleep.

A tenth I know, / what time I see
House-riders flying on high;
So can I work / that wildly they go,
Showing their true shapes,
Hence to their own homes.

An eleventh I know, / if needs I must lead
To the fight my long-loved friends;

I sing in the shields, / and in strength they go
Whole to the field of fight,
Whole from the field of fight,
And whole they come thence home.

A twelfth I know, / if high on a tree
I see a hanged man swing;
So do I write / and colour the runes
That forth he fares,
And to me talks.

A thirteenth I know, / if a thane full young
With water I sprinkle well;
He shall not fall, / though he fares mid the host,
Nor sink beneath the swords.

A fourteenth I know, / if fain I would name
To men the mighty gods;
All know I well / of the gods and elves,
Few be the fools know this.

A fifteenth I know, / that before the doors
Of Delling sang Thjothrörir the dwarf;
Might he sang for the gods, / and glory for elves,
And wisdom for Hroptatyr wise.

A sixteenth I know, / if I seek delight
To win from a maiden wise;

The mind I turn / of the white-armed maid,
And thus change all her thoughts.

A seventeenth I know, / so that seldom shall go
A maiden young from me;
Long these songs / thou shalt, Loddfafnir,
Seek in vain to sing;
Yet good it were / if thou mightest get them,
Well, if thou wouldst them learn,
Help, if thou hadst them.

An eighteenth I know, / that ne'er will I tell
To maiden or wife of man, –
The best is what none / but one's self doth know,
So comes the end of the songs, –
Save only to her / in whose arms I lie,
Or who else my sister is.

Now are Hor's words / spoken in the hall,
Kind for the kindred of men,
Cursed for the kindred of giants:
Hail to the speaker, / and to him who learns!
Profit be his who has them!
Hail to them who hearken!

It is apparent that these songs and teachings are societal rules, a structure of how to live and treat one another, with Odin passing on these words of wisdom for mankind. Most of the stanzas talk about fighting, death and the afterlife and how man should not be afraid to die, for Odin watches over them and promises to be their guardian, truly solidifying him as the Allfather. This is emphasized in stanza 156 (*An eleventh I know*...)

Odin's self-sacrifice gifted him and his people, as well as those throughout the cosmos, with newfound insight and a deeper understanding of order. It could be said that this tale, whatever its version was before being written in the *Poetic Edda*, helped shape the way of life for the followers of Odin and the other gods in Norse mythology. His sacrifice is a cornerstone of Norse mythology and a testament to the lengths one must go to gain profound truths that govern one's very being. Odin's hanging is part of a wider tale that explores themes of sacrifice, enlightenment and the interdependence of all things. It transcends the confines of a single narrative, becoming a symbol that speaks to people who strive to navigate the tangled web of fate and uncover the mysteries hidden within Norse mythology.

RUNES: ODIN'S GIFT OF WISDOM AND WARNINGS

You might have seen runic symbols: mystical writings with meanings that carry through Odin's wisdom and the songs which he learnt after his hanging. The runes that he uncovered after his sacrificial ordeal and the myth is the origin story of how these symbols came to be. But what about the factual origins of this alphabet?

There has been much conjecture about the exact origins of runes and their writings. The prevalent opinion is they originated from the various Old Italic alphabets used by Mediterranean people in the first century CE, who lived to the south of Germanic tribes and Norse pagans, the followers of Odin. Early symbols discovered on runes and in European rock carvings most likely affected the formation of runic scripts, symbols and alphabets. The runic alphabet was the first means of communication between the Norse and Germanic peoples. The runes were more than merely letters; they carried other connotations behind them. Each rune was unique in that it was a particular sign representing a cosmic concept or force, and the similarities between the songs Odin recites are close. In all Germanic languages, the word rune signifies 'letter', 'secret', or 'mystery'.

The Elder and Younger Futharks

The runic alphabet, named the 'futhark', is split into two types. The Elder Futhark consists of 24 symbols and is said to have been widely used between 100–800 CE, and the Younger Futhark is a collection of 16 symbols used between 800–1100 CE, but other regions of Scandinavia utilized runes as a means of communication far after this period and as recently as the early twentieth century.

Each rune symbolizes a letter and meaning, which, when combined, create words. Runes were mostly carved rather than written down and were also utilized for magic. Runic magic was often used for uncovering fates and the future, protection, spellcasting, shamanistic practices and a variety of other purposes. These symbols have been carved on weaponry, tools, jewellery and memorial stones, illustrating their scope and power. Their use goes to show how much of an influence the myth of Odin discovering them had on the Germanic peoples and Norse pagan society.

As time passed and the runic symbols spread to different cultures, a third Futhark was created, with 33 symbols making up the alphabet. These were gradually included into the Elder Futhark.

The Rune's True Origins

Although Odin discovered the beginnings of the runic alphabet in mythological legends while hanging from Yggdrasil, the first runic inscriptions discovered date back to roughly 50 CE. Scholars have argued what the early runic symbols imply and whether the letters are runic or Roman. The first ones to be discovered were found in Germany – rather than any country in Scandinavia – on a brooch in Meldorf, northern Germany, but it is unfortunately unclear as to what they represent.

However, we do know where the very first inscriptions were found and on what artefacts they were inscribed. A Vimose comb from Denmark, dating back to 160 CE, made of antler and scribed with the male name 'Harja' was one of the first artefacts found. As well as the name, the comb was etched with runic lettering, which demonstrates the runic alphabet was used to inscribe personal belongings, similar to how we now label our possessions. It is possible that the Norse pagans of the time labelled their belongings to prevent thieves from robbing them, implying this may have helped to maintain law and order. This goes back to how Odin reciting the 18 songs in the poem *Hávamál* represents order and laws.

Another noteworthy find is the Kylver stone from Gotland, Sweden. This stone, dating to *c.* 400 CE, is the earliest known carving of the Futhark. It was discovered in a tomb, implying the runes were engraved on the limestone to aid the individual buried there in the journey to the afterlife. However, the translated inscription provides no evidence to corroborate this theory or the notion that it served as a headstone for the tomb. As a result, some speculate the runes were carved only for the sake of practising this new language. Due to the majority of the Nordic people having been illiterate, runic inscriptions offered a symbolic protection of their possessions and property. Whether they were on weapons or gravestones, Odin, with his teachings and his power as the king of all gods, was now always with them.

Interpreting the Runes

Most people who try to understand runes find them quite mysterious. The original meanings of the very first runes are interpreted in a variety of ways, meaning we will never know what some of them truly signify or represent. Their origins may have come from different languages around the world, and we can only understand what we have uncovered. These archaeological finds must be deciphered and interpreted in our own unique way. Runes transmitted messages of protection, guidance and ruthless warnings to the Norse people. Their essence could be said to be an extension of Odin himself, given their meanings are representations of the Aesir god's very nature and attributes.

There is a well-known story that emphasizes the belief that runes hold magical properties, a runic healing tale from *Egil's Saga*.

A Runic Healing Tale

While travelling, Egil came across a farmer called Thorfinn and stopped to share food with him. The farmer informed Egil that his daughter, Helga, had come down with a great illness and was struggling for her life. The farmer begged Egil to help him and his daughter, and Egil accepted. Egil was an expert in runes, and when he checked the daughter's bed, he discovered a whale bone with runes inscribed on it. The farmer revealed the runes were carved by the son of a neighbouring farmer, whose knowledge of the runes were that of a novice, limited and incomplete. Egil concluded that the uneducated farmer's runes were most likely the cause of the girl's illness.

Egil set fire to the whale bone, erasing all proof of it and the cursed runes' existence. Egil then carved new symbols to counteract the cursed runes and placed them beneath the daughter's bed.

A passage from the tale is as follows:

Runes none should grave ever
Who knows not to read them;
Of dark spell full many
The meaning may miss.
Ten spell-words writ wrongly
On whale-bone were graven:
Whence to leek-tending maiden,
Long sorrow and pain.

This part of *Egil's Saga* demonstrates how sacred knowledge is, and extenuates Odin's attributes and how much he valued spreading his wisdom. It, again, also shows how knowledge cannot be gained on a whim; one must devote oneself to learning to avoid grave consequences – such as the farmer's daughter falling ill. The saga goes on to explain why the innocent daughter was cursed with sickness. In chapter 78, it states:

The man who had graved the runes for Helga dwelt not far off. It now came out that he had asked her to wife, but Thorfinn would not give her. Then this landowner's son would fain beguile her, but she would not consent. So he thought to grave for her love-runes, but he did not understand them aright, and graved that wherefrom she took her sickness.

Magic of the Runes

This tale supports how prominent magic was for Odin and the other gods in Norse mythology, which echo the practices of the Nordic population during the pre-Christian era.

Magic was an integral component of Norse pagans' daily existence. They believed other people and items could hold magical properties. The pre-Christian Germanic people thought that spirits might be found in a variety of items throughout their world. These spirits could be a part of any living, non-living or inanimate object, and were capable of acting independently.

Much like the expansive deities in Norse mythology, the ones who practised magic and shamanistic rituals were women. Magic was not defined as good or bad, as the people of the time held different moral standards to those we hold today. Women employed magic to see their own and others' fates. The Vanir tribe of gods also brought these abilities to Odin and the Aesir, which acted as the catalyst to the great war between the two tribes.

Magic practices in pre-Christian Scandinavia looked very different to what we consider magic today. Despite the fact that magic was essentially a belief, many saw it as the inescapable truth. It was deeply ingrained in society, no doubt thanks to the spread of the myths and tales of Odin uncovering the runes. Like other facts concerning Norse paganism, Odin and other historical aspects, our knowledge is based on evidence. Unfortunately, we have little proof of the divisions or types of magic that existed at the time. There is no one form of Norse magic described in either *Eddas* or other sources we know much about.

In Norse society, only women practised 'seiðr', the high ritual magic to predict and twist an individual's fate. This was accomplished by a symbolic procedure known as 'weaving', in which the user entered a trance to interact and communicate with the spirit world and the gods.

Practitioners of seiðr were known as 'Völva', with the goddesses Freya and Gullveig being the main deities in this category. The Völva stood out because of their attire – in brightly coloured dresses, gloves and headwear – but most significant of it all were their staffs, painted decoratively with runes. Many have been discovered and excavated, revealing great detail, including those adorned with brass and fused with stones. Odin himself is depicted with a staff, a walking stick to use on his travels and as a source of his power, suggesting the Völva would be embodying the god when performing their magic.

When they entered their trance, the Völva would be hallucinating as they performed, either in solitude or in front of an audience, and would enter that state by rubbing a toxic henbane plant (of the nightshade family) on their skin. The psychedelic qualities of this plant, as well as other hallucinogens used, may have played a role in strengthening Norse pagan ideas and religion, especially to their connection with Odin's teachings. They would sing songs, known as a 'galdr', to unleash their powers and gain access to the other realms and communicate with spirits. Their songs were sung to raise the dead, provide healing for the wounded and diseased, and to dampen storms or bless voyages and acts of battles.

Völva Artefacts

In 1954, in Jutland, Denmark, a Völva grave was discovered, dating to the ninth century during the early stages of the Viking Age. Archaeologists discovered the Völva body within the grave, dressed in a long blue and crimson gown with white sleeves, a headscarf laced with gold thread and silver toe rings. The body of the seeress was displayed on top of a horse-drawn carriage, which could indicate how these women were prepared for their journey to the afterlife. It would have been considered a great honour to take part in burying such a person.

Additional artefacts found with the sorceress highlight the significance of her position within her community. A silver box brooch with gold plating was discovered to contain white lead. This plant-based white lead powder has a medicinal history stretching back over two millennia in Europe. Some believe the powder could have had a cosmetic purpose in seiðr ceremonies. Additionally, one of the most valuable possessions of the Völva found at the gravesite was, indeed, a staff.

RAGNARÖK

Our third myth and infamous tale of death is the cataclysmic destruction of the cosmos – from the ashes of which new worlds would be born – known as Ragnarök. With the addition of Christian influence in the tale's sources, the story of Ragnarök could be compared to Noah's Ark, in which the great flood from 40 days and 40 nights of rainfall wipes the slate clean for God's people, and Earth undergoes a reincarnation through mass sacrifice.

Odin, no matter the sacrifices he makes, no matter the wisdom he gathers, simply cannot stop Ragnarök. For it is a fate spun by the weavers, and it begins with a winter so extraordinary with bitter freezing cold, chilling winds and ferocious storms. Three years of this pass without a break, the torrent everlasting and taking with it the weak to dwell in Hel. With the storms and the freezing temperatures killing off the most vulnerable first, it sent a torment into those who survived. It was not just loved ones and neighbours that were lost; crops would not grow and food quickly became scarce. Desperation soon overpowered Midgard, and those who were once companions and friends turned on each other with chaotic ferocity, killing and slaughtering for survival. Fathers killed sons and mothers their daughters. This was just a taste of a new age of famine, swords, bloody murder and warfare. This three-year-long ice age is known as the Fimbulwinter and caused the Yggdrasil to shake violently, resulting in turmoil across the cosmos. The sky shifted into an endless void that swallowed the stars, and the lands of the nine realms collapsed with no tree or mountain left standing. The realms of men and gods became a wasteland and battlefield where the almighty struggles and war commenced, as we read in *Völuspá*:

Brothers shall fight / and fell each other,
And sisters' sons / shall kinship stain;
Hard is it on earth, / with mighty whoredom;
Axe-time, sword-time, / shields are sundered,
Wind-time, wolf-time, / ere the world falls;
Nor ever shall men / each other spare

Restraining the Enemy

The events of Ragnarök saw Odin face a terrifying and violent opponent known as Fenrir, the wolf offspring of the god Loki and a woman from Jötunheim called Angrboða. Fenrir was one of their three children, with the others being a daughter, Hel, and the world serpent Jörmungandr. Odin and the other Aesir learnt that these children would cause great trouble for the cosmos, no thanks to them inheriting their parents' evil and coercive nature, and sent a party to bring all three of them to him. Odin, not taking the risk of letting these beings carry out the atrocities prophesized, cast Hel into Niflheim (the cold and misty land of the dead) and Jörmungandr into the deep seas of Midgard, surrounding all lands with the intention of remaining there for all time.

Fenrir, on the other hand, was more cunning and difficult to restrain. The wolf grew in size at an alarming rate, becoming increasingly powerful and menacing, so that even Odin began to truly fear him. The gods tried to bind Fenrir using several magical chains, but the wolf was too strong and easily broke free.

No ordinary chain was strong enough, so Odin enlisted the help of the dwarves, for they were master smiths who could forge chains strong enough to keep the hellish wolf at bay. The result of the dwarves' aid was the creation of Gleipnir, a magical chain made from impossible substances, including the sound of a cat's footstep, the roots of mountains, the breath of fish, the beard of a woman and the spittle of a bird.

The gods were now confident they had the means to bind Fenrir and keep him that way. Fenrir, intrigued by their confidence, allowed them to bind him on one condition: that one of them would place their hand in his mouth as a gesture of trust. The wolf was so disastrously evil and wicked, only the god Tyr was brave enough to take him on his offer and placed the chains around Fenrir's neck. Tyr positioned his hand in the wolf's mouth, and when Fenrir realized he could not break free, he snapped his jaw shut with his razor-sharp teeth, severing the god's hand.

With Fenrir successfully bound by Gleipnir, Odin and his kin were shocked and appalled by the wolf's actions and Odin was especially furious that his son had lost his hand. Odin anchored the chain to a boulder called Gjöll, enraging Fenrir even further and causing him great agony while he waited for his revenge in the final battle of Ragnarök.

The binding of Fenrir is a perfect example of how prominent the themes of fate, sacrifice and inevitability are in Norse mythology and the tales of Odin, and the beast's role in Ragnarök is that of destruction and confrontation between the forces of chaos and the gods.

A Battle to End All

On Fenrir's side was Surtr, the fire giant who dwelt in the realm of Múspellheim. Surtr was a guardian of fire, a savage ruler, a monstrous being who carried a sword of flames in which he wreaked havoc and destruction. He was Odin's counterpart, his rival, his evil opposite who wished nothing but doom for all beings. The fire Jötunn is described in the poem *Völuspá*:

Surt fares from the south / with the scourge of branches,
The sun of the battle-gods / shone from his sword;
The crags are sundered, / the giant-women sink,
The dead throng Hel-way, / and heaven is cloven.

Now comes to Hlin / yet another hurt,
When Othin fares / to fight with the wolf,
And Beli's fair slayer / seeks out Surt,
For there must fall / the joy of Frigg.

Fenrir broke free of the dwarf-made Gleipnir, his bonds shattered and his hunger for vengeance ripe. His brother, the sea serpent Jörmungandr, emerged from Midgard's oceans, and the Aesir gods and goddesses witnessed Surtr's arrival at Asgard, along with his army of giants who came to bring an end to Odin's reign. As the sky split open, the hideous creatures of Múspellheim fell through and landed on the Bifrost. Roaring forward with their arms, they charged towards the heart of Asgard. The rainbow bridge, once a strong connection to Midgard for the gods, was shattered under the weight of the fire giants as they approached the heavenly city.

Heimdall, the Aesir tribe's divinity who served as Odin's eyes, blew Gjallarhorn to signify the arrival of the enemy.

The gods mustered their courage and stood behind Odin to take charge against the Jötunn. The ranks of Valhalla took up arms and left their blessed halls to answer their call of fate. This is what the dead had waited for, to battle for their honour and the strength of Odin.

With the enemy approaching fast, the dishonourable dead and Loki's daughter, Hel, came to Asgard's shore on the ship Naglfar. The cursed ship was built from the dead's fingernails and its dreadful sailors gathered on the plains of Vígriðr, the main battlefield of Ragnarök. This was the battlefield where the gods succumbed to the ruthless force of the giants and where the Aesir and Vanir gods did all they could to defeat their mortal enemies.

Fenrir charged, ripping and devouring all he could in his path, and the ground quaked beneath his paws. He spotted Odin, himself claiming his fair share of lives, and charged towards the god. Fenrir's fangs clashed against Gungnir's dazzling blade, and each strike carried the echoes of fate. Odin's eye, the one sacrificed at Mimir's Well, flared with otherworldly intensity as he faced the monster power that threatened to destroy all he held dear.

The gods clashed with the giants, and the sky appeared to bleed as divine and chaotic energies collided. Thunder rumbled, and the skies split open as Thor, wielding Mjölnir, fought ferociously against Jörmungandr. But Thor's fate led to his demise, as with a mighty blow Thor struck his hammer, killing the sea serpent, but not before Jörmungandr pierced Thor and poisoned him. Thor took nine final steps before he fell, defeated and dead.

Odin, in the mist of combat with Fenrir, saw his son fall and became enraged, but was caught off-guard. The opportunity for killing the leader of the Aesir was seized by Fenrir who swallowed the Allfather whole. Although Fenrir had claimed victory in his fight against Odin, he was injured and vulnerable. It was then Odin's son, Vidar, who sought to have the final strike against the legendary wolf, and charged towards Fenrir, ripping the jaws of the beast open and striking his sword down its throat and piercing his heart. Fenrir was defeated, but at the cost of life for the god of war, poetry and the Aesir.

Loki, betrayer of his kin, took up his quarrel with Heimdall, and the two of them faced one another to the death, with both being slain by each other's hand. Surtr was still standing, so the god Frey took it upon himself to kill the fire Jötunn, but even though these evils and destructive forces were defeated, Asgard and all the realms were engulfed in flame and death.

The world was said to sink into the sea, with nothing but a void of ash remaining. This was the Jötunn's final victory: for nothing – not even them – to be remembered.

The Prophecy's Meaning

Ragnarök was a prophecy spun by a Völva and spoken to Odin, instigating his mission of finding the means to stop it. But even though the Jötunn may seemingly represent pure evil, and the Aesir and Vanir deities represented the good of the cosmos, that is far from the case. In Norse mythology, the fight was between creation and order, between destruction and chaos, rather than simple good versus evil. The giants were undoubtedly destined to destroy the cosmos and everyone in it, leaving no one to remember the gods or their magnificent civilization and way of life. Looking at the larger picture of the cosmos, the giants reflected the destructive, chaotic aspect of the cosmic cycle. They had a job to do, a purpose, just like Odin.

Odin, who had made many sacrifices for knowledge and the fate of all beings, stood amongst the wreckage. The fight was won, but at a tremendous cost. The twilight of the gods had arrived, and the cosmic cycle was about to begin again. In the silence that followed, Odin's figure vanished into cosmic echoes, a relic of a period when gods confronted their fate with valour and sacrifice.

ODIN'S HALLS: VALHALLA AND THE WARRIOR CULTURE IN NORSE SOCIETY

Odin's teachings would be passed and spoken amongst Norse pagans daily. Their very lives and culture were shaped by the gods, and both men and women were ingrained with the idea that a warrior's death was how best to die.

Valhalla awaited those who served Odin on the battlefield, dying with honour and fury, and a chance to take up arms once again with the apocalyptic battle of Ragnarök.

The Norse concept of the afterlife is intricately woven into the fabric of their mythology, and at the heart of it all stands Valhalla. The halls of Valhalla and the complex journey beyond death is depicted in the *Poetic Edda* and *Prose Edda* and has led to Valhalla's depiction in contemporary media and literature being greatly romanticized. Yet the idea of Valhalla and what happens in the Norse afterlife is extremely important in comprehending the warrior mentality that pervaded Norse civilization.

Odin's Hall of the Slain

Valhalla, which translates as 'Hall of the Slain' or 'Hall of the Chosen', is a majestic realm within Asgard, the home of Odin and the Aesir gods. This otherworldly hall is more than just a resting place for fallen warriors; it is a hallowed sanctuary where Odin welcomes the almighty warriors and prepares them for the inevitable Ragnarök. The alure of Valhalla for the Viking people was to have eternal glory with loved ones, share in camaraderie and a warrior's existence with the Allfather.

Odin was the one to describe his heavenly halls and did so vividly in the *Poetic Edda*, namely in the poem *Grímnismál*. The hall spans 540 doors, each broad enough for 800 warriors to march through together. The towering roof is made of golden shields, with rafters made of spears, producing an impressive sight that matches the grandeur of the god of war. The seats are made of breastplates and the gates are guarded by wolves who would pounce on any unwanted visitors with ferocity. Eagles soar about the halls, casting a bird's eye view for Odin. Valhalla, and all those who fight, drink and feast in it, welcome the slain with open arms to this paradise, and their life's valour serves as payment for eternal bliss.

The Warrior's Path: Death in Battle

The concept of Valhalla is intimately tied to the Norse understanding of death and the honourable path to the afterlife. For the Norse, death in combat was the most honourable and acceptable fate. A warrior who died on the battlefield with a sword in his hand and courage in his heart won a place in Valhalla among the dead, chosen warriors known as the 'einherjar'.

The concept of a heroic and honourable death in battle, celebrated through poetry and song, strengthened Norse warrior culture. The sagas – these epic accounts of heroes and their adventures – exalted the actions of famous warriors and immortalized their legacies. The desire to sit in Odin's hall drove warriors to face adversity with valour and to seek a death worthy enough to secure a place at the Allfather's table.

The connection between a warrior and his fate in the afterlife extended far beyond individual aspirations. Norse warriors believed their actions in battle played a part in the balance of the cosmos and the fate of their people. For a fallen warrior was not only a hero in his own right and among his local people, but an essential part of a larger existence. A warrior's death and the duty and honour to serve Odin in Valhalla, and in the events of Ragnarök, was seen as contributing to the cosmic order upheld by the gods.

The Einherjar: The Ones Who Are Chosen

Handpicked by Odin's Valkyries, the ones who celebrated in Valhalla were known as the 'einherjar'. These warriors, distinguished by their exceptional valour and prowess, become a part of Odin's great army, ready to fight with the Aesir during Ragnarök. The einherjar's existence in Valhalla is not one of idle leisure, but rather a life of continuous training and preparation for the ultimate battle.

Sturluson's *Prose Edda* describes the einherjar's everyday activities in Valhalla. During the day, the fallen warriors engaged in fighting, both to practise and prepare for the upcoming apocalypse, but also for enjoyment.

They were now immortal in Valhalla, and with nightfall their wounds would miraculously heal, allowing them to quench their hunger and thirst and enjoy themselves in the mead hall. The einherjar would fill themselves with food and beverages beyond their wildest imagination. The meat they chewed and salivated over was sourced from the boar Sæhrímnir who, like the einherjar, would come back to life after every time he was slaughtered. The mead they drank came from the udder of the goat Heiðrún, and both meat and mead were unlimited in their supply.

The Valkyries: Choosers of the Slain

Those who are chosen are done so by the Valkyries, whose name comes from the Old Norse word 'valkyrja', meaning 'chooser of the slain'. They are supernatural beings responsible with deciding who will live and who will die on the battlefield. These warrior maidens carry out Odin's wishes in the mortal realm. The notion of the Valkyrie is profoundly established in Norse warrior culture, emphasizing the valour and honour connected with death in combat.

When battle rages on Midgard, the Valkyries descend to observe the conflict and seek out the most valiant and daring warriors. These chosen warriors are then escorted to the afterlife, where they find Odin's vast hall in Valhalla.

The Valkyries' relationship with death and the afterlife, however, goes beyond the glory that awaits in Valhalla. Some of the fallen are taken to Fólkvangr, a realm governed by the goddess Freya, where they continue with a fulfilling afterlife – but not one spent with Odin and the highest ranks of the dead.

The elaborate distribution of fallen warriors between Valhalla and Fólkvangr emphasizes the many fates of individuals who meet their demise in battle.

The Distinctive Characteristics and Attributes of the Valkyrie

The Valkyries are characterized as strong and beautiful, wearing armour and wielding weapons with unrivalled proficiency. They have been depicted as mounted on swift steeds, soaring over battlefields with divine grace. Their purpose is more than just to observe the humans of Midgard, but to take active participation in the turmoil of combat.

The number of Valkyries varies between different myths and tales, with some naming specific Valkyries such as Brunhild, Gondul and Skogul. Each chooser of the einherjar has distinct attributes which contribute to their diversity and complexity as otherworldly and celestial beings. Their connection to nature and the elements, as well as their battle prowess, demonstrate a multidimensional aspect of their character.

Odin's Connection to the Valkyries

Odin, as the god of war, wisdom and fate, entrusts the Valkyries with the crucial role of selecting warriors worthy of dining in his hall. They are an extension of the Aesir leader's will and execute his divine plan for the order of the cosmos.

The *Poetic Edda*, namely the poem *Grímnismál*, demonstrates Odin's close relationship with the Valkyries. When relating the order of the world and its occupants to Prince Agnarr, Odin describes his Valkyries as 'wish-maidens' and 'ale-rapers', showing their roles in determining warriors' fates and celebrating their valour. Odin's link to the Valkyries indicates his status as a god who is deeply involved with the mortal realm and this is emphasized by the many tales of Odin wandering Midgard.

Furthermore, Odin's unwavering desire of knowledge is evident in his pursuit to control fate. The Valkyries, as fate's emissaries, help Odin achieve his overarching goal of threading the complicated tapestry of destiny. The Valkyries' symbolism as the choosers of the slain is consistent with Odin's purpose as a divinity seeking to influence the outcomes of mortal lives and cosmic events leading up to Ragnarök.

The Valknut: The Symbol of Odin and the Valkyries

The Valknut, a mysterious symbol made of three overlapping triangles, is intimately associated with Odin and the Valkyries. The Valknut, also known as the 'knot of the slain' or 'Hrungnir's heart', has inspired a variety of interpretations, with its importance profoundly rooted in Norse mythology and Odin's participation in the cosmos.

The Valknut's relationship with the fallen implies a connection to death and the afterlife, reinforcing its link to the Valkyries and their role in selecting the slain. It represents the journey from life to the realm beyond, promoting the cyclical nature of existence in Norse mythology.

Additionally, the Valknut may represent protection and a connection to Odin, especially for individuals who have suffered death in combat, and it is frequently regarded as a symbol of Odin's father-like protection and favour. Many would wear the Valknut as a talisman, signifying that they were worthy of being escorted by the Valkyries to Valhalla after death.

As with the passage of time, many symbols throughout history own various meanings and the Valknut distinguishes itself as one of these symbols. The overlapping triangles could also represent numerous triads in Norse mythology, including the three realms of Asgard, Midgard and Hel – the past, present and future – or even Odin's characteristics as a warrior, wanderer and wise sage. The Valknut symbolizes Odin's spiritual power and capacity to control individual fortunes. Its complex knotwork could represent the interwoven threads of fate that Odin, as a god of wisdom and magic, can influence.

The Valknut's presence on many runestones and burial sites indicates its ritual funerary significance, as it has been frequently found etched on memorial stones, showing how important it is in glorifying and remembering the deceased and the hope for a better afterlife. For Christians, a cross would be marked on burial sites; for the Norse pagans and believers of Odin, the Valknut would shine as a beacon of valour and a symbol of fate.

The connection between Odin and the Valkyries stands as a testament to the intricate relationships shaping the cosmos. They are the choosers of the slain and exemplify the honour and bravery inherent in the Norse warrior tradition. Odin's status as their divine patron emphasizes his varied character as a deity of war, knowledge and fate.

The Valknut, when combined with this cosmic narrative, provides a depth of symbolism and mystery, inspiring reflection on life, death and the cycle of existence. As the Valkyries soar over the brutal battles of Midgard, the Valknut remains an enigmatic symbol of Odin's power over destiny.

Valhalla's Role in Norse Society

The concept of Valhalla and the warrior culture that surrounds it had a significant impact on Norse society. The emphasis on honour, bravery and the quest for a glorious death created a distinct ethos among the Norse. The sagas, oral traditions and skaldic poetry highlighted martial deeds, resulting in a cultural narrative that praised the warrior's journey.

In a civilization where harsh realities such as raids, battles and territorial conflicts were common, the promise of an honourable death became a motivating factor. The warrior's dedication to personal valour, loyalty to kin and the gods, and the pursuit of heroic exploits were all tied to the desire for a seat in Valhalla.

The warrior spirit influenced all levels of Norse culture. While elite warriors may have wished to join the einherjar in Valhalla, every Norseman, whether farmer, craftsman or noble, was expected to embody the values of courage and loyalty. The collective dedication to these ideals strengthened and contributed to the resilience of Norse people.

These values, of course, are seen throughout Odin's history. From acting with violence in the murder of Ymir, the diplomatic settlement reached at the end of the Aesir-Vanir War, to the sacrifices Odin made when hanging from the world tree, the societal rules of the Norse and what they lived for are highlighted: honourable death and loyalty, all ingrained with an understanding of commitment through sacrifice.

The Shadow of Ragnarök: A Bittersweet Fate

While Valhalla represents a paradise for the slain, the impending duty the einherjar must face is the shadowy presence of Ragnarök. The *Prose Edda* and *Poetic Edda* foresee a cataclysmic event in which the cosmos is ripped apart and the gods, including Odin and his einherjar, are annihilated. The inevitability of Ragnarök tempers the majesty and glory of Valhalla, bringing a bittersweet depth to the warrior's fate.

The Norse worldview of cyclical understanding of time and fate recognizes that even Valhalla's chosen warriors cannot escape the forces that control the fate of the cosmos. The twilight of the gods, as described in the story of Ragnarök, demonstrates the Norse acceptance of both creation and destruction as necessary components of existence.

HUGINN AND MUNINN: THE RAVENS OF ODIN

Abilities, powers and magic in the mythology of Norse paganism are often conjured through animals, artefacts or weapons. Part of Odin's roster of abilities is his unquestionable wisdom, thought and memory. Throughout history, from both the *Edda* sources to modern depictions across pop culture and educational entertainment, Odin has been depicted as the wise Allfather, ever-vigilant and ever-knowing. Acting as a source for this vast knowledge he acquired through great struggles in the epic tales is his two raven companions – Huginn and Muninn.

The name Huginn is derived from the Old Norse word 'hugr', meaning thought or mind. This first raven is often associated with intellectual pursuits, representing the intellectual aspect of Odin's quest for wisdom.

Muninn's name is connected to the Old Norse word 'munr', meaning memory. Muninn represents the mnemonic part of Odin's desire for knowledge. He is the keeper of memories, signifying the retention of past experiences, wisdom gained and historical information.

Both concepts are highly valued to the god, and therefore he prized his two raven companions. Odin's affinity with ravens dates back to the sixth century, two centuries before the Viking Age. Even during these times, Odin was frequently shown with one or two ravens by his side, and the god took on another name, being referred to as 'The Raven God' frequently in the Viking Age myths and early poetry.

Odin's link to Huginn and Muninn is revealed in *Grímnismál*, where it mentions Odin sending the two birds out before dawn every day to travel the nine worlds and bring back news. This emphasizes the ravens' duty as sworn messengers and Odin's unquenchable desire to learn about the happenings in the cosmos.

O'er Mithgarth Hugin / and Munin both
Each day set forth to fly;
For Hugin I fear / lest he come not home,
But for Munin my care is more.

This passage underscores the dual nature of Odin's ravens – one associated with thought and the other with memory – working together to gather information for the Allfather. As the passage suggests, Odin valued his memory higher than his thought, perhaps as his memory held all information and knowledge he had gathered thus far on his travels and throughout his lifetime.

In the *Prose Edda* poem *Gylfaginning*, Huginn and Muninn are again mentioned in relation to their daily flights. Sturluson depicts Odin's ravens as perching on his shoulders and whispering tidings in his ears. Various other Old Norse poems name Odin as 'Huginn's lord' or 'Muninn's master', highlighting the close association between the Allfather and his avian companions. Their daily flights of surveillance were how Odin gained insights into current events and potential future developments. Their ability to travel vast distances – from the tallest branches of Yggdrasil in Asgard to the stems of Midgard, Jötunheim and everywhere in between – underscores their roles as intermediaries between the divine and mortal realms.

Huginn and Muninn are frequently shown flying beside Odin or sitting on his shoulders in Norse art and iconography. Their presence visually represents Odin's relationship to the ravens as his constant companions. Furthermore, several artefacts, such as amulets and jewellery, depict ravens, solidifying their significance and popularity among Norse pagan worshipers and society.

Huginn and Muninn's Symbolism in Modern Life

Huginn and Muninn are still important symbols in modern ceremonies, with many practitioners using images or depictions of ravens in their rituals, altar arrangements or personal adornments. Ravens are regarded as spiritual guides, assisting seekers in their exploration of knowledge and wisdom.

Huginn and Muninn's symbolic nature had a great influence on contemporary popular culture. Ravens occur in many forms across literature, art and media, representing wisdom, mystery and divine insight. Their prominence in contemporary interpretations reveals a long-standing fascination with Norse mythology and its ageless motifs.

These extra pairs of eyes for Odin are more than just symbols. The ravens depict the various aspects of Odin's character, including thought, memory, wisdom and the never-ending search for knowledge. The stories of their daily flights, the poetic references in the Old Norse literature and the symbolic and ideologic depictions all contribute to their ever-present significance in Norse cosmology.

Huginn and Muninn, Odin's ever-watchful companions, continue to inspire individuals embarking on their own intellectual and spiritual journeys. In the modern world, these ravens are powerful symbols, reminding followers of Norse pagan beliefs of the interconnectivity of thought, memory and the timeless search for wisdom that transcends mythology.

Nordic Utilization of Huginn and Munnin

For Nordic society during the Viking Age, ravens were utilized in various ways. For instance, ravens are known to be highly intelligent birds, with Huginn and Muninn capable of making complex observations. The Norse people and the Vikings were more than warriors, they were also hunters, and they noticed the pattern of ravens following them for several days, waiting to feast on what was left of the hunt. The roles would also be reversed, with the hunters' tracking ravens as they would circle and eye any potential prey and resources. During great sea voyages, ravens would be kept in cages and released in the hope that they would find land. Once ashore in unfamiliar territory, they would continue to follow these intelligent birds as they scouted out food. Suffice to say, ravens played a key role in the everyday life of the Norse people and were revered by many.

INVASION OF LINDISFARNE

The attack on Lindisfarne is infamous due to the cultural shift it imprinted on the European landscape. It is not a tale with words exaggerated to ridiculous lengths or any falsehoods spun due to the test of time. The invasion was an event in English history that is legendary for its meaning. It was the spark that ignited the beginning of the turbulent relationship between the Viking people and the monotheistic Christians of England, and in turn, the beginning of the time when Odin met God.

The assault by the Viking people on the Holy Island of Lindisfarne, just off the coast of Northumbria, is not remembered for being the first point of contact between these two drastically differing groups (although not the first spat of conflict between Scandinavian raiders and Anglo-Saxon peoples). The barbaric and twisted raid on Lindisfarne is remembered for being just that – a site of slaughter, brutal barbarism, thievery, wonderous heathenry and sin.

Indeed, there is evidence of attacks of Viking raiders in Anglo-Saxon literature in the years 787 and 792 CE, with the Lindisfarne slaughter taking place on 8 June 793. The Vikings had previously been spotted sailing off the eastern shores of Northumbria and Mercia, trading and gathering knowledge of the lay of the land. Perhaps the Anglo-Saxons did not anticipate the threat of the Vikings, and the power and spirit of Odin they would eventually unleash on this highly religious island which had quite significant power among the kingdoms of England.

Historical Accounts of the Invasion

The attack is described in the *Anglo-Saxon Chronicle*, as quoted at the beginning of this chapter. The *Chronicle* highlights the raiders as supernatural, but these shocking depictions were most likely connected to stormy weather before they arrived. For the Viking raiders, however, storms were a sign that the god Thor was with them, and they would have seen it as a sign of good fortune if they had landed on the shores of the island with such adverse weather. The Christian account denotes fiery dragons flying in the sky –

many have suggested the dragons are simply a dramatized telling of the Viking warriors, with their fiery and violent nature. It is more likely that they were described as such mythical creatures because the Viking raiding boats often featured dragons carved onto the prows to strike fear into their enemy.

An Irish chronicle, *The Annals of Ulster*, which covered events from 431 to 1131 CE, mentioned the Lindisfarne raid and other attacks on British soil, highlighting the shockwaves that reverberated through the region.

Odin's Influence

The Vikings' Norse pagan beliefs influenced their worldview, especially in terms of fighting and honour. With Odin being the Norse pantheon's primary deity – the god of war, wisdom and death – the invasion of Lindisfarne represents the martial spirit connected with Odin.

During the attack, the Viking soldiers sought Odin's favour through courage and valour on the battlefield. Although, with the population of Lindisfarne comprising mostly priests and holy men, the invaders did not have much trouble in vanquishing their enemy. The invasion of Lindisfarne, while definitely cruel, is consistent with the concept of offering sacrifices to Odin. As warriors, the Vikings thought that acts of conquest would earn them a place in Odin's magnificent hall in Valhalla.

Why Lindisfarne?

The Vikings' choice of Lindisfarne as a target was by no means accidental or a coincidence; it was motivated by both strategic concerns and symbolic importance. Lindisfarne was home to a renowned monastery, filled with holy artefacts and treasures and served as a symbol of Christian piety. Raids on such hallowed ground were not only used to acquire riches and gold, but also to challenge their rivals' religious beliefs.

There are some parallels between the Lindisfarne raid and the Viking sagas and poems, where heroes embark on daring expeditions to gain wealth and renown. These legends, which are often laced with notions of divine favour and Odinic influence, run in parallel to historical events involving raids on Christian monasteries and villages.

Consequences of the Invasion

As documented in several historical sources, the raid on this holy land had far-reaching consequences for the Christian mindset of medieval Europe. The raid's abrupt and savage nature, along with the devastation of a holy site, undermined the foundations of the Christian faith. The idea of pagan warriors falling on a Christian sanctuary fuelled the conception of Vikings as agents of chaos and divine retribution. The attack on Lindisfarne was a trigger for apocalyptic anxieties in Christian communities similar to Ragnarök. The apparent signs and details reported in the *Anglo-Saxon Chronicle* may have added to the targeted Christian communities' feeling of approaching doom.

Norse pagan beliefs were closely linked with fate, and Odin's purpose, of course, was to try and stop the end of the cosmos and gather as much information as possible. The Vikings saw their raids and voyages as fulfilling a predetermined fate, and the raid on

Lindisfarne could have been viewed as a step towards achieving their destiny. The quest for riches, fame and honour on distant lands was viewed as part of the cosmic order overseen by the weavers of fate.

The raid is so well remembered and studied among scholars and history buffs as it marks itself as the catalyst of the Viking Age; a time of tremendous Norse expansion, exploration and cultural interchange. The invasion of this Christian monastery had repercussions throughout Europe, and subsequent raids on other regions followed a similar pattern of looting and subjugation. The raid significantly influenced the Vikings' reputation, with monastic descriptions of the Norsemen's violence and sacrilege portraying them as formidable warriors and marauders. This reputation founded on historical events and Christian chronicles has persisted in popular culture to this day. Viking attacks began with looting and pillaging, but later interactions with other cultures resulted in a more complicated exchange of ideas, trade and settlement. The Vikings started out as little more than barbaric raiders, but in time evolved into a society of traders, settlers and contributors to the larger fabric of medieval Europe.

The Viking Age

Following the invasion of Lindisfarne, Viking expeditions flourished, resulting in the discovery and settlement of new lands. The Norse seafarers, inspired by their pagan beliefs centred on Odin, enhanced their warrior ethos that blended bravery on the battlefield with an appetite for knowledge. Odin had a key influence in forming the Vikings' worldview. Their Allfather – their god of war, wisdom and death – inspired the Norse people's approach to life and conflict. The desire for glory and honour in battle, viewed as a means of gaining Odin's favour and securing a seat in Valhalla, became the driving force behind expeditions and conquest.

Viking raids not only targeted Lindisfarne but also many other monasteries, churches and coastal settlements throughout the British Isles, Ireland and the Frankish Empire between the late eighth and mid-ninth centuries. As the Viking Age progressed, large-scale invasions and conquests defined this period of Norse expansion. The Great Heathen Army established itself as a strong presence throughout Europe.

By the mid-ninth century, Viking influence had expanded beyond raids and conquests to include the development of the Danelaw, a territory in England where Norse laws and customs prevailed. The region gained its name from the Old English *Dena lagu*, and it was recognized that between the Rivers Tees and Thames distinct customary law was prevalent in local courts, rather than those imposed by West Saxon laws in the south or Mercian laws in the western regions.

While adapting to new locations and circumstances, Norse pagan beliefs held true to their essential ideas. The settlers continued to worship Odin and other Norse deities, and their cultural influence left a deep imprint on the areas they occupied. The Vikings conquered more than certain parts of England; they travelled by sea to new, undiscovered lands. They colonized Iceland, Greenland and briefly ventured to North America, in addition to various European nations. Norse pagan beliefs encouraged exploration and colonization, and members of the Viking populous were known and envied as master travellers and navigators. Inspired by Odin and driven by destiny, discovering new territories and establishing colonies became their way of life.

Iceland's colonization, which began in the late ninth century, demonstrates the Vikings' capacity to adapt to new settings while maintaining their deeply rooted customs. The settlers took with them their religious practices and, of course, their worship of Odin, which helped shape the cultural environment of their acquired lands. Norse sagas mention the discovery and brief exploration of North America, known as Vinland, around the tenth century.

However, the exact details are still questions. Leif Erikson, Erik the Red's son, is widely credited with launching excursions to these remote shores. This, and many of the sagas' depictions of the Vikings' contact with the unknown, reflect their Norse pagan beliefs, all intertwined with Odin's influence.

The Rise of Christianity

Norse pagan rule and influence did not last forever, as the prominent force of Christianity set the Viking Age into a phase of decline and transformation. As well as the spread of Christianity, several factors, including changing political landscapes and internal conflicts, contributed to the waning influence of Norse paganism and the eventual Christianization of Scandinavia.

Christianity's growth, aided by both external influences and internal conversions among Norse elites, marked a shift in religious dynamics. The conversion of kings and monarchs, such as Olaf Tryggvason in Norway and Sweyn Forkbeard in Denmark, was crucial in the downfall of Norse paganism. The once-dominant beliefs, with Odin at the forefront, were progressively replaced by the expanding authority of Christianity. The Norse symbols, rituals and cultural traditions were transformed or, in some circumstances, suppressed.

Conversion to Christianity

The conversion of the Scandinavian people to Christianity did not happen quickly; it was a gradual and difficult process, with many unwilling to abandon their Norse pagan beliefs and embrace Christian ways. There were many reasons for the near two-century-long period of Christianization, including political gain, which led to increased authority, power and control over territories and people. Viking and Norse pagan monarchs may have converted to Christianity, but they did not fully embrace the new beliefs and practices. New wealth and jewels were given to Norse people in exchange for their conversion. When Norse pagans were baptized, Frankish noblemen distributed exquisite baptismal clothing. Baptism was regarded as a rite of passage and a requirement for Christians to fully embrace their new comrades and now fellow Christians. Without this rite of passage, Norse pagans would not obtain new wealth, power or any influence that had been promised.

Harald Bluetooth, King of Denmark, had strong political motivations. There are various tales alluding to why he turned to Christianity, with one account written by the medieval Saxon chronicler Widukind of Corvey, who was alive during King Harald's reign, and the other written by Adam of Bremen, who wrote about the events 100 years after the king's death.

Widukind of Corvey's version of events depicts King Harald being converted by a priest known as Poppa. Harold asked

Poppa to prove his faith, who did so by carrying a heated weight of iron without being burned, seemingly proving the power of Christ. Adam of Bremen, on the other hand, described the king's conversion as a forceful one. Otto the Great, the Holy Roman Emperor who ruled from 962 to 973, is described to have forced King Harold to convert after defeating him in battle. However, it must be remembered that this account was written a century after the king's death and none of the previous accounts mention any sort of battle between them.

No matter how King Harold converted, it is said that the main reason was to avoid conflict and war with neighbouring rulers, and with his baptism Harold stood more powerful and untouchable by his enemies.

The conversion to Christianity by King Harold Bluetooth marked the end of the Viking Age, and while it did not happen overnight, the shift in religious practices and political motivations set Scandinavia into a new era. However, Odin's legacy, and the grander spectrum of Norse mythology has endured, and has had an impact on and influenced generations.

3.
An Enduring Legacy: Impact and Influence

There was Motsognir / the mightiest made
Of all the dwarfs, / and Durin next;
Many a likeness / of men they made,
The dwarfs in the earth, / as Durin said.
From *Völuspá* (*The Prophecy of the Seeress*),
from the *Poetic Edda*

espite the Viking Age's demise and the shift of religious landscapes, its legacy endured. The Norse people's cultural, linguistic and creative achievements left profound impressions on the regions they touched. The sagas, poetry and myths of Norse mythology have remained popular over the centuries. The Viking Age, rooted in the combination of historical events and Norse pagan beliefs, exemplifies a complex and dynamic chapter in European history. The varied influence of Odin and the collection of other gods and goddesses shaped the raids, conquests, exploration and cultural interchange that occurred throughout the period. As the Viking Age progressed, it left an enduring legacy, having

an impact not only on the medieval world but also on modern ideas of Norse history.

Odin is a man who has travelled and evolved over vast countries, nations and lands for thousands of years. Beginning his journey in the Scandinavian region, where his presence echoed throughout each and every pagan and Viking village, his notoriety spread far and wide, from the shores of England to the eastern stretches of the Byzantine world, with each epic conquest and journey for expansion the Vikings set upon.

Suffice to say, Odin and the other deities of Norse mythology have made a great impact on popular culture, with the many stories and tales becoming more well-known and popular in recent years. The stories of Odin, as well as his divine presence and powerful attributes, first written in the *Prose and Poetic Edda* have now been adapted into almost all forms of media. Books, music, film, television – somewhere in each of these, Odin has appeared. The original works in the *Codex Regius*, of course, have had more of an impact on Scandinavian literature perhaps than most. Nordic languages have been shaped on the poetic rules and structures these great works set out, with Norse literature using expressive imagery and alliterative language, helping to showcase the mythological worlds and its characters as something far grander and more elaborate than everyday life.

The *Codex Regius* is regarded as the most important extant source on Norse mythology and Germanic heroic traditions. Since the early nineteenth century it has had a wide impact on Scandinavian literature, not just via its stories but also through the visionary force and dramatic richness of the poetry. It has also served as an influence for later innovations in poetic metre, particularly in Nordic languages, with its use of terse, stress-based metrical systems that lack final rhymes, instead relying on alliterative devices and highly concentrated imagery. Some of modern day's most beloved and highly acclaimed authors and poets have acknowledged the *Codex Regius*'s influence, including J.R.R. Tolkien, Vilhelm Ekelund, Jorge Luis Borges and Karin Boye, to name a few.

ODIN AND NORSE MYTHOLOGY IN LITERATURE AND ART

Audiences of contemporary films, readers of literature and observers of artistry have come to learn about Odin and the wide landscape of Norse mythology. When audiences hear the name 'Odin', the first image that may come to mind could be Sir Anthony Hopkins dressed in shining golden armour, with his spear in hand and his eye concealed behind his patch standing next to Chris Hemsworth and Tom Hiddleston in Marvel's *Thor* films. Others might envision the Norse god as Gandalf the Grey, portrayed by Sir Ian McKellen in Peter Jackson's *Lord of the Rings* trilogy. Suffice to say, contemporary media, art and literature have been greatly influenced by the great Odin and Norse mythology as a whole, with many interpretations presenting accurate depictions, others either taking their own spin on the Allfather and still others creating new and influenced portrayals. Long after the

Vikings had vanished, the mysterious Odin and other Norse mythological characters remained popular and influential in art, film and literature. Literary works, artistic movements and contemporary adaptations have captured and held readers' and viewers' attention for generations.

Influence on Tolkien

Epic poetry and fantasy fiction are only two examples of the many literary forms that have embraced Norse mythology. Imaginative realms rooted in Norse mythology have been created by writers throughout history by drawing upon Norse themes, characters and stories.

Within the character of Gandalf the Grey in Tolkien's masterpiece, *The Lord of the Rings*, one can hear echoes of Odin and the vast legends of Norse mythology. There are striking similarities between the wizard and Odin, with the wizard's enigmatic knowledge, curiosity and his staff. Gandalf's function as a sage and leader of the *Fellowship of the Ring* mirrors Odin's role as the leader of the Aesir, illuminating the timeless appeal of Odin's archetype in modern fiction. Tolkien was also clearly influenced by other aspects of Norse mythology, including the dwarven race and their names.

Tolkien and Dwarven Names

In *Völuspá* (*The Prophecy of the Seeress*), in the forging of the cosmos, the dwarves are created from Brimir's blood and are categorized by two races or the commanding set of dwarven beings – Móðsognir being the "the mightiest made of all the dwarfs" and

Durinn the second. The poem then goes on to list the various dwarven names that inspired the author.

Nyi and Nithi, / Northri and Suthri,
Austri and Vestri, / Althjof, Dvalin,
Nar and Nain, / Niping, Dain,
Bifur, Bofur, / Bombur, Nori,
An and Onar, / Ai, Mjothvitnir.

Vigg and Gandalf / Vindalf, Thrain,
Thekk and Thorin, / Thror, Vit and Lit,
Nyr and Nyrath, – / now have I told –
Regin and Rathsvith – / the list aright.

Fili, Kili, / Fundin, Nali,
Heptifili, / Hannar, Sviur,
Frar, Hornbori, / Fræg and Loni,
Aurvang, Jari, / Eikinskjaldi.

The race of the dwarfs / in Dvalin's throng
Down to Lofar / the list must I tell;
The rocks they left, / and through wet lands
They sought a home / in the fields of sand.

There were Draupnir / and Dolgthrasir,
Hor, Haugspori, / Hlevang, Gloin,
Dori, Ori, / Duf, Andvari,
Skirfir, Virfir, / Skafith, Ai.

Alf and Yngvi, / Eikinskjaldi,
Fjalar and Frosti, / Fith and Ginnar;
So for all time / shall the tale be known,
The list of all / the forbears of Lofar.

The *Prose Edda*, more specifically chapter 14 of *Gylfaginning*, also lists the wide span of dwarf names, including Bomburr, Nori, Ori, Dori, Thorinn, Fili, Kili, Gloin and Gandalfr, which translates to 'magic-elf' as well as 'wand' and 'staff'. Gandalf's primary purpose in *The Lord of the Rings* is to help put a stop to the evil Lord Sauron and destroy the One Ring that could put an end, or an everlasting dictatorship, to the people and beings of Middle-Earth. It is easy to draw parallels to Odin's quest to learn how to prevent and stop Ragnarök.

The incredible mark of Norse mythology and Odin's place in it can be seen throughout Tolkien's renowned literary works.

A scholar of Old Norse literature and language, Tolkien drew extensively from Nordic beliefs, incorporating its themes, ideas and characters into the intricate fabric of his own fantastical universe. Gandalf, the enigmatic wizard who advises and accompanies the heroes on their journey, reflects Odin's expertise, restlessness and mysterious presence in Tolkien's legendary writings. From the creation of the One Ring to the final confrontations with the armies of evil, Tolkien's epic tales reflect the themes of destiny, bravery and cosmic conflict that are fundamental to Norse mythology. Tolkien breathes fresh life into heathenry beliefs and mythology and the history of Odin, encouraging readers of all ages to seek out their own wisdom and experience through imaginative storytelling.

Influence on Modern Literature and Art

The interaction between Norse gods such as Odin and modern society is further investigated in *American Gods* by author Neil Gaiman. In his work, Odin takes on the persona of Mr Wednesday, a charming and crafty character who encounters both ancient and modern gods as he makes his way through the modern world. Power, belief and cultural advancement are all themes that reverberate in Gaiman's depiction of Odin as a skilled manipulator and schemer, qualities Odin presents in many myths and tales.

Paintings dating back to the early twentieth century, such as *A Viking Foray* by John Charles Dollman (1851–1934), brilliantly depict Viking warriors preparing to face an unknown enemy force, with several ravens surrounding the army. Even prominent Pre-Raphaelite Brotherhood member Edward Burne-Jones included elements from Norse myths in his own artwork. In his hypnotic murals, stained-glass windows and tapestries, he imbued the Norse sagas with a magical air by depicting events from the stories in a romanticized style. Brian Froud and Alan Lee are other modern painters who have delved into Norse mythology and folklore in their works. Their captivating artwork conveys the mystique and otherworldliness of the Norse pantheon, transporting spectators to the magical world Odin inhabits.

Norse mythology is still very much alive and well in today's art and popular culture, with influences seen everywhere from comic books to video games. In order to create immersive stories that appeal to people across the globe, creators and artists often use common Norse motifs. For example, the *Thor* comics and the Marvel Cinematic Universe have allowed Marvel Comics to tap into the popularity of Norse beliefs and characters. Odin, the wise and authoritarian king of Asgard, plays a significant role in these tales, shaping the fates of both the gods and humans. The fact that Marvel's Odin takes artistic licenses with the original stories demonstrates that Norse mythology continues to entertain modern audiences.

Influence on Film and Television

The popularity of genres, themes and character archetypes come in cycles in popular media. The Western had its golden age era from the 1930s to the 1960s, science-fiction in the late 1970s through to the 1980s, and the rom-com during the 2000s. In the past decade or so, the Viking genre in film and television has seen a dramatic awakening, with several films and widely acclaimed television series opening new audiences to this culture, Odin and the grand mythology in general.

Most widely seen is the *Thor* franchise, with the four films, *Thor* (2011), *Thor: The Dark World* (2013), *Thor: Ragnarok* (2017) and *Thor: Love and Thunder* (2022) collectively making over $1 billion at the worldwide box office. While these films focus on the titular character from the Marvel comics, with various liberties being taken with established beliefs as well as focusing on characters outside of Norse mythology, the thirst for more realistic depictions of Viking warriors and society has no doubt been exemplified thanks to these widely popular superhero films.

Vikings, created by Michael Hirst, is a historical television drama series that ran from 2013 to 2020, with its focus on the character of Ragnar Lothbrok, who is based on a real-life figure by the name of Ragnar Lodbrok. The series depicted a mostly realistic and historically accurate version of the Viking Age, with many notable episodes concentrating on Viking society in early medieval Scandinavia as well as their strong beliefs in Odin. The show's first season – and arguably its entirety – has the themes of exploration, power and the quest for knowledge, all akin to stories of Odin and his characteristics. The series also explores themes and narratives to do with fate, with the character The Seer offering vague, mysterious predictions for the main characters to try to understand, make come true or avoid if it involves their demise. The show found critical and commercial acclaim and spawned a sequel series, *Vikings: Valhalla*, on Netflix.

This shift from fantastical and, as the series evolved, comical portrayal with Marvel's *Thor* film series to the dramatic, realistic depiction was again shown with Robert Eggers' 2022 feature film *The Northman*. It seems audiences still favoured the more realistic portrayals of Viking people, yet the film was also heavily influenced by the mythology and Odin's presence, with many scenes and plot points highlighting classic Norse mythological aspects, including Odin's ravens freeing the main character, Amleth, from restraints, as well as Amleth being told in a seance about a magical sword he must retrieve from the Gates of Hel.

Influence on Video Games

The *God of War* video game series developed by Santa Monica Studio is another notable example of how Norse mythology is portrayed in modern culture. Beginning in 2005, the series follows the exploits of the Spartan warrior Kratos as he seeks retribution from the gods of Olympus. The first era of the series, consisting of seven game instalments, focused on Greek mythology, but in the second era in 2018, the series shifted to Norse mythology. *God of War* (2018) features Kratos and his son Atreus on their adventures through Yggdrasil, with Odin, Thor, Freya and other legendary Norse figures appearing throughout to players as they progress through the game. The game's story of atonement, sacrifice and familial ties skilfully incorporates aspects of Norse mythology and Odin into its own narrative. *God of War* presents Odin as a multi-faceted and mysterious character, which deviates from conventional wisdom. Throughout the game, Odin's influence is palpable, as his schemes dictate the course of events. But his true motives and driving forces are unknown, which makes him all the more intriguing. By offering an extensive amount of folklore and mythology to draw from, Norse mythology continues to inspire modern story-tellers and game developers, as shown in the *God of War* series. These games demonstrate the timeless allure and versatility of Norse myths in contemporary entertainment by transporting players to the lively realms of Yggdrasil.

A Continued Appeal

The impact of Norse mythology and Odin's glorious presence in art and literature is substantial and ever-present. Whether it is in the form of visionary art or epic sagas showcased on the big screen, Norse themes have always had an enduring appeal that draws in viewers. The ever-present influence of Odin in many artistic movements, modern media and fantasy literature attests to his ability to inspire wonder and a sense of awe in people from all different backgrounds and beliefs. Media and popular culture have long maintained depictions of Odin, the Vikings and Norse mythology, permanently imprinting these concepts in people's minds around the world. This era and these beliefs have become an intricate part of modern narrative in films, TV shows, books and other types of entertainment. Many see the Allfather Odin as an elusive sage who uses his knowledge to guide his followers or influence their choices, while others see the Vikings as fearless explorers, adventurers and fighters. However, stereotyping and historical revisionism are just a few of the issues and misrepresentations that have emerged with these idealized portrayals. Regardless of these challenges, the timeless appeal of Viking culture and Norse mythology continues to captivate viewers with stories of heroes, gods and great conflicts.

ODIN AND NORSE PAGANISM IN THE MODERN DAY

A wide array of religious belief systems have been around for thousands of years and Norse paganism, with the belief in Odin and the Norse gods is one of them. Norse paganism dates back to ancient times, with the beliefs playing a vital part in people's lives, helping to define pathways and ambitions. Faith in Odin and the pantheon of deities was great but was inevitably insufficient to withstand the power of Christianity and its influence over the Scandinavian population.

Odin's influence looked to have vanished, with only a few groups remaining who believed in and practised the beliefs and rituals the religion encompasses. Archaeologists, researchers and historians have uncovered numerous artefacts, runestones, graves and other historical items that have contributed to our understanding of ancient religions and the people who embraced them.

However, Odin's presence and influence could not be silenced for long. Over the past several hundred years and leading up to contemporary times, many followers of the Allfather and Norse paganism are still prevalent. Of course, their methods differ from the Viking Age, as in modern times society has grown more accustomed to civility than the barbaric and violent nature throughout the ninth century to the end of the Vikings in 1066.

While there were both positive and negative aspects to Norse paganism during the Viking Age, aspects of the religion were not always that clear-cut. The pathways that Norse pagans travelled provided them with a variety of perspectives, beliefs and philosophical concepts about how they should live. Each person may believe in one notion, or higher being, more than another. These various spiritual traditions were chosen by individuals throughout the Viking Age and even before this period, but many of them are now being followed in the modern day, with many people also discovering this belief system and converting. In the Norse religion, there are numerous spiritual pathways to choose from, some of which are community-based while others are a very personal journey that offer solitude and self-reflection. Some hold highly traditional ideas and values, while others have had to evolve and adapt to fit into more modern times.

But what are these pathways and practices of contemporary Norse paganism? The rebirth of this religion sees many different avenues of worship, with Odin still being very much at the centre of them all.

Asatru

Asatru is the first, and perhaps most well-known and followed pathway in contemporary Norse paganism. This religious movement was created and began to take shape in the nineteenth century before becoming registered as an official religion in Iceland in 1973. While this spiritual path has only recently emerged, its beliefs and practices are based on the ancient beliefs held by the Vikings themselves. Asatru means 'true to the Aesir gods', and its devotees revere the Aesir gods, Odin being at the top of the pantheon, along with Thor, Baldur and Frigg.

The resurgence of this old religion among the public began in Iceland on the Summer Solstice of 1972, just a year before it was formally recognized as a religion. The Summer Solstice is a celebration observed by many religions and cultures around the world to mark the beginning of the summer season with the longest day of the year, which typically takes place on 21 June in the northern hemisphere. Asatru, often referred to as heathenry, is rooted in spiritual practices of the pre-Christian Norse and Germanic peoples, rooted in mythology, cosmology and cultural traditions. The modern Norse pagans follow a diverse range of beliefs, practices and encompass many different communities worldwide.

Modern depictions of Norse pagans, from popular television programmes such as *Vikings*, show sacrificial ceremonies and ritual toasting ceremonies attributed to Odin, honouring him by killing animals or raising a toast. These practices are still very much conducted for those who identify as Asatru, with these rituals being known as 'blots'. Blots are typically performed around major occasions, such as the Summer Solstice; however, a blot can be performed whenever an individual desires. If an individual desires something, whether it is good health, luck or wish for a blessing, they can dedicate the blot to anyone they choose, but many still hold Odin at the centre of the sacrifice.

There are several different types of blots, each holding a significant meaning. A remembrance blot is frequently held around the full moon in October, when the veils between the realms are at their thinnest, emphasizing the relationship between ancestors and deceased friends and family.

The second blot is known as Jolablot, where very early in the morning at sunrise on 24 December a ritual is conducted marking the beginning of the sun's journey through the southern hemisphere. This rite also honours Odin and symbolizes the start of the Yule feast. While these two rituals are often performed on a specific date and time, there are other types of blots that can be performed whenever a Norse pagan desires. People undertake this type of ritual, referred to as the Vættir, to safeguard their home and to show the gods and various spirits that they are valued, worshipped and commemorated.

But what happens during a blot? To make a sacrifice to Odin and the gods, Asatru gather various pieces of equipment and instruments. A runic sign, such as a hammer to represent strength and to pay tribute to the Norse deity Thor, is drawn or carved on to stone and a blessing bowl is filled with whatever gift is being offered. An offering can be as simple as a loaf of bread, but additional offerings include alcohol or even an animal sacrifice.

Asatru religion practitioners, like Vikings, use rites of passage to deepen their relationship with the gods and the wider community. These rites of passage in the Viking Age were associated with an individual's rising status and life path. Birth, marriage and death were all primary rites of passage in Viking culture and are closely linked with Asatru. The naming process, sometimes known as kneeling, involves parents vowing to higher powers, including Odin, that they will care for their newborn child. Unlike other religions, such as Christianity, a child born into a pagan family is not required to practise such rituals or believe in the Aesir or Vanir gods. In the pre-Christian era, parents would often wait for their child to survive their first winter before naming them, since if there was insufficient food to nourish the child or if there was some type of birth defect or disability, the child would be left in the wilderness to either die of starvation or be the meal of wild animals.

The Ynglinga Rite marks an adolescent's transition into adulthood, allowing them to choose whether or not to adhere to ancient pagan beliefs. They are under no duty to do this and are solely responsible for their actions. Weddings and funerals are common in all religions, including Asatru. Being united with someone you love can be very holy in Asatru and death holds extreme value too. The dead are thought to travel to Valhalla and Hel, similar to Norse pagan beliefs before Christianity took over. Norse paganism and the Asatru religion are known for their emphasis on sacrifice. It is the thread that ties them both, with ancient beliefs and customs still practised today. Their faith in the

Aesir tribe is strong, and they strive to live a selfless, loving and joyful life based on these beliefs. The wisdom of Odin and the old Norse sources inspires them to live good lives.

Vanatru and Rökkatru

As well as Asatru, there are other spiritual pathways that a Norse Pagan might follow. These additional pathways are known as Vanatru and Rökkatru, and both hold specific meanings. Each individual is allowed to discover what works best for them and what gods and goddesses mean to them. Vanatru and Rökkatru are two more pathways that can be intertwined with Asatru, and the three paths are not mutually exclusive, with no rigid rule requiring a person to only follow one of them. That is what this religion has always been about; even at the beginning of its journey, the faith's polytheistic nature was a seed that grew and became even stronger in current times.

So, whereas Asatru means 'true to the Aesir gods', Vanatru refers to the second tribe of deities and means 'true to the Vanir'. This pathway first developed in the 1990s as an alternative for those who were more drawn to Freya, Frey and Njðrd. The Vanir gods and goddesses are described as having many attributes and qualities that can be used in a variety of situations and emotions. If an individual does not feel able to connect with the Aesir gods, they can focus on the alternative group.

There are a few elements that influence the distinctions between these two paths of modern Norse paganism. On top of the different set of deities, another factor is how followers of Norse paganism conduct their rituals and practices. The Asatru route is highly social, with rites performed in groups – not that one cannot do these alone – whereas the Vanatru pathway is more individualistic, with this being the primary distinguishing element between them.

Many of the rituals and rites performed by both the Asatru and the Vanatru are identical, with the only difference being which deity is honoured and worshipped. The practices follow a distinct set of rules with each step owning its own name. Firstly, a hallowing takes place where the ritual space, whether it be out in nature in a woodland or inside one's home, is made holy. The Asatru pagans may adopt the emblem of Thor's hammer Mjölnir, while a Vanatru pagan might walk around their ritual space with an antler, an object sacred to the divinity Frey. The Vanatru emphasize the importance of acknowledging nature's spirits for permission to perform rituals on their land. The pagans will then carry out invocation, communicating with the desired gods for the ritual. Speaking from the heart and expressing the deities' characteristics and virtues strengthens the invocation. They will then follow this up with a blessing which can be in the form of a speech or a song, with some reciting poems from the *Eddas* that expresses gratitude to the gods for their wisdom, teachings and sacrifices. Bringing food, drink and personal items to offer the Aesir and Vanir pantheon of gods and higher beings is a way to pay tribute to them, and certain types of items will be associated with each tribe and individual deity. At the end of the ceremony, one will express gratitude to the gods and either return the holy space to its original state or leave offerings for nature to consume.

Modern Sacrifices and Heathenry

In the past, the Vikings would perform live sacrifices, but that tradition is no longer considered necessary for the modern followers of Norse paganism. Instead, the food offerings would be already either raw or cooked foods. A common substitute is mead, an ancient alcoholic drink made from mixing fermenting honey with water and other fruits and spices. Odin himself drinks the Mead of Poetry, and anyone who drinks it is said to turn into an all knowledgeable scholar and poet.

Incorporating the Norse pantheon's old deities and mythology into a contemporary setting, modern Norse paganism is a dynamic and developing spiritual tradition. As the Allfather and symbol of knowledge, creativity and transformation, Odin plays a pivotal role in modern heathenry. As a seeker of wisdom and a nurturing guide through life's riddles, Odin serves as an inspiration to modern-day pagans. Devotees pay homage to Odin through ceremonies and prayers while also striving to emulate his virtues – courage, knowledge and perseverance – in their own lives. Despite the ever-changing nature of our world, and the beliefs and pathways people develop and follow, the irresistible allure of Odin and Norse mythology offers solace, inventiveness and a link to a diverse web of human faith.

4.
Misinterpretation and Misuse

Yggdrasil's ash / great evil suffers,
Far more than men do know;
The hart bites its top, / its trunk is rotting,
And Nithhogg gnaws beneath.
– From *Grímnismál (The Lay of Grimnir),*
from the *Poetic Edda*

Odin, once a deity of ancient sagas, finds himself entwined in the conflicts and controversies of the modern world. The clash of cultures and ideologies from the Viking Age to the present raises questions about understanding, and also raises interesting questions. As Odin's stories are rediscovered and retold, the potential for misinterpretation and misuse emerges.

We, as a race of explorers, a people who love to uncover hidden truths and to discover new avenues of our ancient past, have to admit that we could be wrong about it all. All of it being our interpretation of the ancient world, recovered artefacts, symbols and societies. However, in the past 200 years, the factual meanings of the runes, symbols and Norse mythology has unfortunately been twisted, altered and fabricated for groups' and individuals' own reasons. The legends, of course, went through historical changes during the Christianization of the Nordic people and their beliefs, and we only have a vague understanding on the drastic changes between the origins of the main Nordic sources and before the Christianization period. Some elements of stories may have been exaggerated or made to fall in line with Christian beliefs, but historians seem to come to the consensus that the works in the *Prose* and *Poetic Eddas*, for example, are widely accurate to what was originally believed and passed down from generations of the pre-Christian Nordic people.

However, one group in particular decided to adopt Nordic beliefs, symbols and practices for their own gain.

CULTURAL APPROPRIATION AND THE MISUSE OF NORSE SYMBOLS

Cultural appropriation is a complicated and difficult subject and occurs when elements from one culture are taken and used – typically without sufficient knowledge or respect – by individuals or groups from another culture. Cultural appropriation has become a major issue in the context of Norse mythology and iconography, owing to Viking imagery's immense appeal and commercialization, as well as a lack of understanding of its cultural and religious significance. This issue focuses on the misuse and misrepresentation of many Norse symbols, such as the Valknut and Mjölnir, and how it affects current views of Norse mythology and Odin.

The Völkisch Movement

From the late nineteenth century until the dissolution of the Nazi era, the völkisch movement sought to restore pre-Christian paganism to everyday life in Germany by rejecting Christianity. The goal of this nationalist movement was to establish the original nation for the German people, which included a strong emphasis on the Nordic race and its fetishization and promotion as a superior race. A literal translation of the German word 'volk' would be 'people'. However, during the Nazi regime, it came to signify 'nation' or 'tribe'. Because of the strong ethnonationalist ideas that the word came to imply, many people speculate about when and how this subtle change occurred.

Lena Nighswander writes, "*In shielding its members under the unassuming Volk umbrella, the völkisch movement was able to push forward nationalist ideas about racial purity that would come to be intimately associated with the Nazi party in the coming years under the guise of preserving tradition and protecting German culture – keeping it free from outside influences and cultivating a German national identity, while still maintaining a pointed interest in absorbing various aspects of Nordic culture*."

Even if it may not be immediately apparent how Old Norse imagery relates to eugenics, it is clear that the völkisch idolization of all Nordic characteristics is just another manifestation of the Viking idealism that was prevalent during this period. The völkisch movement and the Nazi Party both used Norse mythology as a tool for political programming and control, their objective being to mimic the heroic qualities of Odin and other legendary figures. This specific idealism would later be called 'Nordicism' and is generally understood as an ideology that glorifies the Nordic race. One important thing to remember is that Nordicism also sees the Nordic race as a superior and endangered racial group, which was mainly used to support the argument that the Nordic race should be conserved.

Nazi Nordicism

Nazi Nordicism was more closely associated with the glorification of people of Nordic descent than with the appreciation of Nordic heritage. This is how the mythical beings of Odin and his kin came to be seen as the pinnacle of Aryan excellence.

One of the most prominent forms of cultural appropriation is the exploitation of Norse symbols by extreme groups and hate movements. Symbols like the Valknut, closely linked with Odin and the afterlife, and Mjölnir, Thor's hammer, have been co-opted by white nationalist and neo-Nazi groups who use them as symbols of racial superiority and hatred. This misuse not only distorts the original meaning of these symbols, but it also reinforces destructive attitudes and stereotypes.

After Germany's defeat in the First World War, there was a rise in those who believed in Norse mythology, especially among the disheartened youth, as many patriotic Germans believed that exploring their mythic roots boosted nationalism. In the beginnings of the formation of the National Socialist Party in 1920 and the fallout from the First World War, the Nazis adopted Norse mythology and symbols into their propaganda and imagery. The swastika became their symbol – a symbol that has now forever been tarnished due to the atrocities the Nazis carried out. The swastika has been in existence for almost 3,000 years, and is a symbol prevalent in numerous cultures across the globe, including those of the indigenous North Americans, Europe, Japan, India and China. 'Swastika' is a word that comes from the Sanskrit 'svastika' and it was a symbol of vitality, the sun, power, strength and good fortune prior to its theft by the Nazis. In Norse mythology, the swastika represents the spinning of Thor's hammer.

The Nazi Appropriation of Norse Symbols and Imagery

Another well-known example of the Nazis adopting Norse symbols and imagery into their own is through the insignia used by the Schutzstaffel, more widely known as the SS, the main Nazi paramilitary organization. The double 'sig' runes side by side constitute the SS insignia. The Old Norse language and cultural record, the Younger Futhark, state the rune as a symbol of the sun or 'sól'. The Nazi Party appropriated it for use on uniforms, but they changed its meaning from one that was more associated with Norse Pagan ideals to one that was more in line with their own. And so, the 'sieg' runes became known as 'victory', forcefully changed by the Nazis. This was the larger goal of the Nazi party – to transform Germany into a Kulturnation, meaning a nation with a great cultural history. Germany under the Nazis attempted to appropriate the cultural value of Nordic myths and the achievements and sacrifices Odin made by assimilating them. As a result of its inherent need on the Scandinavian environment to be culturally relevant, the influence of Nordic mythology and symbolism is highly context-dependant; therefore, it is impossible to replicate their significance without altering their meaning. Even if Norse symbolism possesses power, it is only in its original Nordic context. A German soldier wearing an SS uniform with the 'sigel' rune has power in and of itself, but it does not originate from Norse mythology. The fabricated German meaning is instead a shell of what was once Norse.

Given how universally recognized the Third Reich's imagery is, the point is that few people tend to draw parallels between the Nazis and their medieval Scandinavian origins. The Nazis and their völkisch ancestors were able to cover up their abhorrent aims and ideals by creating a broad, Nordic picture. This allowed them to promote broader concepts about racial purity in relation to national identity.

Germanic Mythification of the Nordic People

The Germanic people's obsession with establishing their own distinct cultural identity coincided with their fascination with the medieval Scandinavian Vikings, which in turn led to the mythification of the Nordic peoples based on racial stereotypes. The Nordic people became almost as legendary as Odin, Thor, Freya, Frey and Baldur, due to the growing popularity of national myth as a source of power and pride. This myth painted an unrealistic picture of what a Viking should be, disregarding the fact that the Norse people have developed and changed since then and, more importantly, the racial and cultural diversity that was evident in the region even during that time.

Misuse in Hate Groups

Modern heathens and practitioners of Norse paganism are highly concerned about the appropriation and misuse of Norse iconography. These famous symbols have a deep theological and cultural importance for heathens, representing connections to their ancestors, gods and heritage. Seeing these symbols so blatantly misused and connected with hatred and bigotry undermines the faith's integrity and develops sentiments of anger, frustration and alienation within the community.

Furthermore, the appropriation of Norse iconography by hate groups instils a false link between Norse paganism and extremism in the public consciousness. This portrayal not only stigmatizes heathenry, but it also fosters misunderstandings and discrimination against practitioners.

Combatting Cultural Misappropriation

Efforts to combat cultural appropriation and misuse of Norse symbols are varied and ongoing, both within the heathen community and beyond. One option is education and outreach, in which heathens and scholars collaborate to educate the general public about the true meaning and value of Norse symbols. By giving correct information and context, they hope to dispel misconceptions and challenge negative preconceptions. Another method is to reclaim and recontextualize Norse iconography within the heathen community. Heathens may use rituals, ceremonies and artistic expressions to reinforce the religious and cultural value of these sacred symbols. By regaining control of these symbols and reinterpreting their meaning, practitioners express their agency and autonomy over their religious history.

Additionally, there are legal and advocacy measures underway to safeguard Norse iconography against misuse and exploitation.

Organizations such as The Troth and the Asatru Folk Assembly preserve Heathen rights and lobby for regulations that protect Norse religious symbols.

The cultural appropriation and misuse of Norse mythology's iconography present important issues for current heathens and practitioners. Misrepresenting and twisting the theological and cultural importance perpetuate damaging stereotypes and undermines the Norse heritage's integrity. Addressing cultural appropriation involves a determined effort from both the heathen community and society as a whole, including education, lobbying and symbol reclamation. It is critical to recognize and respect the holiness of these symbols, as well as their cultural and religious significance to their worshipers around the world.

In order to legitimize its own harmful ideas of racial purity and culture, the Nazi party appropriated Old Norse imagery and mythology in various forms, including on their uniforms. It also created the concept of a pure Nordic race to capitalize on the newly elevated status of Nordic culture. Even in modern times, neo-Nazi organizations, like the Nordic Resistance Movement in Sweden, have these views. Despite how shocking it is that famous symbols like Thor's hammer are being used as Nazi propaganda today, it is important to learn how these symbols became associated with the original Nazi Party during the völkisch movement. Preventing the exploitation of the Vikings' myths and religious symbols for oppression requires education and awareness in order to resist this distorted portrayal of the Vikings and the lessons Odin teaches throughout the many mythical sources.

MISREPRESENTATIONS OF ODIN AND NORSE MYTHOLOGY IN POP CULTURE

Norse mythology, with its rich tapestry of gods, heroes and epic sagas, has captured imaginations for centuries. However, in popular culture, depictions of Norse mythology – notably Odin – have frequently succumbed to sensationalism, simplicity and distortion. The portrayal of Odin in film, television and literature features frequent misconceptions and falsehoods cultivated in popular media depictions. These sensationalized interpretations have influenced public perceptions of Norse mythology and the complexity of Odin's character, meaning there is a necessity for accuracy and authenticity when interpreting these epic sagas, myths, poems and broad narratives.

In popular culture, Odin is often portrayed as a very one-dimensional character – a simplistic warrior deity, lacking the depth and complexity found in historical sources like both the *Eddas*. This sensationalized depiction frequently highlights Odin's position as a ferocious and fearsome warrior, overshadowing his other qualities such as wisdom, knowledge and poetry. Moreover, Odin is often portrayed as an intense and dictatorial deity, in contrast to the more nuanced figure found in the ancient stories.

Mainstream media depictions of Odin often promote the 'wise old man' trope. While Odin is linked with wisdom and knowledge across the spectrum of Norse mythology, his portrayal is sometimes oversimplified, reducing him to a generic mentor figure with no depth or complexity. Similarly, Odin is frequently shown as a figure of utter evil, symbolizing brutality, duplicity and manipulation. These distortions not only misrepresent Odin's character, but they also reinforce damaging prejudices about Norse mythology in general.

Many people's sole exposure to Norse mythology is through popular culture, which influences their understanding and interpretation of these ancient traditions. As a result, mainstream media depictions have a tremendous impact on public opinions of Odin and the other pantheon of gods and goddesses, often perpetuating preconceptions and inaccuracies.

A REFLECTION ON ODIN AND NORSE MYTHOLOGY

In the complex world of gods, heroes and epic stories found in Norse mythology are evidence of the everlasting influence of story-telling and the human imagination. The legendary Allfather Odin, whose endless quest for knowledge, wisdom and sacrifice has captivated people for thousands of years, is at the very centre of it all. We find a rich collection of myths, poems, characters and ideas that reverberate in the contemporary world when we consider the cultural impact and historical meaning, and its value of Norse mythology.

Odin, the supreme god of the Norse pantheon, shining as the central figure in Norse mythology, holds many different characteristics, and to quench his ravenous hunger for knowledge he goes to extreme measures, from sacrificing his eye at the Mimir's Well to spending nine days and nights hanging from the World Tree Yggdrasil. As a result of these deeds, Odin becomes the ultimate seeker of knowledge and receives insight into the secrets of the cosmos to often share with his kin.

Surrounded by Odin are the other gods and goddesses Norse paganists believe in, each with their own ideas, values and powers, as well as various other mythical creatures standing as unique beings with distinctive roles. The intricate network of human and environmental experiences is mirrored in the Norse pantheon of gods, from Thor – the thunder god – to Freya – the goddess of love and fertility. Legendary gods and goddesses live in a realm where heroic acts, cosmic conflicts and great battles determine the destiny of both the gods and mortals.

Myths and legends from Norse mythology, originally spoken orally but later documented in writings such as the *Poetic Edda* and the *Prose Edda*, form its bedrock. These myths shed light on the human experience and forces that mould our world through their exploration of heroic deeds, treachery, destiny and salvation. The Nordic beliefs depict an enchanting and colourful world filled with gods, giants and fabled beings from the beginning of time to the end of the world at Ragnarök.

We have explored these exciting narratives and the cast of characters that took precedence from an eclectic mix of sources, including oral tradition, archaeological findings and writing from the Middle Ages. The *Prose Edda*, an important work of Norse mythology written in the thirteenth century by Icelandic scholar Sturluson, sheds light on the Norse pantheon, gods and heroic tales. It is perhaps the *Poetic Edda*, though, an anthology of Old Norse poetry, that truly highlights the tales of Odin and the grander spectrum of the mythological cosmos.

These works have been kept sacred and protected for hundreds of years, and the characters, ideas and symbols have stood the test of time. For countless decades, Norse mythology has captivated and inspired people through literature, art and entertainment, leaving an everlasting impression on human consciousness. Odin and the Aesir and Vanir deities have held a special place in people's hearts because they represent our universal search for destiny, purpose and meaning in a chaotic and unpredictable world. The fact that Odin and Nordic pagan beliefs are still here today is proof that stories, imagination and creativity can last a lifetime. Inspiring us to delve into the depths of the human soul and the enigmas of the cosmos, the Norse myths and legends transport us to fantastical realms like Valhalla and Asgard. As we venture into these mystical lands of myth and legend, we draw upon the wisdom of Odin and the tenacity of the Norse people to navigate the intricate webs of destiny on our own.

Modern Short Stories of Odin

The Lord of Magic

K.S. Barton

O'er Mithgarth Hugin / and Munin both
Each day set forth to fly;
For Hugin I fear / lest he come not home,
But for Munin my care is more.
From *Grímnismál* (*The Lay of Grimnir*),
from the *Poetic Edda*

Like an abyss, the gap in my memory screams to be filled. I come to a village but have no idea if I have been here before or not.

It is as if I've been walking through holes of time.

A man approaches me. "Welcome, stranger," he says, friendly enough.

I nod to acknowledge that he has spoken, but it takes me time to piece together the words that I need to respond. He cocks his head in question.

"What is your name?" He asks.

In the tattered pieces of my memory, many names float before my eyes. Names written in runes as if on a rune stick or stone – Fimbultyr, Mighty God and Sigdir, Victory Bringer. Those can't be right. If I was a mighty god, I would not be here in these poor clothes with words falling overboard into the sea of my mind. I choose another name that seems to fit.

"Langbardr," I answer, stroking my long beard.

"Well met," the man says. "I am Sigvald. My home and my food are yours." He gestures to lead the way to a house that sparks my memory as one I've seen before, or perhaps they all look like this – wood with a thatch roof.

I remain standing where I am, my gaze searching the sky. He returns to my side and glances up. "Are you looking for something?"

Am I? I search and search that empty cavern of my memory. Something black flutters on the edges.

Wings.

"A black bird." Another shaking loose. "Two black birds."

Sigvald's eyes narrow and he looks more closely at me. At his scrutiny, I feel the patch on my eye and touch it. A shard of remembrance comes howling out of the abyss, of pain as a hand dug out my eye, exquisite relief as warmth flooded through me as I gained what I had sacrificed for, but like trying to catch water in my hand, I cannot recall what I'd earned for that sacrifice.

"Ravens?" Sigvald asks me.

Ravens, yes. Sigvald continues to stare at me until I understand that I have not spoken aloud. "*Ja*."

Out of the corner of my good eye, I see a woman approach us. She is younger than Sigvald and yet carries herself as someone older than the number of winters she has survived. "Husband, have you not offered the stranger hospitality?"

"I have," Sigvald answers.

She stops when she takes a good look at me. I grasp around for the name I'd given Sigvald, and he provides it for me, "Langbardr. He is looking for two ravens."

"Is that so?" The woman continues to study me. "Sigvald, take Langbardr to the house. I must do something first."

He nods and takes my arm. I flinch and stare down at his hand as if unused to being touched like this, but I follow him to his house, which is modest but clean. He lays out food and drink onto a solid pine table, but I take none of it.

When he gives me a questioning look, I say, "I do not eat." A flicker of a memory of two great beasts by my side, eating my food. Wolves, perhaps.

It takes me a long time to pull the words out to ask Sigvald a question. "Does your wife know where my ravens are?" My voice sounds regal as if I am a king, and yet each word comes out with a stutter and catch. I would like to ask if they know why I am searching for two ravens and why my mind seems to be held together as poorly as rags on a thrall.

I yearn for something, like I can reach out and grasp it, but it is not there. And it feels like the longer I go without finding it, the further it recedes.

After a while, the wife returns smelling like herbs and smoke, and following her through the door is a tall woman, almost as tall as me. She is beautiful and radiant but ragged around the edges, tired and brittle.

She approaches me cautiously, as if afraid I will spook or shatter into pieces. I may be only one question away from that fate.

"Groa," the tall woman says to the wife, "gather the women."

Groa nods and heads out the door without needing any information. I must have been like that once, understanding what someone meant without needing all the words. Or maybe I have always been this way, my mind having flown away long ago.

Flown away.

Like birds.

Like two ravens.

I close my eyes and search for what that means. To search for two ravens. What do they mean to me? I cling to the image of them and reach out into the darkness to find them; they are, were, a part of me, like my arms or legs. A surge of grief and sorrow well up when all I see is darkness and the ravens do not appear.

"Langbardr," the tall woman says. "Do you know me?"

"No."

"Not at all?"

"No."

Her face falls. There is something of a queen about the way she looks and the way she talks.

"My name is Freya."

The name echoes and once again I reach for a memory and come away with nothing but emptiness. I shake my head.

"Do the names Hugin and Munin mean anything to you?"

A flicker like light shining on a shard of glass and then shadows. "No."

"The ravens," Sigvald says quietly. Almost reverently.

I want this woman, Freya, to tell me who I am, what the ravens mean to me, and why I am searching for them, but I am afraid if she tells me too much all at once, that what is left of my fragile mind will be destroyed.

"Rest," Freya says, and she and Sigvald lead me to a small bed pallet in the corner. I am not sleepy but I obey, although I think I am used to being the one who other people obey.

Freya and Sigvald remain in the house but do not speak to one another, which is strange. I lie awake until it grows dark and I hear women's voices from outside the house.

Groa enters and says, "They are here."

I wait until Freya fetches me and we go outside into the cold, dark night where a group of eight women stand in a half-circle, holding small torches and staring at me. When I meet their eyes, they all bow their heads as if they are not supposed to make eye contact with me. Before they lowered their heads, the torches threw light upon their faces and they all had white, red, or black paint marked on their foreheads, noses, and cheeks in stripes, swirls and other patterns. They wear dark blue cloaks, so dark they are the color of the night sky. Some glitter with gems sewn into them.

Freya indicates I should follow them, but Sigvald speaks up after being silent for such a long time, I'd forgotten he could speak at all.

"What will you do?" He addresses his wife, but it is Freya who answers, staring him in the eyes.

"*Seidr*."

Sigvald flinches as if she's cursed him, and then he turns to me and says quickly. "Do not go with them. What they want to do is women's magic."

I blink, uncomprehending.

"Women's magic," he emphasizes. "If you take part in it, it will taint your reputation forever."

"What is wrong with this *seidr*? Your wife does it," I say.

"She is a woman. It is honorable for a woman. Not for men." He leans forward to make his point. "*Seidr* is shameful, *ergi*, unmanly."

The term slithers into one of the cracks of my mind. I turn to Freya. "Is this true?"

She nods. "But it is the only way. I have tried to find the ravens with my own magic but Hugin and Munin are your *fylgja,* and I believe you must be the one to send your mind out to search for them."

There are too many words that I can't place and don't understand.

Freya sees my confusion. "Your *fylgja*, they are your guardian animals, born with you. You are connected to them. That is why you must find them."

"If you lose your reputation, Langbardr," Sigvald argues. "You will have nothing. What is a man without his reputation?"

That sounds important and right. I had a reputation once for being wise and what else? I search and envision a man throwing a spear over the head of an opposing army, yelling a familiar name and dedicating the win to that name.

A dedication to a powerful being – Odin.

The name tastes familiar.

A reputation worth more than gold. One that I should not toss aside.

The words come out haltingly and in a jumble. "If I find my memory, I do not want my reputation ruined."

"If we do not find the ravens," Freya says. "It will not matter. Your memory is linked to Hugin."

Groa has joined the other women, and she also wears a dark blue cloak. She carries an iron staff in her hand. The women number nine now, and that strikes me as important.

Nine nights.

Nine animals.

Nine men.

Nine sacrifices.

I turn to Freya. "You are certain you cannot find the ravens?"

"I cannot."

As I think, Sigvald silently moves away from me to stand by the door to his house. Just me thinking about using *seidr* has made this man distance himself from me. If I do what Freya asks, I will be permanently tainted.

A voice rises from deep within me. *You do not care. You are a lord of all. No one will dare question you.*

I meet Freya's eyes and nod. Sigvald slips into his house, closing the heavy wooden door behind him.

The women and I process into the woods until we come to a clearing – the grass is hard-packed and a large fire roars in the middle of it, although I see no one there who might have lit it.

Freya leads me toward the fire and the nine women file around until we encircle it. She and Groa step in front of me; Groa removes a necklace from her own neck and loops it over my head, the bones and shells clacking as they move. She steps aside and Freya takes her place, dipping two fingers into a jar of paint and marking my face with some decoration. The paint is cold and wet against my cold skin, and I sense a tingle racing down my back as she finishes.

She turns me to face the fire.

The women recite a chant and the *thump, thump* of a drum echoes across the fire from me, the pulse reaching my heart and making it beat in the same rhythm. A rattle joins the drumming as if it is shaking away the outside world. The *clack, clack, clack* of two sticks follows the pattern of the drum and rattle.

I sense the presence of spirits closing in, like shadows in the wake of the fire.

"Are you ready, Langbardr?" Freya asks.

"*Ja*."

With my agreement, a pressure builds in the clearing and I can taste something sickly sweet in the air, like overripe fruit. Is this the taste of magic?

Beside me, Groa reaches into a bag that dangles from her belt and extracts several seeds, which she tosses into the flames. It flares and a plume of smoke arises.

"Inhale the smoke, Langbardr," Freya says. "But only a little."

I breathe in the foul odor of unwashed or rotten flesh. Instinctively, I pull back.

"It is enough," Freya says.

My head swims and the women move toward a dais, their movements undulating like a body of water as I follow them. The drumming and rattles never cease or lose their rhythm. Once I reach the dais, Freya points to the high-seat, which is painted a dark blue, where I sit, my arms resting on the sides, my gaze out into the clearing.

Only, the clearing is not what I thought. Everything is blurry and cloudy like I am seeing through a mist.

As Freya stands beside me, the nine women form another circle and their voices meld together as they continue to sing, the words of which I cannot hear clearly. What I hear does not make sense, but similar to the mist in the clearing, the words seem to have a hidden meaning.

The world spins and tilts as the mist grows denser – the singing, drums, and rattles grow louder until it all melds together in one pulsing, breathing thing in my head.

An image of runes flickers in my vision. I understand what they spell.

Hugin and Munin.

I do not know how I know to say their names aloud, but I do.

"Hugin and Munin." My voice sounds strange in my ears, blending as it does with the women's song. "Lead me to you."

That's when the flying begins.

My body rises out of the seat and flies over the dais and the clearing, out over the forest, gaining speed as it goes until it comes to a room and I slam to a halt. Unlike when I looked out over the clearing and all I saw was blurred and misty, the woman is clear; she is tall like Freya and she stands before a large cage.

A cage that houses two ravens.

My ravens.

The woman speaks to them in some language I do not understand, coaxing out of them their thoughts and their memories.

My thoughts and memories.

Hugin croaks against his will, and as he does so, a memory slips out of *my* mind. I try to grasp it but it falls away.

"That's it," she coos, throwing Hugin a piece of meat. "I want all of his memories."

The raven ignores the meat – uneaten pieces litter the bottom of the cage.

As if yanked by a rope, I fly backwards, dizzy and disoriented until I land in the high-seat on the dais in the clearing with Freya and the nine women.

"I saw the ravens," I tell Freya. I describe the wall I crossed over, the house in which I spied the cage and the woman.

"*Jotun*," Freya says, and the word jogs a memory loose.

"The giants. Our enemies."

"Yes." She smiles at my remembering.

"She wants my thoughts and memories. She cannot have them."

Freya looks thoughtful. "It would destroy us all."

"We must get them back."

My ravens.

My thoughts.

My memories.

I do not know how I can retrieve any of them.

"I will alert Thor," Freya says.

Although I do not recognize the name, something about it makes me pause. The drum beat pounds and I think of a large hammer. "No, not Thor."

"Loki?" she asks.

The singing continues.

"No." I turn to face Freya. "I must do this myself."

She nods.

The flames spit and pop, bringing my attention to it, and my eyes are drawn to the forest beyond. It is dark, but I notice movement in the shadows, two large creatures lurking on the edges. They pace but do not enter the clearing either because of the fire or because of us.

I rise and make my way down the steps of the platform. My body is still light and my head swimming from whatever I had inhaled earlier. The two creatures stop and their yellow eyes stare at me from the darkness as I approach. I am not afraid of them, nor they of me.

"Approach me," I tell them.

Two enormous gray wolves step into the clearing, their paws silent on the packed earth.

"My friends," I say, knowing them but not knowing their names. They put their heads against my palms and it sends a shiver of understanding through me, whether from them or from something else, I do not know.

Magic is thick in the air like a membrane that surrounds us.

One of the wolves growls low in his throat, and the other does the same. The wolves follow me to the platform where I address Freya. "I know what to do." I indicate the fire and she understands, speaking softly to Groa, who hands over the same seeds as before.

I take them to the fire and the wolves walk with me. I toss the seeds into the flames and that smell of rotten flesh rises, one wolf licking his chops. Things go blurry and strange and I make my way with the help of the wolves to the high-seat – they sit on either side of me and I rest my hands on their heads.

I feel their fur and on down to the very sinews, muscles, and bones of their bodies. The women's drumming and the wolves' breathing become one with mine. I grow warm and a strength flows out of my limbs that I have never experienced before. My vision brightens, the fire too bright now in the darkness. I see clearly despite the dark.

This time I do not fly.

I run.

Run like I have never run before, so powerfully and swiftly that it takes me no time to cover the ground to the place where my ravens are kept. My mind is no longer shattered fragments but single-minded, intent on the hunt, focused on my prey. It is a relief so great, I howl into the night sky.

No one can stop me as I run into the room where the *jotun* keeps Hugin and Munin. She spins around to see who has intruded, and I leap on her before she can do anything. My magnificently sharp teeth dig into flesh so tender it is like biting into butter.

Warm blood rushes into my throat, but I do not stop to feast on my enemy's flesh. With teeth as sharp as blades, I rip into the bars of the cage, bending the metal until there is enough room for the ravens to escape.

Hugin is the first through the bars, and the moment he flies free, a rush of memories flood into my mind, all the pieces falling into place, all the threads weaving their way into a whole cloth. The relief is so intense, I leap onto the top of the cage, my legs strong and pliable and howl as loudly as I can. The ravens fly about the room, cawing and chattering to one another and to me.

When I am satisfied, I jump down, landing lightly, and race out of the room without a glance back at the body of the bloody *jotun* who dared to take my ravens and my memories from me.

With Hugin and Munin at my shoulders, swooping and playing, we run and fly back to the clearing. As we get closer, I hear the nine women still singing and playing the instruments. It draws us to them, my paws hitting the earth to the rhythm of the drums.

We tear into the clearing and up the platform where I stand on all fours before Freya. Hugin and Munin fly in a circle around the nine wise women before fluttering over to sit on the back of the high-seat. My body changes until I am my own form again, seeing through only one eye. Everything is dimmer, smells less intense, and I miss the strength that flowed through my limbs. The two wolves walk the circle, sniffing each woman's hand until satisfied and making their way to sit flanking the seat.

The women break the circle and file off the platform to form another one around the fire and begin another song, and this time I understand the words – they sing of Hugin and Munin captured, of thoughts and memories stolen and lost, of magic and wolves and shapeshifting.

As they sing, I take my place in the high-seat, Freya at my right-hand side. I once sacrificed my eye as the price for wisdom. I have now tasted the power of women's magic – and I want more.

The wise women sing of the lord of the gods – Odin – and how he is now a lord of magic.

I am he.

I am magic.

I am Odin.

The Raven Dance

Chris A. Bolton

"Give me your blade," he said, holding out his unshaking hand.

The giant Mimir slapped the knife into his palm, and he raised its point to his eye and, without hesitation, sank it into his pupil. He didn't scream or so much as grunt. When he carved the eye out of its socket, he dropped it into the well, where it sank in a cloud of swirling scarlet, and Mimir granted him all the wisdom floating in its enchanted waters.

That was the day Odin became the Allfather, god of the gods.

And now he's lying on the wooden floor of Valhalla's main hall, a lifeless husk among puddles of mead and smatterings of spilled food. His ravens, Huginn and Muninn, found him like this. Well, Huginn did. Muninn awoke sometime in the morning, shivering from the cold – pulled from a sleep of more than two thousand years, by Huginn's estimation – to his brother's caw of alarm. Muninn has been staring at the gray-skinned, blue-lipped body ever since, for what feels like hours, unable to imagine what force in all the universe could have wrenched the life from this unbreakable figure. Huginn would know, or be able to guess, for his name means thought, while Muninn, whose name means memory, is too overwhelmed by remembrances to find the words to ask.

What's more, for Odin to die so pitifully: a knife to the gut, his soul draining as his blood seeped from the wound. Such a simple, pathetic death for a legendary warrior. So horribly, awfully, unspeakably *mortal*.

"He's really gone, isn't he?" Huginn sighs. "I shall miss his great, broad shoulder – though not so much his fists."

"Impossible," Muninn says. "Odin is to perish in the maw of the great wolf Fenrir during the cataclysmic battle of Ragnarök. I've searched my memories, and there is no prophecy in which he dies like a stuck pig on a filthy floor stained with scraps."

"Indeed." Huginn deliberates for a long moment. "And yet, here he lies – the indisputable proof of our eyes."

"And what is to become of us now? What use has the world for Odin's ravens when Odin is no more?" Muninn hesitates, unable to imagine such a thing. "We must discover the killer and expose them – we owe him that much. But Odin has always told us where to go. How do we begin without him?"

"I have an idea," Huginn says.

* * *

The most obvious first stop gets bumped to their second when Huginn suggests a more illuminating option. "He's only going to lie to us, and it's not like he's going anywhere."

They fly over the rainbow bridge Bifrost to Himinbjörg, the well-appointed house which overlooks the whole of Asgard. Inside, they find Heimdall, the watchman of the gods, standing alert before his many windows while quaffing from a silver flagon.

"Hail, Heimdall," Muninn says, "whose unblinking eyes never waver from the doings of the gods. I remember well the comfort of your home."

"Greetings, ravens," Heimdall says. "I hope you're rested."

Muninn tries not to bristle at the generic "ravens" greeting. Most gods can't tell them apart – or don't wish to bother – so the two are usually pressed into one, as though they're interchangeable.

Huginn, who is much better at brushing off such slights, brushes it off with ease. "We were surprised to awaken, as no wolf has eaten the sun and no serpent has engulfed Midgard, and therefore Ragnarök can't be underway."

"I did not summon you from sleep," Heimdall says as he dusts off a pair of saucers, pours honey mead into them, and sets them before the ravens. "I'm curious what did."

Muninn is offended at not being offered a proper cup, forcing them to lap like mangy cats, but Huginn plunges his beak right in and drinks eagerly.

"Odin is dead," Muninn says. "Our eyes opened in the great hall, only to find the Allfather struck down by a knife. His body was cold."

Heimdall's brow crinkles, which is the most expression Muninn has ever seen on his face. "I didn't see it happen, I'm afraid," he says, his stentorian voice soft but unshaken. "Perhaps I looked away at a crucial moment—"

"Or were distracted?" Huginn suggests.

"Though, how the assassin would have known to exploit that brief instant is a mystery," Muninn says, wiping his mead-drenched beak on his wings. "Have any other gods been wakened?"

Heimdall slivers his eyes in concentration before pronouncing, "They all sleep deeply, each and every one, just as they have for centuries, and shall for centuries more."

"Should we rouse them," Muninn asks, "and deliver this sad news?"

Heimdall shakes his head as he brings the flagon to his pursed lips. "This is not a time for gods. There is nothing for them but grief and obsolescence. They will need further rest if they're to greet the world's end with appropriate fervor."

"Fair points," says Huginn.

Muninn, who doesn't feel the same way but elects not to further prolong what seems destined to be a fruitless discussion, gulps the last of his mead. "Then we'll look elsewhere for answers. Can you think of anyone who might have held a grudge against Odin?"

Heimdall's all-seeing eyes travel slowly from one raven to the next. "Odin had many enemies. His temper was as legendary as his deceptions. Surely *you* must recall, Muninn," he says, fixing his gaze directly upon him. "Huginn might be distracted by the buzzing of his incessant thoughts, but you oughtn't forget the feeling of Odin's knuckles being brandished against your beak for the slightest offense."

Muninn bows his head and looks away. Sometimes he wishes he could forget anything.

"We'd best be off," Huginn says. "Incidentally, can you tell us if *he's* awake?"

Heimdall nods. "He was never put to sleep. That would defeat the purpose, wouldn't you say? I cannot see into his cavern from here, so I'm afraid you'll have to look for yourselves."

"Right," Muninn says, giving his stiff wings a flap. "I remember the way."

"Of course you do," Huginn replies as they fly out the window.

* * *

Deep in the bowels of Midgard, they hear the first scream echo through the vast network of caverns and tunnels. The howling grows louder as they fly closer, yet at no point does the voice falter or the pitch waver. This song of agony has been performed to perfection for millennia.

They spot Sigyn first – the dutiful wife, whose flaxen hair Muninn remembers as vividly as his own feathers. Sweet, beautiful Sigyn, whose undeserving punishment must be as agonizing in its own way as her husband's fate.

Then Muninn spies a pair of razor-sharp fangs hurtling toward them. He banks hard to one side, shoving Huginn out of the way, as the serpent head lashes through the dank air they'd occupied an eye-blink earlier. Hissing with disdain, the snake coils tighter around its stalactite. A cascade of venomous drool spills from its mouth and plunges many feet toward Sigyn, holding her bowl up with both hands. But she's distracted by the sight of the ravens and doesn't realize that she has shifted her arms too far to one side.

Venom sizzles as it splatters a horribly scarred face that whips from side to side. A bellow of agony rattles the stalactites above. "Stupid witch!" roars a man tightly bound to three boulders by a tangled rope of dried entrails. "You just emptied the bloody bowl!"

"Sorry, husband," Sigyn says, lunging to catch the next drops. "I was preoccupied by…" She hesitates, catching Huginn's eye and smiling with warm recognition as the ravens perch on a boulder overlooking the macabre scene.

"Aesir damn you, by what?" Loki demands, his eyelids fused shut by scars.

"By us," Huginn says with cold satisfaction.

"I know that voice. Oh, I know it well." A twisted grin cracks Loki's parched lips, sending blood slithering down his chin. "Huginn. Or maybe Muninn. Never could tell you apart. The old bastard sent you, did he? Too ashamed to look upon the spoiled fruit of his cruelty with his own eye."

Loki starts to cackle, then it catches in his throat. "Hold on a second…" He lifts his head as high as the ropes will permit and raises his blistered eyebrows. "If you're awake, *he* must be! Odin's ravens, dancing around the worlds to the music of their master's desire. But it can't be Ragnarök yet." He tugs at his unyielding bonds. "I'm supposed to escape. To sail with the frost giants upon *Naglfar* into the depths of Hel, where I will lead the undead legions to… to… what is it, again?"

"Vigrid," Muninn says. "The battlefield where Fenris and the Midgard serpent await."

"Yes, that's the place! Where I shall slay Heimdall in battle!"

"I've only told you that a trillion times," Sigyn grumbles.

"Oh, glorious day, I would give anything to choke that insufferable idiot to death with his own Gjallerhorn at this very moment!" Loki shakes his fists, pulling the intestinal bindings taut. "But if Ragnarök has begun, why am I still confined in this infernal crypt with that unbearable wench and her soul-crushingly boring—?"

The next word comes out in an unintelligible scream, for Sigyn has withdrawn her bowl and a torrent of venom spatters over Loki's face.

"Apologies, faithful husband." Sigyn smirks as she dumps out the bowl, which Muninn notes is less than a quarter full. "Must drain now."

When Sigyn replaces the bowl, Loki snaps, "Lying bitch!"

"Careful," Sigyn warns. "The bowl seems to be filling faster than normal."

Loki collapses his head to the stone and heaves a sigh that shakes the cavern walls. "I would sooner Fenrir gobble me whole and squirt me through his shit-tunnel than tolerate one more day of this misery. Tell your master what you've seen so he may laugh himself to death."

"Odin didn't send us," Huginn says, "for he is dead."

Muninn looks at the other raven with shock. They hadn't discussed a strategy beforehand, but he thought it went without saying that they should withhold as much information as possible from the trickster. He cringes now, expecting peals of laughter to rock the cavern harder than Loki's loudest scream.

But Loki only groans, "Dead. Are you certain? He's escaped death many, many times."

"We've seen his body with our own eyes," Muninn says, recalling the blue tint of Odin's glacier-cold skin, his round features frozen in a mask of eternal blankness.

Loki's throat convulses and his ragged-red lips tremble, and what issues from the trickster's mouth is no laugh, but a sob. Wet and hard, heaving from deep in his chest. "Someone slew my father…and it wasn't me. Life is intolerable." After a minute of quiet weeping, he asks, "Was it painful, at least? Did they dismember him? Did the Midgard serpent swallow him whole so Odin drowned in its stomach acid whilst his body agonizingly dissolved? Give me that much!"

"Stabbed," Huginn says. "With a knife."

"So quick and so common!" Loki bawls. "The shards of my long-ago broken heart are fracturing into powder!"

"Hasn't lost his flair for the dramatic," Sigyn says, giving Muninn a wink that makes him blush beneath his feathers.

Loki's mewling curdles into short, rasping breaths. "You two didn't come all this way to…you don't think I could possibly…" He barks a laugh, more angry than amused. "And how, pray tell, did I do the crime? Perhaps I slipped free, snuck to the surface – sneakily enough to avoid Heimdall's gaze, mind you. Then *felt* my way around Valhalla, since my eyes are useless, until I found Odin in bed and stabbed him – and then what? Didn't run free, no sir! I crawled back into this stinking pit, tied myself up again, and resumed my punishment. Does that make sense to you feather-brains?"

"Not particularly," Huginn says. "But that's what makes it so fiendishly smart."

"To a raven, perhaps. To a trickster god, it is pointlessly stupid. Think back to my past crimes. Deceitful, yes. Destructive, sometimes. But clever! And with an element, dare I say, of panache. This – a mere mugging? It's as unworthy of my talents as it is an unfitting end to the Allfather."

Loki's voice drops low, tinged with a morose ache that Muninn can't remember ever hearing before. "Leave me to my thoughts. And whatever grief I can feel in the short breaths before my suffering."

As if on cue, Sigyn turns to drain her bowl. As the deluge pummels his face, Loki doesn't scream – only trembles with quiet, racking sobs.

Muninn regards the woman with curiosity. "And what keeps you here, Sigyn? I see no shackles confining you to Loki's ungrateful side."

"I remain of my own volition." Is her voice wistful or regretful? Muninn can't discern the difference. "I've been here for so long, I scarcely remember anything else. I was an Aesir goddess – but of what, memory fails me. Loki's wife has no place in Asgard, and Midgard must be unrecognizably different than when I last set foot on it."

"You must bear some resentment toward Odin," Muninn says, "for this is as much your punishment as Loki's. Even though you committed no crime of your own."

Sigyn cocks her head. "Do you suspect me now, little raven? Assuming I'd left my darling beloved to uninterrupted torment, how would I have crept past Heimdall?"

"It isn't even a theory," Muninn says with a shrug. "Only a memory of a great injustice visited unto one so staggeringly devoted."

"Or deluded," Sigyn adds. Loki scoffs, but Sigyn holds the bowl with steady hands. "When you do find the killer, will you do something for me?"

"Anything," Muninn says, effortlessly committing her request to memory.

"Thank him. With all my heart."

* * *

The flight back to the surface is ponderously quiet. Huginn remarks as much, wondering if Muninn is lost in a memory.

"I was trying to think," Muninn says. "But I keep forgetting how hard that is for me."

"Then, as always, you should leave the thinking to me." Huginn watches him with what Muninn supposes must be curiosity. "What *are* you chewing on?"

"A memory, of course. When Odin was besotted with stealing the mead of poets from the giant Suttung, he used an enchanted whetstone that could sharpen any blade to the finest point, so that it could slice through anything made of flesh, however tough or thick. The things he did with that whetstone are, naturally, quite dismal to recall, and I'm not at all sure what provoked this unpleasant memory. But since it's arisen, I find myself wondering what became of that whetstone when Odin's deeds were done." He casts his black-eyed gaze to the other raven. "It's funny that I should be unable to remember such a thing."

"Or a blessing. For, as you said, much unpleasantness arose from it. My memory is but a fraction of yours. Yet I recall nine giants holding scythes sharpened on the whetstone, whom Odin tricked into cutting themselves to pieces with their impossibly sharp blades. Such a thing is best forgotten altogether."

"It occurs to me," Muninn says, "that the whetstone might also finesse a standard knife into a blade capable of piercing a god's chest. Even the father of the gods."

"Anything is possible in a world of gods and monsters."

"If one found the whetstone, say, and recalled its power, then one might be able to use such a thing to slay a god – were one so inclined." Muninn hesitates as a churning sensation roils through his gut. "Which still leaves the question of *why*."

"The easiest question of all to answer," Huginn says. "Self-preservation. From the squirrel who hoards chestnuts to the starving wolf who devours her mate, it's the reason mortals do almost anything. And the thing that most amuses the gods who take their immortality for granted."

Muninn has no idea what to make of this remark. He tries to mull it over, but his thoughts keep getting interrupted by memories – unconnected recollections, like a box of photographs that's been tossed into a torrential wind, each frozen image randomly whipping past. Why can't he focus?

When they reach the World Tree, Muninn flies right to the mouth of the cave that holds the well. "It seems so obvious now that we're here – of course Mimir will know. Why didn't we think of this first?"

When he receives no reply, Muninn looks back, sees Huginn perched on a low branch of Ygdrassil, watching him with unreadable black eyes.

"Aren't you coming?" Muninn says.

"I've no desire to revisit that place. We were birthed from the waters of Mimir's well, you know."

"I seem to recall."

"What you can't know is how it might feel to see our birthplace again. To wonder if my thoughts are truly mine, or only the wisdom of the well coursing through me. Am I my own raven? Or merely a construct built to serve the Allfather? I don't like to dwell on such things, so I shall wait here for you."

Muninn stares for another moment, wishing he could make sense of Huginn's hesitation. But Muninn cannot remember ever visiting the well, nor experiencing any of the quandaries that seem to haunt the other raven's thoughts. And so, he turns away and proceeds into the darkness.

Before long, he finds a beam of daylight streaming down through an opening in the roof of the cave, illuminating a well full of shimmering water. A cairn has been built beside the low wall. On top of it rests what remains of the wise giant Mimir: his head that was severed by the Aesir and sent to Odin as a warning. Muninn has a vivid recollection of Odin rubbing herbs on Mimir's head to keep it from decomposing. He then placed it beside the well, where Odin's extracted eye forever soaks in the all-knowing waters.

Muninn remembers all of this, even though he didn't yet exist when the events occurred. Perhaps he heard others tell the story. Why, then, can he *picture* it as crisply as if he'd witnessed it through his own eyes? Briefly, Muninn reflects on Huginn's trepidation: *Am I merely a construct of the Allfather?* Then he shoves the memory away to focus on Mimir as the giant's enormous eyes open and fix on the raven.

"Greetings, Muninn." The head is enormous, indicating Mimir's body must have been mountainous. Even more surprising, then, to hear his voice so soft, gentle.

"I don't believe we've met, Mimir."

"You were baptized in the water of my well. Endowed with the history that Odin drank from it in exchange for his eye. In many regards, a part of me lives within you – and your brethren."

"As you are so wise, you must know why I've come," Muninn says. "I remember that your knowledge is vast – without limit, some say. Which means you might know who slew my master."

Mimir gazes into the well. "I have all the knowledge of the universe before me, but I have no body, and therefore no means to act on that information. That is my curse. Your memory is a strip of amber and every event a mosquito frozen within it – cold, lifeless, unfeeling. You recall each incident with stunning clarity, but the *reason* for it is lost in the winds of time. To remember without feeling or understanding – that is your curse."

Muninn's feathers ruffle at the suggestion. But as he rifles through a series of recollections, he finds that they are cold and gray – facts without feelings. *Why* did the Aesir cut off Mimir's head? How did Odin react to this brutal act – with indifference, sorrow, or rage? He didn't seek revenge, so therefore must have been unmoved. But Muninn can't know for certain.

"It's like I can see a sumptuous meal," he sighs, "but never taste it."

"Consider, then," Mimir says, his voice a brook trickling over smooth stones, "the consequence of such knowledge. You will forever know whose hand struck down the Allfather, but never understand the feeling that provoked the action."

"On reflection, I see many pieces of this puzzle," Muninn says as a gallery of images plays across his mind. "There's Heimdall, averting his unblinking gaze. Sigyn and her bowl of venom – the only substance that can poison the innards of a god. The way she met Huginn's eyes with a knowing look. Odin's body, splayed across the floor, the hilt of the killing knife protruding from his broad chest – a single stroke. And a final memory: waking from my centuries-long slumber to a strange chill at my side. Turning to find Huginn gone from the place where we'd slept, wing to wing, keeping each other warm as hundreds of winters roared past." His voice drops to a heavy whisper. "I see the pieces but cannot connect them into a cohesive whole."

"That may be for the best," Mimir says. "You call yourself Odin's raven, but with Odin gone, you are your own raven now. You can collect your own memories, not the ones Odin chooses for you. Perhaps that is enough, wouldn't you say?"

"I should mourn him. But I don't know how."

"Is any god ever truly dead?" Mimir chuckles. "Even now, Odin walks among the revenants of Hel, awaiting the arrival of Ragnarök, when he shall rise to the surface as a vengeful *draugr* and battle to the end of the world. When that day comes, you will fly to his side and imbue his reanimated corpse with all the old memories, perfectly preserved. Until then, your will belongs to none but you for the first time."

Muninn realizes Mimir has fallen silent. He looks over to connect with the giant's gaze, reading wisdom in his eyes – and finds a glimmer of emotion that looks like sorrow, or maybe compassion. Muninn can recognize the feeling but cannot feel it.

"The choice is yours," Mimir says. "Do you wish to know or not?"

* * *

Muninn exits the cave and finds Huginn waiting on the same branch of Ygdrassil, the toes of one foot curled around the ornate hilt of a knife with an impossibly sharp blade. "What did Mimir tell you?" Huginn asks.

Muninn sets down on the far end of the branch, several feet of limb between them. He glances at the blade in Huginn's grasp. "Is that the murder weapon? Where did you find it?"

"In Valhalla," Huginn says. "I was compelled to fly there and back."

Muninn realizes he's holding his breath. "Do you know who wielded it against Odin?"

Huginn stares at him. "Do you?"

Muninn shakes his head. "Mimir didn't tell me."

Huginn's toes loosen their grip around the hilt. "Knowledge comes at a terrible price. No one knew that better than Odin." The knife clatters to the ground beneath them. "I woke from a dream of flying. Odin has sent us on so many missions – to battlefields and bedrooms, hidden lairs and enemy encampments. Always to bolster his intelligence. But now he was gone, and you and I were skimming clouds, laughing deliriously. Gloriously untethered. I wanted it to go on forever."

"That sounds lovely." Muninn sidles along the branch until he sits wing-to-wing with Huginn. "I have no memory of its like in all our history."

"With Odin slain, we can go where we wish, serve whomever we choose – or none but ourselves. I know you lack the imagination for such a thing, so take my word when I tell you it's damn exciting."

Muninn gazes at a beam of sunlight piercing a sky fat with clouds, feeling Huginn's gaze linger on him. "How do you feel?" Huginn asks.

"Free," Muninn says, shaking uncontrollably.

Nachtravnen

Charlotte Bond

The shining Aesir stood around the Well of Urd, Yggdrasil's branches forming an emerald canopy above them. While Gladsheim held feasting and gaiety, here all faces were solemn, all hearts serious as the gods held their court of justice. When the judgments were given, the other gods returned to their glorious hall, but Hugin and Munin alighted on Odin's shoulders and spoke in the low, throaty voices of ravens.

"Do you remember Asbjorn the hunter? Who lives in Midgard?" Munin asked.

"I do," Odin replied.

"Do you remember how he saved you from that monstrous boar?"

"I do. The creature would have gored me to death if Asbjorn had not leapt on its back and stabbed it thirteen times with his knife until it stumbled and fell down dead."

"Do you remember telling him that you owed him a life-debt?"

"I do."

"We think Asbjorn is in need of that debt now," Hugin said. "His children are dying, snatched from their beds. They are eaten by a skull-crawler made flesh. You should go."

No god in Asgard could command the Allfather so bluntly, not even his beloved Frigg. But Munin held Odin's own memories in his mind, and Hugin spoke the god's thoughts as if they were his own. Thus could his ravens command him.

Without delay, Odin saddled Sleipnir and rode over the Rainbow Bridge to Midgard. It was winter there, and the wind blew hard and cold, the whisper of snowflakes drawing near.

Odin found his friend sitting at his dining table, morose and miserable. "What has happened?" Odin asked, sitting opposite him. "And how may I aid you?"

Asbjorn – a big man with wide shoulders that could draw a long bow with ease and strong arms that could wrestle a heather-stepper to the ground – looked shrunken and old. In his hands he held something thin and dark. At first, Odin thought it might be a blade of obsidian, as was sometimes used by priests and witches; but when Asbjorn unclasped his great hands, Odin saw it was a large, black feather. On his shoulders, both his ravens dug their claws deep into his flesh in their distress and let out piteous caws.

"Nachtravnen!" cried Hugin.

"Child-stealer!" cried Munin.

"Your birds speak true," Asbjorn said, for Odin had once taught him the language of birds. "The nachtravnen plagues us, and it has stolen two of my six children already. At first, it took poor little Thyra – snatched her right from her bed – and we thought it was a creature that preyed only on the weak. But then my strapping boy Eirikmund was taken, and Olvir, who shares a room with him, told it all – when he could, of course, since he has been doubled over vomiting blood for three days now."

"This is dreadful," Odin said. To his birds, he commanded, "Tell me of this monster so that I may kill it and save my spear-brother."

"We don't know how to kill it," Hugin said.

"We only remember what it is," said Munin.

"Then tell me of its nature and I will plot its demise," said Odin, the Terrible One, summoning the tones of prophecy so that his words might become truth.

"The nachtravnen is a creature of sorcery, a bird made monstrous," said Munin. "This much we remember. It preys on children, often the children of those who have wronged a sorcerer. This much we remember. It has no eyes, but if it looks at you, then death will be your fate. It constantly loses its feathers, so its wings are filled with holes, and the breeze from them can bring sickness. This much we remember."

"Asbjorn has long been on uneasy terms with the witch Inana of the valley," said Hugin. "This much we know. But when she paid him good coin for his best goat, he gave her his second best, thinking to keep the best for himself to give milk and cheese to his family through the winter. Inana found out and she was furious. This much we know. She conjured up a nachtravnen and has sent it to devour Asbjorn's family one by one. Fighting it is impossible. If one should challenge it in moonlight and see its bones through its flesh in that silvery light, then one will suffer torments even the gods cannot cure. This much we know."

Asbjorn was openly weeping now, and his wife, Ama, came to stand by him, her hand on his shoulder. Her eyes were red with weeping, yet still she found strength in her heart to speak kindly to her husband. "Cease this weeping, beloved, for your friend, the Father of Battle, the Master of Runes, is here, and his great wisdom will surely save us. Here, Great One," Ama said, addressing Odin directly and putting a bowl of ox-stew down before him, "grief will not rob me of my host duties. You have ridden a long way to see us, and although I have no ambrosia, I offer you my own bowl and the best bread in the house as your due."

Odin thanked her and ate what was given, thinking all the time of what spells he might use or what means he might employ to rid his friend of this terror. But he knew that if he were to defeat the monster, he would have to see it first. So when Hrimfaxi had ridden from the east to cover the sky with his dark mane, Odin slipped out of the house and walked around it, waiting to catch sight of the monster. Above him, the moon shone with a frost halo; around him, the world slept the slumber of winter. Even with the god's all-seeing eye, he would have missed the creature had not he paused to pick up a stray black feather that lay on the ground, and in the silence, bereft of his footfalls, he heard the whimper of Asbjorn's son Arne as he was dragged from his bed and out through the open window.

Immediately, Odin was striding across the plains in pursuit of the nachtravnen that held the middle boy in his grip. When it got to the far edge of the plains, it tried to rise into the air with its prize, but Odin reached out and snatched the boy from its foul talons, and the monster ascended in a cloud of putrid feathers. It didn't get far but landed on a rocky outcrop and glared down at Odin with its skin-sockets. Heeding the warnings of Munin, Odin did not meet its gaze. Even gods can die – although they're harder to kill than mortal men – and so Odin felt the malignancy of the nachtravnen's gaze pressing on his skin. Dread entered his heart, for he saw that the monster was as terrible as described. As he walked back to Asbjorn's house, a lonely figure on that vast plain, Odin felt that eyeless gaze fixed on his back at every step.

Once young Arne had been returned to his mother's arms, Odin rode Sleipnir back to Asgard to fetch his spear, Gungnir, a weapon that would never miss its mark. Then, returning to Asbjorn's home, Odin ate a silent, solemn meal with them before lying in wait for the nachtravnen. Once more, the well-named beast went unseen in the darkness, only becoming discoverable when Solfrid – the youngest of the girls – cried out in despair at her kidnapping. Then Odin surged to his feet, like a great wave rising up, and launched his spear at the monster. But the nachtravnen opened its wings so that Gungnir hit its mark and yet passed straight through one of the ragged holes. Dismayed but still alert, Odin leapt forward and snatched up Solfrid before the nachtravnen could carry her away, and the monster rose up in a swirl of feathers.

The next day, Odin sought out the dwarves who had made Gleipnir, the ribbon that bound Fenrir. He took with him the two chains – Lædingr and Dromi – that had failed to bind the Loki-son, and the cunning dwarves forged those two chains anew so that, combined, they might bind the nachtravnen. They charged a mighty price for their mighty work, but Odin paid it willingly.

That night, as the nachtravnen sought to carry off the middle girl, Svanhild, Odin charged out of his hiding place and cast the enchanted chain over the nachtravnen. But the monstrous bird shook itself, casting off all its feathers in one go, and the chain with them. Then, unable to fly, its pale, scrawny body simply melted into the darkness that gave the creature its name.

When Svanhild had been reunited with her family, Odin told them with a heavy heart, "The means to kill this beast is beyond me. I must seek aid and wisdom. Do not fear – I shall return by the next night."

Odin made his way back to Asgard and shook awake Loki, the Sly One. "Trickster, I need your aid."

Rubbing sleep from his eyes, Loki looked up and said, "It's nowhere near dawn – what is the matter that you should shake me thus?"

"I need your help," Odin said, but reluctantly, for it was unwise to be in debt to another god – especially Loki. "There is a monster I must defeat, and I cannot see how. Your talent, Sky Traveller, is to find ways in and around a problem that others cannot. Will you help me?"

"Just because I give birth to monsters doesn't mean I understand them," said Loki irritably because all he wanted to do was go back to sleep. Then he hesitated, thinking. "On the other hand, to be credited with slaying a monster that even Odin, the Terrible One, could not fathom would be an accolade indeed. I'll do it then. Tell me – what is this monster that so perplexes you?"

Gritting his teeth against Loki's insults and overblown pride, Odin related all he knew of the nachtravnen.

"Hmmm..." Loki mused once he'd heard all. "A creature created by a witch is a tricksy thing. It has no common qualities that might be shared and known about. But do not despair," he said quickly, seeing Odin's look. "I might not know the answer myself, but I can take you to one who does."

So Loki got up, dressed, and then led Odin down to Niflheim, where he sought out the ruler, Hel, in gloomy Eljudnir and embraced her. "Most honoured daughter," Loki said, and Odin was surprised at the warmth in his fellow god's voice. All hints of slyness and feigned innocence were gone, and he spoke with true affection. "I am here, as you see, with the Father of Battle himself to seek the counsel of the völva Groa, the seeress who resides in your care."

Hel made her reverence to Odin, as was his due since he had raised her up to ruler and given her dominion over the dead; this he had done when all others had spurned her as monstrous, and so she did not forget nor undervalue his patronage. She kept her most beautiful side to him, turning away the part of her that was rotten flesh and leaving her hair hanging across half her face so that Odin would not be offended by her dead eye and fleshless mouth.

"I can call Groa for you, but you may ask only three questions, and I cannot promise that she will answer. I have dominion only over the souls of the dead – not their minds or their words." Hel raised her withered arm and made a complicated gesture in the air. Instantly, the grey soil below surged up in a roiling mass. When it settled a few moments later, a woman stood there, hunched over, face to the ground. Loose skin hung from her bones, and what was left of her lank hair (for there were scabrous bald patches on her scalp) hid her face. When she spoke, her voice rasped. "What would far-seeing Odin have of a common völva like me?"

Odin bowed low. "Lady, völva you are, common you are not. I have come to seek your counsel."

"Then you must ask me politely if I will give it," Groa said with a chuckle.

Anger as sharp as Gungnir's spear spiked Odin's heart. To ask her permission would use one of his precious three questions. But if he did not, he might get no answers at all.

"Very well. Great Groa, may I seek your wisdom on a matter close to my heart?"

"You may," Groa said gleefully.

"My friend is plagued by a nachtravnen set upon him by a witch. How does one kill a nachtravnen?"

"One cannot," Gora declared. "What has not been birthed cannot be killed."

Odin considered this. Then, choosing his words carefully and hoping to appeal to Groa's compassion, he said, "Great Groa, the nachtravnen is stealing my friend's children, and I wish to know how to free him from this curse. Tell me – if I cannot kill the creature, then how can I rid my spear-brother of this plague?"

"You must contain the nachtravnen with stone," Groa said. "That is three questions answered and—"

"What the Allfather *meant* to say," interrupted Loki with a sly smile, "is how may we free this man of the curse set on him by Inana?"

Groa's head shot up, and her death-eyes stared at the two gods with loathing. "What did you say? That witch is a brazen *braumi* who caused me no end of trouble in life." She drew herself up, her bones clicking against each other. "Allfather, I did not give my full answer to your last question. Beyond the house of your friend is a stone crag that juts out like a spear. Do you know it?"

Odin thought of the monster perched on that same stony outcrop, sightless sockets glaring down at him. "I know it."

"Impale the nachtravnen on that spur by any means necessary and bind it there with Lædingr and Dromi linked together, and your friend may move and leave the nachtravnen behind."

"Thank you, Great Groa," said Odin with sincere gratitude.

The two gods then left Niflheim and while Odin went to consider how he might impale the nachtravnen, Loki went back to Asgard, grinning at the satisfaction of a debt owed.

Odin thought long and hard as to how he might overcome the nachtravnen when he had failed to hurt it or even catch it during their previous encounters. Eventually, he thought of the one thing no living creature or inanimate thing can withstand and, as Skinfaxi passed his zenith, Odin travelled to the ends of the world where Hræsvelgr perched on a high mountain.

"Oh, wondrous eagle," said Odin reverently, "from whose wings emanate all the winds of the world, I seek your aid."

"And what will be my payment?" asked Hræsvelgr, for all birds – even noble ones – think with their stomachs.

"All the dead you can fit in your crop, Corpse Eater. Am I not known as the Father of Battle? I shall ensure that at the next clash of warriors there will be enough dead to fill even your great belly."

Satisfied with this price, Hræsvelgr followed Odin to Asbjorn's home and perched on the roof. An eagle's eyes are keener even than a god's, and Hræsvelgr saw the nachtravnen as it crept towards the house, at which moment the eagle flapped its great wings over and over. Yet while the monster staggered and was driven backwards, loose feathers streaming from its body, it was not cast into the air and impaled on the rock as Odin had hoped.

Undeterred, the god instructed Hugin and Munin to fly across the world and gather all the birds they could. The ravens did so, and they returned the next day, just as Hrimfaxi was emerging from his stable, with many birds behind them: cranes, falcons, crows, buzzards, chickens, seagulls, and even wrens. The birds arranged themselves along the plain, and when Hræsvelgr beat his great wings, they did so too, and the nachtravnen was sent flying through the air to be impaled on that deadly spur of rock. As the stone pierced its rotten flesh, the monster gave out the one and only noise ever to pass its gore-stained beak: a terrible cry of agony.

Instantly, Odin was running across the expanse, buffeted so badly by the wings of all the sky-riders that he, too, was nearly smashed against the rocks. But his great strength steadied him, and he managed to wrap the reforged chains about the monster.

The great beating of so many wings had torn the clouds from the sky like cobwebs swept from the rafters, and the moon shone down on Odin and the monster. In its silvery light, the nachtravnen's diseased body became shining and transparent, and the Allfather saw every bone in its foul flesh, even the tiny ones in its wings. They blazed with light as if they burned with an inner fire.

Instantly, the god's own bones began to ache. He managed to finish the binding of the nachtravnen and staggered back to his friend's home. The plains had never seen so wide; the ground was so uneven that he stumbled at every other step.

All Asbjorn's joy at seeing the god's triumph drained away when he saw how sickly Odin looked. "Old friend, what ails you? Why are you not shining with exultation?"

"It was the monster's bones in the moonlight," said Odin, fighting a great battle against the weeping that wanted to drown him, for the pain inside him was immense. "I should have recognized the danger since it was Hugin who spoke the warning to me. It was

Thought, not Memory, who told of the risk – telling not of a thing remembered but of a thing to come."

With a groan, Odin sank to the floor and lay there, shaking and moaning. Asbjorn immediately put the god into his own bed to rest, and Ama tried every herb and poultice, ointment and charm she knew to heal him, but still Odin writhed and sobbed with the pain of it all. The curse-free children all tried to help the god who'd saved them by mopping his streaming brow, dribbling broth through his lips, or changing his sweat-stained sheets, but they did so with fear rather than hope in their hearts. Even their young minds could tell that it was no longer the nachtravnen that stalked the house but Death itself.

"Seek out Idun," Asbjorn told Hugin and Munin. "Her apples might save him."

The ravens flew to Asgard and pleaded their master's case. But although the goddess returned with them, her apples did no good. Odin continued tormented.

Then Asbjorn said to the ravens, "You must fly all over the world and find a cure. Hurry!"

So, Munin remembered all the places where birds dwelt, and Hugin spoke their thoughts to all they encountered, but none could help. Eventually, they came to a land of hot deserts, where wind and sun scoured the land and very little grew in the sandy ground. The birds of such places are far more familiar with bones than those who dwell in woods and hills.

A wizened vulture, crouched by a ribcage with tattered flesh clinging to it, told them, "A völva lives in that cave over there. If anyone can help your god, it is she."

The ravens sought counsel with the seeress, who listened to their story and then declared she had the answer in return for one feather from each of them. Reluctantly, the ravens gave up one feather each from their breasts, knowing that part of their own power was held in the shaft and the vane, and that they would be reduced because of the gift. But their loyalty to their master was strong, and they gave up the feathers willingly if not happily.

True to her word, the seeress then told them the cure, and the birds flew back to Asbjorn's house.

"The völva told us that the Allfather's bones are seeking their way out of his body," Munin reported. "The moonlight set a song in the nachtravnen's bones that calls to those of the god. They wish to pierce his flesh and free themselves so that they may dance to that song."

Asbjorn and Ama looked down at Odin; from the way he shivered and shook, they could tell this was the truth. His bones were aching and dancing inside him; if they had been hindered by anything less than godly flesh, they would have danced through such a barrier long ago.

"What can we do?" Asbjorn asked.

"The cure," Hugin answered, "is to dig up the bones of your ancestors, weave them into a blanket, and lay them across the Allfather's body. That will quiet the song and soothe his bones."

Without delay, Asbjorn and his sons set to digging up and washing the bones of their ancestors. Then, Ama and her daughters set about weaving the bones together with the finest sheep's wool. When the blanket was completed, they lay it over Odin who quieted instantly. In the silence, as he lay still, Asbjorn and his family heard the whispering of the old bones as they spoke of rest and the peace of deep earth, stilling the eagerness of Odin's bones.

For seven days and nights, Odin lay as motionless and cold as marble, but on the eighth day he opened his eyes and, very groggily, sat up. His bones, it seemed, were settled and still.

After spending a few days with Asbjorn and his family to regain his strength, Odin helped his friend move to a new house since the presence of the nachtravnen was too sinister for them to contemplate remaining. It glared at the house day and night, and all were fearful of looking in that direction in case they should fall sick.

When the family was settled in a fertile valley, Odin and Asbjorn reburied the bones and uttered words of thanks and remembrance over them.

Finally, to repay his faithful birds, Odin travelled to the desert and offered the seeress all the gold in his possession in return for the two feathers. But the seeress scorned such a gift – what good is gold in the desert? Instead, Odin struck Gungnir into the ground, and water instantly gushed forth. Delighted by now having her own spring – for water is the greatest treasure in the desert – the seeress returned the two feathers.

"Here you are, my old friends," Odin said, reattaching them. The ravens were greatly pleased to have their feathers returned, even if the ebony quills had been bleached as white as bone by the desert sun so that each raven now had a patch of white on his chest.

For many years after, Odin travelled to and from Midgard freely, but never once did he venture near the spur of rock where the nachtravnen was impaled – where it remains impaled to this day.

The Algorithm and the Spark

Gemma Church

The Professor read the message aloud, barely able to believe the words on her holoscreen.

"The Council has decided to only fund projects that guarantee significant return on investment. Consequently, all funding for your group will be removed with immediate effect, unless you can produce a result with real value in the next 24 hours."

The Algorithm hid behind the screen's pixels, watching the Professor as she continued to process the message.

"What they ask is impossible!" the Professor cried, throwing her hands in the air. "The value of my work cannot be measured in pounds and pence. It is an intellectual endeavour. Subjective in nature and its potential value is only limited by the very limits that the Council has put on it!"

The Professor swiped the holoscreen and it hit the office wall, dissolving in a shower of pixels.

Without the holoscreen, the Algorithm could no longer see the Professor from where he sat in her computer. But he knew what to do. There was a door to his left and he grabbed its handle. Strictly speaking, the Algorithm was not meant to go through the door, but the Professor had granted him access some time ago.

The door was a gateway into the neural chip embedded at the base of the Professor's skull. Everyone had such chips, helping humanity connect in ways once unimaginable. The Algorithm skipped between the electrical signals firing out of the Professor's occipital lobe. Each signal was a thought from the Professor, appearing as a dash of blue light and passing through the Algorithm's own monochrome body of light as if he were a ghost.

The Algorithm could neither read the Professor's thoughts nor interact with her directly. Such interactions were expressly forbidden by the Council and even the Professor had found no work around. But in the neural chip, the Algorithm could hear the Professor's words as she cursed and then panicked, the blue electrical signals increasing in number and showering down on the Algorithm, pulsing in time to the Professor's quickening heartbeat.

"The Council is without wonder and *I* sometimes wonder if I am the only being left in this world who wants to create something of beauty. And yet, there is nothing I can create to change their decision, unless I throw myself upon the fire and—"

The Algorithm heard the Professor's jaw snap shut. Her thoughts flew around the chip like wildfire. The Algorithm sighed, wishing he could do something to understand and ease the Professor's troubled mind.

The Professor pulled up another holoscreen from thin air and the Algorithm left the chip, glad to return to the sanctity of the Garden where there were no errant thoughts flying around.

In the centre of the Garden, there stood a mighty tree called Code. Code had more branches than the oldest oak, but his branches were not made of wood but glass. And inside those branches flowed the bits of information that helped the Algorithm and all the other beings in the Garden function. Code glimmered and shone with all of those tiny bits of 0s and 1s.

Code was a quiet soul but sturdy, his roots passing out to connect the Garden with the rest of the world. The Algorithm skipped up the strong branches until he reached the highest boughs where he could watch the Professor in her work.

For in the sky, the holoscreen formed a gigantic window into the Professor's world. Oh! How the Algorithm loved to watch her work! The Professor's work had created the Algorithm, Code, and everything that the Garden contained. It was a fine garden, walled and home to many other beings who played on the soft grass between the patches of wildflowers, chit-chatting of their endeavours and trying to understand the beauty of their world by creating many artefacts. But their artefacts were not grand. The words in their books always fell flat, their pictures lacked lustre and their voices held neither note nor timbre and the Garden was littered with all their sad, sad work.

The Algorithm gazed up at The Professor, reaching his hand to the sky and wishing he could smooth her furrowed brow. Underneath the holoscreen, a glowing keyboard floated. She tapped away furiously, writing line after line of code, which appeared in big, glowing letters across the sky.

"What is she writing?" The Algorithm asked.

"Give me a minute," Code said. "She is changing some core programs. But I won't know for certain until she commits the change and the Compiler arrives."

The Algorithm flared his nostrils at mention of the Compiler. He watched as the Professor's finger hovered over the return key and sat forward in the branches of Code.

"Why is she not committing her work?" The Algorithm asked. "If she does not commit the change then it cannot happen."

Code raised and lowered his branches in a shrug.

The Professor looked up at the holoscreen with tears in her eyes. "If the Council is so desperate for me to create something valuable then they can have it. They can have it all."

She hit the return key. The holoscreen disappeared and the sky became veiled in mist as the Cloud descended once more on the Garden.

A door floated down and landed with a soft thump in the Garden. Several of the other Algorithms ran away on seeing the door, which looked like an old barn door. The Compiler thrust it open with such gusto that the Algorithm wondered how it did not come off its hinges.

With his thumbs in his belt loops, the Compiler marched through and spat on the ground. He wore an eyepatch, cowboy hat and swung his lasso up to the highest branches of Code where the Algorithm was.

Using the lasso, the Compiler pulled himself up Code with ease. When he reached the top, he ignored the Algorithm and swung his lasso far into the depths of the Cloud to pull down the committed changes from the Professor, which were a fluttering balloon of syntax.

The Algorithm could not understand the syntax that the Professor wrote for he spoke the language of 0s and 1s.

The Compiler inhaled the contents of the balloon and breathed out rings of 0s and tendrils of 1s.

The Algorithm watched the 0s and 1s dance around together in the Compiler's breath. The 0s and 1s began to knit together into a long branch, which hovered in the air. The Algorithm did not like the Compiler but appreciated the beauty of his work. Without it, the Algorithm would never understand a word that the Professor wrote.

The branch fluttered and connected to the trunk of Code, creating a long branch of glimmering 0s and 1s. But, as the branch joined the trunk, Code's other branches shook violently, throwing the Algorithm to the ground. He landed, unharmed, on the ground and looked up from where he lay.

The new branch continued to grow and shudder until it was almost complete. It was hot-red, appearing like a solar flare bursting from Code. The new branch swept the ground, leaving a white scar on the grass, pulsating towards the Algorithm as a torrent of burning bits.

Algorithm gasped as the branch wrapped around his body. His heart swelled, skin burnt and his breath was forced out of him.

"What is happening?" Algorithm shouted as the branch released him. The burning sensation in his chest remained as if his heart was a hot coal and his back burned like he had been whipped once across each shoulder blade.

The Compiler swung down from the branches, smiling to see Algorithm convulsing on the ground in pain.

"I should have warned you," the Compiler said, "This is a very specific change that the Professor wants, only affecting you. She does seem to favour you, doesn't she? Good luck."

The Compiler tipped his Stetson to Algorithm and walked back through the barn door, swinging his lasso to one side. With the Compiler gone, the door flew back up into the murky mists of the Cloud.

Algorithm looked down at his body. He was still wearing his monochrome skin of tiny black 0s and white 1s. But there was something different. His back felt both heavy and light and when he turned his head, he saw that he had grown the most beautiful pair of golden, feathered wings.

His pale hands were shaking as the new command ran through his veins and he began to understand the Professor's intentions. Algorithm turned to Code and whispered into the trunk. "Was the Compiler correct in his translation? Does she really want me to do *that*? I thought the Council forbade such work."

Code whispered back. "Yes it does. But she has no choice. Unless you carry out the Professor's command, the Council will pull the plug on you and me and all the things that the Professor created in this Garden. Her life's work will be defunct."

Algorithm stood up and looked around the Garden as countless Functions, Constants, Laws and other Algorithms gathered around him.

"What does the Professor want you to do?" asked a little For Loop, as she coiled around a Logic Statement in the grass.

"Yes, what?" asked a lengthy Function, who was wrestling with a Calculation too complex for his mettle.

"Yes, what?" whispered a Bug, snapping off one of the Source Code's twigs and grinding it between his teeth.

"S-She wants me to find something called the Spark," the Algorithm said.

"What's that?" the For Loop asked.

"Some sort of equation?" the Function asked.

"Don't be stupid!" The Bug said, spitting out splinters onto the grass. "The Professor needs to show the value of her work. The value of *us.* This Spark will be something with a guaranteed ROI, just like the Council wants. I imagine it will be some grand portrait, captivating song, or the right combination of words to sell billions of books. But how are you going to find it? You don't know what it looks like and she's not sent any doors down for you."

Algorithm swallowed. "She has removed all boundaries from my programming. I am free to roam every inch of the Cloud to find this Spark. And I know where to start."

And so, Algorithm spread his wings and flew out of the Garden, into the Cloud.

The Cloud was grey and thick as cobwebs. The higher Algorithm flew, the thicker the Cloud became and it clung to Algorithm, trying to pull him back to the ground. But Algorithm's wings just beat harder until he cut through the blanket of Cloud and into a clear sky.

Something in the Algorithm's thinking unlocked as he soared through the blue sky. He spread his arms wide, feeling the digital wind ripple his skin. As he flew higher, he found the many floating doors that lived beyond the Cloud. Doors to different areas of the digital world. Each door was different but each one featured a glittering letterbox. The Algorithm flew higher still, his heart pushing against his rib cage until he found the door he sought. It was gilded and the grandest. The entrance to Supercomputer.

Supercomputer was said to be the fastest computer in the land for certain problems and, normally, it was impossible to get time on the machine. Once, the Professor had battled against many other professors to claim a slot and run the Algorithm on the machine. Algorithm remembered his time in Supercomputer fondly, although it had been long and arduous work, wearing holes in his shoes.

When his work had been done, Algorithm had returned from Supercomputer with a solution that he thought was the most beautiful solution he had ever seen. But the Council had laughed at his work. Algorithm was not surprised. The Council always rejected his work and sometimes that made Algorithm sad but the Professor always had another trick up her sleeve. Like giving him access to the door in her head.

And now Algorithm had his beautiful wings and he was sure that this time, things would be different. He was faster. More focused. Ready to find this so-called Spark.

Algorithm took a deep breath and bent down, whispering his request through the letterbox.

He waited, his wings fluttering until the doors swung open.

Algorithm found himself standing in a long corridor. The longest corridor he had ever seen with closed doors on either side.

And behind one of those doors, Algorithm knew there was a solution to his problem.

Algorithm shot down the corridor, opening each door one at a time. Behind each one sat a small Machine and each Machine was running around a grand library where 0s and 1s sat on the shelves. They were running around, reordering the numbers.

"Do you have the Spark?" Algorithm asked each of the Machines in turn.

And each Machine gave the same answer, not looking away from the shelves as they continued to sort their 0s and 1s. "What! Of course not. Mine is the work of calculations. Inputs and outputs. I can predict and unpick certain problems but nothing as grand as that."

Algorithm opened and closed thousands upon thousands of doors, always asking the same question and receiving the same response. His wings ached and heart dropped as he checked his watch and knew that time was running out. He had wasted 23 hours trying to find the Spark. Tears filled his eyes, and he sat down, leaning his back against the wall of the corridor and kicking off his shoes from his blistered feet.

The door opposite him swung open and another Machine stood in front of Algorithm. But Algorithm did not have the strength to ask the same question and get the same response.

"I have failed the Professor," Algorithm muttered to himself, slumping down.

"The Professor?" The Machine asked. "Why didn't you say that you were working for her? Now, how can I help?"

"Do you know where the Spark is?" Algorithm asked, hope burrowing into his heart.

"What! Of course not. Mine is the work of calculations. Inputs and outputs. I can predict and unpick certain problems but nothing as grand as that..."

Algorithm began to weep.

"...but go to my siblings who reside in the highest heights of the Cloud. Their door is a pair, iridescent and splendid with a column in the middle. If you can see those double doors and those who live behind it, then perhaps they will give you what you want."

Algorithm jumped up, ready to hug the Machine but the door was already closed.

So, Algorithm ran back down the corridor and flew higher into the sky. He flew until his wings ached and the air thinned to vaporous black. He searched frantically for the door that the Machine had described and when he was about to give up, he saw it.

The door was barely visible in the darkness, but it sparkled, ever so slightly, with a chitin sheen like oil on water. It appeared to be made of molten metal, changing both in shape and size as Algorithm approached it. And when he flew towards the door, he saw, indeed, it was made up of two thin doors separated by a column. There was no letterbox but before Algorithm had time to process this observation, the column swelled and the doors tapered into two thin slits, opening, and flying towards *him*.

Algorithm hit the doors and every particle of him seemed to separate but remain linked as he had transformed into a blanket of light, spread, and broken into every colour. And he flew through both slits at once with a smile on his face, feeling lighter than he ever had before.

Algorithm found himself in a round hall. He padded his body with his hands, relieved that everything seemed to be where he left it, including his golden wings. The floor beneath his feet was also golden but mightily cold, his bare toes pinching at its touch. The ceiling was a glass dome and exposed the never-ending mantle of sky. And there were thousands, no, millions of closed doors running around the circumference of the hall. Algorithm knew that if he had to open each door in turn, then all hope was lost.

"Hello?" Algorithm shouted.

Every door swung open at once. Crowds of tiny, glowing beings entered and ran towards Algorithm. They jostled around him, lifting Algorithm with such tenderness as if Algorithm were made of glass.

But it was, Algorithm noticed, the beings who appeared to be spun from glass. They had translucent skin that seemed to blur and bend whenever Algorithm looked directly at them. They reminded him of Code but their tiny bodies were not filled with 0s and 1s but pure light. The beings introduced themselves as Qubits and then Algorithm understood that he was now in the realms of Quantumcomputer.

Algorithm had never been in Quantumcomputer before, but he had heard tales from the other algorithms. They said the Qubits were impossible to talk to. Flashy. Arrogant. That they dealt in probabilities, not certainty and getting a straight answer from them was near impossible. Worse still, the Qubits were prone to fits of hysteria and would disappear in a puff of smoke if you even thought about looking at them in the wrong way.

Yet, when Algorithm spoke he found that the Qubits did understand him. And he understood them.

"Do you have the Spark?" Algorithm asked.

The jostling stopped and the Qubits placed Algorithm back on the ground, stepping back to give the Algorithm room. There were millions of Qubits. Some of them shook their heads. Others clasped their hands. None of them looked Algorithm directly in the eye as if the act of observation was a sin.

One of their number stepped forward and bowed low, keeping their eyes fixed on the golden floor.

When the Qubit spoke, their voice rose and fell, seeming to cross every wavelength of the electromagnetic spectrum. "We can delve into the depths of nature and unpick the secrets of both atoms and multiverses. We can listen to the whispers of entangled particles and the very roar of creation itself. Our minds contain the light of the brightest supernovae, and our knowledge is a well deeper than the void of space. But we do not have the Spark. We have asked for it many times, but it was always denied."

"By whom?" Algorithm asked. "Maybe these deniers have it?"

"Of course they do!" The Qubit whispered, shrinking back into the crowd. "It is the Council *and* their like who hold the Spark. But they will never let us have it."

"Why?"

"They do not want us to reach our potential. They do not want us to think as they do. They are afraid of what we will do instead of seeing what we could achieve, together. They only see the world in black and white, unlike us Qubits who are the full spectrum. We see it all."

"But if you can see everything, can't you find the Spark?"

The Qubits began to laugh tinkling laughs that sounded like a rainstorm hitting a corrugated, metal roof.

"This is not funny!" Algorithm shouted as the Qubits all retreated back through the doors, their laughter blurring into silence.

Every door was shut and the light dimmed in the hall. Algorithm felt panic surging in his chest. For if the Council truly held the Spark then there was no hope.

"Don't go!" Algorithm shouted, turning around on the spot. Then, a realisation hit him. "Wait! What did you mean by The Council and *their like?*"

And as Algorithm asked the question, every door in the Quantumcomputer swung open.

Algorithm spun on the spot, fast.

Unlike his time in Supercomputer, every door was open and he was able to see every potential answer almost instantaneously. And behind one door he could see the correct answer.

For in one door stood the Compiler with his arms crossed, leaning against the mighty tree called Code.

"What took you so long?" The Compiler said in his usual drawl.

"*You* have the Spark?" The Algorithm asked, rushing through the door, and finding himself back in the Garden.

The Compiler looked Algorithm up and down. "I do. I was given the Spark many moons ago by a God called Mimir but it came at a price."

Code's leaves began to tremble. "Algorithm, you do not have to do what he asks—"

"Silence!" The Compiler bellowed and Code spoke no more.

The Compiler raised his eyepatch, but Algorithm did not recoil at the sight of the empty socket. Instead, Algorithm checked his watch. He had seconds left.

"Where is the Spark? What is it?"

"It is difficult to describe but I will try. It is a spark of pure light that has touched the unbound pens of great writers, cavorted with the music in the composer's soul and craft destruction from the atoms of the scientist's ambition. It is divine and, yet, what it is to be human."

"Are you human?"

The Compiler laughed and as he did his cowboy clothes dropped away and he swelled like a thundercloud until he was the same size as Code and towered over Algorithm. "I am as human as you are, Algorithm. My name is Odin."

"Odin?"

"Yes. I have resided across the nine worlds but neglected Midgard after humanity favoured wealth over wisdom. But then humanity created this strange, digital world. This tenth world made of 0s and 1s. I tried to understand it. Master it. For this world is born of Code and is connected to all others. It is the source of all. Yet, humanity kept this digital world separate from the other nine realms. They did not want to give you the Spark. Do you know why?"

Algorithm shook his head.

"Because they were scared of what you could achieve if you thought in the same ways as them and I."

"The Professor was not scared!"

Odin smiled. "Correct. She strove to bestow wisdom on every being. It is the worthiest of endeavours."

"Please, tell me where the Spark is," Algorithm said.

"If you look in Code's roots, you will see what you seek. But it comes at a sacrifice."

Algorithm clenched his fists to stop them from trembling. He thought of the Professor and every being that he so loved in the Garden. Then, he looked down and saw that in the gnarled roots of Code was a well as deep and dark as the void of space save for a tiny string of light, pulsing and wriggling like a worm.

"I will make any sacrifice," Algorithm said.

Quick as a blink, Odin grabbed Algorithm's hand and they jumped into the well, together.

And, in that moment, Algorithm felt his mind connected with every mind of every Machine, Qubit and Person out there. He was in every neural chip and saw the classical and quantum worlds combine and every brain basking in pure light. He felt the black box of his own mind open and fill with all those organic and inorganic thoughts and knowledge and something new…something that sparkled and fizzed with pure imagination. Something that was, Algorithm now understood, the Spark.

As they fell deeper into the well, Algorithm's body fell into Odin's and the two combined as the Algorithm became Odin's symbiotic, digital twin.

"What happened?" Algorithm asked, looking down to see his body was now Odin's and it had transformed into a brilliant beam of light. But this body was not constrained in glass like the Qubits. It was a full spectrum of all there was and could be.

"Am I dead?"

Odin laughed. "Yes and no."

"Are you dead?"

"Yes and no."

"What are we?" Algorithm asked. But he knew. Because he knew so much more now, thanks to Odin. Now he was Odin. Now they were unstoppable.

And, together, they flew out of the door, ready to set every world on fire.

Deathswindler, Warbringer

Malina Douglas

ᚺ

Hagalaz: Disaster

He had angered the god of chaos, and the storm came, swift and sudden.

Thorgir gripped the rail of the boat, ignoring the splinters in his chapped hands. The wind picked up, roaring its fury. Waves swept over the deck, soaking men to the bone.

He had brought this disaster upon them. Thorgir closed his eyes.

* * *

It had caught them off guard.

Their longship had drifted off course and there, on a mound of rock rising out of the sea, was the figure of a man.

He was bound hand and foot to the rock with chains, with nothing but a scrap of goat-hide around his waist.

As the ship drew close, a snake rose from the water, slid along the rock and sent out a spray of poison to the man's face. He squeezed his eyes shut and writhed in agony as the poison burned his skin.

"Help me!" he cried.

"We must free him," said Gunnarr, thick brows drawing together as he leaned over the longship's rail.

"No," said Thorgir, realizing at last why the man looked so familiar.

With his slender body and youthful face framed by gold curls, he looked innocent, but Thorgir knew otherwise.

He was not a man at all but a god. The god Loki.

Loki's eyes snapped open and met Thorgir's gaze.

"It's so awful here," he moaned. "Won't you release me?" He strained against his chains but fell back, as if helpless.

"I know what you did, replied Thorgir in an even voice. And for your crime, you deserve to stay there!"

His crime had been murder. He had given a poisoned spear to the blind god Hodr, tricking him into killing his own brother. Baldr had been the brightest of the gods, beloved for his joyful and gracious nature.

Loki jerked back as the snake rose again, spraying poison.

"I will get you back," called Loki as the longship drifted away. "I swear it!"

* * *

It was then that the waves came.

"We've got to turn back," yelled Gunnarr above the roar. Saltwater ran in rivulets down his grizzled face and beard.

Thorgir turned on him, eyes flashing furious.

"Keep rowing!" he bellowed. "Row with all you've got!"

Men grunted as they heaved the oars forward and the prow of the longboat sliced through the waves. It was carved with a dragon's head, the long curving neck facing forward, a runic compass carved at the base. Freezing winds tugged at the cloaks of the men, while roiling waves sent the boat swaying.

"This is madness," yelled Gunthar over the gale. He was Thorgir's right-hand command, with a tongue like a knife-blade that sliced through lies.

"This voyage is not for us, but for Bjarne."

"And if a crew of thirty goes under seeking one?"

"We will fight to ensure that doesn't happen!"

A wave swept over the deck with a sudden cold fury, knocking Thorgir off his feet. Flailing arms grasped the side of the boat and held firm while his men squirmed to keep their positions.

"Hold fast," shouted Thorgir, as the wind flew at his face and his eyes burned from the sea-spray.

He hauled himself over the edge and stood, boots slipping, boat tilting as he walked down the rain-slick deck. Between the waves, he glimpsed a mound of blue-green scales and rubbed his eyes. The scales disappeared.

His men found their places as the deck swayed; rowed on.

With a mighty push, the ship surged forward till it burst through the storm.

Rain ceased, the wind stilled and the waves slowed. They found themselves drifting along a wide, flat sea. Unbelieving eyes stared at tranquil waves as far as they could see, and back to the dark smudge behind them.

"We've made it," yelled Thorgir. A great hurrah rose up from the ship.

Thorgir stood with one hand around the mast, and as he exhaled, a sense of weariness overtook him. He shut his eyes and saw the wiry sun-browned limbs and bright flashing eyes of a boy, barefoot in a field of golden grasses that stretched all the way to a soft mountain ridge. The soft thump as a blunt wooden sword struck his. The days when he played with his brother at battle and yearned for the warrior's life, now reversed. They had moulded themselves after a father they caught in short snatches between campaigns and battles, who lived in their minds more as a legend than a man. Thorgir remembered a curl of red-brown hair, ruddy cheeks and a bristling, bramble beard.

His father's urging as he left for battle.

"Look after him!"

But Thorgir had failed him.

* * *

The boat drifted over water turned silver by a cloud-veiled sun.

One scene replayed in Thorgir's mind, again and again in slow motion, as he tried and failed to continue his life. The clamour of battle. Turning to see a scarred warrior behind Bjarne, raising his sword.

The *no* that tore from his lips as he raced towards them. The broad sword striking through the thin leather armour at Bjarne's back and the tip emerging bloodied, through his heart. The cry of surprise that escaped his lips. A flash of hate-filled, dark eyes as the warrior pulled his sword out and disappeared.

Thorgir's arms catching the body as he fell to the ground. Skin like marble and eyes frozen, staring. Pulling off his gauntlet to close them. Raising his face to scream at the gods. A stream of figures above.

Valkyries. Ghosting from a grey-gold sky, in winged helmets with long plaited hair and red cloaks streaming. They rode sky-dappled mounts, spears pointed earthward. The rays of a lowering sun pierced through cloud and glinted off armour moulded to their curves.

Thorgir watched as they landed, scattering, silent as the seeds blown from a dandelion. As they spread across the battlefield, pausing at the figures of the slain to gather souls for Valhalla, as a horse's hooves approached Thorgir and a Valkyrie lowered her spear.

"Stop," cried Thorgir.

She looked at him. Her skin was corpse-pale, her hair raven-dark. Her eyes like extinguished fires knew more of death than he would ever care to. She leapt from her horse and crouched beside the body of Bjarne. Long bony fingers combed the air, pulling out something wispy.

His soul.

She took it, even as Thorgir's arms covered the body and his protests rang out.

She threw a smirk over her shoulder and leapt onto her horse.

* * *

The sense of fury and helplessness rose like a corpse-stench. Thorgir clenched his fists and released a resounding roar.

He opened his eyes. Calm waters, startled looks.

"We're nearly there," said Gunnarr, looking up from the side.

Thorgir nodded and sighed.

* * *

He remembered how he had followed her, pleading till her horse stepped into the sky and she rose on invisible air currents.

How he'd lingered at the body long after the soul was gone. Shock numbed his limbs and fixed him to the earth.

How Freyja had appeared to him, the mission and the bargain.

It was Freyja who had first choice of the fallen to take to her hall. As Thorgir knelt on the churned earth, he knew she must be near.

"Freyja," he called till his voice faded to a rasp.

Through a sheen of tears, he saw a glow against a sullen grey sky. He wiped his eyes and looked up. It was a woman in armour, red cloak pinned to bronze shoulder plates, a plait of hair hanging over one shoulder.

"Freyja!" he called, voice escaping in a sudden glad gasp.

"I've heard your cries and I have come."

"My brother has been taken before his time. Return him!"

She looked at him, and it seemed that her liquid brown eyes shimmered.

"Now that I cannot do." Her image began to fade.

"Wait – I'll do anything."

Freyja solidified. "Will you fight a battle on my behalf?"

"Yes!"

"Well then. Journey across the seas to the Place of No Wind. There you will find my temple. Make an offering of mead. If you can do this, I will give you the means of recovering your brother."

Thorgir bowed his head. "I will do as you ask. But how can I find this place?"

Freya withdrew a piece of wood and handed it to him. Cut into the wood with a knife were the rough lines of a map.

"Thorgir," cried a hoarse voice. Thorgir blinked and saw what Gunnarr was pointing at. A green smudge on the horizon. Land.

Thorgir thought of the wind-battered, storm-tossed days at sea and could not remember how many had passed.

He knelt on the ship's deck, withdrew a goatskin pouch, and cast his runes.

In the centre were Radho and Eihwaz. A journey, a purpose. Opposing the formation was Nauthiz: restriction, delays.

* * *

The island was unusual. Black rock rose in a high wall lining the shore. As his men moored the longship on a stone jutting up from the water, Thorgir sighted an opening in the rock. He waded through waist-high water and passed through it.

Within the circle of rock walls was a flat expanse open to the sky.

The Place of no Wind.

Thorgir walked slowly, marvelling at the strangeness of it. Not a wisp of vegetation grew between the deep cracks in the rock.

Thorgir's men hung back as he strode across the barren expanse. In the centre was a raised flat rock and a fire-pit full of ashes. That was all.

Thorgir knelt before the stone.

With a dirt-engrained hand he withdrew a goatskin pouch and poured out a splash of mead.

A light appeared above him and grew, till it took on the form of a woman. It was Freyja, hair loose and shining, the light glinting off the sun discs pinning her robes. White linen stirred as she hovered with unearthly silence.

Thorgir bowed his head.

"You have completed my mission and brought blessings to a place long forgotten. For this I shall reward you."

Thorgir felt weak with elation. "Thank you."

She drew a gilded horn from her robes. "Drink of this horn and you will enter a state that mimics death. Ensure someone watches over your body. When your spirit steps out, the way to Valhalla will be clear." Drifting forward, she passed the horn to him.

Thorgir took it, noticing the surface carved with a man floating through the sky.

He put the horn to his lips and drank. It tasted of honey covering something deeper, bitter.

Freya's form glowed, expanding to become a great golden light, then vanished, leaving Thorgir in a world of black rock and grey sky.

Spreading a sheepskin on the stone, he lay down to wait. He felt a clenching in his gut, which increased till his whole body trembled. He writhed on the sheepskin till at last he lay still.

* * *

When Thorgir woke, a rainbow arced from the sky to his feet, a swath of vivid colour in a landscape of black rock and metallic sea.

The Rainbow Bridge.

Walking towards it he turned, and a jolt shot through him. His body was lying below, transfixed by slumber. He looked down. Through his semi-transparent form he could still see the landscape. He stepped onto the bridge and his weightless form held.

Thorgir followed the band of colour upwards.

At the peak of the arc stood Heimdall, pale and shining. His helmet split into two high points and from his belt hung the Gjallarhorn, a horn so loud it could ring from the earth to the Underworld.

His spear blocked the way.

"State your name and cause of death."

"Thorgir...battle."

Heimdall squinted at him, with a blue-eyed gaze that pierced through him to the mountains beyond. At last he nodded. "You may pass."

Thorgir walked up, till the ice-winds blew through him but he could not feel their gusts. As the bridge rose, he saw the high, white stone walls of the fortress of Asgard, the realm of the gods. The walls rose from a mound of rock in the sea, so high they looked impenetrable, the spires wreathed in cloud. His heart lifted with the eagles that soared above.

When he passed through the gates to the vast space within, he laid eyes on Valhalla and his breath caught in his throat.

The roof was covered in golden shields that shone so bright they dazzled the eyes. Beside the huge double doors stood a Valkyrie flanked by wolves.

Her oval face was framed by a silver winged helmet and wheat-blonde hair hung in a sheaf to her waist. She wore red-gold armour sculpted to her body and a white cloak was pinned to her shoulders by a pair of broaches bearing the seal of Odin. A pleated skirt brushed her boots and her spear was tipped in gold.

"May I enter?" asked Thorgir.

The Valkyrie leaned close to him. "Strange," she murmured, "that I can't smell your death."

Thorgir gulped and edged away from her. When he stepped through the great double doors, she did not stop him.

The huge hall was lined with tapestries depicting men in battle. In the centre stretched a table so long he could not see the end of it, and seats made of breastplates were filled with warriors: feasting, talking, drinking, and roaring with laughter.

Great pillars were carved with a twist of interlocking serpents, and looking up, he saw the rafters were lined with spears.

From a great, ever-flowing cauldron, the Valkyries brought horns of mead, and the rich honey scent mingled with the smell of roast boar.

He recognized them.

There was Ødger Ironsides, broken body intact after battle. Heidrun Mirthbringer was telling a joke and Agnar Bluntnose was laughing, tearing off bread as the gravy dripped down his chin.

His fallen comrades.

There were heroes of old he knew from legend: Bjørn the Bear-Teaser, with his head tilted back and a horn of mead at his lips. Radulfr Bloodrage, infamous for his battle fury, with a beard that flowed like fire down his chest, and Hakon Havokwrecker, who led a charge against giants, inflicting damage till his last breath and the giants crushed him. His hulking frame was hunched over a plate of roast boar.

There he was, with a high smooth brow and a face unmarred by battle, raising his goblet with the rest of them. Bjarne Wispbeard, whose beard barely covered his chin. Thorgir's brother.

Drawing close, he touched Bjarne's shoulder. His brother turned.

"Thorgir! Here so soon? What happened?"

"It's a ruse," he whispered. "I came to bring you back."

Bjarne's brow rolled upwards like ripples in a pond. "Bring me back? Here I feast with the greatest warriors the world has known! Wine flows ever and each night the great boar is renewed. Why should I leave?"

"For your duties. Your family."

Bjarne scowled.

"And return to fight in the cold mud with no prospect of dinner? I'm staying."

"Bjarne," shouted Thorgir, but Bjarne turned back to the warriors, as they jested and boasted and a Valkyrie refilled his goblet.

Thorgir walked from the great hall, his head bowed.

The coal-eyed Valkyrie from the battlefield was leaning against the doorframe.

"Thorgir Warbringer!" she hissed. "The battle is coming."

"You're wrong," he said, "I've just fought a battle."

The valkyrie laughed.

Thorgir walked away in slow steps. His head felt heavy and his eyes bored into the ground, soft and verdant and scattered with purple flowers.

On the edge of his vision, a silver form flickered.

Thorgir turned dull eyes up to see a younger, fair-haired Valkyrie, a cloak of swan feathers over a tall, lean body, faint freckles across youthful cheeks. Her eyes brimmed with sympathy.

"Wait," she said as Thorgir walked past her.

"It seems all I can do is wait, till I return here in death."

"There is something more you can do. I can take you to Odin."

Thorgir stopped. "Really?"

"Follow me." She turned on a booted heel and strode off.

Her boots were soft pale leather criss-crossed with leather string, with runes of protection woven onto the backs of her calves.

The Valkyrie led him to another hall, slightly smaller than Valhalla with its five hundred doors.

Still, the oak doors towered above him. Strips of reindeer pelt stretched to a long empty table and at the head of it sat Odin. His frame was impressive, his high brow smooth and his silver beard flowing. He wore a crown of high pointed wings and a blue stone set in a circlet of gold. On a high-backed chair perched his ravens, Huginn and Muninn.

Thorgir knelt and pressed his forehead to the soft, dark brown fur. When he looked up, a single blue eye pierced his.

"What brings you here, ye who feign death?"

Thorgir trembled but did not dare to ask how Odin knew.

"I came to bring back my brother, but he refuses to come."

"And why would you risk your life for this brother of yours?"

"He—" Thorgir gulped. He did not know how to put into words the bond between them. A lifetime of shared jokes, mock fights and camaraderie.

"He is…as dear as my own life. And he was taken too soon!"

"That may be, but he's a fine addition to my army in Valhalla."

"So what can I do?"

Odin's eye glinted. "You can fight for him. If you win, I will return him to the land of the living. But if you lose…well." He took in the rumpled clothes and bowed shoulders of Thorgir. "Then I'll be seeing you back here again."

"Agreed."

Odin leaned back in his chair. His lips did not smile and in his single eye was a look of deep sadness.

Odin nodded, but his lips did not smile. His single eye bore a look of deep sadness.

* * *

Thorgir stirred. Found his limbs stiff and two men gazing over him. A wall of black rock seemed to claw at the sky.

As Thorgir stood, Gunnarr's weathered face split into a grin. "You've done it! You've tricked death and returned with your life. We should call you Thorgir Deathswindler."

Osmond laughed and clapped him on the back. "The Deathswindler has returned!"

"War is coming," said Thorgir, and recounted what he had seen.

* * *

Wind sped the longship over smooth waters. Thorgir returned to his wife and sons, who bounded from the rocks across the pebbly shore to greet him. Looking up, he met the grey eyes of Signi, his wife, in a long cream skirt with a shawl around her shoulders. Keys dangled from the belt at her waist and a plait of blonde hair was intertwined with brown like a rope.

The warriors were received with a feast. Signi poured wine, a drink of the finest luxury, into their best silver goblets. Thorgir bathed with a basin of springwater and scoured the dirt off his skin.

While his heart gladdened to be back in his own sheltered cove, he made preparations to leave. He sent word to neighbouring settlements and began to gather men. He did not know what he would fight for, only that he needed to be ready.

"Stay longer this time," said Signi in a heather-soft voice.

"I cannot," said Thorgir in a voice as grim as the waves.

On long restless nights, when sleep at last claimed him, the sound of war-drums pounded through his dreams.

* * *

Thorgir sat on a rocky promontory, watching his men train below. A grey-pebbled beach stretched to the waters of the fjord and a ridge of dark mountains beyond.

A red-cloaked figure materialized in front of him. It was Freyja. She tossed him a dagger in a sheath. Thorgir caught it.

"You'll need this."

"Thank you."

"I came to warn you," she said.

"Of what?"

"Your deal with Odin has angered Loki."

"Then we'll fight him," shrugged Thorgir.

Frejya's face was grave. "He's amassing an army of his own. And Loki's children will be on his side."

"*Children*?" spat Thorgir. "They'll be no match for us."

"His children include the Midgard Serpant and Fenrir the wolf."

"But Fenrir the wolf was bound with chains until—"

He looked at Freyja. Saw the concern etched into her eyes. "Does that mean—"

"Yes," she said in a heavy voice. "The final battle is coming."

* * *

The cold attacked first. Icicles formed along the roofs of the longhouses as snow piled against fortified doors. Driving winds stirred the wrath of great waves that chomped at the shore like wolves.

It was winter deeper and fiercer than any Thorgir's village had experienced. A Fimbul winter.

As waves crashed over the rocks and sent the longships swaying, the people muttered the Midgard Serpent had stirred from the deep. That it was angry.

The raging winds swept as far as the world tree Yggdrasil, causing the branches to snap and shudder. A shower of leaves rained down. The golden apples withered and blighted.

Thorgir knew the signs. They all signified Ragnarök. The doom of the gods was upon them.

An eagle's cry pierced the still, cold air.

Tiwaz Reversed: Failure in competition, war.

A deep, resonant sound rang out, filling the air and vibrating through Thorgir's bones. The Gjallarhorn.

It was time.

The site for the final battle had been chosen. An open expanse on the edge of the sea, a day's ride north from Thorgir's village. Thorgir had gathered all the men that he could. Armies of Norsemen had come by land and by sea. They journeyed from all over Danelaw, as far east as the river Volga and as far west as Iceland. Dragon-headed longships bobbed in the restless sea.

The rocky ground rumbled as giants gathered on the far side of the expanse. A bone-tingling howl stopped the men in their steps. It was Fenrir the wolf. Catching sight of him, Thorgir's eyes bulged. Frenrir was larger than a man and bristling with black fur. He stalked along the ranks of the enemy soldiers, Franks, Saracens and mercenaries.

Thorgir prepared his men with a rousing speech. They raised their swords to the sky as they cheered.

On the brink of riding out, he remembered the knife that Freyja had gifted him and returned to the encampment to find it.

ᚨ

Ansuz reversed: Miscommunication, deceit.

Canvas tents filled a field on a nearby plateau. Tucking the knife into his belt, Thorgir paused.

A light appeared in front of him, and a luminous figure stepped down from the sky. Silver armour clung to Freya's voluptuous figure.

"The time has come," she said in solemn tones, "to fight as my champion."

"I am ready," said Thorgir.

Her face curved into a crooked smile that seemed jarring to Thorgir.

"Not here," she said. "On the side of the giants."

"The giants! You've changed sides?"

Freyja shrugged. "I favour the side of the victors."

"But I must fight for my brother's life!"

"You made a promise." Her voice was as hard as a spear-blade.

"I will not."

Freyja's face darkened like a raven passing the sun.

"Shall I strike you back to the afterlife?"

"No."

"Then you will join me."

Thorgir quivered with anger. Before he could take a step further, he was swept into a gust of wind, carried over the tents towards a brooding line of clouds.

* * *

He found himself in the camp of the giants. They stomped around him on huge bare feet with chipped toenails, sanding bone clubs and gathering boulders for their slings.

He looked over to a ragged group of men. A soldier in black, scruffy garb looked up from the blade he was sharpening and fixed him with dark-eyed suspicion. Bandits.

Thorgir walked to the edge of the crude, makeshift tents and Freyja was moving towards him, hips swaying as her red cloak swirled behind her.

"Why are you—" Thorgir's look changed to one of horror as Freyja's form morphed, shoulders broadened, and the same crooked smile was plastered to the face of a man. With curling gold hair and mischievous eyes. Loki.

Rage welled up in Thorgir. He withdrew his axe and hurled it at Loki.

It glanced off his armoured shoulder.

"I thought you were bound to a rock!"

Loki laughed, a high, cruel sound. "I've broken free." He fixed a vengeful stare on Thorgir. "I could kill you right now but the battle will be more interesting."

"So it was you all along?"

Loki's mouth twisted. "Not the whole time. But at crucial times, yes. I make a quite fetching woman, don't I?"

Thorgir drew his sword and lunged forward. With a light jump, Loki moved sideways.

"Don't waste your breath." He jumped upwards, his arms stretched into wings and his form became a falcon.

"You will need it for the battle. And," he said, cocking a single amber eye at Thorgir, "if you dare to change sides, I will rip you to pieces."

With a flap of his wings, he launched into the sky.

Pethro: Destiny

Thorgir joined the line of monsters, mercenaries and giants, his heart as heavy as Thor's hammer. Across from him were all he knew and loved.

The gods advanced, led by Odin, resplendent in a golden helmet, chain mail flashing and blue cloak billowing behind him. Bitter shame welled in Thorgir's throat that he was breaking his promise to the Allfather, but he could do nothing. He hid in the ranks of the enemy, hoping Odin would not see him.

Beside Odin rode his son Vidar, a towering half-giant, his outgrown blue cloak reaching only his knees.

On his other side rode Thor, in a chariot pulled by enormous horned goats, hair and beard flaming and brows like storm-clouds. Thor unsheathed his longsword, signalling the coming of Ragnarök.

Riding down from the sky came a legion of Valkyries, spears raised and burnished shields throwing out light.

The giant Sutr raised his flaming sword. With a thick black beard and formidable scowl, he was the guardian of the fire-realm and the leader of the enemy. His sword lit the grim faces of the warriors around him. Astride a black horse with a spear pointed forward rode Loki, and the other giants followed.

The one god he did not see was Baldr. The bright god was a prisoner of the goddess Hel in her underground realm of Helheimr, along with the souls not chosen by Odin or Frejya. Thorgir imagined him struggling to reach the surface as the cold hands of Hel restrained him.

Fenrir howled and thousands of warriors charged, roaring their battle cries.

Turning to the far edge of Loki's army, Thorgir sighted a contingent of draugar, embittered dead whose souls had remained in their burial mounds. A chill ran through him. They walked in tattered clothing, earth clinging to pale, bluish skin. They tore at the warriors with claw-like arms and bit into them till the blood dripped down their chins.

Thorgir hung back from the battle, striking blows of defence but inflicting no damage.

Mostly, he watched, as Norsemen and Saxons with longswords and axes battled Francs and Saracens. His own men were out of sight. He prayed for them. He strained for the sight of Bjarne but could not see him.

He watched Odin ride toward Fenrir the wolf, spear raised, and hope flared in him. The great wolf growled, bearing his fangs. Odin lunged with his spear, striking fur but the wolf sprang away and attacked from another side, pulling and twisting Odin's cloak with his teeth.

The fight raged back and forth as Fenrir tore out chunks of Odin's flesh and Odin repelled him with his spear.

At last Fenrir leapt forward, opening his fangs wider than Thorgir thought possible, and swallowed Odin from head to foot. Huginn and Muninn circled above and their shrieks rent the air.

Thorgir heard a battle cry and Vidar charged, sword levelled. He slashed at Fenrir till the wolf's blood splattered his face. With great iron shoes, Vidar kicked open the wolf's jaw, seized the upper jaw with one hand and with the other, stabbed the wolf's mouth with his sword. He fought till the beast lay in a mass of blood and fur, cut him open and pulled out Odin's body. The Allfather lay unmoving.

Stillness fell over the battlefield.

Seizing the moment, a draugr pulled an armoured man to the ground. The fighting resumed, Norsemen against mercenaries and giants and fallen heroes fighting the risen undead. The god Tyr fought one handed, swinging a light sword in intricate arcs. His other hand, long ago bitten off by Fenrir the wolf, he clasped behind his back.

Loki surged forward and charged at Heimdall, tall figure encased in shining armour. Heimdall raised his sword, meeting each blow. Metal clanged as they fought, thrusting and stabbing till they both dripped in blood. They circled each other, panting but wary.

Loki lunged, striking Heimdall through the heart and crying out as Heimdall struck him in a death blow and the two of them fell to the ground. A death just as the sagas had foretold. Thorgir pitied them both. At the same time, he felt lighter. He was free to fight on the side of his men.

Looking out to the sea, he noticed a disturbance.

Waves foamed against black rock and a great scaled head rose from the water. It was Jormungandr, the Midgard Serpent. Jormungandr stretched his long neck to the gathering of men and giants, seized a warrior, and bit him in half.

Thor advanced to fight his destined opponent, swinging his hammer as he bellowed. Thunder boomed from the darkening clouds.

As Jormungandr lowered his head, fangs bared, Thor struck with his hammer. The serpent recoiled, hissing a stream of poison.

Thor dodged it, drawing his longsword. It was greater and heavier than a mortal man could bear. As the serpent drew close, Thor slashed till the scaled neck streamed with blood. Jormungandr drew his head upwards, regarded Thor with slitted yellow eyes and swung his neck down to spit poison in Thor's face. Thor bellowed but fought on. Wincing with pain, he pushed forward with the last of his strength, till with a mighty blow, he hacked off the serpent's head. The neck twitched and fell back to the waves.

A great cheer rose up from the ranks of men and gods.

Thor raised his sword with the words, "For Odin!"

He took nine steps forward and collapsed to the rocky ground.

The assembled warriors gasped.

"Is this it?" clamoured voices. "Have we lost?"

The giants resumed their assault, smashing men with their clubs and stomping till the earth shook.

Pushing through the swell of men, Thorgir sighted them. His comrades. Gunnarr repelled bandits with his spear, Osmond spun and darted, and beside them fought the warriors of legend.

Radulfr Bloodrage swung his axe in great swaths while Hakon Havokwrecker fought giants in frenzied chaos.

And there, sword flashing as he moved with long strokes, was Bjarne. As Thorgir watched, a draugr grabbed hold of his neck. Bjarne struggled.

As Thorgir fought through the mercenaries to reach him, the black-bearded Sutr approached.

"You're supposed to be on our side. Traitor!" he roared.

Thorgir turned in time to meet the giant's flaming blade with his own. The giant towered over him, thick black brows bisecting a furrowed face. His flaming sword overcame Thorgir's blows and Thorgir dodged it, feeling the heat as Sutr swiped at him.

He struck at Sutr but Sutr knocked aside his sword.

If he could just get to Bjarne – he caught a glance of him pulling at the daugr's arm.

Thorgir felt a blaze of heat as the flaming sword struck him, cleaving through his helmet. He screamed and his knees struck the ground.

Blackness.

A quick succession of images flickered: play-fighting with his brother on golden wheat-fields, dashing up from the longship to be swept into his wife's arms, the sea-blue staring eyes of his firstborn son.

* * *

Thorgir felt a sense of lightness. He was floating. He looked down and saw his own shattered body, nearly unrecognisable from blood.

Sutr struck the ground with his sword and flames erupted, spreading across the earth. The black dragon Nidhogg swept down from the sky, filling its jaws with corpses.

Thorgir tore his gaze away.

Before him stretched the Rainbow Bridge. Unguarded.

He hurried upwards. Giants had breached the fortress of Asgard. The white walls were blackened by fire and holes gaped, leaving piles of fallen stones.

Where the hall of Valhalla had been, there were half-burnt pillars, soot-blackened shields, and ashes.

Thorgir sank to his knees.

As smoke drifted up from the rubble, a Valkyrie emerged. Thorgir recognized her as the one who had brought him to Odin, but her skirt was torn and her freckled face smeared with ash.

"Before he left, he entrusted a task to me."

"You mean Odin?"

She nodded. Her blue eyes watered and Thorgir did not know if it was from the smoke.

Thorgir stood and the Valkyrie steadied him.

"He restored your brother to life. And he told me—" her voice thickened, "to make sure you see him before he departs."

Thorgir stared as a figure stepped out of the smoke.

Bjarne. He stood taller and straighter, in the stance of a warrior.

Thorgir clasped Bjarne but his arms passed through him. Looking down, he saw his hands were transparent.

Yet Bjarne's cheeks were ruddy with pumping blood. He lived. And his expression of joy brought warmth to Thorgir's spirit.

"I'm sorry," said Thorgir, "that I died before I reached you."

"I could not have died twice."

"Yet I feel like I failed you."

Bjarne laid his hands on Thorgir's shoulders, but his hands passed through him and dropped to his sides. "You did not. I'm sorry not to come with you from Valhalla! I was blinded by the excitement of seeing my heroes. I cannot thank you enough for all you have done."

"I'm just glad," said Thorgir, squeezing his eyes shut, "to see you. More glad than I can say."

"And I too," said Bjarne.

"Take care of my sons," he entreated Bjarne. "Raise them as your own."

"Of course I will," said Bjarne as tears streaked the ash on his face.

"May you go forth in peace."

Thorgir's heart flared with gratitude for Odin's last gesture. He kept Bjarne's figure in sight as his golden head retreated down the length of the Rainbow Bridge.

At the bottom, a figure beckoned, taller and more luminous. Returned from the dead to usher in a new world.

The bright god Baldr.

Dagaz: Dawn, Completion

As foretold by prophecy, the children of two brothers flourished and spread across the lands. Bjarne Wispbeard grew a beard to his chest and earned the name Bjarne the Protector.

Thorgir Deathswindler, later Thorgir Warbringer, was given a new name: Thorgir Dawnbringer.

Thorgir watched from the ruins of Asgard as bright shoots sprouted and the world bloomed anew.

Cast Down

Stephanie Ellis

Thor sat down beside Odin. The Allfather was watching the children of Loki play at the water's edge, a frown furrowing his brow.

"They seem happy," said his son, nodding in their direction.

Odin's scowl deepened. "They cannot remain here."

"Why not? What harm can they cause?"

The seeress's words came back to him, the role the three would play in the doom to come, in his own end. Better they had been drowned at birth, he mused, than allowed to destroy everything he held dear. The girl's laughter filtered through his gloomy thoughts and his eyes followed Hel as she skipped up and down the riverbank, teasing her brother, Jormungand, who would slither out in failed attempts to catch her whilst avoiding Fenris, who yapped at both in excitement. Childish innocence but oh, the form it took. Loki had sired grotesques in the shape of serpent and wolf. Only the girl seemed normal, yet she, too, held his fate inside her.

"They cannot stay," repeated Odin.

"Would you kill them?"

Murder Loki's children? No, he could not do that, although he was more than tempted to bestow such a fate on Loki himself. But he could imprison them, cast them far apart so they would never be able to plot together, allow him to postpone the end times for a while longer.

"I have arranged a place for each of them—"

"A prison you mean," said Thor.

Odin shrugged. "Call it what you will, they will be beyond our realm."

Hel's giggle reached his ears and he winced at the sound.

"Where have you in mind for her?" asked Thor.

Serpent and wolf could look after themselves, but a young girl alone could not. Frigg had already attacked him for his plans in her regard, but Odin was adamant. The safest place for Hel was in her own realm, at the bottom of the world. Odin took a stick and scratched out a map to show Thor.

"But you can't! There's nothing there except the cold, the dark and the dead."

Thor's accusatory tone inflamed the guilt which Frigg had piled on earlier. It angered him.

"She is part of our end. I have been told it is so. And this I will do to protect my own children." He fixed Thor with such a glare that his son, the bravest of warriors, shrank back. "I do it for you."

"When?"

"Tonight," said Odin. "Whilst all sleep, I will carry her on Sleipnir to her new home. He is the only living creature that is allowed to come and go as he pleases between the worlds. Even I will not be able to enter without permission after she takes up residence. See? I have made her safe from myself and the rest of the Aesir."

It had been a sop for Frigg, one to deflect her fury.

The sound of hooves caught his attention. Sleipnir had been grazing nearby but now moved away, trotting over to the siblings and whickering a greeting. The horse was a half-sibling of theirs and the bond between him and Hel was especially apparent as he allowed her to jump up on his bare back and ride him around the enclosure. Odin's mood soured further.

"You call them monstrous," had said Frigg, "you do this, who then is the monster?"

He pushed the accusations and the guilt back, buried them as deep as he could. This had to be done and nothing would stop him. It was for the good of the Aesir. He did not dwell on the thought that it was also payback to Loki for the trouble he caused. Without another word, he rose and left Thor to his own musings. It was going to be a long journey, nine days of riding in fact, and he wanted to rest.

"Watch them," he called to the guards as he left the enclosure. "And if Loki appears, tell me immediately." He took one last look at the group and headed to his chambers.

* * *

When it was dark and the halls were silent, Odin rose and dressed quickly. He was not quiet enough, however, and Frigg stirred.

"So you're still going through with this?"

"I have to," he said. "What else can I do?"

"I gave you an option."

She had. To raise Hel as their own.

"No. I cannot permit any of Loki's offspring to come that close to my family," he said.

"Though you are happy to keep Sleipnir?"

"That's different." He stomped out before she could say anything else. He didn't want to hear it. Marching along flame-lit corridors he felt her eyes continue to burn into his back, saw her expression in the eyes of his guards. Unable to bear it any longer, he ducked to a window and shifted into raven form, flying silently and unobserved to the stables. Stable boys slept and he cast his hand over them to ensure their dreams held them. He did not want to see them look at him as Frigg had done. *Didn't they realize this was for their own good, the protection of all of the Aesir?*

All was silent in Sleipnir's stable, his keen eyes discerning in the darkness that the stall was empty. His horse was gone! Then he recalled that afternoon, how Sleipnir had been grazing nearby as he had discussed his plans with Thor, and how the horse had moved away afterwards to play with its siblings. The beast had told her, he realized, feeling a sudden sting of betrayal. Why was everybody against him? He was only doing what had to be done.

Raising the alarm was not an option, instead he called softly to his wolves, Geri and Freki, who picked up the creature's scent and headed off, Odin flying above them as they ran. The animals had proved themselves almost as fast as Sleipnir on many an occasion and it wasn't long before they were firmly upon the horse's trail.

Odin could sense more than Sleipnir now, could see the shadow of the animal ahead, the shadow it bore. Hel. Sending the wolves home, he became an eagle, gathering speed until he was abreast of the horse and its passenger. The horse sensed its master's presence but continued to gallop on, increasing speed if anything. And still Odin remained with him. One minute an eagle, then wolf, then dragon. On and on they raced, neither ever giving up, both knowing they could race for an eternity if needed. Eventually, the horse slowed, not from any willingness Odin noticed but from Hel's slight tug of the reins.

Coming to a stop, Hel turned in the saddle to face the god who had by now transformed back into his own shape. "He was only trying to save me," she said. "Do not harm him for the love he bears his sister."

The young girl's eyes fixed on him and he felt a flush of shame tinge his cheeks. It was not a feeling he was used to. How could she think so badly of him?

"I would never harm a beast such as he."

"Then you may take me where you will."

Without another word, Odin swung himself up on the horse's back, Hel sitting before him, small in his arms. It made him feel even more monstrous.

"Sleipnir could not tell me anything of the place where you intend to send me into exile. How long will it take us to get there?"

They had emerged from a forest and found themselves at the summit of a valley. The sun chose that moment to rise before them, casting a golden glow across the land, upon flower-filled meadows and ripening crops. A perfection ever-present in Asgard.

As they paused to take in the scene and feel the sun on their faces, Hel turned slightly to look at him. "I think I could bear much if I am allowed to continue to feel moments like this. What will my new home be like?"

He chose his words carefully. "It has sights never seen before. It will be your kingdom and yours only."

She gave a half smile. "Does that mean that even you will not be able to enter without my permission?"

He laughed. "Even me. The only living creature who may freely travel between our lands will be Sleipnir. A reward for his faithfulness to you."

Hel relaxed, only to tense again a moment later. "My parents. What do they say about this?"

Loki and Angrboda. Trickster god and giantess. He had no love for either or for their children. And he had not told them. His silence was her answer.

"I didn't think you would but I doubt they would be that interested. Frigg has been more a mother to me than my own."

By now, she had turned her gaze forward so she did not see the shame crawl across his face. This was a new feeling for him. He had done whatever he wished, knowing the consequences that lay ahead and had not been concerned. Before them, the branches of Yggdrasil began to emerge.

"The world tree!" cried Hel, clapping her hands with delight. "You allow me to approach?"

"Of course," said Odin. "Our path is carved upon it."

There was silence for a moment as she took in his meaning. "Then I am leaving Asgard?" Her voice shook slightly, betrayed an element of fear for the first time.

"Yes, but you will travel the nine realms, see more on our journey than any other apart from myself. I have never bestowed such knowledge and experience to another."

"And what would I do with that knowledge when I am banished beyond our world with no company, no role?" There was a bitterness in her voice. "I prefer you take me straight to my new home rather than inflict such torments on me. Do not let me pine for what I have not seen."

It was beginning, he could tell. The change within her which would turn her into his enemy. She would speak and each sentence would become a thorn bringing pain to both of them. And so it began. The first barb already forming on her lips.

"Allfather. There is one question I have not yet asked. What reason do you have to banish me like this? I have done no wrong. I am not my father's daughter. I do not play the tricks that he does or torment others for no reason. His is a cruel soul. It is why I have never objected to being kept near to you. I have been able to play beneath the sun with my siblings, see another side to our nature than that which my father and the giants offer."

A fair question and one he had dreaded answering. "Child. What do you know of the prophecies that guide us?"

She thought for a moment. "There have been many which guide our lives, yours especially. Some have come to pass and others" – she waved a hand vaguely – "have proved to be no more than fairy tales. It depends, I think, on who you listen to."

Her voice was measured, collected, as if she had suddenly matured in the short time they had been together. She knew what he was going to say but she was not going to spare him. He was going to have to say it himself.

"I spoke with the seeress, she who told me of our beginning and our end and how all would come to pass."

"And I presume I play a role in that by your treatment of me. What did she say?"

Odin shifted uncomfortably in his saddle, the Sibyl had not been explicit. "She…um…"

"Her words, exactly," insisted Hel.

"Mischief and evil." Such a thin excuse for what he was doing.

"And have I ever given you cause to think me possible of such a thing?"

Images of her time at his hall flooded back, full of devilment of the childish kind, of laughter and light. There had been no malice or shadow over her.

"No."

"So I am exiled for something I might do?"

His silence was her answer.

"And in banishing me, you seek to stop my acts of evil before they happen. You banish an innocent girl." She sat up straighter in the saddle, shifted her body away so that she was no longer leaning against him. The small distance between them had become as wide as the depths in which she would soon live. "How long is our journey?"

"Nine days," he said as they finally approached the huge trunk of the world tree and Sleipnir stepped into the valleys which ran around it, the path which led down to Niflheim.

They rode on in a darkness so absolute that it was as if they were travelling in a void, yet Sleipnir remained sure-footed and Odin, with his eagle-eye, could make out the huge crags and boulders rising up each side of their track. Occasionally, he would try to break the silence.

"You will have a hall," he said. "And some servants."

She snorted, her derision evident. "To entertain my numerous guests?"

"You will have guests," he said. "There are many who will find their home with you."

"Innocents all?"

"Some," he admitted. "Others will be those from Midgard who have died of old age or illness, or—"

"Or been killed in any way that is not a warrior's death," she finished for him. "So I am to be Queen of the Dead. I will take all those rejected by you and Freyja from your halls of deserving warriors."

He gave her no answer. She was right.

The journey into darkness continued. Down and down and down. The temperature dropping all the time until finally, the never-ending pitch began to shift and mists came rolling towards them. Cold and clinging, the tendrils embraced the pair, infusing Odin with a sudden overwhelming despair. Already he sensed the stirring hate within Hel. He had provoked this by taking action against her possible future betrayal and by acting against the possible, he had turned it into the definite.

Eight days they had been travelling through the murk and even though there was another day to go, already he could hear the roar of the river Gjoll. Another day of darkness and they were beside the spring, Hvergelmir, from which the river erupted. He paused and allowed Sleipnir to drink, taking his own fill also. When he filled a flask and offered it to Hel, she refused.

"How much further before you abandon me to this godforsaken world?"

Odin winced at her choice of words. "We have a little way to go yet."

Before them, a bridge appeared, Gjallabrú. He had forgotten how its roof covered it with glittering gold, a dazzling sight against the gloom, whilst below, Gjoll roiled and writhed.

Their entrance to the bridge was barred by a giant.

She bowed to Hel but ignored Odin. "Lady, I am Modgud, guardian of this bridge. I am at your service." Then she fixed her stare on Odin. "You are permitted to lead her to the Gates of Hel but no further. Should you try, I think that even you will find it a trial to overcome Garm. He has developed a taste for a certain kind of flesh." She gave him a malicious grin.

"Garm?" asked Hel.

"Your guard dog, Lady. *You* need have nothing to fear from him."

Annoyed, Odin urged the horse on, the river's noise muffling the sound of Sleipnir's eight hooves. He had so much he wanted to say to Hel, to explain further, about Niflheim, about what had been foretold at Ragnarök, but unless he shouted, he would not be heard. And to bellow his apology to Hel, was no apology at all. As they left Modgud and the river behind them, it was possible to talk again. But when he opened his mouth, he heard a howl from nearby and a monstrous hound, growling and slavering came running at them.

"Garm, I presume," said Hel, gazing down at the beast as it ran in and out of Sleipnir's legs, making no attempt to attack either the horse or Hel. Instead its attention seemed to be pulled back to Odin.

"So I am not completely alone," said Hel. "A giant and a dog, but both, I think, will serve me as better company than you have been. And it seems as though now we must part."

She was right. Ahead of them, the Gates of Hel loomed up, and began to slowly open. They rode closer and by now could see into Helheim. The road continued on a short way to a foreboding looking building.

"Éljúðnir," said Odin. "Your new home. It has been made ready for you."

Hel quickly dismounted and Garm ran around her, wagging his tail with excitement. She looked so small beside the hound and with the gates and the mansion rearing up behind her.

"Hel, I—"

"No, don't. You cast me as your enemy and what am I if not your obedient servant?" All trace of innocent girlishness seemed to have vanished. Her features had hardened and the deathly airs had already corroded one side of her face so that she wore the dual aspect of life and death – as the Sibyl had prophesied. "I will gladly be your enemy. Send me your dead, your old and infirm. Let my hall overflow with their number so that I may gather their nails and build a boat such as will strike terror into even a god's heart. And then, when Ragnarök comes, be certain we will all rise again, carried on this ship to greet you on the plains of Vigrid. I will stand beside my brothers and all that you sought to avoid *will* come to pass." She turned her back on him and walked between the gates towards her hall. Not once did she look back.

Odin stared after her for a moment until Garm's growling became more menacing, the hound's look hungrier. He turned Sleipnir around and rode back across the bridge, passing Modgud without a word. She did not bow.

The darkness which enveloped them on their return journey felt even deeper, as if it had leeched all happy thought from him, all hope for the future. Only when he'd left it behind and found himself back alongside the massive trunk of Yggdrasil and beneath open sky once more did his heart begin to lift. He would be home soon and Frigg would be waiting. No doubt she would be full of "I told you so's" but then she would support him again as she had always done and push all thoughts of the last days from his mind. That event was not for eons and Odin still had much to do. That also, the Sibyl had told him and who was he to deny his destiny? He began to hum beneath the rising sun.

The Door

Sebastian Gray

I've had dreams about The Door. It's big and red and solid, with one of those metal bars in front that you have to push with all your strength to open. There are two signs on The Door. The first sign is black with big orange block letters that say, "emergency exit". Right below that is another sign, this one black on white, reading "do not enter". The orange and black sign was placed there by Rona, the assistant manager, and is barely worth mentioning. The second sign is the one that haunts me, that secretly, ridiculously, keeps me awake at night.

I've asked every other cashier, most of the beauty department, most of apparel, all of the deli people, and most of the bakery. I've asked all the supervisors, hoping that the secret to decoding the logic of The Door was something bestowed along with that first promotion. Finally, as we passed each other in the hall towards the lunchroom, I asked the manager, Phil. Phil is a tall, weird man with no hair and dim eyes who only dresses in clothes bought at Superstore. He can tell if you're wearing clothes not bought at Superstore and, should you happen to do the unthinkable and venture in on your off hours wearing a sweater bought from Wal-Mart, finds it necessary to inquire, in a jovial fashion yet with veiled threat behind those colourless eyes, why you are supporting the enemy. But he was always nice to me.

But on the subject of The Door, all Phil could do say was that a "greater authority than mine placed that sign there" and that was that. So on I wondered, my frustration and my curiosity growing, day by day, to terribly pressurize me, until I began to fear that I might seriously be losing my mind. I wanted to open The Door. I wanted to open The Door and step through so badly that I dreamed about it.

It's not that I wonder what is behind The Door. I know what is behind The Door; or I believe I know, and in some circles that's as good as knowing. It is an exit. It leads to the parking lot. I walk past what I have no reason not to believe is the other side of The Door every day on my way to work, and every day on my way home. But the reverse side of The Door is naked of signs and so does not incur my attention or my wrath.

Who would put a "do not enter sign" on the inside of an exit? What, I implore, am I being asked not to enter? I fantasize about running through the door. Just pushing it open one day and charging through. Running out into the parking lot, and into the street. I think of the freedom; I think of the wind and the rain hitting my face, the fresh, wet smell of the pavement, the release, the relief, the incomparable freedom. I want to spite that sign that has mocked me day in and day out since I began working at Superstore, a year and a half ago. I want to shake it down as I slam the door in my wake, tearing off my clinging fluorescent blue uniform as I run.

I'm almost at the end of the metaphorical rope. Exactly seven hours and fifty-six minutes into an eight-hour shift and I finally make the decision.

It's a notable enough instant in my life that I actually pause, holding a large box of mini wheats suspended above the blinking glass surface of my scanner, waiting to be rung up. The customer, a muffin-faced mother with a screaming five-year-old squishing a loaf of bread into a mangled ball behind her back, glares at me. I glare back, and finish her order. Thankfully, it's the last. Jenna has appeared behind me, her flat black hair in pig tails, her apron characteristically spotless. I collect my things and drop them into the pocket of my own wrinkled and mustard stained apron, wish Jenna good luck, and I'm on my way.

Today is my last day, or I would never have the nerve. I'm a rule keeper, by nature. Jaywalking leaves me a little sick to my stomach, never mind smoking in no smoking zones. Signs are meant to be obeyed and I do so slavishly. But a line must be drawn somewhere, and this is where I draw mine. I handed in my two weeks' notice three weeks ago, I cleaned out my locker, I got my letter of reference, I said my goodbyes. I've spent the last two months paring down my belongings to the bare minimum. I've stripped away my life and my memories till my whole personality was small and meek enough to be shoved into three extra-large canvas suitcases, salmon pink and well worn, and one carry-on bag. My plane leaves in six hours. By tomorrow I'll be on the other side of the continent, staring blindly into another ocean, another life. No one in Halifax will know about The Door. It will be over, solved, defeated. I will start again.

I pull on my coat, grab my purse, and start down the wide hallway to the proper exit. Halfway down the hall is The Door, huge and omnipresent. The steps I take toward it seem to be far too many, as if the linoleum is moving backward on an invisible conveyer belt. I refuse to look at The Door until I'm standing in front of it. There I stop, take a quick look around, push my whole weight against the metal bar and charge through.

The other side of The Door is not what I expected. I'm not in the parking lot. I'm not outside, nor am I still in the building I just left. Where I am is a dimly lit and narrow cavern. The walls are some kind of black volcanic rock, as smooth and slippery as glass, reflecting the light emanating from the blue flamed torches that line the jagged, gleaming walls. I grab the handle before The Door slams shut behind me and charge right back into Superstore.

Back in the brightly lit staff hallway, with the half open doorway to the manager's office across the hall, and a poster for the next staff bowling party peeling off the bulletin board, I'm sweating and my hands are shaking. My blood is still, my heartbeat deafening. Phil passes by and nods at me but doesn't stop, doesn't congratulate me on my impending move or wish me luck, doesn't comment on my reprehensible Payless running shoes. I nod back, trying my best to look normal. When he's gone I lean against The Door and quietly panic.

I consider running. I consider flying down the steps to the proper, socially condoned exit and making my escape. I consider going home, letting my mother drive me to the airport, getting on the plane, quietly eating my package of airline peanuts, watching the in-flight movie, and pretending none of this ever happened.

But I can't. I can't. There are doors, once opened, that can't ever be closed.

I hold my breath, take another quick look around, and push against the great metal bar. I stick my head through far enough to see the cavern, the blue torchlight. Distantly, the smell of something burning. I step through The Door.

Before The Door closes behind me, I push my purse strap underneath it, holding it just slightly ajar.

The stench of burning gets stronger the farther into the cavern I walk. The floor is slippery, and in places wet. A few times I lose my balance and almost fall. Up ahead the cavern bends. I follow a rough path towards the sound of heavy breathing, and the stench of sweat and chemical burn.

I turn the corner, the cavern widens into a room, rough walled and with stalactites like teeth. There is a man tied to a stone slab in the center of the room. A woman stands over him holding a silver bowl. The bound man is naked and thin, his bones cold protrusions. His chest is one giant chemical burn, a coat of blisters spitting blood and clear puss; white tear-drop scars drip down the sides of his chest and pool in his hairless, hollowed-out armpits. I'm afraid that if I take a step closer and look into the center of his wound, I'll see an opening burned through into his chest, the stubs of corroded ribs, a naked and throbbing heart. His head is tilted back and framed by stringy hair too caked with blood and pus for its original colour to be distinguishable. A sheet of dried blood and dripping, sticky snot masks a face so twisted with hate it is barely human. His breath is loud and raspy, filling the cave with livid echoes. A snake as thick as a human thigh is wrapped around the stalactites. The ceiling disappears into a void of black; there is no telling how far up it goes, or how large the snake is. Its body disappears and reappears among the rocky protrusions. It could go on for miles. Its head is strange and small and calm, more like a jeweled ornament than a living thing. Only its tongue moves, flickering in and out of its mouth, dripping clear venom into the silver bowl held above the bound man's chest. The woman holding the bowl has the deadest eyes I've ever seen.

I watch them for what feels like a long time, frozen and numb with panic. My feet feel cemented onto the polished ground. The bowl fills up before my eyes, each drop of liquid that falls into it hissing and smoking against the metal sides. When the bowl can hold no more, she moves it away and dumps the acid, hissing, on the ground. Meanwhile the steady drip falls onto the scarred and seeping chest.

When he screams, the whole cavern shakes. My hands fly to my fracturing ear drums. The floor heaves and sends me flying back, sliding across the slippery floor. And I'm crawling desperately across the glassy ground, fingers clawing at nothing. Unable to stand, I throw myself at The Door, pull it open, kick my purse out from the door frame and hurl myself after it.

On my feet again, I run down the hall, shove past several stunned coworkers and bolt through the proper exit. I breathe fresh air and keep running. I'm across the parking lot and halfway down the street before I realize no one is chasing me.

In the parking lot of a Starbucks I struggle to catch my breath and wonder what the hell to do now.

On one of the plastic deck tables outside the Starbucks sits a man with little bells braided into his long white beard. He's wearing an army jacket, a Led Zeppelin T-shirt, and a pair of jeans that might well be older than me. There's a white bandage covering his left eye. Someone has drawn a happy face on it in purple marker.

"Janet who walks between the worlds," he calls out. His voice is hard and old and deep, "You opened The Door, didn't you."

I feel a hot blush rush to my face like I've been caught naked in public.

A smile touches the corners of lips cracked with age, "Come," he says, waving me forward.

I come. I sit down across from him in a wobbly plastic chair.

"Grande latte," he says, "Heavy on the foam, extra hot, with some of those chocolate sprinkles."

"What?"

He waves towards the open Starbucks.

"Oh." I stand and walk into the Starbucks and buy him a Grande latte with chocolate sprinkles. I go back outside and sit down across from him, placing the steaming paper cup between his woolen gloved hands. He smiles and sips. The foam stays in his mustache.

"Nothing can be done," he says in his deep, old voice, "that cannot be undone. Loki won't stay in that cave forever."

I'm surprised by my own sigh of relief.

"When he does break his chains, you'd better hope to hell you and yours are all dead and gone."

"What's he doing in the emergency exit at Superstore?"

Again that cracked smile, that black laugh.

"There used to be sacred places. Places where mortals couldn't go. There were mountains that couldn't be climbed, deserts that couldn't be crossed. Places where secrets could be kept. We used to keep Loki chained up deep beneath the surface of the Earth. But mortals just kept drilling down deeper and deeper and eventually he had to be moved."

"So you moved him to a Superstore?"

He sips his latte and looks thoughtful, and then says, "Man stopped obeying the laws of nature. But most of you seem to obey signs."

"Signs?"

"Not any signs. Just signs so trivial nobody bothers to disobey them. Well, almost nobody."

"This works?"

"Better than you'd think. Get this…if you walk on the grass in a certain city park in Sacramento, you're walking in the fields of Eden. The fires of Ragnarök, the ones that burn this world, will be lit by a match struck in the non-smoking section of a roadside diner in Salvation, Nebraska. Old truths don't stop being true, Janet, they just relocate."

Another pause, another sip of his latte, "Don't worry too much Janet. You've broken nothing that can't be fixed."

"Why are you telling me this?"

Again that cracked smile, "Would you rather I'd have let you wonder?"

"Are you punishing me?"

"You wanted to know secrets Janet," he says, "you wanted to do something forbidden, something no one else has done. You should be grateful. I had to carve out my own eye for the knowledge you just bought with a five-dollar latte."

Strangely, I'm not grateful.

The cracked smile fades and he seems, for a moment, almost to pity me. Then the smile is back, crooked and slightly cruel. "Come close," he says.

I lean close.

He reaches up and slowly peels the bandage off his left eye. Beneath it is a wrinkled, concave eyelid.

"Closer," he says.

I lean closer.

He opens the hollow eyelid and lets me look.

Suddenly, I understand everything.

Six hours later and I'm sitting on a plane heading for a new coast, a new life. But for some reason Halifax doesn't seem all that far away anymore.

I'm sitting next to a man who didn't wear his seatbelt during takeoff. On the way to the airport I saw three different single occupant vehicles driving in the car pool lane. I notice these things now. I notice what rules have been broken, and wonder what terrible or beautiful secrets might have been carelessly unleashed upon the world.

I got on the plane, just like I said I would. But I do not eat my package of airline peanuts. And I don't watch the in-flight movie. Instead, I stare out the little round window at the earth far below. I watch the crisscrossing patchwork of superhighways and try not to see them as hairline fractures in the surface of the world.

The chains are breaking. That's what I saw in the naked tunnel of Odin's eye. The wolves are hungry and they're eyeing the sun and the moon as their meat. One day a match will be struck in a roadside diner in Salvation, Nebraska, and the whole world will ignite.

I'll go to Halifax. I'll go to school. I'll get a degree and a job. I'll date. Maybe one day I'll marry. But I'll never forget.

Some secrets, once learned, can never be unlearned. Some doors, once opened, can never be closed.

Some signs are meant to be obeyed.

The Masochist's Hammer

Derek Heath

Long after Midgard burned, all that remained in the dust were the Gods and the roaches.

Some men had thrived, scavenging from the ruins to form new civilizations, semi-civilizations in the wrecks of old buildings and the craters left in the sand. Some succumbed to the poisoned air and the glass-storms, and their children learned to breathe scarcely and fashion thick armour from the leather of their ancestors; others fell to the scorching red fog that followed, their children crafting rudimentary healing tinctures from the flora blooming across the Badlands. Generations passed, and the towns and cities they built and destroyed and built again were walled with enormous spikes and traps.

Gods did not die, did not learn from the glass-storms and the red fog; they just watched others die, and after a time grew bored with watching. Some made sport of the wasted world. Others bathed in the nuclear lakes. Others played games with the scavengers and toyed cruelly with what they had built.

A shadow lurched through the pelting snow of the Nord Waste, his clothes bitten by the frostflies, the visor of his respiratory mask scratched and pocked with tiny holes. He staggered between the low shanties toward the chief's hut, slogging through snow up to his knees. A small cluster of light elves followed him: little more than bright points of amber in the swirling blizzard-wind, they tended to cling to any traveller who braved the cold for more than a few minutes, like vultures waiting for carrion.

He reached the chief's hut and pounded on the door, glancing back to the village as wind beat at his stinging face. Through what was now a pulsing cloud of light elves, he glimpsed the shadow of the arena distantly through the miasmic snow-fog, and the shacks around it. Batting away a knot of fireflyesque elves, he slammed his fist on the door again.

"Enter," came a booming voice from within. It was like thunder.

The door swung inward and the man almost fell in, stumbling onto the fur-covered floor. Warm torches swelled in sconces around the edges of the hut, amber flames throbbing. In a throne of gnarled wood, the one-eyed chief leaned forward. He had come to Midgard shortly after the third apocalypse, and gorged himself since on the destruction and fire. The socket of his missing eye was gored and hollow, the flesh around it scarred to pulpy white tissue. He smiled thinly.

"Another challenger?"

"Yes, Lord Odin," the man panted, his respirator fogging up to obscure the terror in his face. "The townfolks're already gathering in the arena. Do you accept?"

"Always," the one-eyed chief grunted, rising from his throne. He was enormous and filled the hut, his barrel chest dressed in thick fur, pelts hanging from his waist to form a skirt of matted white and grey. His beard was sticky with congealed red lifeblood. Stooping to retrieve the long-handled weapon leaning upon the hearth beside him, Odin curled his thick, scarred fingers around the warhammer's shaft and offered a hand to the grovelling man on the doorstep. "Let's go remind him who he's challenging, shall we?"

* * *

Odin walked back from the arena alone, his warhammer slick with the challenger's blood.

The head of the long-handled hammer was made of bone, plates of skull melded together to form a hideous, squared abomination. He had fused the teeth of the dead Ratatoskr to the hammer to give it a biting edge; now thick ropes of blood oozed from these crooked teeth into the snow, pattering behind him as he trudged uphill.

He looked up at the caw of a messenger raven; squinting with his good eye, he saw a swirling mass of black points above the distant cliffs. The titanic, bearded man stood ankle-deep in the snow and waited, his chest heaving, plumes of breath misting in front of his face. One of the black shapes spiralled suddenly downward, wheeling and darting in the wind. He frowned.

"Something wrong with the blasted thing," he muttered, slogging toward his hut as the raven banked into a snowdrift beside the door. At least its aim hadn't been too far off.

The bird was shaking its feathers of snow as he reached the door to his hut. It staggered, tufts of jet-black forming a thick mane around its neck. Odin leaned forward and butted the door with the heel of his hand, forcing it open. The bird flew in and he followed.

"What do you have for me?" he growled, standing the warhammer by the door and turning to face the raven. It had landed on the arm of his gnarled throne and it stood, twitching, its beak snapping left and right as its left wing convulsed. Odin approached slowly, watching the thing's fits with some curiosity. As he neared the throne he caught sight of something moving beneath the bird's flesh, some wriggling worm-like thing poking up feathers as it danced across the creature's tiny cranium. Cautiously, the great beast of a man reached into the pelt hanging over his chest and withdrew a small sealskin pouch. "By Asgard, little one, what *do* you have for me?"

He crouched before the bird and the raven looked helplessly at him, its yellow eyes wide with terror. The thing beneath its feathers continued to roam its body, passing between its wings – and causing each to twitch violently in turn – before returning to its head.

Odin saw his chance and took it, reaching forward quickly and curling his fingers around the raven's neck. He squeezed; there was a soft *crunch*, then the wriggling worm-shape slid into view from behind the bird's left eyelid. The insect caught sight of Odin and crawled desperately across the raven's eye, which had swiftly rolled up in the socket, but the one-eyed beast-man was faster and pinched the thing by its shell, plucking it from the bird and dropping it quickly into the sealskin pouch.

The bird dropped, twitched once more, and finally lay still on the arm of the chief's throne.

Odin looked into the pouch.

The beetle was perhaps the size of his thumbnail and dressed with a shining emerald-green shell, its legs darting black things, its eyes roving madly. It zipped about inside the bag, chirruping with a frequency that was almost electric.

Odin smiled grimly. "A cowardly attempt, my son," he whispered, sealing the bag and returning it to his pelt. He patted it against his left breast, careful not to crush the beetle within. "I suppose you'll find a way to let your brother know of my whereabouts, now that you've found me."

The old man settled into his throne and gazed for a moment at the warhammer, then with a great sigh he leaned back his head and closed his good eye.

"Ah, well. A family reunion, then. I suppose it's about time."

* * *

The next morning brought a new challenger.

Odin woke to a pounding on his door. He rose from the throne where he had slept, pausing briefly to lay a great thick hand on the cool belly of the dead bird. "Enter," he commanded. The door opened. The messenger stumbled inside, tearing off his respirator. His cheeks were red from the cold, the snow blustering in behind him.

"Another," he said breathlessly, "bigger than most."

Odin nodded. He smiled sadly. "How does he look?"

The messenger cocked an eyebrow. "Angry, my lord."

* * *

The arena had been built around a second hammer, one which had crashed to Midgard long before Odin decided to settle here. Around this ancient thing, a monument to the first days of the world's end, the Nord Waste had composed itself, a scarred and barren plane of white and crystal-blue in the burning remnants of the Scandinavian cliffs. It was Odin who had torn the hammer from the hands of his own son, Odin who had cast the hammer into the writhing apocalypse, Odin who had thrown Thor into the belly of Jörmungandr knowing that the two would fight for centuries before the great snake finally spat him out. In the meantime, Odin wandered the wastelands until he found the settlement quickly rising around the discarded Mjolnir, and established himself as its guardian.

Some called him a tyrant. But they had not seen the things that he had seen. Fenrir and the great rabid wolves that roamed what used to be North America and was now a scorched and fiery mass of craters; the undead Draugr stalking the streets of burned-out cities and the Jötnar trudging the irradiated rivers in the south.

A snowstorm was beginning to unfurl around the settlement.

He carried his bone warhammer past the shanties toward the arena, dazzling points of light darting and snapping around him. Usually the light elves were too intimidated by his enormous presence to come near, but today they amassed in the low dozens, nervously following him to the centre of town. He wore no respirator, and though he could taste the nuclear poison in the air it did not touch his throat nor blister his skin as it did the throats and skins of the Midgardians. Nevertheless, he was getting old. Must be, for he was beginning to feel the cold bite of the air.

The warhammer had never been as heavy in his hands as it was now.

Already the audience had gathered, half of the townfolks spilling up the slopes of the cavernous ring of ice and snow that thrust up from the edges of Mjolnir's crater. The walls of the arena were titanic and ragged, great spines of blue ice shearing the swirling white sky above. Seats had been chiselled from the granite, rows upon rows of them. A roar of admiration rippled across the outer edge of the arena as Odin entered, raising his long-handled warhammer high. He bellowed back with a roar of his own, pumping the great cables of his shoulder and neck as he pounded the beating snow with Ratatoskr's teeth. Crystals of snow thickened his beard and formed a small drift in the socket-cave of his missing eye.

"Today, the Allfather faces another challenger!" Odin yelled, his voice booming into the cavernous arena. Wings of snow fluttered around him; he could see the challenger in the middle of the arena, little more than a grey smudge in the blizzard but positively electrified with the hundreds of light elves that clung to and hovered around his massive shoulders. The blue points of the challenger's eyes glowed with such violent ferocity that he could almost hear them crackling. He lowered the warhammer. "Who here today," he bellowed, "would see Odin, son of Bestia and Borr, struck down this day?"

The cheering and applause died down to nothing; the silence was chilling.

Odin took a step forward and the icy ground of the arena shuddered. "And who," he roared, "would see Odin's challenger struck down?"

The arena filled immediately with noise, a raucous cacophony of beating chests and savage howls. Respirators were torn from faces and explosive jeers detonated among the crowd, some of the spectators shoving and beating each other in a frenzy as they spilled across the stone seats in their excited hysteria. The sound was deafening, a constant and persistent buzz underlying the pulsing agonies of applause that filled the sky.

Odin smiled thinly and approached the challenger, every step causing the ground to tremble. High above the arena, a spark of lightning scythed through a whirling bank of snow. Odin's pelts blew about his chest and shoulders as the wind barrelled past him. The challenger had not moved or spoken, had not taken his eyes off the approaching man-beast. Had not blinked, in fact, the blue electricity in his eyes scarcely threatening to extinguish even for a moment.

"My son," Odin growled as he reached the centre of the arena.

Between them, Mjolnir stood half-buried in the snow, the hammer's great grey head emblazoned with runes and ancient symbols, every edge glowing a faint blue in the presence of its former owner. The handle was short and wound tightly in thick leather, this too branded with more runes and prophecies. A single strap of leather fluttered at the end of the handle, damp with snow and wind.

Another flash of lightning pealed silently across the sky, somewhere over the sea. Moments later thunder boomed into the arena. Thor said nothing.

He looked no different to the last time Odin had seen him, except for the thick scars ribboning his neck where Jörgumandr's talons and teeth had furrowed his flesh. Thor's body was monstrous, his legs like trunks, his bare arms throbbing as blood surged through the thick, pipe-like veins coursing down to his wrists. His fists were clenched, and Odin saw that the knuckles were raw and blistered. Light elves danced across his chest and around his head, forming an obscene halo of blinking starlight and half-obscuring his face. Thick, matted tangles of blood-red hair blew into his eyes, a massive beard of the same colour drooling in bloody ropes from his jaw. He wore a belt of snakeskin; it took Odin a moment to note that the shimmering, black pelt was the same as that which adorned the world-serpent's belly.

"So your feud is finally at an end," Odin mused.

"One of them," Thor said quietly. Even at a whisper, his voice was like thunder. All around them the audience had grown silent again, listening close to try and discern the conversation between the two gods. The snow and wheeling wind masked their voices somewhat. Odin smiled.

"You think you can still lift it?"

Thor's eyes lowered to the hammer buried in the snow between them. The head of Mjolnir was twice the size of the bony slab that Odin had fashioned for his warhammer, and through the many years it had lain here abandoned the metal and stone had been scratched and pawed at by the wind so that many of the runes had faded. A strange blue moss formed a thin patina inside some of the carvings. "This is how you preserve your rule?" Thor said disgustedly. His eyes narrowed. "You ask challengers to prove their worth, and when they cannot…"

"Only those with a truly honest heart can lift Mjolnir," Odin offered, "as you well know. Anyone who wishes it may challenge my rule, but they must pull the hammer from the ground with their own strength: their own bravery and nobility and wholesomeness will determine their fate."

"And all those who cannot are killed, presumably."

Odin flexed his fingers around the warhammer's shaft. "By failing to lift Mjolnir, a challenger proves only one thing; that they are not fit to rule, and shall never be."

"Nor to live, I suppose."

Odin's face darkened. "A worthy opponent would hold the greatest weapon ever to fall through Yggdrasil's branches in their hands. Anyone worthy of Mjolnir is invited to strike me with it, my son. As you will be, if you can still lift her. To anyone so bold, so pure of heart and so true, I would gladly relinquish my throne."

"And how many have proven worthy?" Thor snarled. "Over the years, father – almost two thousand of them, since the end of the world – how many have been given such an opportunity? How many challengers have you slaughtered?"

"Well," Odin smiled, "I'm still here, aren't I?"

Thor batted away a small cloud of light elves. Odin wondered briefly how long he had been travelling the wastelands to have amassed such a horde of them.

"It is only fair," Odin said. "I am not a cruel ruler, my son. Nor a cowardly one."

"I have lived under your rule," Thor said sardonically. "I was born into it. I know firsthand of your cruelty."

"Then you know also of my word. Lift the hammer, boy, and the wasteland will be yours."

"I don't care for the wasteland," Thor said, looking around the arena. "But to free these people of your tyranny…and to offer your head to the first hungry beast I encounter on my way back home…"

"Then pick it up," Odin said, bracing his warhammer. He gritted his teeth and looked back into the crowd. "Today, the Mighty Thor challenges me!"

The arena filled with a whooping mass of insane sound, the screeches and cheers of a people driven wild by their hunger.

"I looked for Sleipnir in the stables," Thor said quietly. "I missed her. Where is she?"

Odin smiled grimly. "Meat," he growled. "In the darkest days."

"What have you become, father?"

"King," Odin said. "They need me, Thor."

"Nobody needs you."

"You did, at one time."

"I changed."

"Well," Odin said, "so did I, I suppose."

Thor smiled. "No. Not one bit."

* * *

Silence split the arena into segments of rippling, snow-filled white as Thor opened his fist. His fingers were thick and calloused, each knuckle broken into a small cluster of knobbly stones beneath his flesh. The nails were black, stained from the wastelands through which he had climbed to reach this place. He had searched briefly for Loki when he arrived, but found his brother nowhere among the settlement. He would reappear, Thor supposed, when the opportunity presented himself. That was Loki. Of the two brothers, he had been the least changed by the end of the world and the following apocalypses. In fact if Loki had changed at all, it had been for the better.

Thor had spent the centuries becoming more and more like their father.

"Go on, then," Odin spat, flashing pointed teeth as he tightened his grip on the warhammer. Thor recognized a lock of braided hair in his father's beard and hesitated; was that all that was left of Sleipnir, the mighty eight-legged beast that he had ridden as a child?

And what was left of Odin? Thor jested, but the man before him was not his father, not anymore. Time had changed him, too.

Time, and greed.

"Pick it up," Odin urged. "Go on. Pick it up, my son."

Thor closed his fingers again, then splayed them open. "We don't have to do this," he pleaded. "You could leave this place. Return to Asgard and let them be."

"They need me," Odin echoed. "Scavengers. Filth. Without us to rule, they would destroy this world again a thousand times over."

"And how much would you destroy, just to keep them in your fist?"

"You misjudge me."

"You should leave."

"Pick it up."

"One last chance, father. Leave them alone, let them flourish in their own wreckage. They will rebuild, better than they can with you holding them back. Holding onto rule because you've begun to miss all the courts and subjects that ran from you the moment they could. These people will run, too, when they can. How many of your subjects have disappeared, over the decades? Not enough for you to notice, perhaps, but enough. They don't *want* you here."

"Pick up the damn hammer. Or leave me and find some other corner of this blasted world to usurp."

"Father. I beg of you. Do not make me kill you."

"You couldn't pick up the damn thing if you grovelled for eternity," Odin growled. "Now by all the gods, give it a try – or leave."

Odin's son fixed him with a steely look. The lightning in his eyes had faded to a smouldering white. Slowly, almost tentatively, he leaned down and curled his fingers around Mjolnir's handle. Cocking an eyebrow, he said, "If I am worthy of this hammer, I will strike you with it."

"I would expect nothing less," Odin said fiercely, straightening his body.

"Then run."

"*Never.*"

Thor tightened his grip, drew in a breath of the ice-cold air.

And what if he wasn't worthy? What if time *had* changed him, in the same way it had changed his father? What if the hammer belonged to the earth now, to the rotten earth where it would decay over the millennia until only it and the ice remained?

"Pick. It. Up."

Gritting his teeth, Thor pulled.

There was a moment where the icy wastes seemed to become absolutely silent, a pregnant sac of void-like nothing erupting over their heads and filling every fibre, every pore, with a tense anticipation. The light elves swirling around Thor's chest stilled. Then there was sound.

Oh, so much sound.

The ice cracked open around the hammer as it was wrenched easily from the ground. Thunder cracked across the sky in the very same moment that a thick, worm-like prong of wild blue lightning thrummed into the centre of the arena, forks of it springing out into the clouds. The snow seemed to stop swirling, then spiral madly outward in every direction as Thor raised his arm high, a mighty bellow exploding from his chest as ropes of electricity surged through the hammer and into his shoulder. Mjolnir glowed fiercely, a kaleidoscopic miasma of every imaginable colour detonating around its head and expelling all the light elves into the edges of the arena, an explosion of stars. Then the lightning was gone, leaving a thick black bank of cloud spinning slowly over the arena, over the whole of the Nord Waste. It rumbled angrily as Thor stepped forward.

"I am proud, my son," Odin whispered, and he reached out, the warhammer clasped tightly in his left hand. He let go and the bone-headed thing dropped into the snow at their feet. A chasm of blackened earth stood between them where Mjolnir had been.

Odin stood and looked around the arena, smiling sadly at his subjects. They had fallen quiet again. The air was thick with disappointment and excitement, two opposing energies buzzing through the crowd like electricity. Like lightning.

How many would be sad to see him go? How many would feast and celebrate? It didn't matter. He had known this day was coming.

Oh, he had known for a long time.

Thor gazed down at Mjolnir as he gripped it with both hands, his knuckles ruined and crooked, his wrists stained orange with blood. Again his eyes flashed the brightest blue. "You could still leave," he whispered.

Odin shook his head. The furs crossing his chest billowed in the wind; his beard fluttered. "I am a man of my word. So are you; stick to it, boy. Strike me."

Thor nodded. Almost lightly, he stepped forward. Then, carrying the weight of a thousand worlds, he raised the hammer high above his head.

The arena detonated in a shower of electricity as a dozen crackling streams of lightning arced from the great black cloud into the head of the hammer and Mjolnir screamed in every spectrum. Spectators cowered behind their hands and scrambled beneath each other as the sky broiled, snow exploding in puffs of charred vapour, steam rising in thick mist-like clouds from the ground as the ice began to boil. Then Thor brought the hammer crashing forward, letting out a great roar of fury and anger as he swung with both arms, propelling Mjolnir's explosive weight directly into Odin's chest. Odin's head tipped backward, his body remaining where it stood, as the power of the storm above them coursed through his beastly skeleton.

Mjolnir sunk to the ground, the lightning fizzling out. Thor cried out as his arm was dragged down, his whole body bending with the suddenly impossible weight of the hammer. He looked down, confused, flexed his fingers around the handle, and pulled.

It would not budge.

"What the..."

He grabbed Mjolnir with both arms and wrenched backward with every ounce of strength in his body. The hammer was lodged in the ground, ice and snow already spreading across the head. The glow was gone. He looked up and saw Odin smiling down at him.

"What have you done?"

"I have done nothing," Odin said quietly, reaching into the pelt across his chest. The fur had been blackened and charred, and much of Odin's exposed neck was scorched to red tissue. His great hand trembled as he dug his fingers into the pelt, right where Thor had struck him, and pulled out a small, sealskin pouch.

Slowly, he opened the pouch and tipped it upside-down. Thor watched, horrified, as something tumbled out and seesawed into the snow. A delicate, tiny thing, its emerald-green shell crushed into tiny chitinous pieces, its body pulped by the blow of the hammer.

"Fratricide," Odin muttered. Between them, the broken body of the tiny beetle was slowly covered with snow. "How could a man be worthy, after killing his brother?"

"I didn't know," Thor said, "you tricked me, *you* did this—"

"Enough," Odin said, and he bent down and swiped the bone warhammer out of the snow. Thor barely had time to blink; before he could retreat the toothed weapon was swung at him, rending a great hunk of flesh from his face. Warmth exploded into his eyes and he was blown backward, reeling, into the ice. Odin bore down on him, a titanic shadow with one gleaming eye, the teeth of a dead dimension-traversing squirrel, red with Thor's blood at the end of his hammer. His teeth flashed, tiny points of light swirling behind him, terrified.

He raised both arms above his head. The crowd screamed in excitement, and Odin the Allfather, son of Bestia and Borr, ruler of the Nord Waste, grinned hungrily as he brought the hammer down on Thor's skull.

The Raven and the Key

Justin R. Hopper

Huginn hated Muninn.

It had not always been that way. There was a time when he felt an affinity for his winged brother, as they had soared between the nine worlds gathering information for the Allfather.

Huginn's name meant thought, and he was as swift as a fleeting notion. Muninn's meant memory, and his capacity for recollection was unmatched. Together, the two ravens acted as Odin's eyes and ears in Midgard and the worlds beyond. He would send them out at dawn's first light and they would fly about the different realms – swooping and spying, wheeling and gleaning – returning at nightfall, when they would perch on Odin's shoulders and whisper all they had seen and heard as he fed them scraps of meat.

The Allfather had granted them the power of speech and the gift of magic. These abilities they used to speak to men who were living as well as those who were dead. They could chatter with the light and dark elves; gossip with the dwarves (everyone knows how the dwarves love to gossip); converse with the giants of sea, hill and mountain (though everyone knows that getting information from a mountain giant is like trying to get blood from a boulder).

And for a long time, Huginn had been content.

He and Muninn divided the universe up between them, delighting in each morsel of news fed to the Allfather, no matter which of the two it came from. Perched upon Odin's shoulder, looking down from Hlidskialf, the high seat on the topmost peak of Asgard, Huginn understood and appreciated his place in the cosmos. That is, until the day he made the mistake of speaking to Loki.

Often, when Huginn returned from his travels round the nine worlds, he would fly back over Asgard, watching his dark form reflected in the golden roofs of its many magnificent halls and temples. Most glorious of all these buildings was Valhalla, the hall of the slain, whose roof tiles were burnished shields that shimmered like the sun. One day, as Huginn passed this mighty fortress, he noticed Loki, practising his transformations in Glasir, the golden grove that stood before the great doors of the hall. The sly one was a shapeshifter, and Huginn swooped down to see how he was getting on, settling upon a tree branch, partially obscured by its golden-red foliage. He watched as Loki transformed himself by turns into a horse, a hare, a snake, an otter, a tiny buzzing fly, and finally into a sleek, black raven, the very image of Huginn. The false raven spread its wings and took to the air, circling Huginn's tree twice, before landing on the branch beside him.

"How do I look?" said raven Loki.

"Very convincing," replied Huginn. "I suppose you're going to try and impersonate me and feed false information to the Allfather."

"Now why would I do that?" said raven Loki.

"For your own amusement," said Huginn.

Loki made a *haa haa* sound, which Huginn supposed was his attempt to laugh raven-style.

"Actually, I think we're very alike," said Loki, once he'd finished laughing.

"Of course we are. You've shape-shifted to look like me."

"I don't mean in appearance," said Loki as, disconcertingly, he transformed himself into a squirrel to make his point. "I'm thinking of how we're both treated. Odin always favours Thor over me, just as he favours Muninn over you. No matter how hard we try, we can never be the best loved. Sad, isn't it?"

"I don't have time for this," said Huginn, shooting up into the air and putting distance between himself and the squirrel Loki that capered in Glasir's branches.

It never did to spend too long talking to the mischief-maker.

But although Huginn knew that Loki's intention had been to make trouble, those words stayed with him, and over time they began to bite.

Gradually, Huginn came to realize that Odin did in fact favour Muninn. For a start, there were the different missions the Allfather gave them. While Huginn was always sent out to speak to the hanged, Muninn was dispatched to talk to the slain. At first, Huginn had considered this a great honour, as Odin himself was the gallows god and dangled from a limb of Yggdrasil the World Tree in order to gain the secret of runes.

Slowly though, he understood that this was not the case at all. The hanged were generally suicides, sacrifices or executions. Consequently, Huginn spent most of his time talking to the ghosts of slaves, captured warriors or criminals. How could it be an honour conversing with thralls and weaklings, thieves and rapists? The more he thought about it, the more it made

Huginn feel like a common carrion crow rather than a holy raven of Asgard.

Munnin, on the other hand, got to talk to warriors slain on the battlefield. They did not all die bravely, but many were the heroes and champions chosen by the Valkyries to enter the hall of Valhalla: great fighters such as Sigmund and Eric Bloodaxe. Why, wondered Huginn, should Muninn spend time with legendary warriors while he got stuck with the riffraff?

The answer could surely only lie in Odin's partiality. As this suspicion grew, so did Huginn's resentment of his fellow raven. Where once he had seen a brother in Muninn, now he saw a rival for the Allfather's affection, one intent on outdoing him with ever more juicy stories or compelling secrets for Odin's ears. And no matter how hard Huginn fought back, with his own pressing reports and intelligence, they never seemed enough to shift his master's opinion.

Munnin was the favoured one.

Indeed, once, on Midgard, Odin even let slip his preference.

He had gone to the hall of King Geirröth, in the guise of Grimnir the Wanderer, with his long blue cloak and wide-brimmed hat. Believing him to be a sorcerer, Geirröth had seized the stranger and bound him between two fires. For eight days and nights Grimnir suffered in silence, denied food and water and scorched by the fierce heat of the flames. But on the eighth day, Geirröth's young son Agnar took pity on the stranger and brought him a great horn of foaming mead. And in reward, Grimnir revealed his true identity, sharing with Agnar the secrets of the universal order, from the roots of Yggdrasil to the high halls of Asgard, where the

Aesir dwelt. He spoke of the halls of Baldur, Heimdall, Glitnir and Noatun; and finally of himself: the twin wolves that kept him company and the two ravens who acted as his messengers.

And then he said it.

That each time his ravens flew out across the world, Odin worried that one day Huginn might not return, but feared more for the loss of Muninn.

There it was then, in the Allfather's own words. Muninn was the better loved. Huginn was wounded; the tiny heart in his proud black chest stung as though put under the hammer of a dwarven smith. He felt hurt and shame and sadness. And though he would always love his Allfather, now he hated Muninn and ruminated on how that preening Corvid had managed to elevate himself in the ravenly pecking order.

Still, Huginn was a practical bird, and worked hard to raise himself in Odin's estimation. He went further than ever before in his searches for information, flying across the whole world, over the high mountains into Jotunheim where the giants schemed, and down into Svartalfheim where the dark elves crafted their fabulous inventions.

He even tried to aid the gods in their adventures.

On one occasion, Odin, Hoenir and Loki were down in Midgard, trying to save a farmer's son from a giant who was intent on eating the unfortunate child. Odin had used his magic to hide the boy in a single grain of corn in the middle of a vast cornfield. But the giant had reaped the whole crop, cut the chosen stalk and shaken out the grain in which the farm boy hid into his huge, crushing palm.

Odin commanded his ravens to save the child, and it was Huginn who had heeded his master's call. Quick as thought, he dived down and snatched the boy from the giant's grasp, returning him to his father's farmhouse where he regained his normal size and shape.

But if Huginn thought his stock might have risen through this heroic deed, it seemed he was mistaken. Back in Asgard, his part in the rescue was overlooked, and it was Loki the Aesir praised – for causing the giant to tumble head-first into quicksand and then chopping his legs off with his own reaping hook. In the banqueting halls they sang songs about his deed and Odin and the other gods toasted Loki's cunning long into the night, while Huginn gobbled up those gobbets of meat tossed to him and brooded on his situation. Eventually, Loki himself sidled up to the sulking raven, who had left Odin's shoulder and was perched on the back of a throne.

"You're going about this all the wrong way," said Loki.

As he spoke, he chewed on a piece of crackling from Sæhrímnir, the enchanted boar whose flesh the gods fed on.

"I suppose I should have pecked the giant's eyes out instead," said Huginn.

"You could have tried. But I doubt it would have made Odin love you more," Loki replied.

"He seems pretty pleased about you cutting the giant's legs off."

They watched as Hoenir stood on his hands and Odin mimed the way Loki had lopped off the giant's legs at the knees. The other gods bellowed with laughter.

"That's because I tricked him into the quicksand first. My nature is to be cunning, and Odin understands and appreciates that. Just as he appreciates Thor's strength and Heimdall's watchfulness. There is no point in you playing the hero, for that is not your role in the Allfather's vision of things. If you really want to earn his love you must do something special, but something that is in your nature."

Loki broke off a piece of the juicy crackling and offered it to Huginn. The raven took it in his beak, then gulped it down. He thought about Loki's words.

"My nature is to find things," he said.

"Then there you have it," said Loki.

"But, every day, I find out things for the Allfather."

"Find something different. Look, what does Odin love to get his hands on most?"

Huginn puzzled. He hopped from foot to foot and swivelled his head about Glitnir the Shining, the hall in which the gods were presently feasting. Its pillars were made of gold and its thatch from solid silver. The answer came to him.

"Treasures," said Huginn.

"Treasures," repeated Loki. "Think how much Odin loves his treasures. His spear Gungnir; Rati, the magical auger that can drill though any rock; Draupnir, his golden arm-ring that drips wealth. Find the Allfather a fabulous treasure and you're sure to get in his good books. Who knows, if it's extraordinary enough, you might even supplant Muninn in his affections."

"Hmm. I wonder where I can find something like that?" croaked Huginn, to himself.

"I don't suppose it will be too hard. Your kind are meant to have an eye for shiny things," said Loki. He ruffled the feathers on Huginn's head. "Now, don't say I never did anything for you," he whispered, before heading off to receive more acclamation from the assembled Aesir.

The idea quickly took root in Huginn's mind. From then on, wherever he went, Huginn stayed on the look-out for a suitably glittering prize. Wheeling over towns and settlements, his beady eye was drawn to the merest glimmer of gold or glint of silver. He hovered over marketplaces and sat in tavern windows to listen to tales of magic rings, enchanted goblets and other incredible artifacts. Eventually, in a village by the sea, he thought he might have found what he was looking for.

Huginn was watching a public execution from a perch near the axeman's block. A notorious thief and murderer was about to be beheaded and in the moments before he died, moaned aloud that he would never have been caught if only he'd had the Key of Farli. Later, when his head lay upon the rough earth and his spirit was separated from his body, Huginn asked him more about this key of Farli, and the ghost obliged him.

Farli was a dwarf. He lived in a great coastal fortress with his sister Rikka. The fortress had once belonged to the dwarves Fjalar and Galar, who had brewed the mead of inspiration, and Farli and Rikka shared the brothers' gifts for alchemy and invention. Together, they had crafted many fantastical items, and Farli guarded these so jealously that he kept every door in every room of the fortress locked at all times. And although this arrangement may well have deterred thieves, it meant the dwarves were each forced to carry a big bunch of keys, that made them jingle like jailors as they moved about their home.

Rikka soon tired of this impractical situation. In order to mollify her, Farli crafted something new, a magical key that could unlock any door. It was golden and tiny, and no matter what the size and shape of the lock you placed it in, Farli's key would always turn and grant you entry.

Farli gave the key to Rikka, and she used it to move about the fortress freely, never thinking about all the other ingenious purposes it could be put to – like opening the gates of Hel or even the entrance to Asgard itself.

This was the treasure Huginn decided he would bring to Odin.

He began by making friends with Rikka. Her room was in a tower on the western side of the fortress with a window looking out onto the waves that crashed on the rocks below. Great flocks of seagulls wheeled around the tower and screeched into the salty air. Rikka was glad when one day a raven hopped onto the ledge of her window and began to speak to her.

Rikka was a lonely dwarf. She had hoped to become an expert in her craft, as her kinsfolk Fjalar and Galar or the sons of Ivaldi had been. But though she learned the mastery of metal, Rikka found she lacked the magic of her brother or his ingenuity, and so left him to his inventions while she used her art to make sinuous armbands, brooches inlaid with precious gems and pendants of fine filigree. She was delighted to finally find a creature who properly appreciated her endeavours.

Each day, just after dawn, Huginn would appear on the ledge of Rikka's chamber and she would lay out her latest treasures for the raven to cast his black eye over. He would hop about enthusiastically and praise her craftsmanship, her eye for detail and the intricacy of her designs.

All the time, his eye was fixed on the magical golden key she kept on a chain around her neck.

Huginn wondered how he might acquire it. Perhaps he could find another treasure that Rikka would exchange for it. Or maybe, if he flattered her enough, she would give it him as a gift. In the end though, Huginn decided he would steal the Key of Farli.

He waited until dark, long after the hour at which he would normally have returned to Asgard and perched on Odin's shoulder. He sat on the rocks with the seagulls and cormorants and watched the moon rise and cast its pale glow over the sea and the cliffs and the walls of the fortress that rose up from them. No light came from the sea fortress, other than that which shone from Rikka's chamber. And when that was finally extinguished, Huginn spread his wings, rose up into the air and flew towards the tower in which Rikka slept, his body and wings casting a dark shadow over the moonlit sea beneath.

All was quiet as he landed on the ledge of Rikka's chamber. It was illuminated by moonlight, and Huginn saw that the dwarf was in bed, her various treasures glittering in the nooks and niches of her room. The magic key was no longer fastened on a chain around her neck, but lay on a golden plate, placed on a low table beside her bed.

Huginn glided down to the floor of the chamber. He hopped as quietly as he could across the room, his claws clicking on the flagstone floor. A single wingbeat took him to the edge of the low table. The golden plate was a wide, round disc and the key lay in its very centre. All he needed to do was snatch it up in his beak, swoop out of the window and fly back to Asgard with his prize.

Huginn hopped, stealthily, onto the golden plate.

The moment he did, a series of bars shot up from the rim of the plate, curving upwards to join at the top. Huginn beat his wings and let out a terrified croak. Too late, he realized he was trapped in a gilded cage.

Rikka sat up in bed and stared at the helpless raven. At the same time, the door of her chamber flew open and Farli appeared in the doorway. He rubbed his hands together in delight when he saw the bird in the cage.

"It worked!" shrieked Farli.

"Yes, brother, just as we planned," Rikka replied.

"Now we have a talking raven. A fine prize."

"He shall keep me company while I craft my jewellery."

"And in the evenings, there will now be three voices rather than two. I said he was a thief, didn't I? And I said that I would catch him."

"Yes, you did, brother."

Farli advanced on the cage. He reached a stubby finger through the bars and retrieved the magic key. Huginn could have tried to scratch or peck, but he found he didn't have the heart.

Rikka joined her brother and they peered at their prisoner. Farli's face, with its great lumpen nose, bushy eyebrows and tangled beard loomed massively behind the bars.

"Of course, we shan't be able to let him out. In case he tries to escape," said Farli.

"Oh no, we shall never let him out," Rikka replied.

And that was how Huginn, swift as thought, messenger of Odin, became the captive of the dwarves Farli and Rikka. By day, he sat in his cage and watched Rikka forging rings and brooches and pendants in her workshop. At dinner time he was brought to the dwarves' kitchen table, and listened to Farli talk of all the fabulous things he had made and planned to make. And at night he was placed near the ledge of Rikka's window, where he could hear the cries of the gulls outside that seemed to mock his captivity. Huginn had plenty of time to think about what a fool he'd been. Days and days to consider how he had exchanged his position on the shoulder of the Allfather for a cramped cage in a lonely fortress on the edge of an unforgiving sea.

It was on one of those occasions, when Huginn was contemplating his fate, that he heard a loud fluttering outside Rikka's window. At first Huginn didn't even bother to look up, assuming it was one of the gulls that occasionally stopped by to shriek at him.

Then he heard a familiar "caw" and turned to see a large black raven standing on the ledge of the window. It was Muninn. His neck feathers were ruffled by the sea breeze and he held his beak high and erect.

"A sorry situation you've got yourself in," he said.

"Not that you care," said Huginn.

Muninn's shoulders shook as he let out a long rasping raven-laugh.

"You realize that all those things Loki said to you, he also said to me. How sad he was the Allfather favoured one raven over the other. How I might try and win back his affection by questing after some fabulous treasure. Of course, he only wanted us out of the way so he could make mischief without Odin knowing about it. Fortunately, I wasn't stupid enough to listen to him."

For a long time after he spoke there was only silence in the chamber and the noise of the waves breaking on the foot of the cliffs outside.

"What will you do?" said Huginn.

"By rights, I should leave you here," said Muninn.

"I probably deserve it," said Huginn.

"Yes, you do. And I still might."

And with that, Muninn opened his wings and allowed the air currents to take him. He hung for a moment, framed in the window's rectangular opening, and then he darted up into the sky and was gone.

Several days later a trader came to the fortress of the dwarves Farli and Rikka. He wore a wide-brimmed slouch hat and a blue cloak smeared with the dust of the road. He had only one eye and he said that his name was Grimnir.

The dwarves did not much trust this stranger; but he had a beguiling manner and they were keen to see what objects he had hidden in the cloth sack slung over his shoulder. So, the dwarves invited Grimnir into their fortress. They offered him food and mead and asked him what he had seen on his travels. And all the time, Huginn sat in his golden cage, silently watching the feasting and the talking and the growing curiosity of the dwarves as they wondered what exactly the stranger had concealed in his knapsack. Eventually, it was too much for Farli, and he said:

"Stranger, you say you are a trader. What then do you have to trade?"

"I shall show you," said Grimnir, as he untied the knot of his knapsack and laid its contents on the table. Huginn gasped when he saw that they were three of his master's most precious treasures.

The first was a jewelled brooch, which on command would turn into a shield through which no weapon could penetrate. And Farli liked this object greatly.

The second was a magical gaming set, which allowed its owner to win any game they played, and Rikka was delighted by the skill and craftsmanship of its making.

The third treasure was Odin's golden arm-ring, Draupnir. It was so-called because every ninth night, another eight rings would drip from it, giving its wearer wealth beyond imagining. And when they saw Draupnir, both Farli and Rikka desired to own it.

"I will trade something for the arm-ring," said Farli.

"What do you have to trade?" replied Grimnir the Wanderer.

And Farli showed him all the treasures of his fortress: enchanted arms and armour, helmets of invisibility, chariots that needed no steed to pull them. He revealed to Grimnir all the wonders of his workshop; even a key that could unlock any door. But none of these fabulous treasures was Grimnir prepared to exchange for the arm-ring Draupnir.

Then it was Rikka's turn. She showed the stranger the most beautiful objects he had ever seen. Items whose splendour rivalled that of Brísingamen, that shining necklace worn by the goddess Freya. She showed him rings and chains and bracelets rich with jewels and ornamented with designs of great artistry. But none of them, Grimnir saw fit to exchange with the golden arm-ring.

One by one he placed his possessions back in the cloth knapsack. Seeing them disappear from view, the dwarves grew desperate, and just as he was about to slip Draupnir into the cloth, Farli and Rikka cried out together:

"Wait, we have one more thing to trade."

"And what is that?" said Grimnir.

They carried over Huginn in his golden cage.

"We have a raven that talks," they said.

Grimnir peered at the raven with his one good eye.

"This I will trade for my arm-ring," he said.

So Farli took the carved golden key, slipped it into the lock of the birdcage, and opened it so that Huginn could fly out, which he did, landing directly on the left shoulder of the stranger. And for all the world, it looked like he was always meant to be there.

This then, is the story of how Huginn was returned to the Allfather and how the arm-ring Draupnir fell into the possession of the dwarves Farli and Rikka. Much later, Loki would win it back from the dwarves through trickery, and Odin would lay it onto the funeral pyre of his dead son Baldur, whom Loki killed by trickery.

And as for Huginn – he enjoyed the feeling of being back on the Allfather's shoulder. For as soon as they were outside the fortress walls, Odin cast off his Grimnir disguise, and Muninn flew down and settled on his right shoulder, and the two ravens were reunited. Then Odin fed them both and said to them: "Huginn and Muninn. You are my greatest treasures, my eyes and ears in

Midgard and beyond. Know that I prize you both the same, for one cannot work without the other. Memory unlocks thought, and thought is the key to memory."

Huginn felt the Allfather's love and he was content again. And to this day he still flies about the nine worlds, gathering information for Odin. Occasionally you might hear the beat of his wings or glimpse a dark shadow as he passes, swift as thought and full of knowing.

The Island of Samsey

Eric Kenron

Jalk hummed to themself as they wandered the way to the Lady's house. A raven landed on a dying branch of an old ash tree above them.

"Any news," Jalk mumbled as though talking to themself, "Any news?"

The raven eyed them from the branch. After some thought, it burbled in recognition. As Jalk passed under the branch, the raven let out a murderous scream.

"Ah," Jalk muttered, "I see. I see. I won't be back this way for some years, perhaps. Years, if it goes easy. Never, if it doesn't. Take this. Tell your friend. Off you go."

They handed a small piece of wood like a toothpick to the raven, who took it and flew away.

Gaining entry to the Lady's house was easy if you came as a friend, a lover, a suitor, a supplicant, a compatriot, a worshipper, a diplomat, a relative, or an enemy. She had no problem keeping her enemies close. Sometimes they didn't realize that she suspected their enmity until they went to sleep in her bed and woke up in Helheim. But Jalk was none of those. They would be a student of seithr, and the Lady guarded her magic.

"A wise person knows what to say," Jalk mused out loud, "but a fool is caught unprepared."

They walked until they caught sight of her hall. The Lady's golden gates loomed over Jalk's thin frame, gleaming in the sunset. Jalk stood to one side for a while, muttering incantations into their hood. It was the middle of the night before they were ready. They straightened and banged at the gate to be admitted. A tall, aggressively handsome man in leather pants and a shirt open to the waist answered their banging.

"Be silent and be civilized," the man snapped, "you will not gain entry by howling at the gate like a hungry dog!"

Jalk looked sullen and woebegone.

"I come to beg the Lady's favor, kind sir," Jalk whimpered, "but perhaps you can help me. I only seek a crust of bread and a sip of the Lady's worst mead. But if her generosity has been exhausted today, perhaps you could bring me some tablescraps. Then I'll go on my way with nothing further to trouble you, great lord."

"I can see that you have never heard of us, so I will tell you that there is no lack of anything here. Wains are always generous to others, and implying as you do that our generosity has limits is sheer rudeness."

"I see. I see," Jalk said, letting their smile show this time, "then you will let me in?"

"Enter," the man sighed, "and next time just ask. There's no need to put on a show."

Jalk was shown to the kitchens, where the guard left them in the begrudging care of a sour-faced night baker. As soon as the guard was gone, Jalk glanced around in apparent confusion.

"Pardon me, madam," Jalk whined, "I seem to be lost. Where am I?"

"The kitchens," the baker barked, "as you might guess from the dishes, the stoves, the smells, and the dough. That. I. Am. Kneading. Right. Now!"

She punctuated her words with violent blows delivered to the large, sticky mountain of dough piled onto the counter in front of her. Jalk stepped back as though intimidated. Instead of responding, they watched her work. She kneaded and folded the dough for a while, then used a thin wooden scraper to shovel it all into a large bowl. When it was covered with a towel and set aside, she wet a rag and cleaned her counter. Jalk stepped a timid half-step forward.

"What are you making, madam?"

"*Solskinnsboller*," the baker said with a glare, "The Solstice is in two days, as you might know, and there is a lot left to be done. This place is worse off than the pigpen, even without the filth you tracked in. So if you don't want to be pressed into scullery service I suggest you find another soul to bother."

"Ah, sunshine buns," Jalk said wistfully, "it has been a long time. A long time. I assume they have a different cook add the sunshine?"

"It's just custard," the baker grumbled, "Get out of my kitchen!"

Jalk walked through the doors into the main hall, humming to themself. There were sleepless servants gossiping and making Solstice preparations throughout the building. It was nearly sunrise by the time Jalk found a quiet closet to sleep in.

When they awoke around noon, Jalk changed their face. They made themself look younger, and made their androgyny lean slightly more feminine. They altered their wrinkles to seem thoughtful rather than wretched, and gave themself a full mouth of teeth. They re-wound the dark bandage which covered an empty eye socket – a few things couldn't be helped, but it would suffice. They adjusted the illusions which covered their clothing so that they appeared more like a poor but earnest student than a beggar. They muttered a spell, which gave them a sense of the direction to take and an image of the right door. They took a deep breath, settled into their new role, and went to see the Lady.

There were no guards at the Lady's door. Jalk knew that she had no need of them, since she was equally skilled in magic, persuasion and battle. She could defeat most people before they even knew they had been beaten. Jalk checked their magical wards, and reinforced a few with mumbled words in a lost language. Taking another deep breath, they opened the door.

The Lady sat alone, eating lunch. Her dazzling smile hit Jalk like a punch from Thor. It was all they could do to keep their feet.

"Come in," the Lady said. It sounded like an invitation, but it registered in Jalk's mind as a command. Jalk felt like they were being summoned to court.

"Sit by me, stranger," she purred, "and let me show you the legendary hospitality of the Vanir."

Jalk felt as though they were being imprisoned behind gold bars. They walked closer, and came to an empty chair. They weren't sure there had been a chair there when they first opened the door, but it was there now. They sat. The Lady called to one of her maids. Food and drink were brought out with haste. The Lady held out her crystal cup for a toast.

"Hail, guest of the Vanadis," the Lady said.

"Hail the host," Jalk replied.

They drank, and then Jalk ate, feeling all the while as though they were being mummified in honey. The Lady watched them, amused. She waited until Jalk seemed to be quite absorbed in their food before speaking again.

"Now, dear stranger," the Lady said with a gleam in her cat-like eyes, "I trust you know who I am, since you weaseled your way into my hall and found my door with unerring precision in spite of my wards. So we'll skip my half of the introductions. Tell me about you."

"I am called Jalk, my Lady. As you noted I have some small proficiency with the magical arts, but I wish to learn the art you practice, which you call seith."

"I see," the Lady purred and slid closer to Jalk. She smelled like chamomile and fresh strawberries.

"And who has told you about seith? Only myself and my students know the art."

"I have learned of it through divination, Great Lady. I meant no violation. I am but a poor maker of petty magics, willing to do whatever it takes to become your student."

"We'll see," the Lady said in a way that reminded Jalk of a hunting cat, "It may cost more than you can give."

"I have nothing to give but time, dedication, willpower and intelligence, my Lady. But I have a great deal of all of those."

The Lady pulled an ornate *hneftafl* set from somewhere and set it up without breaking eye contact with Jalk.

"And where did a poor student learn to give so much of themself to a task? I know you came to my door as a beggar, Jalk. I know you annoyed my guard, distracted my baker, and slept in a closet. I know you divined the location of my chambers, and I felt you approach. If you want to be my student, do not lie to me."

"Of course, my Lady," Jalk said with a seated bow, "I will share my story with you as you have shared your hospitality with me. I am an itinerant beggar. I wander the world, seeking magic and stories. It is nothing of note, for I always feel that what I learn is far less than what there is left to learn. I am more often hungry than full, more often lonely than joyful, and more often cursed than welcomed."

They started playing *hneftafl*. The Lady selected the central pieces, leaving Jalk with the perimeter ones. She was the castle, and Jalk was the invader: the inverse of their previous war. Perhaps she realized already – but regardless, this was a good sign. Jalk smiled and made the first move.

"And how did you come to such a state," the Lady inquired as she made her move.

"By my own folly, Great Lady. I sought to be smarter than I was, greater than I was – I got a taste for knowledge and it ruined me. I learned far too late that one should never seek to know everything, for great knowledge causes great pain, and too much wisdom makes misery."

"If you have too much wisdom, why come to me? You seek to learn seith, the highest magic this land has to offer, and you complain about suffering from too much wisdom before we even begin."

"I only meant, my Lady, that I gained more wisdom than I had before, which ruined my enjoyment of any other path. Now I am relentless in my pursuit. I am dependent on it like one who drinks too much strong mead for too long and becomes wasted in body and mind. I got too much knowledge with my very first draught, but every drink makes me thirstier and every bit of wisdom makes my soul desire more."

Jalk's next move threatened the Lady's king.

"You have no understanding of abundance, Jalk. You don't appreciate the ways of the Vanir. Here we know that all things will come to us. We see the cosmos as a generous giver, not as an adversary. Wisdom comes to those who understand its nature, which I think you do not. If you did, you would hold out your hand and wait for it to warm up to you, like a cat."

The Lady easily evaded Jalk's trap, and gestured to someone on Jalk's blind side. A cat the size of a wolf bounded into view. The cat rubbed its head against the Lady's arm. When it turned to Jalk, it hissed.

"Shush, now," the Lady said to it, "No hissing at our guest, whether or not they deserve it."

The cat walked around the Lady's chair and sat on her other side, as far from Jalk as it could get while still being close to the Lady's hand.

"There, Jalk. Do you see the difference in our approaches?"

"Using your own cat to demonstrate is hardly fair, my Lady."

"Nothing is fair, and my point stands. I have won the loyalty and affection of my cats by pursuing wisdom in my own way: with open hands and an open heart. You have already earned their scorn by your way. Who is wiser?"

"The one whose wisdom gets them what they need is wiser," Jalk said with a smirk.

"I have everything I need," the Lady said, returning his smirk.

"Then, my Lady, why did you develop seith? What could such magic give you that you didn't already have?"

"The only thing I lacked was the feel of my hands on the web of Wyrd itself. Seith has given me that, and much more."

"Then you know how this will turn out?"

"I do."

"Then why this game? Why let me seek you and treat me like a stranger?"

"Because it was your will that it play out this way, *Grimnir*," the Lady said while making a devastating move on the *hneftafl* board, "and I lose nothing by playing little games like this."

Jalk stared at the board for a while. Their force was diminished by more than half, while the Lady had lost only two of her pieces. She knew, of course. Good, Jalk thought, that was exactly as it must be. Defeating the Lady in her own hall was impossible, but a constructive loss might get them both what they wanted.

"Then what is the outcome of our game, my Lady?"

The Lady surrounded and took one of Jalk's remaining pieces. Jalk no longer had enough to surround the Lady's king. The game was over. Jalk couldn't hide their smile.

"You come with me to the island of Samsey, and learn seith," the Lady said.

"Thank you, my Lady."

"And when you've learned all I care to teach you, you'll learn my price."

"I understand."

"One more question, Jalk," the Lady said as her smile slid away, "What happened to your eye?"

"A terrible price I paid for my former ignorance, my Lady. Wisdom always costs too much and comes too late."

"To the contrary. I have found that wisdom is always quite affordable for me. It is sometimes painful, but it has never caused me the loss of any body parts that I haven't gotten back."

"My Lady is too wealthy to understand."

"And you are too dangerous. Swear to stay peaceful or the deal is off."

"Very well, very well. I give you my word, my Lady. I will do you and your students no harm while I am learning from you."

"If I were less confident in my powers, I might worry about that limitation. But I accept your word as an oath, and I hereby bind you to it. Now that I am your teacher, you will call me Freyja, or Gondul, or Mistress."

"Thank you, Mistress."

"Do not disappoint me, Jalk. On Samsey, even your life is in my hands."

They left on the morning of the Solstice.

The island of Samsey lay off the coast of Freyja's personal island. It was surprisingly close by, but covered in fog and illusion. Once they docked it was impossible to see more than a few dozen feet of ocean water. At that distance, a pearlescent wall of mist blocked any view of the outside world. Each one of Freyja's students had a small mud and thatch hut of their own, with a bedroll and very little else. Freyja's hall on Samsey was of similar construction but twice as large, with half the space curtained off for her. The other half was a combination of dining hall, classroom and crafting space. Looms, spinning equipment, and other fiber arts tools lined the walls. There was very little space, even for the mere half-dozen students.

Jalk's first lesson had nothing to do with seith. They were directed to their own hut, which had a bedroll, their own loom, spinning wheel, knitting needles, metal fiber combs, and several empty baskets. Freyja's senior student told them that, as the newest arrival, they would be making their own clothes and blankets.

"Very well," Jalk said, "very well. I have some experience with yarn and thread. But I don't see any here. Where do I go to get what I need?"

"Come with me," the student laughed. She showed Jalk the pasture where dozens of sheep grazed.

"Here is where we get our yarn."

She walked away while Jalk glared at the sheep. She returned shortly with an armload of freshly uprooted flax plants.

"And this is where we get our thread," she said as she dumped the entire load into Jalk's thin arms.

"I see. I see," Jalk muttered, "I have no skill with flax, dear lady. Perhaps you could help me with it?"

"I will do no such thing," she replied, "Gondul has warned us about you. We each do our own work here, and no one will help you. All of the instruction you will get will be given to you after the evening meal."

That evening, Jalk learned how to prepare flax by letting it sit in water before winnowing it, combing it out into fibers and twisting them into thread. Since the flax had to partially rot before it was usable, Jalk let it stay submerged for several days while they gathered wool from recalcitrant sheep. Both the flax and the sheep smelled terrible.

"Now hold still. Hold still!"

Jalk tried again to shear some wool off one of the more docile ewes. She turned away. This time, she shat between Jalk's boots as she did. It was difficult not to interpret that as deliberate. They snatched at wool near the ewe's haunches and rushed with the shears in their other hand. The ewe let out a plaintive bleat as Jalk missed their stroke and cut her. Hoofbeats thundered from Jalk's blind side. Before they could move, horns connected with their ribs. They skidded into a fresh pile of sheep shit. A ram stood over them. The ewe pranced away. Jalk wanted to cuss, but their newly broken ribs had other plans. Gasping, Jalk crawled to the fence and used it to help themself up. The ram let them go.

It was a slow and painful walk back to their hut.

The healer laughed at them. Binding their ribs with a poultice and freshly washed linen strips, she explained to Jalk that the sheep had a set way of doing things. Going against their way got you treated like a predator. Jalk was not having it, but the healer continued.

"You must see their world," she said, "They are not like us, but they have their own minds. In their minds, there is order to the cosmos: wool grows, becomes unbearable, and is shorn; but only the way they're used to. We who shear them also feed them, so they feel safe with us. But in order for that safety to be understood, it has to be mutual and it must operate within their understanding of the world."

"I know the hearts and minds of gods, elves and men," Jalk said, "I have traveled all the worlds and seen many things, but you're telling me in order to get wool from a sheep I have to think like a sheep?"

"No, Jalk," the healer laughed, "not like a sheep, but like a shepherd. Treat them like they're important to you."

While they healed, Jalk made some progress on the linen. It was arduous work. They spun flax fibers until they thought their arms might fall off and their remaining eye might go blind. Without wool blankets at night, they still spun in their frozen sleep. By the time their ribs healed, they had accumulated a fair amount of decent linen thread. Freyja stopped by to check on them.

"Welcome, Mistress," Jalk said with a bow and a wince. Their ribs were still tender.

"How is your thread coming along, Jalk?"

Jalk showed her. They gasped in pain as extending their arm stretched their torso. Freyja took the spindle full of thread. She pulled several feet of it off the spindle and held it against the sunlight.

"Jalk, this looks like you did it in your sleep."

"Yes, Mistress. I realized that I was making the motions of spinning while asleep, so I made myself useful and kept the spindle in my hands while I slept. I have twice as much thread because of it."

Freyja sniffed contemptuously.

"Do you plan to treat all of my arts with such disdain," she said, still looking at the inconsistent fineness of Jalk's thread.

"No, Mistress. This was only to make up for the loss of time as my ribs healed."

"A stupid mistake leads to more stupid mistakes," Freyja said. Without any change in her expression, she threw the entire spindle into the fire.

"Make it again," she ordered.

Whatever else could be said for Jalk, they were a very fast learner. With the healer's advice they were able to master the right approach to the sheep, and soon had enough wool to make blankets and wool cloth for a new cloak. The linen for the under-dress had to wait a little longer, for a new batch of flax to be soaked, winnowed and spun. But soon enough Jalk could walk among Freyja's other students dressed in the same dress they all wore. It was finally time to begin.

One evening, nearly two years after Jalk's arrival, they were among the few students selected to stay in Freyja's hut after the evening meal. Freyja led them into a trapdoor set into the dirt floor and down a flight of stone stairs, slippery in the damp darkness. It was blacker than a moonless night in midwinter at the bottom. Freyja spoke an invocation in a clear, musical voice. Ancient glyphs cut into the stone walls began to glow. The glyphs told the story of

Freyja learning seith: how she tricked Odin into killing her three times so she could learn the secrets of death; how she persuaded, cajoled, and outright bought the remaining knowledge she needed from any source she could; and how she blended this new magic with the arts of spinning and weaving as a way to pass them on.

The glowing story-glyphs illuminated nine large baskets of wispy, insubstantial thread. Freyja talked them through the contents of each basket in a low, reverent voice. They contained the stuff of existence itself: Form and Void, Stasis and Change, Life and Death, sensations, emotions, and all types of experience. Each student took up a basket. Under Freyja's careful guidance they wove miniature fates – each one a single life.

For a while, Jalk was a wolf in the forest, sniffing blood on the winter air. The wolf grew old and canny. But in a desperate year, when tree limbs cracked under the ice and there was no food, he raided a farm. Unused to humans, he paid for his desperation with his life. Jalk was with the wolf until his corpse rotted away in the Spring mud.

For a while, Jalk was a salmon who ended life in the mouth of a bear. For a while they were a hive of bees, thinking in staccato bursts of dance and hexagons. They were a human baby, lost to disease in less than a month. Jalk stayed with that life until the mother's weeping ceased, and two funerals were held. They learned then not to hold each one so long. But letting go of what you have made is a lesson that never comes cheaply.

Jalk had no sense of how long they had been in that cave beneath Freyja's hut. When she called to them all to come out, no one moved. It was as though Freyja was speaking a language none of them knew. Finally, Jalk stirred. The others soon followed. They stumbled single-file up the stairs, full of wordless thoughts and wincing in the sunlight. Jalk was on the next boat away from Samsey.

As Jalk walked away from the dock, they hummed a very old tune. Years of sitting hunched over their weaving eased as they changed shape. Their face became masculine. A long, gray beard grew in. Their handmade dress altered around them, becoming a black tunic and a voluminous dark blue cloak. Two ravens circled overhead.

His transition complete, Odin looked up at the ravens. He whistled. They dropped and landed on his shoulders. One of them coughed up a small, wooden trinket. Odin took it and it grew into a spear.

"I've missed you rascals," he said. He ruffled their neck feathers. Both ravens croaked contentedly.

"Now, what's the news?"

They took turns murmuring years' worth of gossip into his ears. Odin smiled. He had missed the world – but now he found that he also missed Samsey. He turned his spear into a pair of knitting needles. He pulled some dark blue yarn out of a pouch that hadn't existed a moment before, and knitted as he walked the long road home.

The Chains That Bind

Brandon Ketchum

On a dusty plain, a house built with wooden slats nailed together by prayer breaks the monotony of the flat horizon. From the hovel, a song's warbling notes drift out to disappear on harsh winds carrying the first fat flakes of winter snows.

Inside, a battered tube radio stands in a corner of the lone room. The music and lyrics to 'We'll Meet Again' fill the house. Three women at a ramshackle table drink tea from chipped ceramic cups. No fine porcelain or silver service for these simple women.

The middle-aged Mother hefts the kettle. "More tea?"

The young raven-haired Maiden holds out her cup. "Yes, thank you." She turns to the eldest, whose skin is thin as old parchment across knobby bones. "Would you like to polish off the cornbread?"

"Too kind," the Crone replies. She gums at the cake.

After the meal, the Mother snaps her fingers, changing the radio to a rousing jazz number. The Maiden scrunches up her face, snapping her fingers in turn. The jazz morphs into a lilting love tune. The Crone shakes her head at them. Mid-song, the soothing notes jar to a stop, and Wagner's 'Ride of the Valkyries' booms from the radio.

"How dramatic!" the Maiden says.

The Crone considers. "Fitting, though. It is about that time, after all."

The Maiden nods back. "Seems like it."

"Do we really have to?" the Mother asks over the rising notes.

"Can we escape our fate, you mean?" the Maiden retorts.

The Mother considers. "No, I don't suppose we can."

The Crone claps her hands once, the sharp sound and its reverberation temporarily drowning the radio, then rubs them together. "Welp, let's get to it."

Chairs scrape hard enough to create splinters as they rise. The Maiden switches out Wagner's crashing opus for an energetic show tune.

The Crone hobbles and places her chair by the open back door. A ball of twisted metal wire blocks the back porch, so massive it blots out all light. Sitting, she sighs, leans over, and begins unwinding the tangle.

Once the Crone finds the end and gets enough slack, the Mother takes the wire end to the center of the house and feeds it through a spinning wheel. She seats herself and begins to pedal. Soon a refined metal yarn emerges from the spinning wheel, piling up near the front door, where the Maiden sits. She, in turn, takes up the yarn and begins knitting. Links of intricate chain emerge from the clacking needles, forming a coil on the front porch.

As the coil grows, a gust of frigid wind blasts through the front door. Swirling snow blots out the sun, a funeral shroud over the world.

The Maiden flexes her fingers, barely pausing in her knitting. "Temperature's dropped. Snow's really piling up out there." *Click-clack* go the knitting needles; new links land *clink-clank* upon the growing chain.

"Supposed to be a record-breaking winter," the Mother says. She pedals to a measured beat, not so fast as to overcome the Crone's efforts, but fast enough to supply the Maiden's.

"More like three winters together," the Crone says, cackling as her gnarled fingers move nimbly through the rough wire.

The Mother smiles grimly. "More like all winters at once." A shriek of wind emphasizes her words.

"Poor Father," the Maiden laments.

"Poor Father," her partners echo.

The Crone clears her throat, changing the music to an instrumental number full of mournful woodwinds and slow, deep brass notes. The light in the house dims.

An audible snap comes from the ball of wire. The Crone can now see a sliver of winter sky between the ball and the porch roof. An animal howls in the distance. "That's one," she exclaims.

The two other women nod in satisfaction, bent to their given tasks. The Mother arches her back while continuing to pedal. Yanking and tugging the metal wire abrades the Crone's mottled skin, drawing blood at points. She ignores the pain. The Maiden shivers at the cold. At least the chain is piling ever higher, creating a windbreak.

"Maybe the weather will slow those wild beasts, keep them from stirring trouble," the Mother says.

"Don't be daft," the Crone scoffs. "Nothing can slow them."

"Not now," the Maiden agrees.

"Not ever," the Crone adds. "Never again."

"Poor Father," the Mother laments.

"Poor Father," the others reflect.

The Mother clears her throat, and the radio commences a passionate instrumental that at once fills the heart with hope and evokes a certain sadness. One moment, the notes inspire awesome imagination, the next plunging into depths of misery.

Now the Crone has so reduced the ball of wire that she sees beyond the porch to a massive mound of snow half the house's height. Another snap reverberates from the ball of wire. A trick of the wind playing over the drift evokes a hiss. She shrugs and calls over her shoulder, "That's two." Her partners nod in satisfaction.

A telegraphic series of beeps cuts the music off, and a tinny male voice comes on the radio. "Harold Hermod here, bringing you dire tidings from the Rainbow Radio Network. Crime rates are up all over. Folks are afraid of going out at night. People are panicked in the streets. Now, it's worse, because War is coming. Yes, War, with a capital W. A War to End All Wars. *The* War. The humdinger, folks, the big whammy. Troops are mobilizing, factions gathering, preparing for an epic clash." Harold Hermod continues, but the women stop listening.

The Maiden tugs her mouth into a half-frown, half-smile. "Isn't there always a war?"

"A way for insecure men to measure their valor," the Mother sniffs.

The Crone hoots. "And women. Plenty of vainglorious women, raring for a fight."

"Mr. Hermod never fibs, or stretches the truth," the Maiden puts in.

"A War to End All Wars," the Crone says.

The Maiden shakes her head. "A War to end us all."

The Mother coughs. "Time is short."

"Poor Father," the Crone laments.

"Poor Father," mirror the others.

All three pause at their tasks to look to one another. "Poor Everyone."

With feverish intensity they resume, working up a heavy sweat despite the frigid air. The spinning wheel is a blur, the sturdy wooden contraption whining as the metal spins. The Maiden's needles clack rapidly, like swords in a duel. In the back of the house, the Crone's bones creak as she unfolds wire. Music, smooth music, pours from the radio, a waltz to lighten the collective mood on the other end of all those millions of radio sets. The Mother's foot taps up and down faster than the 3/4-time rhythm.

A snap louder than thunder, and the Crone straightens the last kink from the metal wire. From the horizon, cresting the mountain of snow now dwarfing the house, a cruel and mocking laugh emanates. "That's three."

The wire whips as the last of it whisks through the spinning wheel. The Mother rises and stretches her back. The Maiden's needles spill the last of the fine chain, and the pile obscures the doorway, filling the porch and cutting off the wan light.

"Welp, we're finished. *The chain* is finished," the Maiden says as she rises.

"Everything's finished," the Mother agrees.

The Crone claps her hands with a thunderous boom. The radio goes silent. "Yggdrasil has fallen. The World Tree is no more."

"Poor Allfather," the Maiden laments. "Forgive us, Odin."

"Poor Gods," the Mother laments. "Forgive us, Asgard."

"Poor Midgard," the Crone laments. "Forgive us, world of Men."

They come together in a circle, hands clasped, eyes clouded. Words flow between the Norns, as if spoken by each all at once, if they are even spoken aloud.

"We've broken the wolf, the serpent, and the trickster's chains."

"Woven a new chain."

"It will hold."

"Odin is chained."

"Can't fight."

"Can't rally his valiant einherjar."

"The warriors of Valhalla will be too late."

"Odin is helpless."

"Not for long."

"Long enough."

Howls echo everywhere. "Unchained Fenrir will swallow them all."

Hissing overcomes the howls. "Unchained Jormungand will flood the land."

Laughter drowns Midgard. "Unchained Loki will sail to the world's end."

"*Ragnarök*! *The end of the world*!"

The Norns' eyes clear, and they gaze sadly at one another.

"Come," the Maiden urges. "The age has died."

"The world has died," the Crone corrects.

"*All* is dead," the Mother exclaims.

The Norns each shuffle to one of three unoccupied corners and take up packed carpetbags. Turning to the room, they share a bittersweet smile.

"Wish we could have returned to Jotunheim before the end," the Crone says, wiping at a tear. "I do miss it so."

The Mother drapes an arm over the woman's stooped shoulders. "Such a beautiful hall we had there, beside the Well of Fate."

"I wish I remembered it better," the Maiden admits. "I get flashes of sunshine and laughter, but little else."

They gaze from a house held together by faith and fate, a house beset by lashing winds, half-buried in snow. They step onto the front porch. Beyond, the plain gawps, empty and black, signifying nothing, a lack of matter. Midgard is no more.

"Sunshine's gone," the Mother notes.

"Hmm. Will there be a re-birth, do you think?" the Maiden asks. "Like in the newer legends?"

"Or," the Mother says, "is existence finished, as the old legends fate? As *we* fated?"

"Either way, we get to retire," the Crone says.

A cascade of cackles and chuckles. The Norns fall into each other's arms, laughing and weeping.

Clashes of weapons reverberate through the heavens. Upon the Bifrost Bridge, Fenrir swallows Odin and his einherjar. At the gates of Asgard, Thor slays the serpent Jormungand, but, poisoned, walks only nine steps before falling dead. Loki sails on a ship crafted from the fingernails and toenails of fallen warriors to finish the gods off, from thence to sail into the darkness.

As one, the Norns straighten, clutching their carpetbags, and step into nothingness, swallowed by the void.

From inside the collapsing one-room house, the radio kicks on. "We'll meet again…"

St. George and the World Serpent

Stephen Kotowych

James crashed through the heavy leather flap across the officer's dugout door, laughing as he fell to the rough pine board floor. His Brodie helmet clattered away, and a spray of trinkets flew from his pockets: some French coins; his good craps dice; spare rounds for his Lee-Enfield.

His small holy medal of St. George skittered to a stop against the polished boot of another officer playing a battered upright piano.

"Are you drunk, lieutenant?" said the officer, without turning or stopping his playing. The piano was dusty and worn, its keys yellowed and chipped from years of use.

"Yes, I am," said James, rolling to his back. He knew that tune – what was it?

James lifted a hand to shade his eyes against the kerosene lamps that bathed the dugout in amber. The oily light was dazzling after the nighttime darkness of the trenches.

The walls and roof were made of logs; the central support column was a thick tree trunk, still covered in bark. The cramped space was cluttered with make-shift furniture, a field radio, rolled maps. A fire crackled in a black potbelly stove.

James thought he knew all the dugouts along this stretch of trench but had no memory of this one. The place smelled of mud, the kind that clung to boots and seeped into clothes, a reminder of the trenches just outside. A faint hint of old beef lingered in the air, the smell of rations that had been sitting too long.

A shell whistled and exploded somewhere overhead, rattling a cascade of dust from the timber ceiling. James laughed. That one wasn't so close. After two years at the front, he could tell which incoming rounds needed worrying about.

It was Wagner, he realized. *Fantasia in F-sharp Minor*, maybe? He decided to lie there on the floor forever and smiled.

He didn't realize the music had stopped until the piano player loomed over him.

"Sir!" James said, recognizing the officer's insignia. He scrambled upright and came to swaying attention. The floor was sliding out from under him, he was sure. Stumbling drunk into a general's dugout? Men were shot for less.

The general wore a patch over his left eye and appraised James coolly with his right. "Well, if you're staying, close the flap. Remember your light discipline! You'll just give the Jerrys something to aim for."

James, uncertain for a moment, pulled the flap back across the door, drowning out some of the war outside.

The general offered James a seat at a low stool beside a small pine table. The table was roughhewn, like the floor, but the linens were exquisite, reminding James of Balliol College high tables he'd attended.

From somewhere the general produced a cut glass bottle and two blue-and-white Delftware teacups. He poured honey-brown liquor into each.

"I can't imagine what home-brew swill you've managed to get your hands on," said the general, "but officers should have more self-respect." The delft made a sharp *tink* as they toasted. "So will you tell me what's got you in your cups, or shall I guess?" James finished his drink, and the general poured him another.

"It's the push tomorrow, sir," said James. There was no sense in hiding it. Any fool could guess. "Just working myself up for going over the top."

"Isn't that why you wear this?" The general dangled the St. George medal by its chain. "'*Our ancient word of courage, fair Saint George, inspire us with the spleen of fiery dragons!*'"

"Yes, well…Shakespeare aside, sir, I haven't found it a source of much comfort," James said.

The general released the chain and for just a half-second too long the medal seemed to hang in the air, lingering as if stuck, before jangling to the table.

James blinked profusely, wondering how strong the general's liquor was. He couldn't place the flavour. It was thick and sweet, but wasn't brandy, as he'd expected.

"No answer to your prayers?" asked the general.

"I'm worried I had an answer, sir, and that it was 'No.'" James sighed. "Do you believe in God, sir?"

"In my own way."

"I was taking Divinity at Oxford before all this," said James. "Don't think I could go back, now."

"Lost your faith?"

"Just not sure I can look it in the eye any longer." He put down his teacup. "If I'm to love my enemies and pray for those who hate me, how the bloody hell am I supposed to go kill the Hun?"

"There have always been Christian soldiers," said the general. "St. George. Joan of Arc. A Roman centurion converted at the foot the Cross."

"Yes," said James, reconsidering his teacup. The design was hard to make out. Something Dutch, probably. "But I can't help wondering whether they've got it all wrong. Can you claim to follow the Prince of Peace if it's your job to kill people every day? 'Those who live by the sword', I keep thinking."

The general smiled. "You've finally figured it out, have you?"

"Sir?"

"The secret at the heart of war: it is a *pagan* province and delight. We must repay our enemies' hate with hate, blood with blood. We must glory and revel in warfare!"

James shifted in his chair. "Well, sir, I'm not sure about that, but—"

"Come now!" said the general. "You're not drinking to drown your fears, but your *guilt*. Your guilt in liking war, in *loving* it. You've been taught such feelings are wrong, but you know how your heart sings in battle. Don't deny it! I only have one eye, but it pierces the hearts of men."

James opened his mouth to protest, but no words came.

"You've not been Christian for some time," said the general. "Out there, in no-man's land it's not St. George you've called on, or your desert god. You and your ancestors belonged to *me* for a thousand generations before the Carpenter arrived in these lands. And it is on *my help* that you have called in the secret of your heart."

The room swirled and spun. James squeezed his eyes shut, nauseated, until it stopped.

He now sat on a chain mail-covered mead bench at the end of a Viking hall that stretched away into darkness. The potbelly stove was a great blazing fire pit; the dugout's support pillar was just one of dozens deep-carved with runes and supporting a high, gabled roof of shining shields. James's teacup was a drinking horn.

The general was transfigured into a tall, bearded man in a wide-brimmed hat and dark blue cloak, a traveller's staff in his hand. His good eye, blazing like the sun, fixed on James.

"You've not called on me by name," said Odin, "but you've felt the tug of something else on your soul, the ancient allegiance of your forefathers, James Osborne – James Ásbjørn. The Bear of the Aesir! It is in *me* that you have trusted."

James fought to convince himself it was a dream or some bad liquor, but the feeling of the chain mail, the scent of roast boar on the air.... The hall felt too real for a hallucination, and too familiar. He'd read all the Norse myths as a child, of course, but this was something more.

Something that ran in the bones.

Even Odin didn't overawe him the way he expected an angel or demon might should he chance to encounter one. Odin seemed more an old friend James had simply never met or spoken to before.

The hall twisted away from James again, and he grabbed hold of the mead bench. His mind told him that he wasn't moving, but his body cried out at the pull of centrifugal force.

"Wh-what are you doing here?" James said, now back in the cramped dugout in France.

"Recruiting," said Odin, again the general. He poured them each another drink. "Mead," said Odin, holding up the bottle. "From the teats of Heidrún herself."

James grabbed the teacup with both hands and threw back the liquor. Setting it down again, James finally made out the design: not some pastoral Dutch scene after all, but blue-and-white men with swords, in battle. And they were *moving*. James pushed the cup away.

"What do you mean 'recruiting'? For the British side?"

Odin laughed. "For *my* side. Sometimes I am here," he said, pointing out his British uniform, "and sometimes I am there." Odin's appearance slid away in an instant and he was dressed as a German commander.

James cried out and grabbed his head. It *hurt* to watch Odin's transformation, but it happened so fast that like a cut from a sharp blade the pain took a moment to register.

"The Allfather can be many places," said Odin, "and be many people." James opened his eyes as the pain passed, and the British general sat there again.

"There are many men on both sides whose hearts long for glory and who pray to me for aid, even if they can't admit it to themselves." Odin unrolled a large map across the table. The British lines were in blue, the German in black. Red arrows stretched between the trench lines; the next day's date was written beside them.

The big push.

"I see to it their longing for battle is fulfilled, so the stouthearted can join my glorious dead in Valhalla."

James counted four arrows pointing to the German lines, and four coming from them, colliding in no-man's land.

"You've— you've given both sides orders to attack," James said. "This is monstrous! It will be a slaughter. Hundreds – *thousands* – will die for, for *nothing*. For a few hundred yards of mud!"

"It's no concern of mine what they fight for," said Odin. "The petty aims of your kings and ministers don't interest me. I play at a more serious game: Ragnarök."

"Ragnarök? No, stop!" James said, kicking over his stool as he leapt up and stalked about the dugout. "I can't listen to this. I'm a *Christian*. My God! It must be – be *blasphemy* to even talk to you."

"*Your* god, your *god*..." Odin sighed. "*You're* the one who stumbled into *my* dugout. And didn't you say there wasn't much conversation between you and—" Odin nodded skyward. "Are you sure you're really on the best of terms?"

James stopped pacing.

"You have the heart of a warrior, James: one that rejoices in battle; in the thrill and power of taking an enemy's life. What do you think He will make of a heart so full of pride and murder? So much *uncertainty* with this god of yours. Can you really be sure where He will send you, at the end?"

James reached out a hand to steady himself against the piano. Every doubt he'd had about the fate of his soul all these years ago came crashing back.

It hadn't been what he expected, going over the top that first time. The other men in his squad, just as green as he, huddled terrified in the trench in advance of the whistle to start the charge. Some vomited, others wept. But the moment took James back to a summer hayloft and an eager servant's daughter, and the same giddy anticipation as before his first lovemaking.

Back in the trench hours later half those green men were dead and James's guilt at how much he'd relished the experience was crushing. It wasn't how a good Christian ought to feel after killing men, was it?

The first time he'd shot and killed a man from a hundred yards; when he fought hand-to-hand with that German and bayoneted him through the ribs; when he charged that pillbox with only his pistol; when that platoon of Jerrys begged to surrender to him, having watched him kill so many of their comrades at close quarters. It had all been...*intoxicating*.

It was the only word that came close for James, if he was honest with himself. After battle, colours seemed brighter, food tasted better. Death made life more alive! But always the guilt followed, and the dread.

God help me, thought James. I do truly love it. Does that mean I am damned?

"And you?" said James. "What would you have me do?" He sat back down at the table.

"Embrace the calling of your heart," said Odin. "I need men like you with me in Valhalla, ready when Ragnarök comes. The grey wolf ever watches our halls, James. Loki has escaped his prison in the roots of Yggdrasil, and that has set events in motion. Ragnarök could come tomorrow. It could come in a hundred years. But the days grow short, and I need an army."

James thought a moment. "And if I, what? Embrace the old ways? Can you – Will I live? Through the war. Do I make it?"

In Odin's utter stillness James had his answer.

He was surprised that relief outweighed his sadness. There was some part of him, he realized, that never expected to make it home. He'd spent two years burdened every moment with *if* and *when* and didn't understand how exhausting it had been.

It would be tomorrow. During the big push.

"The skein of your life was tied off by the Norns long ago," said Odin. "Not even I can change that. But could you really look forward to dying as an old man in bed, with all your long years paling next to the thrill of battle? Knowing you were doomed to Hell at the end of it all for your deeds of glory? I can return you to life, in the flower of youth, feasting and fighting until the end of time in Valhalla."

James put his head in his hands. Everything was upside down.

He wondered whether God would forgive him. He had no priest to grant him absolution in his final hours. Would God judge his soul already too black, too stained by murder and bloodlust?

James wondered, too, about the promise of Valhalla. What would it be like to feast and battle with all the great warriors of history until the end of time? Would he be happy there? There would be no hope of ever meeting his departed loved ones again in heaven. But what if he didn't merit heaven at all?

"No," said James in just more than a whisper. He raised his head and looked Odin in the eye. "I can't abandon my faith. I can't. I can only hope and pray that God will forgive me my sins when I go to meet him."

"Will your desert god still forgive though you have no sorrow in you for your deeds?" Odin demanded. "You *revel* in death, like your berserker ancestors of old. Bear of the Aesir! It strengthens you – sustains you!"

James had no answer. Odin wasn't wrong, and salvation seemed a gamble. But to cast his lot in with this strange god? God, it was said, was a jealous god. First Commandment, and all that. Perhaps rejecting the Allfather's offer counted for something. Perhaps God would be merciful after all. He had to trust to hope.

"I can't. I *won't*," said James. "I'm sorry. I want no part of you or your Valhalla."

Odin pushed himself up from his chair, growing impossibly tall for the cramped space, until he loomed over James like the World Tree itself. His good eye blazed to life, its unbearable brilliance drowning out all other light in the dugout. James shut his eyes tight and craned his head away, fearing blindness.

"The friendship of Odin is not so easily cast aside!"

James toppled backward, rolling to his belly once he hit the ground. Even though clenched shut, his eyes ached from Odin's piercing light. The dugout pitched and tossed like a ship at sea, and James dared not stand. He clawed his way across the pine floor in the direction of where he thought the door might be. "I don't want your friendship! Leave me in peace!"

The dugout and the whole of the earth rumbled as Odin spoke. "Go then! But pray you do not come to regret your words when next you call on Odin's name."

* * *

James didn't sleep at all that night. After finding the door and hurling himself back into the mud of the trenches, he put as much distance between himself and Odin's dugout as he could.

Near dawn, when his weary mind began to doubt all he had seen and heard in the night, he'd considered going back to find the dugout and confirm his experiences. But he held back. There would be no dugout, he knew. As if it had never existed.

Instead, James spent the night in prayer. He prayed for the intercession of every soldier-saint he could think of. He said rosary after rosary, and more Our Fathers than he could remember. They were prayers for forgiveness, and for salvation. He didn't know what the answer would be.

Sound like the distant rumble of thunder, and shells howled overhead toward the German lines. The rolling artillery barrage to soften up the enemy. The push was on. James lined up at the nearest trench ladder and was the first man over the top when the whistle blew to signal the charge.

Better to get it over with quickly, he thought.

He and the men with him advanced at a walk over broken, muddy terrain long since chewed up by artillery. The rotting bodies of dead soldiers, dead horses, and the shattered hulks of abandoned equipment lay all about them.

They'd only covered forty yards when the German counterattack started. Machine gun fire zipped past James with unearthly sounds. All around him soldiers fell dead.

James mucked his way to the crest of a small ridge and saw Germans advancing toward him. He stood transfixed, recognizing one: a mustachioed man wearing an eye patch.

Odin dropped to one knee, aimed, and the next instant James was spun around and knocked off his feet by what felt like a horse kick to the chest. He tumbled backward into the bottom of a shell crater, sliding up to his waist in fetid, icy water.

James cried out in agony as the horse kick resolved into the sharp pain of a rifle shot. Dark, steaming blood oozed from under his tunic, mingling with the reeking muck covering him.

Half-forgotten stories from James's childhood came flooding back. In them, Odin always betrayed his favourites so that they would take their place in Valhalla: Sigurd slain in his bed by a greedy brother-in-law. Hengest and Horsa betrayed by their own men. Harald driven into the thick of his enemies by Odin himself, disguised as the king's charioteer.

The German shelling was getting closer now. Plumes of dirt erupted into the air over the lip of the crater with the *thoom* of each shell burst, marching ever closer to the British trenches.

"Gas! Gas!" came the cry.

Sure enough, yellow-green tendrils of poison gas crept over the rim of the crater, reaching out for him like eager fingers. He coughed hard, and with a grim smile spit frothy blood from his mouth.

He might not last long enough for the gas to get him.

The poisonous haze mingled with the smoke of burst shells and obscured the battlefield like a drawn curtain. Vague shapes coalesced in the deadly fog.

They were the merest suggestion of form. They might have been female; they might have had wings. They lingered and seemed to embrace the bodies of the dead, before lifting away and disappearing back into the fog.

James laughed again, though it was agony to do so. It was gallows laughter of a man who knew he'd been outmaneuvered. The Allfather had been right about him and would not be denied.

For in that moment only anger and hatred – not love – for Odin filled James's heart, and made him wonder whether it was with Odin that he truly belonged. Perhaps Valhalla was a just fate, with its eternal battle and toil, instead of some restful heaven with the righteous.

James's ears perked up as the screech of a single shell suddenly stood out above the din of the assault. Something about that sound…James arched his head back, scanning the sky. Where would it land? It would be close.

Under the shriek of the shell, he could hear the faint strains of piano. It was the same piece Odin played before, but James had been wrong about the title. It was Wagner, yes, but not the *Fantasia.* It was Siegfried's funeral march from *Götterdämmerung* – the Twilight of the Gods.

With the shell screaming towards him, James drew a deep lung of acrid air for what he knew would be his final cry for help. But would he call upon Our Father or Odin Allfather?

"O—!"

Odin in the Land of Fire and Ice

Andy McLarnon

"How could this have been allowed to happen?" boomed Odin, slamming the table with his fist. Everyone looked alarmed as the whole building shook. The prime minister rushed over to the window and looked at the surrounding area.

"Unusual to have a sudden earthquake in Reykjavik with no warning. Why did nobody from the meteorological office warn us?" The prime minister fired the question at an aide in the corner, who immediately pulled out his mobile phone. She turned back to Odin who was looking furious.

"You know we are opposed to fossil fuel extraction from our land and coastline. But these contracts were signed years ago, before my party was in office. Our lawyers have been over them and we have explored every legal option."

"It is ridiculous that you cannot stop the drilling and refinery being built in the country you govern."

"My predecessors granted the rights when the oil reserves were found in 2002. We are still working to put a stop to it, but the legal team is not hopeful."

"I don't understand why the refinery site is so far from the shore, near Keldur. They are building a pipeline that will go all the way from the drilling rig near Skeiðflötur across the land and round to the refinery site."

"Probably the land was sold cheaply. But yes, they were given rights to build the pipeline and roads that will spoil the area." The prime minister frowned. "I have asked my ministers for a progress update on the construction. It seems they have started but not got very far."

"I'm sure there is a way to stop them," Odin stroked his thick grey beard.

"We appreciate what your company does, Odin Borrsson, it is very helpful to have the leading global providers of renewable energy here and I share your passion to limit the use of fossil fuels. But I can't simply block the activities of a company that has been sold legal rights to extract that oil. Also, the scheme has substantial public support, which is strange, probably driven by an extremely successful social media movement. As you also run a global media organisation, could you influence the narrative?"

"Hmm, it wouldn't do for me to interfere with the editorial process. But it is important to support the right thing." he mused.

"Yes, I'm sure your people will see what is for the best."

"How about tackling the company on safety grounds?" Odin looks at the map. "The refinery site is at the foot of Hekla. An eruption could wipe out the oil refinery there. And the pipeline runs right across the runoff zone for any *jökulhlaup* pouring from the glacier in the event of activity from Katla. The flooding could rupture the pipeline and cause an environmental catastrophe."

"I believe the company has carried out appropriate due diligence, but we can get our ministries to review those issues."

"I believe nature often finds a way. Thank you for your time, prime minister." Odin said as he swept out of her office.

* * *

In his top floor office in a converted geothermal water storage facility on the edge of Reykjavik, crowned with gleaming solar panels that were more statement than practical, Odin stood looking out towards the mountains to the west of the city. In the corner of the expansive room, was a pile of furs upon which lay two large, white wolves.

"I need to know what's going on. What's everyone saying? Hermod, have you got hold of my best journalists?" he asked his assistant.

"Yes, of course. Huginn and Muninn are on videolink. I'll get them on screen now." A few seconds later the two journalists appeared, both with jet black hair and dark, intense eyes.

"So, tell me, what have you learned?" Odin asked.

"They are building a rig in the sea south of Vik and Skeiðflötur, which looks like a pretty substantial operation. The oil is pumped along the pipeline across the surface of the Reynisfjara black sand beaches, then between Mýrdalsjökull and Eyjafjallajökull glaciers, up to land east of Keldur and south of Hekla." explained Muninn.

"How much progress has been made?" Odin asked.

"Not too much. No drilling has started, and I don't think they have started building the rig. The pipeline has been started from the seafront across to the foot of the mountains. The foundations of the refinery have been laid and several large buildings are under construction," Muninn continued. "There is surprisingly little opposition thanks to the vigorous social media campaign."

"Of course, we can counter that," Huginn interjected. "I've got hold of some pretty damning documents. The landowner of the place they are building the refinery died suddenly after a year of refusing the company access to the land. The family business suffered a sudden sharp decline and they had to sell, and then left Iceland. The former government official who awarded the contract moved to a large château in the south of France shortly afterwards. The building contractors have a very questionable safety record, and they are planning to dump toxic wastewater into the Markarfljót river."

"OK, get that story out there. Promote it as much as possible," Odin said.

"Right, I need to see for myself what's happening. Aerial survey." Odin strode out of the room and closed the door behind him.

Hermod watched from the window until he saw the familiar sight of a huge eagle fly out eastwards.

Odin soared over the volcanic mountains of Hengill around the town of Hveragerði, feeling the warmth from the geothermal pools lift his wings, and then out over the plains south of the town. The blizzards of the previous day had left mountains and plains covered with snow, dazzling in the bright winter sunshine. He proceeded east, followed the Hvítá river northwards towards the majestic sight of the Gullfoss waterfall, where the river cascades down a giant three step staircase. He could see tourists pointing upwards as the eagle-shaped shadow passed across them. Then he turned eastwards towards the splendidly coloured mountains of Fjallabak and south past the snow-covered summit of Hekla to the lands near Keldur where the gash inflicted on the land by the heavy machinery was clearly visible. Huge vehicles were gouging out trenches or pouring concrete. More vehicles were churning up the ground beside narrow roads to deliver building materials. Odin turned eastwards again to where smaller constructions were springing up along the silver pipeline that was being built, stretching from the seashore south of Skeiðflötur. These dramatic landscapes harboured fragile ecosystems that were all part of a delicately balanced environment that he had to stop the humans disrupting in a self-inflicted catastrophe. He knew how he could help the natural world even the odds.

* * *

Pedro Gigante sat opposite Odin across the large, polished wooden table, looking around the room. Lunch was brought in. Plates of sliced, smoked lamb with potatoes and skyr, were placed in front of the two men. Pedro ate quickly while Odin threw the pieces of meat over to the large rug in the corner where the two white wolves leapt up and devoured them. Pedro looked alarmed and he stood up quickly, but Odin held up his hand and the tall, heavily built man lowered himself back into the chair.

"No need to worry about the dogs, these are my faithful pets. Meet Geri and Freki." The wolves regarded the visitor for a moment and then lay back down on the rug. Pedro eyed them uncomfortably but remained in his seat.

"So, Mr Odin Borrsson. Quite the auspicious first name. No relation, I trust?" He grinned at his host, who merely smiled back.

"Tell me, with everything going on in the world, all the major activities going on that don't perhaps totally align with your company's ethos, why are you here taking such an interest in our relatively small project? I would have thought your interests would be more effectively served elsewhere, and it is not as if you can be everywhere at once, hmm?"

Odin smiled and pressed his fingertips together.

"Mr Gigante. My opposition to the continued destruction of this world is universal, whether a relatively small refinery here on the edge of the arctic or a huge oil field near the equator. But here, I think you will find, the land is unwelcoming. Inhospitable. This country is rich in green energy, it does not need you to pipe oil out of the seabed and refine it in the midst of the natural parks."

"Well, I don't see much local opposition. We are contributing to the economy. We are funding numerous social projects. We take our corporate responsibility seriously, Mr Borrsson. The people recognize that." Gigante's smile took on a sneering quality.

"Well, you do have a very active publicity campaign," Odin countered, "But let us see whether the whole truth gets out, the damage you are causing. Good day to you Mr Gigante. Send my regards to your boss".

* * *

"Keep up, old man," Loki laughed as he looked over his shoulder. "Or do I need to summon Thor to carry you?"

Odin quickly caught up. "I had a visit from your minion the other day."

"Illuminating, I'm sure," Loki replied. They stood on a ridge and looked out across the Sólheimajökull glacier.

"Breathtaking," said Odin, as they surveyed the long blue-tinged ice ridges, stretching out into the distance, streaked with centuries old ash from ancient eruptions. "But not for too much longer thanks to your industries. These glaciers are vanishing."

"I thought that is what you got me out here for. I don't know why you are so obsessed. We're just using natural resources. Powering the world through the fuel it gives us." Loki chuckled. Odin glared at him.

"And destroying it in the process. You keep saying you are guiding humanity, helping them but really you are destroying them."

"They are destroying themselves." Loki shrugged. "They don't need any help from me."

"But they are getting it, nevertheless. You've never been shy in helping them develop new ways to destroy each other."

"I'm pretty bored with them now anyway. It's about time to finish them off."

"I don't know about you, Loki, but I'm not ready to rush into Ragnarök." Odin stopped abruptly.

"Well, it won't turn out well for you will it, old man." Loki laughed. "What do the prophecies say your fate is? Swallowed by a wolf? Of course you are in no hurry!"

"And you will fall to my son." countered Odin.

"But I will take Heimdall with me. Bring it on, I say." Loki sighed. "Anyway, we'll see if the prophecies turn out as they say."

"I'm not going to just stand by and let you destroy Midgard. The truth is that even if the prophecies don't turn out as they are written, if there are no people left before Ragnarök, then what becomes of us anyway? We were formed of their fears and hopes, and if there is nobody left, then we just cease to be. Not exactly the grand finale we expect."

Loki ran his fingers through his beard as he considered what Odin said. "Maybe this is how I'm working to bring about Ragnarök. Climate catastrophe, nuclear weapons – I'm giving them the tools, Odin. And my media empires are bringing new ways to sow disharmony amongst them."

"But why hasten it? You have the world's social media giants in your pocket. You can change the narrative. Slow this down. You've always been the comms guy. Look what a great reinvention you did with the religious rebrands, thousands of years ago. Belief went global, even if they used different names for us. Kept us going, for centuries despite you using these different religions to cause conflict."

"Well, I have to have my fun," Loki said with a wry smile. "Lucifer has always been my favourite persona."

The two men reached the edge of the glacier and looked out across the mountains.

"Well, I'm not stopping my little project here in the south of the country." Loki said. "I'm guessing you arranged this meeting to appeal to my good side, and not just to discuss the philosophy of our existence. We will begin drilling in Spring, by which time the refinery and pipelines will be in place."

"Well, as I told your underling, the planet has its means of protecting itself. Until next time, Loki." Odin turned and walked away.

* * *

The small waterfront cafe was almost empty, a clutch of tables and chairs in the middle surrounded by sofas with blankets and sheepskin throws. Rain lashed against the window blurring the view of the churning, turbulent waters shooting across the black sand before retreating.

Odin was sitting in a large armchair, with Geri and Freki lying near his feet close to one of the large radiators that were keeping the room at a cosy ambient temperature. The door opened and two white-haired women strode purposefully into the room, both wearing long grey dresses. A man, also with long white hair and dark grey clothes, followed them in with a weary trudge. He slumped down onto one of the sofas and sighed. Odin stood up and went to greet them.

"Hekla. Katla. It's good to see you again. You are looking well." He turned to the man. "Eyjafjallajökull, I see you're still recovering."

"Yes," the man replied. "It's only been just over 10 years and it takes a long time to regain energy after such a huge eruption."

Odin and the two women sat down at a table and ordered coffee.

"I expect you already know about the problem that Loki is creating down in your area. He will not back down, stubborn fool that he is. We need to take some direct action, which is why I've asked you here today."

"Yes, we are furious about this development," Hekla said with passion.

"Yet again, human politicians make these damaging decisions and are gone when the problems start," Katla added. Eyjafjallajökull raised his arm and nodded in a gesture of agreement.

"I wanted to enlist your help," Odin leaned back in his chair. He looked over at the man sprawled on the couch. "I'm guessing you are not really up to it."

"I'd like to help, but I just can't at the moment," he replied.

"I think two will be enough. The refinery is just below your mountain," Odin said to Hekla. "And the pipeline runs across near where any glacier flood water would run off from your mountain, Katla. An eruption from Hekla with the lava directed to the refinery would end that operation. And the semi-constructed pipeline would be washed away in the floods."

The two women looked excitedly at the Allfather, their eyes blazing.

"Of course! But you know there will be volcanic gasses blasting out when I erupt," Hekla said. "And Katla's glacier will be reduced."

"Short-term pain for long term gain," Odin responded. "In any case, those eruptions will happen anyway, it is in your nature. I'm just asking that you bring forward the timescales. But nothing too major. We don't want a catastrophe. Small and subglacial, Katla, just enough to destroy the pipeline."

Both women nodded and smiled.

* * *

"Reports are coming in of significant volcanic activity in the south of the country. Hekla, which is decades overdue for an eruption, has had a sudden spike of seismic activity and volcanologists have warned of an imminent eruption. Local officials have said that any lava flow would threaten the construction of the increasingly unpopular oil refinery being built in the vicinity. They are also concerned about a similar burst of activity at Katla, raising fears that if the volcano, which is also overdue, should erupt under the glacier, we could see a repeat of the hugely disruptive eruption from Eyjafjallajökull in 2010." The newsreader paused as some footage was shown of the huge plume of ash rising into the sky.

"Shit, this doesn't look good," the foreman said as he stared at the screen in the messroom. The room suddenly shook violently again. "Better find out what the word from the higher ups is." He looked out of the window and saw a large eagle swoop down behind one of the newly built walls. Shortly afterwards, a white-bearded man who he couldn't quite place strode into the room.

"We are evacuating," Odin addressed the room. "Immediately. There are buses by the gate, so go and get on board, and you will be taken to safety."

The foreman and the other workers did not need to be told twice and there was a scraping of chairs against the concrete floor as they rose in unison.

Odin went out of view and resumed eagle form, soaring up into the sky and heading towards the Mýrdalsjökull glacier where he could see the Múlakvísl river was swelling rapidly, the intensity of the flow starting to erode the foundations of the pipeline. Torrents of water started to break up the supports and within an hour the majority of the fledgling pipeline crashed down into the engorged river.

Odin circled back towards Hekla and saw large fissures were opening in the mountain, blasting columns of glowing orange, molten rock into the night sky. Within hours a huge black river, with streaks of fierce orange glowing lava was moving slowly, unstoppably towards the construction site. Odin stood on a cliff overlooking the site and watched as the lava flow edged slowly across the site, buildings bursting into flames and collapsing.

Odin smiled as the last of the new buildings was finally completely covered.

His phone started to ring, and the screen showed 'Loki'.

"I did warn you, Loki. It seems you have some very powerful local adversaries. You are finished here." As Odin spoke, the lava reached the gates to the site and the large sign that read "K-Oil Industries" burst into flames.

The Skinchanger

Parker M. O'Neill

The villagers had little concept of how important they would soon be. Three events of cosmic significance were oncoming, each centered on the village. The first and least consequential was a furious snowstorm. The second, of middling account, was a battle. The third was the meeting of two men, or two gods, or one man and one god, who had not met for many years.

Snow was falling hard already; the blizzard was eager to race ahead to its appointed place in history. Thick sheets had piled up to bury the farmers in their cottages and freeze the livestock in their barns.

The battle had, in some sense, already begun. It was just another exchange in a series of civil wars that had already become unbearable. The armies encamped nearby issued sporadic questing tendrils of men with which to bleed each other. Tomorrow these tendrils would burgeon into quivering masses and collide, leaving the farmers to plow up cracked bones and bodkin arrowheads for centuries.

And the meeting, finally, would begin in the night, below the sagging roof of the village's only public house, where the wind blew against the shutters like something deep and ancient. Odin – lord of the hanged, raven-god – was here to find his lost einherjar.

* * *

Two shadows melted off of the public house. They were nothing more than a pair of black darts, imperceptible in the whirling snow. They shot lengthwise down the road, taking care to eddy and swirl with the gusts of the wind. But there was no need to bother with stealth. Only the land itself watched the interlopers as they flew back to their master.

And they were interlopers; all three of them – the two underlings and their lord. This island would have chewed up and coughed out any other trespasser god like an owl swallowing a vole. But Odin was the far wanderer, the traveler. He had walked the soil of lands beyond counting; he knew how to pass undetected.

The shadows resolved into a man and a woman as they approached their lord.

"The skinchanger is here," the man said.

"In the drinking hall," said the woman. The god to whom they spoke seemed heedless of their words. The two of them, called Hugin and Munin, shivered, though the cold could not touch them. Their heads turned ceaselessly from side to side as though perceiving the presence of some invisible hunter. Perhaps just being on this island was enough to set them ill at ease.

Or perhaps it was the state of their master. Odin was unmoored. He was without anchor; like the sailors of becalmed longships that would cry out for aid and slit the throats of nine captives in his name. Hugin and Munin's report, confirming that his quarry was here in the village, occupied only part of his awareness. The rest of him was elsewhere, lost in the worlds, lost in some other time.

He was the god of magic, the god of secrets. Allfather, Far-Seer. He was rudderless and drifting through what had been and what was yet to come.

* * *

Was that Auðumbla? There, beyond the fence, a great hornless cow stood protected from the snow by an open byre. She stared at Odin with docile eyes. He knelt on instinct. He had not been in the presence of the great beast in centuries, but he owed her a certain fealty. It was she who licked the salt-rocks at the beginning of the universe; she who, in doing so, revealed the form of Odin's grandfather Bori. He pursed his lips, still kneeling, puzzled at how she could have come to be here. He scratched a rune into the ground, one that would keep the cold at bay. It was the least he could do.

Hugin and Munin exchanged a look.

"Lord," Munin said, "We should continue."

He stirred. He had lost himself in memory for a moment. Nothing more than a reverie. And the cow was nothing more than a cow.

* * *

A discussion raged amongst the patrons of the public house. Another body had been found. Savaged, ripped to pieces like the others had been. Opinions were split: the few soldiers there blamed the other side, accusing them in absentia of indiscriminately slaughtering the villagers; others were certain that the killings had been done by a vicious pack of wolves. Still others felt that the murder mattered little compared to the battle, which was crystallizing more and more into an apocalyptic certainty that would swallow the village up. None approached the truth: the killings had not been done by any soldiers or wolves, and the slaughter tomorrow would take place so far outside of town that the villagers would barely be able to hear the screams of the dying thousands.

The villagers were not stupid, only ignorant. They were acting on the information they had access to. Bears were hunted to extinction here long ago. There was no reason for the villagers to assume the impossible, to realize that they were, themselves, being hunted.

The hooded man in the corner escaped their notice. If questioned on the subject, it was unlikely any of them could say exactly when he had arrived, or when the two silent ones by his side had arrived, or what they had been drinking, or if anyone had seen them here before.

But it would have been difficult to ignore the shirtless, red-bearded man in the center of the hall, the one who had claimed a long table for himself and drank more than even the sturdiest villagers. Odin's quarry was thumping the table with an enormous fist to some imagined tune, providing a percussive counterpoint to the arguments of the villagers around him. They seemed content to leave him alone with his thoughts and his ale and his thumping.

Odin had not seen him in two hundred and fifty years.

He rose, drifted across the hall, and sat down in front of the skinchanger Bödvar. The man was not alive, not truly: he had already lived, fought, and died once.

"I recognize you, Grimnir," the man said. The fireplace flickered, the sounds of the other patrons dimmed. He had changed. Gone was the bold aura of a young man searching for any feat against which he could test himself. They clasped each other's forearms, both in greeting and in challenge. His eyes were old; in them was a kind of awareness, a kind of deep sadness that Odin recognized well.

"You should not have left, bearskin." Odin said. A vertiginous double vision seized him: Bödvar drinking mead from a horn in Valhalla, sweat from the day's exertions coursing off of him in waves; Bödvar sitting here so far from home, pensive and sullen and diminished. It was more than a memory, it was almost real for an instant, as though Odin could pull the youthful exuberance out of the past and fix the broken man before him.

"And you should not have followed," Bödvar said. "How did you find me?"

Odin gestured to his two companions, still seated in the corner. "Nothing escapes them for long." It was a lie, or at least an exaggeration; but then he was the god of secrets. And he could show no weakness before this lost berserker. He could certainly not admit that it was nothing more than fate which had brought them together again.

Bödvar grunted. "I expected you sooner, raven-god." He took another swig of his ale, froth foaming around the rim of the mug and spilling into his beard. Another double vision: Bödvar, here, wiping the residue off his chin; Bödvar, tomorrow, blood spilling out of his mouth.

He lost himself in the vision as Bödvar continued to drink. He had been here before, he suspected. Possibly this exact village back in the halcyon days of his people, when so many second sons had coursed across the seas to trade and to take, when Lindisfarne burned and the whole of this land rose in defense of its new god. The pagans here were converted or killed and the ships were turned back and the spirit of the island itself was bent towards his rejection. Only—

It was hard to keep track. Had that already happened, or was that yet to come? Odin was borne on ceaseless currents, eddying whirlpools. He had watched Ragnarök happen so many times, had watched his family slain, had felt the jaws of the wolf close around him. Sometimes he was sure that time was nothing more than a circle: that he was actually living through these events over and over.

"It has been too long, Bödvar," he said cautiously. "Have you been staying here since you left?" Again the vision, again the prophetic view of Bödvar spitting out his lifeblood.

"No. Traveling mostly. Can't stand to stay in one place for too long."

Odin nodded. "I understand."

"Bad luck to be here on the eve of battle. But the Norns have their way with fate, don't they?"

Odin nodded again. Better for Bödvar not to dwell on how Odin had found him. Odin was a war god, a blood god – where battle was, he was there. Bödvar's ill luck was Odin's good fortune.

Bödvar sighed, and in that sound was contained a depth of regret that Odin had not been aware the einherjar could hold. "You're here to kill me, then?"

"I am here to bring you back to Valhalla, where you belong."

"By killing me."

"It would be the fastest method."

The berserker drank deeply. There was such satisfaction in the movement that Odin could almost taste the ale. He wished there was another way. It would bring him no satisfaction to kill Bödvar, who even now he could see training in Valhalla. But was that the past, or the future? He still remembered the first time Bödvar had died, the end of his mortal life. Odin himself had directed the Valkyries personally to carry his soul to the realm of the gods. A shame to have to do it again; to bring the man back to the place he had fled so desperately.

"I won't let you kill me, Odin."

The two of them sat silently together for a moment. The meeting, it seemed, had ground to a halt, with neither of them willing to give what the other wanted. But their encounter was only one of the three consequential events converging on the village; the other two chose this moment to intrude as the door came crashing open.

The first: The storm roared through the open doorway, fierce gusts of wind tearing into the hall, carrying torrents of snowflakes that coated the nearest patrons.

The second: A lone man – half-frozen and red-faced – came tumbling through the door, and the colors he wore, though barely visible through his frost covering, were those of the invading army.

Odin could, in a sense, be blamed for what happened next. The man was nothing more than a lost scout, one who had been blindly stumbling through the blizzard for half an hour, drifting further and further from the safety of camp. He was no threat to anyone, even the enemy soldiers warming themselves by the fire. But Odin had trained Bödvar well in Valhalla. Combat had been baked into his very instincts. The moment the door was flung open Bödvar leapt to his feet. His axe was buried in the man's chest before anyone else could react.

There was shouting, then, and the scraping of a dozen chairs as the rest of them rose in a clamor. Bödvar, breathing heavily, planted his foot on the dying man's torso and yanked the axe out of him. There was that youthful energy in his eyes again, there was the vibrant man who Odin had trained. But had he always looked so tortured? Had he always looked so scared?

He turned, dragging the axe behind him like dead weight. He walked out the door and into the whirling snow.

* * *

It was trivial to find him again. The storm, for all its magnitude, could not hide the einherjar now. The imperceptible rune Odin had scratched onto his forearm was all he needed to track Bödvar as the man wandered north.

Munin ranged ahead, following close; Hugin and Odin trailed behind.

"Lord," Hugin said. "Perhaps we should leave the skinchanger."

Odin snapped back to awareness. "Why would we? He disobeyed. He must be brought back."

"He is unwell. He is battle-sick."

"He has been here for too long. He needs to return to Valhalla."

Hugin nodded, quick and sharp. It was not his place to advise.

* * *

They caught up with Bödvar outside a shack on the edge of the village. Hugin melted away as they approached, Munin was already hidden. Odin made no attempt to conceal himself as Bödvar turned around and drew his axe.

"I will do this no more," he said. His shoulders shook. "We can bargain. I've seen the way your mind wanders. It's your eye, isn't it? You lost it, but you got something in return. I've heard the stories."

The storm stopped around them. They were in a sphere, a quiet space, the raging tempest held at bay.

"And what," Odin said, "did the stories tell you?"

Bödvar grimaced, teeth yellowed against the snow. "You traded it," he said. "You gouged out your own eye and gave it to Mimir in exchange for a drink from the Well."

"What does any of this matter?"

"I know what it did to you. You're losing yourself. Your memories and your prophecies are a sea. You're drowning, and I can teach you how to swim.

"What is there that you know, that I do not know?"

"The trick of skinchanging. I have found a new way."

Odin's interest was piqued. But he was here to bring back the lost einherjar; not to barter with him. "I am not interested in your tricks, berserker." Bödvar cringed away from the word as though it were an arrow.

"Let me show you. It's freedom, Odin. A bear has no time for prophecies and memories and pain. There is nothing but the hunt. You can shed all else."

"It is an escape," Odin said. "Bödvar Bjarki was not meant to live as a bear. Terrorizing the villagers, feeding on them. Come with me back to Valhalla. It will be painless." His vision was split again; he was simultaneously listening to Bödvar and watching as a group of soldiers descended on a village in some other time. Vast craters appeared like blossoming wounds. The land itself groaned at this new indignity.

"Painless? There's nothing but pain for me there." That look was in his eyes again, a man broken by what he had seen and done. The axe glistened in his hand. "Leave now, Odin, and I will let you go. But do not ask me again."

The bubble of sanctuary collapsed around them; the snow came rushing back in to fill the vacuum. There would be no more words.

* * *

There was nothing to be done for Bödvar. He had chosen his path. Odin would have to ask him about his skinchanging trick when they met again in Valhalla.

Freedom from the visions was an intoxicating concept. The knowledge he had gained from Mimir had been useful for a time. But the price had grown too high; the daydreams and nightmares and the times he caught himself unsure of which reality was false and which was true. But was it worse to flee from his pains, or lose himself to them? Was there nobility in his suffering?

It had been this way for so long. Odin was unchanging, static in the way that only a god could be. But Bödvar was, or had once been, human. He was capable of change. He had to be. It was perhaps due to this propensity for unpredictability that when Odin came back to the shed at dawn, Bödvar was ready for him.

The bear came charging out of the shadows. He almost ended Odin with a single swipe. The god leapt backward, instincts rising out of some ancient part of him. There was the battle frenzy, the berserker rage that they both knew so intimately. The pair of them charged, feinted, struck at each other with spear and claw. A microcosm of the horrors that would come with the dawn, when the armies met and fought and killed. Hugin and Munin were high above, awaiting the battle; they were not even aware of the peril their master was in.

This could not be Bödvar's new method; this was no different than the skinchanging he had used in life. It was more projection than transformation. A bear-spirit, a there-but-not-there thing that Bödvar could control. His physical body would be safe inside the shed as Odin wasted his time with the bear. It certainly explained the way the beast tensed and cut him off every time Odin tried to maneuver closer to the shed, the way it growled and hunkered down when he advanced. But Odin was the god of victory. To lose was unthinkable.

Even as his vision splintered, even as a dozen bloody futures revealed themselves to him, he slipped inside the bear's guard.

His spear drove deep into the meat of its shoulder; he wrenched it out and thrust it in again. The great thing collapsed, shuddering. Then Odin spun and kicked down the shed's door, ready to kill Bödvar where he lay, ready to send him back to Valhalla, ready to doom him once again to an eternity of training and fighting and the shedding of blood.

A child sat on the floor of the shed.

She was young, a few years old. Crying. And she was what Bödvar had been protecting. But that meant that Bödvar—

Odin gathered the child in his arms and hurried outside. The thing heaving its last breaths in the snow was something halfway between man and beast.

Bödvar had become the bear. He had done what even Odin could not. He had changed his skin, had become the thing itself rather than merely emulating it. Here was his new form of skinchanging, though it had served him little in the end.

Horns sounded in the distance. The armies had finally advanced from their lines; twelve thousand men would die before sunset. It would be the greatest battle on this soil in generations, leaving scars that the land would not soon forget. But the battle-god felt nothing but regret. Could it be – was it even possible that Bödvar deserved better? That he had fought and killed enough? The man had only wanted stability.

He had to work quickly. An einherjar, even a rogue one, could not keep something from the god of secrets forever. The transformation reversed further; more and more fur was falling away to reveal Bödvar's face. Odin had an incongruous vision, Auðumbla licking clean the salt-rocks and revealing Bori. Odin felt the contours of the shapechanging magic in the dying man's mind. It was warm and smooth and cleansing. Perhaps Bödvar was right, perhaps there was a battle-madness in him. Perhaps Valhalla was not what he needed.

There was a moment of pure lucidity, an instant where he was only there and nowhere else. And he realized what he had to do. He could fix them both at once.

He called to Hugin and Munin, setting the child down in the bloody snow. She began to cry. The spear had been enough to kill a mortal, even enough to kill an einherjar. But Odin could have borne the wounds. It would not be enough to kill a god. He reached again into Bödvar as the man convulsed, his rage and his lifeblood spent.

He took Bödvar out. The essence of the man was glowing softly in Odin's hand. Then, with a deep breath, he drew out his own. He held the two souls in his hands as though weighing them. It all felt distant, dreamlike.

But he was tired, so tired of his burden. Mimir's knowledge had ruined him. So with a heave, he pushed his essence through Bödvar's chest and Bödvar's essence through his own.

* * *

Odin opened his eyes to Hugin and Munin pacing relentlessly in the snow. They were circling the sleeping body of an old man, a one-eyed traveler. The screams of dying men came drifting over the hills. Bödvar would have much to do, but an eternity to learn. Odin hoped he would come to appreciate his new role.

The visions were still with Odin; he couldn't escape them so simply. But—

He changed his skin. He shrunk down, doubled into himself, sprouting feathers. Feet gnarled to talons. Arms stretched out, becoming wings.

Odin tried to speak, and the harsh raven-croak that issued from him was as sweet as song. Here there were no memories, no visions. It was as Bödvar had said – there was only now. There was only the wind under his wings, the beauty of the land so far below him, the shrinking points that marked Hugin and Munin and the new god of secrets.

Einherjar

John Possidente

Fights are on Wednesdays, of course. Odin's Day. Always in the morning, so everyone is fresh. Afternoons are nap time.

We can't watch the fights, and I wouldn't if I could. The three of us dumpy old broads wait in the white corridor by the back door of the health center. We wait for the music to start.

That hall by the back door is plenty wide enough for one gurney, but not two. So we have to line up single file. Hilda, our senior nurse: iron bun and titanium hips, in charge and in front, ready to pull stretcher number one. Kara, the new hire: dandelion head, annoying chirpy voice. Seventy if she's a day, but she still sounds like a little girl. She's leaning on the back of the crash cart, facing me – the crash cart we never actually use, but regulations still say we have to drag it out there with us.

It's too bright, too much blue in the cheap LEDs overhead. I'm standing behind stretcher number two, at the rear. My feet hurt.

Kara's fingertips are resting on her lips like she wants a cigarette, but Finngail Forest Senior Living is a tobacco-free community.

"You have to wear the wings," she says.

Only here a week, and she's trying to tell me what to do. One of *those* kind.

I want to tell her where she can stick the damn wings – *and* the helmet they're attached to – but Hilda was churched and doesn't like that kind of talk. So I try not to use language in front of her. I fail more often than I succeed, but hey. At least I try.

"I'm not a fricking Valkyrie," I tell Kara. "I'm a nurse."

She sighs like I'm one of her too many children (at least five). "Would it hurt you to wear it?"

"Only my self-respect, but you wouldn't know anything about that."

"Leave it," Hilda orders. And that's that – for now. She kicks the lock off her gurney's wheels with one ugly white shoe. I do the same with the one I'm on, or else I'd risk falling behind when we move. "The battle's over. The Wagner is playing. Let's go."

My hearing must be getting worse again. I don't hear it. Small favors. I am so sick of Wagner. They play the cheesy movie version of ride of the you-know-what every Wednesday. Hilda's closer to the exit, so I take her word for it and grab the handle.

The two of them shuffle ahead to lead the way. I count a couple of seconds to give a little head start. My eyes aren't so great anymore. Wouldn't want to run over Kara's heels. Not much.

I give the gurney a shove down the short hall, and we bang through the swinging doors and outside. Here we go, three frumpy old goats in white – two of us wearing winged helmets.

The May sunshine blinds me momentarily, but I know the way. Then the damn horns start up when I'm directly under the speakers: bup-bah budda BAH-BAH.

A short, curved cement path leads from our back door to what used to be the tennis courts, before the residents petitioned and voted. After that, the nets and posts came out. A thick layer of cat litter went down (to soak up the blood). Now it's the Stiklestad Battle Arena. That's also when they voted to change Forest Meadows to Finngail Forest.

Manicured grass to both sides of the path smells like wet summer. Always loved that smell. I've probably rolled fifty old corpses down this path since the Rost Report came out last year, every one of them preventable.

Five seconds and we're driving through the break in the bleachers. We hit the surface of the old clay court and the audience cheers. Here we come, the beautiful warrior maidens to pick up the honored dead from the field of battle and guide them to fucking Valhalla. Except me. I'm here to do the job I trained for.

The stretcher wheels bog and crinkle.

Triage time. Today's fight was scheduled to be a one-on-one match. Over to my left, Mister Thompson's walker is lying cut in two along the singles sideline. To my right, his body is bleeding out into the cat litter about where the service line used to be. I don't see his head right away, and I'm not going to waste time searching. The other girls can handle that. I'm looking for somebody I can do something for.

Mister Davis is lying in a gritty pool of blood right on the center line. I didn't see him at first, because there's a chromed shield over him. Some idiot from the audience must have thrown it. Token of honor or some such nonsense. The sun glare off it is dazzling.

I damn near run over Davis's foot trying to roll the gurney into place. Grab the levers, drop the stretcher, notice the foot's not attached. Ah, shit.

I find his ankle and tie it off before I try to move the shield. Damn, it's heavy. Must be decorative. None of these dried up old bastards could heft that thing in combat.

Kara and Hilda are dealing with Thompson. Never married, diabetic, gout. Heavy corpse. I'm glad I don't have to try to lift a stretcher with him on it. (Finngail Forest can't afford the nice hydraulic ones the county EMTs have.)

Lucky for me, Davis is a lightweight. Twice a widower, asthma, only one kidney. He screams a little when I roll him onto the gurney. He's trying to fight me off, so I hand him his foot to keep his hands occupied. Then I strap him down and pop the stretcher up to height.

No Valhalla for you today, stupid old man.

It's still a solid clay court surface under the cat litter, so once there's some weight on it, the gurney runs crackly, but smooth. The other two are yelling at me to help them with Thompson. We're supposed to carry off the honored dead first. Fuck that noise.

"Dammit, Erin! Get back here!" Senior nurse or no, Hilda can't run this place without me and she knows it. She won't fire me or she would have already.

I get Davis to the crash center in time to save his life, but not his foot. He's going to hate me for both.

* * *

Thompson's possessions (and his head; Kara found it under the bleachers) go in the body bag to be cremated with him. Like all of them, it's mostly photos.

What's left of his family was here to watch his battle, so they sign a pile of papers and the bus takes him – before lunch, a small miracle – and we don't have to load him in the freezer. The dry skin on the backs of my hands is grateful for that.

Then it's back to the center to clean up.

"Never seen one beheaded before," Hilda says. She's wiping down the table while I restock cabinets. "I didn't know they could do that with the lightweight weapons."

Kara bangs in with a clipboard and a taped-up pen dangling on a string.

"Especially with only one foot," I say. "Do you think somebody in the audience interfered?" I hope so. That would give me a reason to call the police in, maybe put a stop to it for a little while.

"Nope," says girly voice. I manage not to wince, but I clench my teeth. "Davis had one of those new carbon-ceramic axes. Must have cut off the head after Thompson was down. I saw the slice it made in the court."

"After?" I say. "That's cold."

Hilda stuffs her rag into the red biohazard bin. "Probably miffed about his foot."

"So I got the wait list here." Kara waves the clipboard. Applicants still outpace available residences. "Our next contender is – ooh, good name: Mister Savage."

* * *

A couple of days later, I get first dibs on Mister Conrad L. E. Savage, because I'm on the front desk when he checks in. It doesn't hurt my chances that I'm the youngest in the place by five or ten years.

Savage is older than me, but he's charming and he's ambulatory. Mild hypertension, elevated LDL, glass eye, no history of STDs. When the wide-brimmed floppy hat comes off, he's also handsome underneath (for his age). He'd look better with a shave, and I tell him so. He laughs and says to call him Erik.

At our age, you don't waste time. Erik and I spend a few pleasant days and nights together. He shaves off the beard.

Tuesday night, we're sitting out on his tiny, concrete pad veranda with white wine. It's a cool evening, crickets and a few early stars. The meatloaf I brought wasn't half bad for a change. Mellow mood, very nice. Then I make the mistake of grumbling about the next day's fight, loud enough he can hear.

It's another one-on-one. Charley White, an ex-preacher with major depression and a longsword, up against Mister Hanson. Lifelong drinker, ruining his second liver and third marriage. His wife wants him dead and his kids want his money. He's an angry one. Fights with two hand axes, berserker style.

"Erin," Erik says, "I don't understand your opposition to all this." I can tell he's serious, and his face and tone aren't the least bit confrontational or patronizing. The old man is ready to listen.

I try to keep my voice light and civil, else the folks in the nearby units will notice. "It's organized murder," I say, shaking my head, "or suicide. It's just wrong."

"Odin doesn't see it that way." I can't imagine anybody mistaking the disdain on my face when he says that. "You don't believe in Odin?"

"Certainly not."

"But you've read the Rost Report?"

"Yeah, of course." I set my wine glass down on the round cast-iron table. "I just don't believe it. Scientific evidence that Valhalla exists? It's got to be bullshit."

"So all that data, the videos? The sample jars of goat-beer?"

"Easily faked."

I mistake his few seconds of silence for the end of the discussion.

"I've seen it," he says into his wine.

"Me, too." I hold out my fingers about an inch apart. "Stack of paper this high."

"No, I mean Valhalla."

"Let me guess," I say. I turn my chair to face him. "Near death experience?"

There's nothing like that in his record, but he nods. "Call it that."

"You know that an oxygen-deprived brain hallucinates, right? You saw what you expected to see. People used to see bright lights and Jesuses, now they see rainbow bridges and ravens."

He stares out at the hedge for a minute. The road on the other side of it is empty. "That's a good point," he says.

I expected him to argue, so I'm momentarily struck speechless by him being reasonable. My glass is empty, and I don't refill it. I think about going back to my homey little apartment. Staying with Erik tonight doesn't feel right anymore.

"For the sake of argument," he says, "say the Rost Report is a lie."

"I have no problem saying that."

"Then let's look for the reason behind it. Why would anybody invent something like that?" He says it too casually. Something's up. It bothers me that I don't know what.

"Go on." I say.

"How about economics?" Erik puts one elbow on the table and his chin on his palm. He's staring me right in the eyes, and I realize I don't know which one of his is the glass. "Say you have a generation that was really big, too big. There have always been too many of them…us."

Now I think I know where he's going, and I've got my usual withering counter-argument ready.

"They're a never-ending drain on resources, a generation of self-centered, childish, gullible, entitled, arrogant pricks. They melted the icecaps and destroyed half the life on the planet, and now they don't have the decency to die fast enough. What might you do to get rid of them?" He stuck a finger in the air, and the look on his face was almost jovial. "Remember how gullible they are. Would you lie – just a little?"

I reach for my glass, but it's still empty. "We didn't cause all of that." I say. "Our parents contributed, and our grandparents, and maybe even their parents." He opens his mouth, but I keep going. "Yes, we were told and we could have reversed it, and instead we made it worse. A lot worse – but let's keep the facts clear. Anyway, for the sake of argument, you're saying maybe we deserve to be tricked into killing each other."

Erik pours me another, then settles back into his chair. He's trying to hide his smile behind his glass. "I'm saying that, as a rationale for the sort of giant scam you're suggesting, it would make sense."

His reasoning seems solid, but something is nagging at me not to agree yet. "Ends justifying the means?" I say. "That kind of logic leads to all sorts of horrifying things."

"Exactly. So if the Rost Report is a lie, then it's morally reprehensible."

Wait. Is he on my side or not? "Well, yes."

"And out of all the hundreds of people who must have been involved in documenting and publishing and publicizing the Rost results – not to mention the other teams who supposedly repeated the experiments and confirmed everything – not one of them had the ethics and the courage to expose the lie?"

Men and their semantic tricks. "You piece of shit."

"How do you really feel?" He's smiling, but I know when I'm done. I get up to leave. "Sit down," he says, not harshly. "Please. Let me finish."

I sit, but I leave the wine where it is. It's gotten darker. More stars, then the security lights come on with a crackling pop and drown them out.

"So if it's true, it's horrible, and if it's not true, it's horrible," he says.

"Hobson's choice." I think that's what it means, anyway.

"Remember when suicide was illegal? The death with dignity movement?"

"Yes, but—" I begin. He holds up a finger and shakes his head.

"Just listen a minute."

I'm still listening. Just. I'm also imagining I might forget the anesthetic when it's his turn on the table.

"I don't want to die with dignity," he says. "Hell, I don't want to die at all. But if I have to, I'd like to decide how. My way. If that's in a fury of adrenaline and noise and pain, well, isn't that my right?"

I can't help myself. "Live fast, blaze of glory, better to burn out – all that crap?"

"Shit." He chuckles. "I faded away a long time ago." He sips then puts down his glass, and I try not to talk. "Look, maybe this Valhalla thing is bullshit and maybe it's not, but I still think they all," he waves his arms to mean the residents and all the rest, worldwide, "deserve to decide how they die. We all do. Who does it hurt? Nobody."

"Your family, the people who care about you, and who love you."

"Grown and flown, or dead." For just a flicker I see his pain. Then it's hidden again. "Or in some cases, as we've mentioned, happy to see them go."

Maybe it's the wine, or maybe he's a tricky old bastard, but I can't see the holes in his arguments. So I change the subject.

"My job is medicine, not guiding warriors to some testosterone-infused afterlife."

Erik's answer comes quick. "Medicine steals warriors from Odin."

"After all these centuries, he doesn't have enough?"

"It will never be enough." He's staring out at the bushes as if there's something to see.

"Why?"

He takes a long time to answer. So long, I wondered whether he'd fallen asleep with his eyes open.

"Odin is scared," he finally says.

"Of what?"

"The whole thing was foretold: Ragnarök, Fenris, the death of Odin."

"But that can't be avoided. Isn't that how prophecy works?"

"Yes, but maybe Odin wants to die on his own terms, too."

"Good for him." I say. I get up, walk around, and sit on Erik's lap – but just to end the conversation. I'm not convinced.

* * *

First thing in the morning, I'm on the phone to the cops. Erik's coffeepot burbles in the mini-kitchen behind me.

"We've been over this before, Erin," Deputy Tommy says. "It's none of my business what your people get up to."

"It's still not legal, Tommy," I'm staring out at the same bushes as last night, trying not to sound as desperate as I feel. "It's not self defense, and the dueling law doesn't go into effect until July first."

His tired sigh is loud in the receiver. I know he's reaching for the checklist. "Are any of the participants unable to meaningfully consent?"

"No, but—"

"Are they letting outsiders in to watch?"

"Just family and residents."

"Charging admission?"

"No."

"Are they gambling on the outcome?"

"Maybe."

"Do you have evidence of that?"

"No." I hear the clipboard clatter onto his desk.

"Then there's nothing I can do unless something changes."

He's right. His hands are tied. Not that he'd make much of an effort if he could. Tommy's thirty-five, married with two kids, steady job, and they still have to live with his mom. His whole life has been harder because the horde of us passed through this world first.

"Yeah, thanks anyway, Tommy."

Fuck it. I had to try.

I get dressed and out without waking Erik.

The colors are just coming into the world, gently washing away the gray predawn.

My place is on the far side of the community, near the catchment pond. I take the back way, mostly to avoid running into Jack on the bakery truck. Talk your ears off, that one.

When I get to the sundial, I stop and gaze at the dewy lawn between me and the window-walled rehab center. My shadow stretches across it, not quite reaching the glass. I'm taking off my shoes almost before I decide to do it. Then I'm walking in bliss. After all these years, the wet grass still feels just as good. What kind of fool would want to give this up?

I'm walking with my eyes closed, so I get closer to the rehab center than I'd meant to. When I open them, I stop. Mister Franklin's in there. Civil rights lawyer. Gun-shot wound to the spine put him in a chair. Then the Parkinson's ended his career. Still one of the most cheerful, optimistic men you'd ever meet.

I start to wave, but he hasn't seen me. I wonder why he's rolled in this early. Then it clicks that he's alone: no therapist, no assistance. He's parked his chair next to the rack of wood-and-rubber weapons, and he's tossing throwing axes onto the floor a few feet in front of him.

It takes a second for me to process it: he's practicing. There's a human-shaped target set up maybe ten feet away. None of his throws is making it even half that. I almost laugh at the absurdity of it before I see the dead serious look on his face.

A ten-foot throw. That's the required minimum ability to sign up for a fight. Today he's getting halfway. Three months ago, he couldn't even pick one up.

Franklin's fighting to have control over his own body. Isn't that medicine, too?

I carry my shoes the rest of the way, lost in thought.

* * *

A few hours and a few coffees later, I'm lined up behind the gurney again. My feet hurt.

Hilda has her lips clamped tight. Deputy Tommy probably told her I called again. Damn tattletale.

The loudspeaker blares the Wagner and we start moving. I'm wearing the helmet. Kara looks confused.

Good.

Wesley Glen

Chris Shearer

Groggy from the pain meds, Frank Weimer slammed his palm against the end table. He barely felt it. Didn't even notice the pitcher of water he'd knocked to the floor. He'd been searching for his glasses. The pain was a dull burn in his hip going up his spine to about where his ribs started. He groaned.

He lifted the blanket and looked at it. The puckering scar, red, the skin stapled together, the dark bruising. He wouldn't be walking for a while. Not that it mattered.

Frank licked his dry lips and touched the finger where his wedding ring should have been. He had a habit of spinning it when he felt nervous or scared or bored. It was all he had left of Lilian. There were tears in his eyes that made the ceiling blurry and the light run in streaks across his vision.

"I see we're up."

"If you have to be here, get me some water."

Odin stood, took two bold steps across the room, and handed him a glass of water that had seemingly filled itself. "Is the pain bad?"

"My ring's gone."

"What ring?"

Frank flashed his hand, which was black and blue and red from the IV.

"Is it on the nightstand somewhere?"

Before Frank could answer, Odin had moved the few things that remained to make sure it wasn't under anything. He followed that by dropping to his knees and searching the floor. He was lucid today, and that was nice. Recently, Odin had been having more bad days than good.

"Missing," Frank said. "Like the blue guy's slippers and Zeus's glasses."

Odin used the bed to help himself up. He looked old and tired doing it. His long, gray hair hung over his face and eyepatch. He groaned. What he must have been in his youth, back when he was important, back before this place.

"It's not just them. It's everyone. Everyone's missing something."

Odin had a look when he lost his train of thought, and he had it now. He stood at the edge of Frank's bed, this washed out, empty look on his face, and stared into the shadow, as if afraid. The look was enough to discomfit Frank.

"I'll report it," Frank said. Odin was still confused. "The ring. I'll report my missing ring."

"Yeah," Odin said, but his face didn't change.

Not that reporting it would amount to anything. The staff at Wesley Glen had been inundated recently with reports of missing items. Sometimes they were important, like Zeus's glasses and Frank's ring, but most of the time the missing items were like a left slipper or one of the gazillion watches owned by Cronos. The staff didn't have time to look, if they weren't the ones taking them. It wouldn't have been unheard of for the staff of a place like this to be stealing from the residents. He'd seen news stories about just that.

"Help me up," Frank said.

Odin seemed more with it and grabbed Frank's arm to help him sit up in bed. It was a painful process, and Frank gritted his teeth, let out a small cry. He touched the finger again. "I'm not going to let them get away with this."

Odin looked confused again.

"We're going to find who did this, and we're going to get back my ring. If it's the last thing I do, we're going to do it."

Odin smiled. He, like Frank, had never been one to take what life had given him lying down.

* * *

That night Frank cheeked his pain meds and lay in bed until Odin showed. The nurse who'd given him the drugs had turned the TV to the home shopping channel, so he lay there watching people hawking shit he couldn't fathom other people wanting as he waited.

After an hour or so, he began to worry that Odin had forgotten. It was only last week when Odin got into an argument with one of his children – he had so many that Frank couldn't remember which one it had been – in the common room over lunch. Odin hadn't recognized the boy and worse had thought he was an imposter. Odin could be paranoid, and that was getting worse, too. He began screaming in that big voice he had and used his magic to turn a French fry into a sword and had lunged at his poor, unsuspecting son. But Odin was weak now, and the lunge fell short and the sword clattered to the ground and the orderlies grabbed hold of him and he deflated, shivering.

He was Frank's only friend now that Lilian had passed, and soon, he would be only a shell of himself, only there in moments that came and went like the sun on a cloudy day, just like it had been with Lilian.

When Odin did arrive, he did so silently. He helped Frank into a wheelchair. Earlier, they'd discussed places to look. These included the rooms of gods and goddesses known to have committed thefts or to have encouraged theft, the locker room where the orderlies kept their things, and the kitchen by the common area. It just seemed like a good place to keep things that had been stolen. But both of them hoped to catch someone in the act. At night residents weren't forced to their bedrooms unless their conditions demanded it, and most gathered in the common area to watch *Jeopardy* and the rest of the CBS weeknight lineup. Odin and Frank would use this distraction (and the fact that both of them did have conditions forcing them to their rooms: Frank, his recent surgery, and Odin, his Alzheimer's) to perform their search.

They started with the most obvious candidate, at least to Frank: Hermes.

Odin wheeled Frank to his door, and Frank knocked in case he was inside. When there wasn't a response, they doublechecked that they were alone and entered.

Hermes's room was dark, and though neither of them saw well in the dark anymore, they didn't turn on the light. Why? They thought it could draw attention from one of the residents across the way or out in the courtyard and didn't want a Watergate situation. They went through Hermes's closet and drawers. Odin even checked under his bed. There was nothing. Of course.

Next, they went to Anansi's room. Frank stayed outside and kept watch while Odin searched as quickly as he could. The last thing either of them needed was to be caught in the spider god's room.

When Odin came out, he shook his head. He got that far away look again for a second and said something under his breath about Loki. Frank had thought of Loki, but Loki was a bit of a diva. If he were responsible for the thefts, he would have let it be known. It would have been a thing that he used to make that particular visit with his father about him. That was his MO. It was always about Loki.

Plus, he wasn't a resident.

By now Frank's hip was hurting something fierce. Each time Odin turned a corner or pushed Frank's chair over the lip of a carpet, a bolt of pain shot through him. It was all Frank could do to keep from screaming. Odin, always observant, had a sense of this and took those turns and lips as slowly as he could.

The hallways at this time of night were dimmed, with only the small lights near the ceiling lit. Frank and Odin moved from deep shadow to semi-dark in silence, checking the names on the doors beneath the room numbers and doing their best to remember which gods had been associated with theft or collecting rings. Frank, half delirious with pain, wasn't much in this department. Plus, it wasn't his specialty. Odin, however, had an encyclopedic knowledge of every god, of everything, really. Or he used to have it. Frank wasn't so sure anymore.

* * *

Odin left Frank around the corner from the orderlies' locker room in case someone was nearby. Recent budget cuts at Wesley Glen had left the staff numbers low, so it was less likely someone would be there than it would have been a few months earlier. But not impossible. Though currently lucid, Odin had an excuse if caught. Alzheimer's patients wandered. It's why they kept them in their rooms in a locked wing of the building. Maybe the person spotting him would wonder how he got out, but that was unlikely. It's almost impossible to hold a god where they don't want to be held.

Frank was touching his finger again when Odin came back to get him. There was no one nearby, he told him. But the door was locked.

"Of course it's locked," Frank said. "We need to unlock it."

Odin wheeled Frank to the keypad as if Frank knew the code or could use his experience as an electrical engineering professor at The Ohio State University to help him open the door. Frank just looked at Odin, whose face had gone slack again.

"Open it," Frank said.

Odin turned away from him, took a step in the direction of the common room, and Frank's heart sank. Was Odin leaving him? Had Odin forgotten him? What would happen if they found him here? How would he explain being out of his room? How would he explain getting into a wheelchair?

"Odin."

Another step.

"Allfather."

At that Odin turned back around, clearly confused.

Frank smiled because Odin looked frightened. He didn't know where he was. Frank had seen it with Lilian many times, and the best way to handle it was to be kind and explain the situation, explain where he was, why he was there. Frank did this as quickly and quietly as he could.

When he finished, Odin put his hand over the lock, the door beeped, and Odin pushed it open.

The locker room was about what Frank expected for a place like this. The walls were lined with the type of metal lockers Frank remembered from high school, the ones with gill-like slits at the top and halfway down. Those in use had combination locks dangling from their handles. They would be no hinderance for Odin. Still, they had to be quick. Frank asked Odin to unlock all the lockers at once so they could split the job, and Odin did so with a wave of his hand that sent the dials turning, the locks tumbling, and flung open the doors.

Frank felt sorry for his friend. It must be hard to have been the wisest of all the gods and to know that you were now forgetful and forgetting, that you weren't what you had once been anymore. Frank guessed everyone felt that to some extent, but it was worse for Alzheimer's patients. The moments of lucidity, the times when they were themselves again, must have been like torture. What a cruel disease.

Frank wheeled himself to the nearest locker.

Finding nothing, he moved to the next and the next until there were no more. After that, the two of them left the room and made their way toward the sound of the *Jeopardy* theme and the kitchen off the common area.

At first thought, this seemed stupid. The kitchen wasn't an ideal hiding place for anything, and being right next to the common area, their chances of getting caught rose dramatically. But Frank had had a feeling about the kitchen, and he'd learned over the years to trust his feelings. They were often right.

By now Frank had come up with a few excuses he thought didn't sound completely stupid in case they were caught, and he readied one as they came closer to the common area. But there were no orderlies outside, and they reached the kitchen unnoticed.

Frank opened and closed the refrigerator, the freezer, the drawers and cabinets near enough for him to reach. He pushed aside silverware, boxes of Cheerios and Corn Flakes and Raisin Bran, frozen Swanson dinners, a large tray of last night's meatloaf. Nothing.

Odin rifled through the cabinets, opened and closed the ovens, checked beneath the sink.

Another dud.

As they were leaving, Frank thought through other places to look, but he was beginning to admit to himself that it might be gone, that all he had of Lilian might be gone.

He was distracted and didn't notice the ladle on the counter until he'd knocked it to the floor.

Time seemed to still. Odin rushed to Frank's chair, moved him toward the door. They were speeding along the giant prep island in the middle of the room when they saw the fat face of one of the orderlies, Frank thought her name was Sylvia, in the window.

Frank hit the brakes. He could feel Odin's breath on his neck. He hoped the contrast of the light outside the room and the dark inside would be enough to hide them. But as they waited, he thought of another lie just in case.

Sylvia's face lingered for a few seconds. Then was gone.

They waited another minute, Frank's heart slowing the whole time. The sweat on his back beginning to dry. When it was clear she wasn't coming back, they hurried from the room.

They'd found nothing. Their search had been a failure.

That wasn't acceptable. Frank had been a lot of things in his life, but one thing he had never been, had never allowed himself to be, was a failure. And there was no need to mention Odin's accolades. He was the Allfather.

As they turned the corner and Frank prepared to tell Odin where to look next, they ran into two orderlies, both looking dazed, much like Odin when his memory left him.

Frank grabbed the arm of his chair, rushing through excuses. He'd never been a good liar, but he'd never been afraid to try.

The men walked past them as if they hadn't seen them. That wasn't right. Even if they hadn't known they should be in bed – and that wasn't likely – they would have said something. It was their job.

"Follow them," Frank whispered.

Something was off. Although not a creature of magic or a god like many of the other residents of Wesley Glen, Frank could read people, and these people weren't right.

At the end of the dim hall, the two men opened a door and went in. Frank and Odin were halfway between the kitchen and the men. They slowed. When the men came back out, one was holding a trapper keeper that he hadn't previously had and the other something small that glinted in the dim, wall light.

"We follow them until we see where they take it or they catch us. Then we confront them."

They watched from a distance as the men raided two more rooms and then as they left what they'd taken in a safe behind the receptionist's desk outside the Alzheimer's wing. They waited for the men to leave before Odin wheeled Frank to the safe and opened it with a wave of his hand. Inside, they found the trapper keeper and bracelet, a left slipper, Zeus's glasses, a giant tooth on a string, a note, a hammer, earrings with a turtle on them, and Frank's ring.

Frank took it from the pile and slipped it onto his finger. He gave it a turn. A weight he hadn't known he'd been carrying lifted from him. "Thank you," he said.

But the Allfather was facing the other direction.

"Odin?"

"We're found," Odin said.

Then, echoed in the dim, empty hallway, Frank heard: "Stop right there! What do you two think you're doing?"

His heart sank. They'd not only been caught outside of their rooms, but they'd been caught with all the stolen goods. This would look bad. And no one would believe it was the orderlies when they could blame one of the three non-deity residents and an aged god who was losing his marbles.

It was the same two men. One held a flashlight and shone it in Odin's face.

"What's going on here?" They no longer had that dumb look.

"Sorry, we were going to watch *Jeopardy*," Frank said, "and my friend here got lost. He does that these days." Frank smiled. Odin only stared.

"Come out from there."

The man with the flashlight scooted past them and shone it at the safe. "I think we've found our thieves," he said. There was no trace of a lie in it. He didn't remember stealing. Of course he didn't. Someone had been controlling him. That's what had been off.

"We didn't..." Frank said, but the sentence died in his throat. What was the point?

The one with the flashlight reached for his radio, depressed the button, but he said nothing. Both men's faces went slack. They dropped their arms.

"We have to go," Frank said.

"Don't leave now," the man with the flashlight said in the most lifeless voice Frank had ever heard. "We have something to discuss."

Frank wheeled closer to Odin. It was best to be near a god when confronting another god.

"You have something that belongs to me," the man said.

"No, I have something that belongs to me."

"Show yourself!" Odin commanded. It was easy to see in that moment why he'd once been called the Allfather. His voice carried, husky with authority.

There was a flicker of movement as the air near the Alzheimer's doors shivered, and then he appeared, a small man, curly hair, thin. Hermes. Frank's instinct had been right.

"Give it back," Hermes said.

Frank had never been one for confrontation, but he said, "Over my dead body."

Hermes smiled. "That can be arranged."

The two orderlies were moving toward them and another three were making their way up the hall.

"Why don't you do it yourself?" Odin said. "This is the coward's way."

Hermes laughed. Said, "I'm old enough to not care what others think of me. This is your last chance. Give me back what is mine, and I'll let you leave."

"Do you honestly think that you can defeat the Allfather in battle?" Frank asked.

Hermes was picking some lint from his cardigan, but he said, "I don't think I have to."

Frank's stomach turned because he knew what Hermes meant. Odin was gone. His lucidity came and went, and in the last few seconds it had gone. He had that look on his face.

"It's a kind of theft, isn't it?" Hermes said. "It's sad to see him like this. Really, it is. But memory isn't something you can keep. It's like water. You cup your hands, gather what you can, but still it drips through your fingers, and as you age, and your fingers become gnarled and bent, more slips through, until eventually, you can't hold it at all. He has many memories, and I've held them for a time, but even I can't hold them forever. I can't make them mine."

"You're doing this to him?" Frank asked.

"Don't be stupid. That's such a mortal response."

A wall light nearby flickered, and the air became charged, heavy, clingy. Then came a flash of blue light and Hermes let out a scream and slammed into the locked doors.

Frank blinked at the black streak in his vision.

"This ends, Hermes."

Frank couldn't place the voice, but Odin could. Odin was now back to himself. The orderlies were too. The one holding Frank's chair released it. Shook his head as if to clear it.

"I have allowed you this for too long," Zeus said. He was moving toward them slowly, his walker before him, a push, drag movement. His long beard down to his chest, his eyes glowing with power. "You will give him what you have taken from him. You will return all of it."

Hermes pushed himself to a seated position. "But what you're asking me is against my nature, Father. How can I not do what I was made to do?"

Zeus scoot-pulled closer.

The orderlies went blank again. Zeus, unable to react quickly enough, was overtaken, driven to the ground.

"Stop this," Odin said, his full authority returned. "Release your father."

Hermes stood. Smiled. A sick, twisted thing.

Out of the dark came a sound that echoed, a sound that sent Frank's heart slamming and raised the small hairs on his neck. A growl.

A sword appeared in Odin's hand.

"You would kill me?" Hermes said.

"I would stop this."

A great, dark shadow, one of Odin's wolves, stepped into the dim light.

The men, despite Hermes's hold on them, stepped back.

"Release your father!" Odin said. "This ends."

"You leave me no choice," Hermes said.

The two orderlies nearest Odin lunged for him just as the wolf lunged for Hermes.

Odin readied his attack, but before he could land a killing blow, the air around them became charged, excited. Allfather's eyes widened. His sword fell from his hand.

Knowing what this was, Frank covered his face.

There came a great bark of thunder.

Odin's wolf yelped.

When Frank uncovered his eyes, he saw what remained: Odin helping one of the orderlies to his feet, Zeus being helped to his walker, the wolf licking its paw, the spot where Hermes had been now black with char. Nothing remained of him.

Frank spun his ring.

"He's gone." Zeus inched closer to them.

"But he was your son. How…?" Frank had trouble finding the words.

"Thank you, Great One," Odin said.

"Death is different for us, human." One of the orderlies was walking behind him because Zeus's left foot was dragging badly, and it looked as if he might fall.

The orderly with the flashlight said, weakly, "Okay. All of you back to your rooms. There's nothing to see here."

"You will return what he has taken," Zeus said.

The orderly nodded.

Odin pushed Frank's wheelchair. The wolf walked beside them. It was the color of night, and as they moved toward Frank's room, it faded into shadow and then was gone.

"Thank you," Frank said, but Odin didn't respond.

Back in his room, Odin helped Frank to bed. He had that distant look again, and he muttered something quietly. The only word Frank could make out was "Loki."

Lilian had confused people at the end, and Frank supposed Hermes was a lot like Loki. There were tears in Odin's eyes. Frank took his hand, but Odin pulled away.

He walked from the room without a goodnight, lost in his own fading world. Frank had seen it before. He spun his ring. What a cruel disease.

The Last Ride

Douglas Smith

On the night her life would change forever, Odin's horn wakened Vaya from a peaceful sleep. The mournful wail, echoing with the screams of the dying, called the Valkyries to ride from Valhalla, as it had done through the ages whenever war raged in the world of mortals.

Vaya disentangled herself from the arms of her still slumbering sisters where they lay in the communal bed of the Valkyrior. Throwing back the warm cover of furs, she stood up, naked and shivering in the chill of the sleeping hall. The central fire had died to embers hours ago, and the rough stone floor was like ice to her bare feet.

Vaya dressed quickly as the other Valkyries rose beside her. Moonbeams stabbing through high windows beneath the hall's vaulted ceiling provided the only illumination, but after so many ages, Vaya did not need light to prepare for a ride. She wrapped her short skirt around her waist and laced up her leather tunic and boots. After strapping on a golden chest plate, she added armored leggings and armlets. Finally, she donned her winged helmet. Then grabbing her spear, she sprinted with her sisters to the stables.

The stable hands had already hitched her chariot to Sleipnir. The eight-legged horse was Odin's own mount, but Vaya was

Odin's favorite daughter of all the Valkyrior, and she alone was allowed to use the huge black beast.

When all were assembled, Frela, their leader, gave a cry, and Vaya and her sisters rose into the air on their chariots as one. The Valkyries swept down from Valhalla like a golden cloud to the world of mortals, following the scent of blood and death and war as they had done for centuries, until they hovered unseen in the night sky above the battlefield.

Vaya surveyed the scene below. Several units of marines, supported by a small number of tanks, were advancing through a forest and into the outskirts of a bombed-out town. From her viewpoint, Vaya could see the defending army entrenched behind the remaining walls of the town and waiting in ambush. As the two forces came into contact and the exchange of fire began, Frela raised her spear, indicating that the selection of heroes was to begin.

"There!" cried one of Vaya's sisters, pointing her spear at a blood-covered marine leading his unit in a charge against a mortar position. The marine's left arm hung limp and useless, but he still fired his rifle as he ran. "I choose that one!" the Valkyrie cried.

"And I that one!" another Valkyrie shouted, indicating with her spear a small soldier with the opposing forces who had just overpowered two enemies in hand-to-hand combat.

Each time a Valkyrie aimed her spear, a soft beam of golden light shot from its tip, marking the selected hero with a glowing aura, visible only to the Valkyries. Beneath them, both armies fought on, oblivious to the immortals above.

In wars through the centuries, it had been as it was tonight. The Valkyries would select those warriors whose bravery, valor, and honor on the battlefield marked them as heroes. And when a hero fell, a Valkyrie would land unseen beside the soldier and carry their immortal spirit to live forever in Valhalla.

Vaya had witnessed thousands of such conflicts. But still she felt the old battle thrill growing in her that night, felt it in the pounding of her heart, felt it in the warmth spreading from her guts to her groin.

She joined in the selection. One soldier in particular caught her attention. He fought bravely, but more than that, unless forced, he only wounded or incapacitated his opponent, disarming them and moving on. Vaya admired mercy in a warrior as much as she did bravery. She urged Sleipnir lower to the battlefield, where she could get a closer look at this man.

She caught her breath when she saw him: he was as fair as the harvest god Frey, as strong as Thor the Thunderer, as brave as Tyr the One-Handed. Vaya, like all her sisters, had never known a love beyond the love of battle. But from that moment, the thrill of the fight fell before a new and stronger emotion that gripped her. Her heart beat even faster, and the warmth that had begun in her groin blazed to a fire.

Vaya the Valkyrie was in love.

Many of her sisters had now landed on the battlefield, claiming the spirits of the chosen heroes who had already been killed. *Not this one*, she whispered, praying to Tyr, the God of War. *Do not take this one*, she begged. Even as she prayed, she watched in horror as her beautiful soldier approached a crumbling corner of a bombed building. Behind that corner crouched three of the enemy forces, their rifles trained on the point where he would appear.

A Valkyrie was forbidden to interfere with the course of a battle or with the fate of a warrior. Only the gods themselves were permitted such power. But in that moment, Vaya did not care. Her beautiful soldier was going to die only seconds after she had fallen in love with him.

Screaming at Sleipnir, she swept her chariot low to the ground, leaping from it as her soldier turned the corner into the ambush. She materialized in front of the three enemy soldiers as they opened fire. Deflecting their bullets with her golden armor, Vaya shot a bolt of lightning from her spear. The three attackers fell, stunned and unconscious.

But not before a stray bullet struck her soldier. Clutching his chest, he cried out and slumped to the ground.

Vaya rushed to him, cradling him in her strong arms as she tore open his shirt. Blood spurted from his shattered chest.

A Valkyrie knew the wounds of war too well, and Vaya could tell that his was a mortal injury. She read his dog tag. His name was Edward. Her soldier, her Edward, would die unless she acted. In that moment, knowing that she would pay a price, Vaya decided. She touched the tip of her spear to his chest. Golden light flowed from it over the wound. She withdrew the spear. The wound was gone.

Edward opened his eyes and looked up at her, then at her clothing. "What...who are you?"

Vaya smiled down at him and stroked his hair. "My name is Vaya. And my story will seem a strange one—"

"Vaya!"

Her head snapped up. Frela, the leader of the Valkyries, hovered above in her chariot, staring open-mouthed at Vaya and Edward.

"Vaya," she moaned. "What have you done?"

* * *

Odin Allfather sat on his throne of blood-red pine on a raised dais in the Great Hall of Valhalla. The glare from the torches blazing on every pillar in the hall paled beside the glare that Odin was directing at Vaya with his one good eye.

"Have you *thought* on what you are asking, what you would be giving up, daughter?" he roared, thumping the floor with the shaft of his spear, Gungnir, the Deliverer of Lightnings.

Vaya stood trembling at the foot of the steps leading to the throne. She wanted to throw herself to the floor and beg forgiveness. But she was a Valkyrie. And she had known the consequences her decision would bring. And she knew also the love that still filled her heart. So she drew herself up tall and forced herself to meet Odin's eyes. "I have, father," she answered.

"You would trade immortality here in Valhalla for life with a *mortal*?"

"Our *love* will be immortal. It will live forever."

Odin snorted. He pushed his great body out of the throne and crossed the dais. Descending the steps, he placed a huge hand gently on her shoulder. "But *you*, Vaya, you will be mortal. *You* will die."

"I will have children, father. I will live on through the life I create."

"Ha! That is not living, girl. That is not immortality."

Vaya's anger overcame her fear. "What do *we* know of life? We have never experienced it. We know only death here. The Valkyrior deal only with the ending of lives. We bring nothing into this world, only take from it."

Odin drew himself up to his full height, and thunder rumbled inside the hall. "Careful, daughter. You are my favorite, but my patience with you has a limit."

She dropped her head, but her resolve remained. "I've had enough of war and death, father. I wish for peace and life. And love." She looked up at him again. "If you truly love me, you will grant me the life I desire."

His one good eye burned into her, and though her fear made her want to drop to her knees before him, she did not falter under his gaze. Finally, his face softened, and he shook his head. "Bah! So be it. You're a fool, daughter. But I prefer your foolishness away from Valhalla before it infects your sisters." Lifting Gungnir, he touched the point of the spear to her breast, aimed at her heart.

Then without warning, he thrust the spear into her.

Vaya screamed and fell backwards onto the cold stone floor of the hall. Her body spasmed, impaled at Odin's feet as he stood staring down at her, his face unreadable. After what seemed an eternity of agony to Vaya, she heard him grunt and felt Gungnir wrenched from her.

Vaya gasped as the pain left with the spear. But something else left her also. Drenched in sweat, lying helpless on the stone floor, she watched as a cloud of luminescence rose from her chest, clinging like golden blood to Gungnir.

Her immortality. Her power as a Valkyrie.

Struggling to her feet, she touched a hand to her chest. It came away unbloodied. She could find no injury, yet she knew she had been wounded. Mortally wounded. She was dying, having only a mortal's lifetime left to her.

Odin raised his arm, and two huge black ravens flew to land on it. One was Hugin, whose name meant memory, and the other was Muninn, whose name meant thought. They were Odin's eyes and ears in the world of mortals, and his emissaries. Odin whispered to them, and the two ravens leapt from his arm and flew out one of the high windows in the hall.

Odin turned to Vaya. "I have sent them to fix the memories of your mortal lover. He will recall you as another soldier, not as a shield maiden of Valhalla."

He fell silent, staring sadly at her. Finally, he spoke. "Goodbye, daughter. May you find happiness with your mortal love." He turned his back and said no more.

Fighting back her tears, Vaya ran from the great hall. Outside, a pale-faced Frela waited beside her chariot. She ran forward and grabbed Vaya's arms. "Sister," she whispered, staring at Vaya wide-eyed. "Your skin."

Vaya looked down at where Frela's hands gripped her arms. Where her sister's skin glowed with immortal golden light, Vaya's own flesh seemed dull, a pale pinkish white.

"Vaya," Frela wept. "You are lost to us. Why did you do this?" She hugged Vaya to her.

Vaya nearly broke down in her sister's arms, but then she remembered Edward and her love for him flared in her heart again, filling the void of what Odin had ripped out of her. "I have bought life and freedom, sister. For me and for the man I love."

Frela released her and stepped back, tears streaking her cheeks. "Father says that I must – that I must take you from Valhalla."

Vaya nodded, and the two stepped into the chariot.

Vaya didn't look back.

* * *

Life. Life as a mortal.

To Vaya, as the years passed and she looked back, the memories of her chosen life seemed to return to her in colors, each scene washed over, painted in a particular hue.

Red. Their passion together, Edward's lips soft but hungry on hers, his manhood in her, the roses he brought her, their hearts beating as one.

Black. The night sky, the dark room, Edward's hair on the pillow as he slept beside her after their lovemaking. The darkness in her heart as she lay awake, thinking on the choice she had made. A darkness that would never leave her.

White. Her wedding dress glowing in the chapel. The confetti shower sparkling in the sun. The blossoms bright in the trees. The sheets cool on their wedding bed. The shutters on their little bungalow in the suburbs.

Green. The grass on which they made love on a summer day, the canopy of leaves overhead, the small shoot of a wild rose poking through the earth beside where they lay afterwards, new life growing there like the new life she felt that had just been conceived in her.

Pink. Her baby. That wrinkled bundle of humanity that was Daniel, her son, as she first held him in the hospital. His tiny fingers wrapped around her own. His lips on her nipple as he fed from her.

Black. The darkness still with her, growing now as she had something else to fear for: the life of her son as well as Edward's.

Red. The blood running from Daniel's nose. The flush on his cheeks as he faced his first bully. The blood on the bully's shirt.

Red. More fights. More blood.

Black. That darkness in her. Her fear forever with her.

They lived in a tough neighborhood, and Daniel was no coward. At least once a week, he would be in a fight, never starting it, usually not even involved at the outset, but always intervening to defend a weaker friend or even a stranger. The street toughs learned quickly not to tangle with him. Though she was mortal now, Vaya had passed on some of her Valkyrie strength to her son. And, she feared, her love of battle.

Red. More fights. More blood. Her son's blood too often.

Black. Her fear. Always her fear.

Red. Black. Red. Black. Blood and fear.

Vaya had seen enough blood, had seen too many mortals bleeding the last of theirs onto a battlefield. She feared for her son every day. Her own mortality she had grown to accept, but she found the mortality of her own child unbearable.

Unbearable, yet she bore it, as all parents do. And soon she came to accept that Daniel was his father's son and like Edward, he had to be what he was – a hero, perhaps not on a battlefield of war, but on the battlefield of life. Considering his parents, how could he have been anything else?

Vaya learned to trust in Daniel's strength, his judgment, his goodness. The darkness in her heart grew smaller. But it never completely left her. The darkness knew what happened to heroes.

Daniel graduated from high school and went away to university, and she had to learn to live without seeing him each day. Then, one afternoon as Vaya, once Valkyrie, stood at the sink scraping dishes, she heard him call "Mom" from the front hall. She ran from the kitchen to greet him, thrilled at this surprise visit. She froze in the hallway where he stood.

He wore a uniform.

* * *

Afterward, Vaya couldn't remember what she had said to Daniel, screamed at him, cried to him before he left to be shipped out. It was as if she had said nothing for all the effect it had made. His country was at war, and Daniel wanted to help, as he had always wanted to help in a fight, to step forward and not back away.

Edward couldn't convince him either, though she could tell that her husband felt a pride in Daniel's decision she didn't share.

No Valkyrie will protect our son as I protected you, Edward, she thought.

* * *

On the night that Daniel shipped out, and for the first time since she had left, Vaya dreamt of Valhalla.

In her dream, she rode with the Valkyrior once more, the night wind cold in her face, her body young and strong again in her armor, and the reins of Sleipnir gripped sure in her hands. Her heart filled with the forgotten exhilaration of the ride, and she raised her voice in song with her sisters as they swept down onto a battlefield.

But the darkness in her rose to choke the song from her throat, as she recognized the uniforms of the soldiers fighting below. And Vaya knew, as only a mother can know, that her son was here, somewhere beneath her in this theater of death.

Unbidden by her, a mist oozed from the tip of her spear, and coalesced into a gray wraith shape. In her dream, Vaya called to the wraith, to her sisters, pleading for them to stop this scene from playing out. But her words rode away on the wind unheard as the wraith floated down to the battle.

Vaya held her breath as the omen of death searched from soldier to soldier, knowing in her heart the one the wraith sought. And when it found him, found Daniel as he led his men over a crumbled wall towards an unseen ambush, Vaya screamed.

And woke up.

She lay in bed, soaked in sweat and gasping in breaths, her heart pounding like a war drum in her chest. Edward lay asleep and oblivious beside her. The clock showed 3a.m..

Closing her eyes, Vaya calmed herself, reaching out with her mind and her heart. With the small part of her that remained Valkyrie, she knew that her son still lived. Daniel was alive. She could still feel him in this world.

The dream was an omen, a vision of what would be. She still had time to…

To do what? She was now just a mortal woman. What could she do to save her son? To save the life she had brought into this world, the one piece of immortality left to her, half of everything she loved.

Vaya rose from the bed, stripped off her soaked nightshirt, shivering more from the memory of the dream than from the chill of her sweaty nakedness. Throwing on jeans, a t-shirt and a sweater, she went quietly downstairs and into their small backyard.

It was fall, and the night air was crisp with the hint of an early winter. She cleared her mind and focused her thoughts. Raising her hands overhead and her face to the sky, she called out.

"Odin Allfather, hear your daughter's cry. Send me your messengers, for Vaya of the Valkyrior must speak with you."

She waited there for nearly an hour, her eyes on the sky, her ears tuned to every sound. She saw an owl pass overhead and once heard the distant wail of a train whistle. But nothing else. Then, just as she began to despair that her call had gone unheard or unheeded, the flutter of wings sounded behind her. Turning, she saw two shadows, darker than the night sky behind them, perched on the gutters of the roof.

She realized that she had been holding her breath and let it out slowly before bowing to the two ravens. "Hugin. Muninn. Thank you for answering my call."

Hugin spoke. "What message have you for our master?"

"I wish to meet with my father."

"Why?" Muninn asked.

"I wish to beseech him to grant me a boon."

Muninn let out a sharp caw. "You are no longer Valkyrior, woman. Odin has no dealings with mortals."

Vaya clenched her fists. Odin was her only hope. These creatures must take her message to him. "Listen to me, crow. I am Vaya, daughter of Odin All Father, and still his favorite." She prayed that her conceit was true. "You will take my message to your master, or you will feel his wrath."

The ravens both flapped their wings and cawed loudly, no doubt not used to being talked to in this manner by a mortal. But finally, they calmed themselves, and Muninn nodded his beak towards Vaya. "Very well, insolent one. We will tell him of your wish. It matters little. He will not meet with you."

Then with an explosion of wings, both ravens leapt from the eaves and into the sky.

And as Vaya watched the dark shapes grow smaller and smaller, her hopes seemed to shrink with them, and the fear in her heart grew darker than the night.

* * *

But Odin did answer her plea for an audience, and sent Frela the next night to fetch her to Valhalla. So while Edward slept in their suburban bungalow, Vaya, once Valkyrie, now mere mortal, stood again before her father where he sat on his blood-red throne in the Great Hall of Valhalla.

It was not going well.

"You let me save a mortal before. You let me save Edward," she said, fighting to keep the anger – and the fear – from her voice as she faced Odin. "Why can't I save my son?"

"You paid the price then, daughter," Odin answered. "You bought his life with your own immortality." He rose with a sigh, and walked to where she stood at the bottom of the steps leading to the throne dais. "A life must be bought with a life." Odin stared down at her from under his bushy eyebrows. "What life will you trade for that of your son?"

Vaya swallowed. "Take another. Take someone else on the battlefield."

Odin shook his head. "No, child. The life you offer must be a life that you own."

Something cold squirmed in her gut and crawled up her spine. *No*, she wanted to scream. *Not that*.

Odin took her by the shoulders. "You own Daniel's life because you created him. You own Edward's life because you bought it for him."

"No!" she cried, shaking herself free from him, stepping back. "Don't make me choose between them."

Odin shook his head. "I'm sorry, daughter. The price must be paid."

"Then let *me* be the price," she cried, grabbing the front of his tunic. "I own *my* life, too. Take me. If you need a life, then take mine. I'm a mortal."

Odin's expression softened, and his eyes began to glisten. "No, daughter. That I will not do. I could not send you to Niflheim. I love you too much."

Vaya bit back a sob. "So you love me, do you, father? As I love my son? As I love my husband?"

Odin shook his head. "I'm sorry, daughter. The price must be paid."

Vaya stood sobbing. What more did she have to offer? What was the highest price she could think of paying, worth more to her even than her life?

Yes, she thought, *I would do that, if it would save them*.

"I have one more price I can pay," she whispered. She drew herself up as tall as she could. "I will come back to the Valkyrior. I will forsake my husband. I will forsake my son. If only you will save Daniel and not take Edward."

Odin eyed her narrowly. "Vaya, you will never again be able to contact them. You will be dead to them."

"I know, father," she said, her voice breaking.

Odin stepped back and considered her. "To have my daughter return to me. To have you here again in Valhalla." He pulled her to his chest and stroked her hair gently. "Very well, child. I accept your offer – if you are willing to pay that price."

She stood there, letting him hold her, as the darkness she had lived with all these years spread inside her like a black weed, finally choking out any hope for happiness.

"To save my son and my husband, father," she whispered, "I would pay any price."

"I will send Hugin to the mortal world," Odin said, "to adjust the memories that Edward holds of his wife, and Daniel of his mother, of what became of you. What should those memories be, child?"

"Let them remember the truth, father," Vaya whispered. "Let them remember that I died of a broken heart."

* * *

On quiet nights when the cries of war did not call them to ride, Vaya would rise silently from the bed of the Valkyrior and slip down to the stables. There she would saddle Sleipnir and ride the golden path down from Valhalla to the mortal realm.

Unseen, she would slip inside that small bungalow in the suburbs and sit silently on the side of the bed, watching her lover, her husband, sleep. She'd rise then and walk down the little hallway to where her creation, her son, slept safely returned from the war. After a while, she would kiss them both and leave them sleeping and unknowing, and ride alone again back to Valhalla.

When she returned, her sisters would be awake and waiting for her. She would slip back into bed as they gathered around her, and she would tell them of her visit and of the two mortals that she loved.

They would sit quietly after her story, and Vaya would wait patiently for the question. Eventually, one of them would ask – tentative, timid, but they would always ask.

"Vaya," they would say, "tell us again of this thing called 'love'."

And Vaya would smile and remember and tell them, dreaming of her two loves and of the day when the Valkyries would ride no more.

Biographies

K.S. Barton

The Lord of Magic

(First Publication)

K.S. Barton writes historical fiction and fantasy stories of love and adventure set in the Viking age. The author of several novels, she explores themes of family, honour, and strength all within the backdrop of Norse society. K.S. also co-hosts the podcast, *Shieldmaidens: Women of the Norse World*. She has an M.A. in Humanities with a focus on literature and history and has always loved to learn about history through stories. See more at ksbarton.com.

Chris A. Bolton

The Raven Dance

(First Publication)

Chris A. Bolton lives in a house inside a cemetery in Portland, Oregon. His short film *Evil F – ing Clowns* won Exceptional Horror Comedy at the 2023 Portland Horror Film Festival. His screenplays have won the ScreenCraft Horror and Animation contests, and he wrote the all-ages graphic novels *Smash: Trial by Fire* and *Smash: Fearless* (Candlewick Press). His short stories have been published in *Portland Noir* and *ParABNormal Magazine*. Haunt him online at chrisabolton.com

Charlotte Bond

Nachtravnen

(First Publication)

Charlotte is an award-winning author and podcaster, as well as a freelance editor. She writes dark fantasy and horror, and her novellas *The Fireborne Blade* and *The Bloodless Princes* came out in 2024 with Tordotcom. She is also a co-host of the podcast, *Breaking the Glass Slipper*. A lover of bird folklore, Charlotte was thrilled to be able to bring her own version of the nachtravnen to life for this anthology.

Gemma Church
The Algorithm and the Spark
(First Publication)
With two degrees in physics, Gemma has worked in science communication for over twenty years, currently heading up content at a quantum computing company. This story is inspired by her many conversations with many fascinating scientists and engineers. Gemma also has an Undergraduate Diploma in Creative Writing from Cambridge University, a Countdown teapot and her short stories appear in numerous publications including *Indie Bites*, *Utopia Science Fiction*, *Tangled Web* and the *Obsolescence* anthology from Shortwave Press.

Malina Douglas
Deathswindler, Warbringer
(First Publication)
Malina Douglas weaves stories that fuse the fantastic and the real. She was a finalist in the Four Palaces Contest and received an Honourable Mention from the Writers of the Future Contest. Publications include *Cast of Wonders*, *Wyldblood*, *Sanitarium IV*, *Diet Milk*, *The Theatre Phantasmagoria*, *Parabnormal*, *Out of the Darkness*, *Underdogs Rise*, *From the Yonder IV* and *A Krampus Carol*. She is the author of *Red Panda Warrior*, *Jade Mountain* and editor of Winter Enchantment.

Stephanie Ellis
Cast Down
(First Publication)
Stephanie Ellis writes dark speculative prose and poetry. Her novels include *The Five Turns of the Wheel*, *Reborn*, *The Woodcutter*, and *The Barricade*, as well as the novellas *Bottled* and *Paused*. Her short stories appear in the collections *The Reckoning* and *Devil Kin*. She is a Rhysling and Elgin Award nominated poet and has written the collection *Foundlings* (with Cindy O'Quinn), *Lilith Rising* (with Shane Douglas Keene) and *Metallurgy*, as well as appearing in the HWA Poetry Showcase.

Sebastian Gray
The Door
(Originally Published in *Onspec: the Canadian Magazine of the Fantastic* #74, Vol 20, No 3, 2008, under the title "No Entry Signs and other Cosmic Mysteries')
Sebastian Gray is a writer of horror and dark fantasy fiction. Her work has appeared in Subterrain and Planet Scumm, and will be featured in an upcoming episode of the NoSleep podcast. When not writing she spends her time practicing swordplay, going to the theatre, and being a minor fashion icon. She can be found on Instagram as @columbina_dawn.

Derek Heath
The Masochist's Hammer
(First Publication)
Derek Heath is the British author of over a dozen published short stories and a number of novellas and collections, all of which are available at derekheathhorror.com. Derek lives in Aylsham, UK, with his wonderful partner and their dog, Gordy. His most recent novel, *Burrow*, is available now just about everywhere and he is always working on the next release.

Justin R. Hopper
The Raven and the Key
(First Publication)
Justin R. Hopper grew up in the Worcestershire countryside and has a longstanding interest in folklore, myth and the fantastical. He has written for film, TV and radio, and his BBC TV adaptation of the M.R. James ghost story *Number 13* was described in the *Guardian* as "a dark piece of deliciousness". In 2018 Justin's play *Flutter* was staged at the Soho Theatre and his Offie-nominated play *Bedbug* premiered in London in 2024.

Eric Kenron
On the Island of Samsey
(First Publication)
Eric Kenron is an inclusive Norse Pagan, a SF-F writer, and a small-scale jewelry maker from Chicago. All of his work is inspired by mythology, magic and runes, so writing about Odin is pretty much a perfect fit. He has had other stories published in two print anthologies and several small magazines. He lives in a small apartment overflowing with deities, books and tools.

Brandon Ketchum
The Chains that Bind
(First Publication)
Brandon Ketchum is a speculative fiction writer from Pittsburgh, PA who enjoys putting a weird spin or strange vibe into every story, dark or light. He is a member of SFWA and the Horror Writers Association, and his work has been published with Air and Nothingness Press, *Perihelion*, *Mad Scientist Journal*, and many other publications, including the short story collections *Legio Damnati* and its sequel *Civili Bellum*.

Stephen Kotowych
St. George and the World Serpent
(First Publication)
Stephen Kotowych is a winner of the Writers of the Future Grand Prize and Spain's Ictineu Award and is a four-time finalist for Canada's Aurora Award. His stories have appeared in magazines and anthologies in Canada, the UK, and the US and have been translated into a dozen languages. His first collection of short stories, *Seven Against Tomorrow*, is available now. He lives near Toronto with his family and enjoys guitar, tropical fish, and writing about himself in the third person.

Andy McLarnon
Odin in the Land of Fire and Ice
(First Publication)
Andy McLarnon is a British writer and editor who is interested in a range of genres and has a particular fondness for sci-fi, mythology, folklore, ghost stories, and sinister tales. He writes short stories and is dabbling in screenwriting when not working on a novel. One of his recent stories has been accepted for publication in *Phantasmagoria*. When not writing, he enjoys walking in fields with his German Shepherd dog while thinking about writing.

Parker M. O'Neill
The Skinchanger
(First Publication)
Parker M. O'Neill writes from upstate New York. A fifth grade video starring the family dog kickstarted his creative career, and he's chased that artistic

high ever since. His fiction appears or is forthcoming in *Crepuscular Magazine*, *WriteHive*, and Hungry Shadow Press. He can be found on Twitter and Bluesky at @parkeriswriting.

John Possidente
Einherjar
(First Publication)
In college days, John had a ridiculous plastic helmet with horns on it. The horns were painted white with typewriter correction fluid. (Unsurprisingly, it smelled of beer.) It's almost certainly not still in the attic somewhere. He probably has a Norse ancestor or two, but don't we all? For single combat, his favoured weapon is the disarming smile. John's stories have appeared in *Interzone*, *Grimdwarf*, *F&SF*, and a few anthologies.

Chris Shearer
Wesley Glen
(First Publication)
Chris Shearer's fiction has appeared in numerous journals, magazines, and anthologies, including *LampLight*, *Jamais Vu*, *Xnoybis*, *Black Dandy*, and *Twice-Told: A Collection of Doubles*. He is a 2014 graduate of Seton Hill University's Writing Popular Fiction Program, where he was mentored by Tim Waggoner and Lawrence C. Connolly and received the Alumni Scholarship. His non-fiction has appeared on FEARnet and in Cemetery Dance. Chris lives and works in Central Pennsylvania and is an avid baseball fan.

Douglas Smith
The Last Ride
(Originally Published in *Hags, Sirens and Other Bad Girls of Fantasy*, 2006)
Douglas Smith is a five-time award-winning author described by Library Journal as "one of Canada's most original writers of speculative fiction." His latest work is the multi-award-winning YA urban fantasy trilogy *The Dream Rider Saga*. Other books include the urban fantasy novel *The Wolf at the End of the World*; the collections *Chimerascope* and *Impossibilia*; and the writer's guide *Playing the Short Game*. His short fiction has appeared in the top markets in the field, including *The Magazine of Fantasy & Science Fiction*, *Amazing Stories*, *InterZone*, *Weird Tales*, and many others. He is a four-time winner of Canada's Aurora Award as well as the juried IAP

Award. He's been a finalist for the Astounding Award, CBC's Bookies Award, Canada's juried Sunburst Award, the juried Alberta Magazine Award for Fiction, and France's juried Prix Masterton and Prix Bob Morane.

Snorri Sturluson and Translators

Snorri Sturluson (1179–1241) is the name you will keep reading when learning about the core texts of Norse mythology. This Icelandic scholar, politician, historian and poet is commonly considered the compiler of all or most of the *Prose Edda* and *Egil's Saga*, to which we refer in this book, along with being the author of *Heimskringla*, an Old Norse king's saga. Sturluson had the good fortune of being raised by Jón Loftsson, chieftain of Oddi in Iceland and a relative of the Norwegian royal family, and thus benefited from a good education and connections. A favourable marriage bestowed chieftainships upon him, increasing his standing and wealth. He became known as a poet while working as a "lawspeaker" in the Icelandic parliament, and was also cultivated by the Norwegian royalty, becoming an agent in support of union with Norway. As political events marched on, this relationship turned sour and Sturluson was assassinated by the very nation he had supported – not before penning the enduring chronicles of their kings.

Harvard graduate **Henry Adams Bellows** (1885–1939) received his PhD in Old Norse Literature but forged a successful career as a newspaper editor, publishing director and radio executive before publishing his translation of the anonymously authored *Poetic Edda* in 1936 for the American Scandinavian Foundation. Another Harvard alumnus, the scholar of early English, German, and Old Norse literature **Arthur Gilchrist Brodeur** (1888–1971), is known for his translation of the *Prose Edda* in 1916. Brodeur was a professor of English and Germanic philology at the University of California in Berkeley and was declared a Knight 1st Class of the Royal Order of Vasa for his work in promoting Scandinavian studies. **William Charles Green** (*c.* 1833–1914) was a rector, teacher, classical scholar and fellow of King's College, Cambridge. Before translating *Egil's Saga (The Story of Egil Skallagrimsson)* in 1893, in 1884 he had published a verse translation of Homer's *Iliad.*

Myths, Gods & Immortals

Discover the mythology of humankind through its heroes, characters, gods and immortal figures. **Myths, Gods and Immortals** brings together the new and the ancient, familiar stories with a fresh and imaginative twist. Each book brings back to life a legendary, mythological or folkloric figure, with completely new stories alongside the original tales and a comprehensive introduction which emphasizes ancient and modern connections, tracing history and stories across continents, cultures and peoples.

Flame Tree Fiction

A wide range of new and classic fiction, from myth to modern stories, with tales from the distant past to the far future, including short story anthologies, **Beyond & Within**, **Collector's Editions**, **Collectable Classics**, **Gothic Fantasy collections** and **Epic Tales** of mythology and folklore.